Ann: A Story of Intolerance

Ann: A Story of Intolerance

JOHN MOEHL

RESOURCE *Publications* · Eugene, Oregon

ANN: A STORY OF INTOLERANCE

Resource Publications
An Imprint of Wipf and Stock Publishers
199 W. 8th Ave., Suite 3
Eugene, OR 97401

www.wipfandstock.com

PAPERBACK ISBN: 978-1-5326-5587-6
HARDCOVER ISBN: 978-1-5326-5588-3
EBOOK ISBN: 978-1-5326-5589-0

Manufactured in the U.S.A.   MARCH 12, 2019

"You have your way. I have my way. As for the right way, the correct way, and the only way, it does not exist."

Friedrich Nietzsche

"We may have different religions, different languages, different colored skin, but we all belong to one human race."

Kofi Annan

Contents

Author's Note

THIS IS A TALE of three generations of an American family. It is a work of fiction. The story, its actors, and their actions are fiction. While some of the sites are fictitious, in other cases, incidents may take place in real, at times well-known geographic locations. However, the story recounted at these locales is fiction. Similarly, at times historical persons or events are incorporated into the story to complement its telling. This does not imply any relationship between the story and these true historical personages or these real historical deeds.

While this story is fictitious, to some readers it may strike cords of truth and reflect upon what, in some instances, may be seen as true human emotions. Sentiments often transcend fact and fiction—this oneness is hopefully captured by the telling of one family's tale.

This story has been greatly influenced by my loving wife, Elisabeth. She has taught me the importance of telling a truthful tale—even if fiction. She has stressed the value of looking at an argument from all sides and helped me realize how crucial both forgiveness and patience are to all facets of life.

Finally, I would like to thank our dear friends Marie and Jim for their help with this work, as well as, Jacqui for all her efforts in polishing the raw stone.

Preface

We grow up attributing what we do not understand—or do not care to understand—to changing times. With ever-evolving technologies and lifestyles, we can be twice bitten. On the one hand, we can excuse ourselves as being out of step because we are from another time. On the other hand, we can blame all the ills of the present on those of the latest generation who have no link to or appreciation of the past. Some would argue our inconstant environment produces altered cultures—changing social norms. Others would counter that, transcending these dynamic stages of human development are truths—some things always right, others always wrong.

Our story is a story of change and resistance to change. It is a tale of seeking right and wrong in the face of personal loss and personal gain. It is a look at people who are both good and bad, more complex than they wish to be, and thus, more difficult to judge.

In the less abstract, this is also a story of racism. Many may feel racism has been defeated—that we are all one happy melting-pot family. But the truth is that racism is alive and well in most places—even places we least expect to find it.

Race can ultimately be a factor, among others, used to abuse, marginalize, and take advantage of others. Racism can be a gut feeling. It can elicit extreme emotions—even extreme hatred. It feeds on ignorance and intolerance—devouring the souls of even the most unexpecting.

Knowledge and understanding are the best remedies.

Alone

THE WIND WHINED INTO *the night, whipping dry leaves into small funnels, twisting upward.*

The aging house stood stoutly against the onslaught—its rafters and joists creaking in protest.

Slivers of moonlight managed to penetrate the sea of clouds sloshing across the heavens, eerily casting pulsating glimmers across the mirrored dresser to the side of the bed.

The mistress of the house, in spite of the hour, sat upright, the covers falling about her waist.

Her mate of four decades, not feeling the cold draft that swept across the mattress, continued to sleep soundly.

The lady of the house, the unquestioned head of the household, stared at her shimmering reflection in the mirror, shocked at the wreckage time had heaped upon her as she had fought the good fight.

The true cost of her sacrifice was not written in the wrinkles on her face, but the cracks in her soul—being right and standing upright came at no small price.

Like the old house, she alone was steadfast against the ill-placed flurries of change.

She alone was the standard-bearer, the wife, the mother, the judge and jury, the touchstone.

She stood not knowing where she wanted to go.

A gust shook the house and its mistress fell, her spirt carried on the wind—still alone.

Prologue

LUCY WAS A SHEPHERD mix. She had a shiny black coat, intelligent eyes, and a sensitive personality. To her great surprise, she had recently been relocated. She had spent her life loving a lady who took exquisite care of her—fed her, walked her, bathed her. She had been spoiled. Her loved and loving *patronne* had left. Lucy did not know where she had gone. Unlike when she went to the grocery store or the beauty parlor, this time it seemed she was not coming back.

Some people she knew, but not well, had taken her to their home, some sort of sprawling but chaotic place with all sorts of other animals. She really had not liked this place and wanted to go home—go home to her *patronne*.

Then she had moved again. This time it was far, and they had put her in a crate on an airplane and she had been really scared. At the new home — this time calmer—she had felt more at ease. Here she had two keepers—one whose scent she seemed to know.

Her new custodians—her new family—were different. They were not only different from the previous family, they were different from each other. One had a pale complexion like her first beloved *patronne*. The other had very dark skin. They were different. But they fed her, walked her, and bathed her. They spoiled her. Lucy loved her new family.

1

Meet Ann

ANN WAS DEAD.

She had lived to what used to be called a ripe old age. One night she just fell over dead.

This was, of course, quite a shock to her family. She had been a strong, stocky woman of Anglo-Saxon decent, scarcely ill a day in her life. Now she was dead.

Her family diligently sought material to use in her obituary. They had not realized this would be a problem. When it came down to it, there was not much to say about Ann. She had left few tangible markers along her road. Finally, they took the picture from her high school year book and wrote, "Beloved mother and wife".

Ann was gone, seemingly without a trace. But she had left a spore, some would say a scar, that would survive long after her internment. Ann was gone and maybe even forgotten, but—more than by her family—she was survived by her spirit.

Ann had left this world as we all do: alone, possession-less, and naked in the eyes of her God. She passed through the portal that had greeted millions before her—millions of men and women—millions of Europeans, Asians, Hispanics, Africans, and all the world's people—millions who were her equal in death. Yet, up to her last breath among the living, Ann had felt— had imposed on others her belief—that all are not equal. There were truly, those who were better, those who merited more, those who were simply superior to others. She carried to her casket a belief, honed by seventy years of shaping and molding by her family and her community, that she was one of the chosen few. One of the elite who need not concern themselves with the conditions of the masses. One who could not tolerate the commonness of the Philistines. One for whom the end justified the means. Her exclusivity endowed her with the inalienable right to be right. In life, Ann had been an unbending bastion of being right. In death, her survivors wondered about what she had done right.

Ann had been born under the cloud of war, two years after the armistice between Nazi Germany and the French Third Republic, almost a year after the bombing of Pearl Harbor, in a midwestern city that had been geared up to supply the front through the president's Lend-Lease program. Her father, for some reason not draft-able, was a supervisor of an assembly line at a munitions factory while her mother worked in a plant that made canvas tarpaulins. With the end of hostilities, her father's brothers and sister who had been in action returned— the family luckier than thousands of others, with everyone returning home of sound mind and body.

Her father was the grandson of German immigrants who came to America before the first Great War. Her grandfather had been born on the Plains, hard at work at a small-town lumberyard before his fifteenth birthday. Her mother was French-Irish in origin, her mother's mother an intellectual who had outlived two husbands.

With the war ended and the family reunited, all efforts refocused on the family's new-found trade—the lumber business. Grandfather started a small business concentrating on providing doors and windows to the booming post-war housing industry; his sons assumed various tasks from operations through sales.

Ann's family lived in a small home her father had built—comfortable but far from lavish. Ann's early years had been spent secure in a large family web. She had been surrounded by grandparents, uncles, and aunts. The whole family had snuggled close to the paternal grandparents' home, near the primary school attended by all members of the family for the past two decades.

Christmas, Easter, Fourth of July, and Thanksgiving, the extended family would celebrate, and Ann would play with her cousins. Through a child's eyes, all was harmony. Everyone loved everyone and everyone loved cute little Ann.

While memories of infancy can be a panoply of snapshots, she would remember most her grandfather's scent of cigars and the ripe-apple-doggy aroma from his faithful English Setter. She would recall the wonderful bouquets that filled her grandparents' home as her grandmother baked a luscious array of German cakes, cookies, breads, and pies.

Looking back from adulthood, she would, in her mind's eye, see shadowy images of romping in the yard, ducking into the playhouse her father had lovingly built, of being amazed at her grandmother's knick-knacks as the morning sun set the cut glass on fire, of being enthralled by her grandfather's horses that he kept in a wonderful-smelling barn, of getting groceries with her mother who seemed to know everyone, of cold, cold winters, hot, hot summers, and kaleidoscopic falls. There were these and other rose-colored flashbacks making her early years seem like something out of the pages of Stevenson's *A Child's Garden of Verses*.

But before her sixth season her sublime world was ripped apart. The post-war economic explosion was taxing traditional supply channels, too many people wanted the same things. Grandfather was not able to get enough lumber for his windows and sashes. He needed to go closer to the source. "Go West, young man" as Horace Greeley reportedly extolled a century earlier, seemed to be the only solution in Grandfather's mind. So, he sent his first-born, Ann's father, out west to buy a small sawmill that could supply the company with all its needs. With the force of a Midwest tornado, Ann felt her roots ripped from the fertile soil as she was sent spinning in the direction of the setting sun.

It was a very un-spring-like spring day when Ann first saw her new home. Nestled, or more correctly, jammed into the eastern slopes of the Cascades, the town reflected a dozen shades of brown from the scrubby brown hills, to the trees with leafless brown branches and the brown grass, to the brown air impregnated with the arboreous fumes from more than a dozen sawmills of all shapes and sizes. The mill where her father was to assume responsibility was along a muddy canal. The mill, seemingly coated with inches of adhesive mud, continuously stirred as equipment and horses moved boards from place to place. To Ann, it all looked like the faded woodblock prints from the old copy of *Struwwelpeter* her father had given her. If spun, the images blurred like a sepia pinwheel, spinning into obscurity–or so it seemed to a little girl's eyes. It was an unwelcoming colorless place, one to be shunned, not embraced.

This less-than-enthusiastic opinion was shared by her mother who saw her rough and dirty surroundings in great contrast to the conformable, well-worn, and clean environment she had been forced to leave; leaving behind life-long friends and family for the muck of a western sawmill did not seem like a very good trade.

The change was more than cosmetic. From centuries-old midwestern farm land, the family now found themselves in what could, with a bit of a stretch of the imagination, be called the wild west. From the well-heeled by-ways where cultured people politely went about their daily affairs, they were now living in a mill town. The mill site, now effectively a ward of the growing community, had initially been a self-contained borough unto itself—workers paying in company chits to use the company store, company barbershop, or company-run dancehall. While it was no longer a closed economy, the site retained a feeling of isolation; the houses, built by the original owners, clustered on one margin of the mill. The Twenties, when the mill was built, was not an egalitarian period. The mill houses reflected the positions of the occupants. The big white house at the center of the residential lattice was for the boss. The good-sized homes on the next loop for the supervisors, and so on to the small but well-built homes on the periphery for the common hands—an expanding spiral resonating power and wealth at its core.

Ann lived in the big white house. Even for a little girl, it was hard not to let the imagination roam.

The Grants, who had sold the mill to Ann's grandfather, had had a regal life, even in the dun-colored hills, right up to Mr. Grant's death a few months prior. The five-bedroom home, overseen by a live-in butler and maid, had an expansive solarium, a vast underground root cellar for storing food, a small fishpond, a half-acre vegetable garden, stables, a corral, and detached servants' quarters. Quite a change from the small home her father had built.

The silver lining, therefore, to the dreary surroundings was this house that Ann soon saw as her castle. She had her own grand bedroom and another bedroom where trunks of old clothes were stored and where she would go and play dress-up. There were huge walk-in closets and a myriad of secret places where a little girl could hide and immerse herself in her imaginary world filled with great finery and noble subjects.

Ann's mother, and Ann always called her "Mother", was not able to play dress-up and have an imaginary world, although she may have wished she could. She was flung into the central role of managing the household without the staff who had assumed these duties for the previous residents. It was a major undertaking and a double-edged sword. While she probably would never have admitted it, and maybe never even thought about it, she liked living in "the big house". Much like her daughter, she had an avid imagination and had wished for more opulent lodgings when living in the apartment with her mother or the small home her loving husband had built.

In some ways, this was a dream come true, even if it was taking place in a sordid mud-infused mill town. She could finally be mistress of the manor.

But it was a lot of work and, more importantly, it was the center of attention. While the mill's management had changed hands, by and large the workforce had stayed the same. Thus, all the layers of houses that surrounded her were occupied by people who had been living there for a long time, some for a lifetime. She was now in their sights. For many, she was the focus of their envy. Who was she to occupy The Big House? Was she the aloof matriarch, despite her youngish age? The overly-sophisticated easterner, the bleeding-heart Samaritan, or even a new generation Suffragette? Going and coming, from the house or yard, she was under the microscope. This was no small price to pay for being the Lady of the (Big) House.

Mother's charge was all the more daunting because her husband was never there—truly so near yet so far. The mill had fallen into disrepair, slipping backward as Mr. Grant's health slipped away. To turn it around was a big job. The mill had to be able to compete. The valley's forests were vast, but nonetheless limited. Mills competed for the best logging sites, for the best logs, for the best workers, and the best equipment. There was a lot to do. Ann's father was at work six days a week. This meant mother had to not only set up and maintain the household, but also do this in an unfamiliar environment.

Zelda was the first break. Zelda's husband Jimmy worked in the mill, but was a relative newcomer, and had not been able to get company housing. Zelda was an innovator who knew how to get things done. She noticed the empty servants' quarters adjacent to The Big House and approached Ann's mother. For relatively modest compensation, she would be happy to help with all the housework if she and Jimmy could live free of charge in the quarters.

In the bat of an eye, the deal was done. Zelda was at the backdoor early every morning to get the washing going, iron clothes, clean floors, dust fixtures, polish silver, wax furniture, or undertake any of the long list of assignments required to keep the house spick-and-span. Ann's Mother was keen on clean—not just superficial neatness, but real deep-down sparkle.

As the days and weeks passed and the house became a home, Zelda became indispensable. Regardless of her newness, she became the needed entrée into the community. Zelda was able to guide Mother, indicating where to get this or that done—who to trust and who to avoid. Where to buy meat, vegetables, eggs, and milk. Who to contact for dry cleaning, painting, or plumbing. Who to service their 1948 Ford Woody Estate they had driven out from the Midwest. And, even where to find a good doctor, dentist, or pharmacist.

Real spring was slowly settling into the valley and Zelda recruited Jimmy (for a bit of extra pocket money) to get the garden into shape as well as to clean out the stables and tack room. Soon there were rows of carrots, cabbage, green beans, and peas. Mother was a happy spectator to all the outside goings-on. While still the chief, she was citified with no notion of gardening, let alone what one would do with a sable or a tack room. She gave Jimmy a free hand and soon there were chicks and ducklings running about the yard.

However, the family's poultry adventures were curtailed when Father came home one evening with a golden retriever puppy, Chip. The guy who sold the machinery that sharpened the mill's saws had a cousin who had a golden who had just had a litter. He felt a pup would be a good way to get Father to upgrade his equipment. While this ultimately never happened, Chip was received with great joy all around.

Chip would pick up the little chicks and ducklings and proudly strut around the yard with a squawking bird in his mouth. While the fowl were not injured, they did not appreciate the free rides and soon learned where and how to move about so as to stay out of Chip's reach.

As her mother strove to organize her household and her father fought to organize the mill, Ann was a free spirit covering the whole two acres that constituted The Big House's fenced-in compound. Indoors and out, she played make-believe, romped with Chip, scampered through the garden, harassed Zelda, or hid in the basement. During those early days in what she saw as an unwelcoming milieu, she was almost forgotten as her parents were totally preoccupied with major tasks. Yet, ironically, in retrospect she would view this period as one of her happiest. A time when she felt totally free—willing and able to explore strange surroundings, treading where she had never stepped before.

Sunday was really the only day when the whole family was together, and on Sundays they went to church. Not to a specific church, but to any one of the number of houses of worship that dotted the valley. Her parents had decided with this new life to turn over a new leaf—to ignore their religious upbringings and to attend the parish, regardless of the denomination, where they felt the most at home.

This desire to join a religious group was based on more than religion. They were, in every sense of the word, strangers in a strange land. The valley had been populated by white men since the end of the Civil War. Some of those original families were still there, strongly influencing the area's growth and development. The progeny of the first logging and ranching families still, in many ways, held the reins of power. Ann's family was the outlier—no contacts, no champions. Her parents wanted to change this equation. For both the benefit of the family and the mill, they needed a firm footing in the community and a good church seemed like the first door to open to start down this pathway. Consequently, every Sunday they sat in another congregation, not necessarily listening to the words of solace from the altar, but examining those seated in the pews with them, trying hard to imagine who had the strongest hold on the strings of power.

After weeks of sitting on hard benches, struggling to keep awake as the voices of reason droned on and on, the family tentatively settled on the Congregational Church. Based on her parent's scrutiny, this flock seemed well-heeled, with deep pockets, and deep roots. The nonconformist puritan spin embellished by the Congregationalists apparently appealed to the remnants of the pioneering spirit as many of the old families seemed to be followers—followers who now counted Ann's family among their own.

There was then a convergence of events that affected greatly Ann's free spirit. By the time they had chosen their church, her family had gone through the first phase of getting settled. The house was organized. The grocer, butcher, cobbler, mechanic, and beautician were identified. Zelda had satisfactorily completed her break-in period and was able to do a lot more with a lot less supervision. Chip was house broken. And, most importantly, in a few months, Ann would have her sixth birthday.

Ann was an autumn baby. She had arrived after the deadline for school registration. While most children started first grade at the age of six, Ann had to wait almost a year and would start just before her seventh birthday. Now, as she approached her sixth, her family began to think seriously about school.

Unbeknownst to Ann, her family also began to think seriously about another child. This was a sensitive, if not heart-wrenching, topic for them to broach. After Ann's birth, her mother had had two miscarriages. She had convinced herself she would never again deliver a healthy child. Coming from a small family herself, she felt she had more to gain from concentrating on the child God had granted them rather than raising hopes, only to have them once again dashed. However, her husband, a product of a big family, wanted more children; he wanted a son. Even though he scarcely had time for his family, small as it was, he wanted, he really wanted, at least one more child.

Ann's mother loved her husband dearly. They had grown up together. Their life was but one life and he was staunchly in the driver's seat. Mother was from the old school where the man was the head of the family; the wife's job was to protect, encourage, shore-up, and assuage the husband. She would do all she could to fulfill her husband's expectations. She prayed, because her religion was more than just a community anchor. She asked

God for a healthy baby, hoping this new world of western mills would yield a strong new life.

Their recent and ongoing rigors had pushed the once idealistic newly-weds closer and closer to pragmatism—even if much of this new practicality was based on seeing the world through a very small window—it was time to think about Ann's schooling.

There was a public grade school not far from the mill where all the mill family kids went, but should the boss' daughter go there? Ann's mother was still very uncomfortable in the local social setting, feeling she was being constantly watched with less than friendly eyes. It was as though, if she fell down the stairs when carrying a great heap of laundry, spontaneous applause would erupt from the entire mill camp. As an educated woman, she did not see this as paranoia, just part of life as the boss' wife. But she did not want her daughter subjugated to this non-stop scrutiny. She felt schooling with the same group with whom you lived from the first to the thirty-first was just too much. Her daughter needed exposure to other things, other ways, other families. She should go to school elsewhere.

As with many communities, there was a neighborhood more frequent-ed by the elite—the business and professional families who were on the way up, who drove nice cars, who had nice houses, who tended nice rose gar-dens. And so, it was here. On one of the higher slopes overlooking much of the valley, there were The Heights. Smack in the middle of The Heights was a grade school that was the spitting image of the school near the mill—same building, same playground, same books, and probably same style of teach-ers—but, not the same families. This was where Ann would start school.

Fortunately, they had time because this was a unique case that re-quired special arrangements. Moving between school districts was possible but frowned upon. The specific circumstance would ultimately mean the request would be approved, but there was no bus service, so Mother would have to drop-off and pick-up Ann every day.

They had the time and the means—the school decision was made. But Mother wanted to do more. She wanted her little girl to start piano or dance lessons immediately—you are never too young to learn. You are never too young to expand your horizons and begin developing good habits.

Ann's father was less insistent on immediate training for his daughter, public or private. He had news and he felt this would impact not only on work, but also, on family life. His brother and his family were coming. They would, in fact, move into the vacant supervisor's house immediately across the street from The Big House.

Ann's grandfather had decided the mill assignment was, indeed, too big for one man. They desperately needed the old replaced with the new and the new producing more lumber to supply his Midwest factory. So, he had assigned, in his role as patriarch, a second son to help with the job. This was almost old-world rule, but none of the family would ever overtly contradict the family's head. As much as some would like to, it just was not done.

Thus, at the end of summer, Uncle Steve and Aunt Christine moved in across the street with their daughter who was just two years younger than Ann. In a matter of days, Steve sat at Ann's father's side with all kinds of new ideas about how to expedite the mill upgrade and quickly get the needed lumber on the road.

Ann's father had had a notion of creating a family module to counter the hard-to-penetrate cliques of the locals. He had a vision, perhaps driven by a slightly tarnished retrospective view of his own childhood. He fore-saw establishing a personal family faction that would generate its own sort of mini-society—its fun, its games, and its fraternity. Aunt Christine and Mother would become inseparable twins as would Ann and her cousin, Sara. While the mothers shopped together, cooked together, organized par-ties together, gardened together, and played bridge together, the cousins would go to school together, go to camp together, go to church together, and play tennis together. They would be one big happy family—even happier than it had been in their, now, far-off hometown.

Since the longest journey begins with the first step, even if a stumble, Ann's father tried to start a tradition for the two families: having Friday sup-per together. It was a valiant effort and it lasted for a surprising two months before one or another of the anticipated participants began making ex-cuses for absences. This did not cut the cord that bound them. The brothers worked together on a daily basis, the sisters-in-law inevitably found them-selves at the same place at the same time. The cousins even played some together. Nevertheless, the families moved slowly and inevitably apart. In a new community and a new job, the glue that held them together began to shear. No longer was it two brothers working for their father, it was now one brother as the *de facto* boss and another as his lieutenant. Only one family could occupy The Big House.

The shearing manifested itself as Steve and Christine forewent Ann's family's offer to introduce them to the community. They preferred, they stated emphatically, to explore for themselves. They, too, hunted for a house of prayer that could help them integrate—avoiding the Congregationalists and ultimately settling on the Methodists. Christine signed up as a substi-tute teacher for the city schools. Steve became an active Mason. Ann rarely saw Sara other than to wave to her as their cars crossed going in or out of the lane that was the main byway for the housing area.

As Ann reached her first anniversary in the West, there was a new normal. Father was still at work six days a week. Mother still felt she had her house in order, her relationship with her sister-in-law arranged, and her daughter ready to start school. It was time to expand her focus. While her in-laws sought their own footing, for her own family's interests, she herself could and should now start thinking about how she would better merge into the community. She looked not to the mill estate nor the surrounding neighborhood, but to The Heights. Here she would find her people.

Mother felt she could take a few afternoons a week off from her domestic charges to devote to her quest for access to what would pass for the upper echelon of this sad mill community. She joined PEO, Book Club, and DAR. If anything worked in the tight-knit community, these forums would open the doors.

From an early age, Ann had lots of two things: books and dolls. She adored books. From her infancy, she was attracted to the pages, quietly collecting them in spite of an inability to grasp their content. Dolls seemed a natural thing for a girl. Her mother's mother was a great traveler and began sending Ann dolls from far-off places. Dolls from other sources seemed intuitively to follow and she soon had a small village that lived in an old glass-fronted bookcase.

Ann's actions and reactions to these two collections were very different. She demonstrated keen and open affection for her books, willingly sharing with others; either to experience together with them a photo or drawing that caught her attention, or in the hopes of getting someone to read to her. However, her dolls were hers. It was almost as though they were indentured to her. She would dust them off, clean their faces, arrange their clothing. Each had a name. To Ann, each had a unique personality. And all were hers, and hers alone.

Both her books and her dolls took her to special places, but very different places. The books took her to special, selected parts of the commons. The books were, after all, in the public domain—those she so carefully selected offering insight into other places, other times, other people—but all shared with a larger population of consumers. Even at a young age she seemed to understand this shared ownership and did not interject herself completely into a story or fable.

Her dolls, however, were a different thing all together. They were her entourage—her consorts, her escorts, her coterie. They were the occupants of her world. They were not shared with others, but they did share her world with her. She went to Greece or Ceylon or Siam or wherever her dolls would take her. She circumnavigated the globe with her dolls. But—because she had never been to these far-off lands, because she knew nowhere but here, because she spoke nothing but her mother-tongue, because she knew nothing but her God—she visited these places without seeing. Instead, for all her companions she created tiny mental boxes, each labeled with the names of exotic foreign territories—tiny boxes that were identical, all reflecting her life in the brown hills of the West. Tiny boxes that began to build a foundation for an outlook on life—an outlook that was self-contradictory, seemingly at first glance to be worldly and broad, but actually, upon careful inspection, narrow and introspective.

As she grew, her books and her dolls continued to be pivotal parts of her life, but they, too, evolved as she moved through the stages of childhood. Initially, her dolls and her books were foci heavily dependent on others, her family explaining the dolls' origins and attire as well as the books' subjects and locations.

At this point in her life, she was, like all young children, absorbed by her family, her home, and her garden—her world stopped at the chain-link fence that separated The Big House from the rest of the neighborhood. Her domain held many secrets to be discovered and many make-believe microcosms to create.

However, as she grew older, she would cling to the chain link, watching children her age playing in the lane—running, jumping, laughing, cavorting. She wanted to expand her world, to go through the fence and to play with children her own age. But she could not. She was captive in a sphere that did not extend beyond her fence—a sphere with a wealth of things—dolls, books, food, clothes, all any child could want. But a sphere populated by a very small, select group of people: her parents as well as Jimmy and Zelda, and, of course, Chip.

As she grew older and could read to herself, her books changed. They were no longer adorned with colorful and exotic pictures, but with intricate and lavish tales. She became an avid reader, reading volumes of romance novels and similar fictitious narrations that took her to strange places if not strange lands.

As she grew older, her dolls remained her companions, but in a static state. She no longer took them out of their mental boxes. She cared for them, kept them prim and polished. But she no longer talked to them, and they no longer talked to her. Nonetheless, they were still hers and no one else's.

As she grew older, she and Chip would sit inside the fence watching as though they were at the cinema. In fact, as time passed, this became in some ways their cinema—whereas, to the outsider looking in, it was a picture of a very sad and lonely little girl, alone with her dog.

As she grew older, she observed that people were different. She observed even her family members were different. On the rare occasions when she went to the garden or to roughhouse with Chip, instead of wearing selections from her wide variety of dresses, she would pull on her trousers, then put on her socks and shoes. She noticed her father would put on heavy woolen socks and his heavy leather work boots before he pulled on his heavy gabardine pants. She had asked her mother why this was so? Mother had replied simply, "God makes us all different, but we are all His children."

This answer did not answer her question, but she pretended it did so as not to push her mother into an even longer more tortuous invented explanation that still would not answer her question.

Pretending and pretenses became part of her lonely world.

It was unclear why her parents did not want her to break through these barriers. Certainly, this was not a subject which would ever have occurred to Ann herself as she simply reacted to the guidelines the adults set forth for her day-to-day routine. Her isolation, physical and psychological, was not a decision made intentionally by a little girl nor her parents—it was a creeping and pernicious phenomenon that sprouted in defiance of everyone's best efforts (or what they considered as their best efforts).

At later dates, some would say the miscarriages her mother had experienced made her overly protective of her one living child. Others would say her parents felt, as shown with their selection of schools, that it was necessary to separate the royalty from the peasantry in the mill town community. Still others would point the finger to Ann herself, who was so worried about being overshadowed in one way or another by others that she chose self-isolation.

Whatever the reason, or reasons, by the time Ann was ready to enter into grade school she was already a little girl whose best friends were characters in books and dolls from around the world.

Even with this seeming sequestration, Ann had impeccable manners—one could easily have thought by her remarkable correctness, politeness, and sociability that she had grown up in a large clan of cronies and kin and not the confines circumscribed by The Big House's chain-link fence. These talents were not due to Ann's innate desire to know how to do things in a way that was considered as socially acceptable to those who measured such performance. In fact, the genialness was, in truth, a veneer that hid a great pool of shyness and apprehension. However, this reality aside, Ann's mother was a real stickler about manners—speaking faultless English, having good posture, maintaining excellent hygiene, knowing how to set the table (put from the left, take from the right), how to use a fish knife and desert spoon. Her mother wanted her daughter to know all that Emily Post subscribed in *Etiquette*[1]. These were the skills her mother had learnt from her mother—skills that were held with great pride. Skills that were an important part of being a correct woman and eventually a correct wife.

With this indoctrination from an early age, when Ann finally entered primary school, not only was she almost chronologically a year older than her classmates, but in terms of what might be deemed as socially acceptable behavior, she was ahead by a decade. But socially acceptable behavior does not apply on the playground during recess in the first grade.

That late summer, as the schoolyear neared, the mother was more excited than the daughter.

Ann had been the princess of The Big House. Often, when alone in her domain, she commanded all and was overseen by none. When her mother was away in town and Zelda had gone to her small house in the northwest corner of the property, Ann dominated the palatial, in her eyes, Big House—even the only other animate object in her realm, Chip. Now the princess was in school.

Ann was not happy to go to school. She was happy surveying her dominion.

The week before school started, Ann informed her parents she was not going to go to school. She was learning all she needed to know at home. With Mother, Zelda, and her books, she was sure she would be able to do all she needed to do when she grew up.

Ann had never been an emotional child. She did not throw tantrums. She did not scream and yell. She was generally obedient and did as she was asked until she reached a point where she would not do as asked. But when this hurdle was reached, she did not make a fuss. She did not have a conniption fit. She was like a mule that would balk at pulling a plow. She would just stop. She would not budge. She simply would not do it—whatever *it* was, as

---

1. Ann's later life would demonstrate no small irony in regard to Emily Post's well-known quote: "*Manners are a sensitive awareness of the feelings of others. If you have that awareness, you have good manners, no matter which fork you use.*"

long *it* was something she adamantly resisted. And right now, *it* was going to school.

Her parents tried the "it's the law" approach.

Ann did not budge.

They tried the "you'll make a lot of friends" tactic.

Ann did not budge.

They tried the "this is the beginning of learning" strategy.

Ann did not budge.

They even attempted the "if you don't go to public school, we'll send you to Catholic school" ploy.

Ann did not budge.

Ultimately, instead of the child going to her room, her parents left an undeterred Ann in the solarium and went to their room.

The next morning, when her father had gone to the mill and Zelda was hanging clothes outside on the line, Ann's mother sat Ann down on one of the chrome and vinyl kitchen chairs and fixed her in a glare that was seldom used, her thick eyebrows peaking on her forehead, "Young lady, you will start school next week. End of story."

Ann's mother was rarely severe and almost never captured her child in a threatening glare. As these moments of demonstrated force were so rare, they were very effective. Ann had no defense. She could and would sulk. But she would also start school the next week.

The following Monday, Ann took her seat at the hardwood table in Mrs. Altman's first grade class that would double as a desk and workbench, and next to which she would lie on her small but plush pink and black rug at naptime. Mrs. Altman was a slender red-headed, middle-aged lady who appeared to Ann to be the picture-perfect image of—from what she had been told by her cousin last Thanksgiving—the sinful heroine played by Jean Harlow in the movie *Red-Headed Woman*. She wondered how such a bad lady could be a first-grade teacher. She knew she should have stayed at home.

Ann adapted quickly if begrudgingly to first grade. She already read and wrote at a level far superior to this grade, thanks to her long attraction to books. She managed to undertake all the artistic challenges—finger painting, papier-mâché, clay modeling—under duress. Because she lived outside the school district, her mother had to drop her off and pick her up. This meant as soon as the final bell rang, she was out the door and in Mother's car. This also meant she did not walk home with classmates, get involved in after-school activities, or in other ways socialize with her peers.

Every morning, just before the bell rang, she kissed her mother good-bye, jumped out of the car, and ran down the hall to her classroom. The process was then repeated in the afternoon, culminating with giving Chip a hug as she walked into The Big House. Quickly it all became routine.

School to Ann seemed neither good nor bad. Even from her early grades, she appeared indifferent to school, be it the academic or the social side. It was more something to be tolerated. Ann was not the most tolerant of people. She gave the impression she sought a state of stasis, balancing her obligation to attend school with her desire to be elsewhere—in a world controlled by her own self and not her detached teacher.

However, this state was disturbed, nearly irreversibly sidetracked, when her life changed forever. Her mother had a baby; she had a younger brother. The shock was nearly a physical blow. She was no longer the centerpiece. She was no longer her parents' only child. She was no longer the be-all and end-all. She had to share the spotlight. In fact, she had to surrender the spotlight to this young woebegone, fighting to regain a bit of its illumination.

The only slight bit of good luck was that her baby brother was nearly a decade younger than she, meaning they neither had, nor likely would ever have, much to do with each other. When he entered grade school, she would be in high school. She would not need to put up with a young sibling following her around everywhere. She could continue leading her life as she wished, only she now had to compete for her parents' affections.

During grade school she had established few if any real friendships. On the family side, outside her nuclear family, she begrudgingly saw her across-the-street cousin once or twice a year—generally at Thanksgiving and sometimes the Fourth of July.

When there was a family celebration, the brothers alternated hosting the event. When the celebration, such as it was, was held at her house, Ann was expected to entertain her cousins—cousins, plural, because her aunt had also recently had a baby boy to add to the ephemeral clan.

Sometimes Ann could maneuver things such that they spent all their time playing dress-up in the spare bedroom where all the trunks of clothes were stored. But sometimes she was forced to bring out some dolls and this was a troubling time. Once Sara had picked up two of the dolls, declaring she was going to change their clothing—dressing the Greek as a Spaniard and vice versa. As Sara picked up one of the dolls to undo her dress, Ann flew at her, flipping the doll from her grip and pushing Sara away so hard her cousin hit her head sharply on the corner of the glass fronted bookcase. Sara was not seriously wounded but burst into tears, running to her mother. The family celebration was terminated early. Suffice it to say Sara and Ann were never close friends.

Ann's life was not only rocked by the arrival of a sibling. There was another stunning arrival. This seconding coming was, however, much more gradual even if, at the end of the day, more influential. Ann's maternal grandmother, Isabelle, came to town for a visit—a *prise de contact* with her Western family, as Mother explained.

This started almost imperceptibly. Her father told Jimmy to clean out a shed near the corral and began referring to this large locker as "the Mother-in-law House".

Her father then told her this heretofore unused structure would be for her grandmother.

Ann was confused. The shed was not even as big as her bathroom and had no windows. How could someone live there? How could it be someone's house?

Her questions were not answered when a truck came, and two men off-loaded a whole bunch of stuff into the "house"—big cardboard barrels with metal tops and cardboard boxes tightly closed with yellow tape, all labelled in wax pencil. By the time the men left, the entire "house" was more than half full, floor to ceiling. Where would her grandmother stay?

But no one seemed to care. Her grandmother's house was locked with a big black padlock on the door and no one seemed to wonder where grandmother was or where she would stay.

Ann asked her mother but was told not to worry, her grandmother was still far away and would not be here for some time to come. Mother added that Grandmother Isabelle was first sending a few things for them to keep for her—soon she would be showing up herself for a short stay with them. Ann could then introduce her grandmother to her new dolls that had arrived since Grandmother Isabelle's first visit.

This, of course, did not at all answer Ann's questions. However, if Mother did not think it was anything of concern, there was no reason Ann should think any more about it. She promptly picked up her latest read, Charlotte Brontë's *Shirley*—a novel from the mid-1800s about a man trying to manage an inefficient mill and a woman trying to make something of herself—the appropriateness of this tale to Ann's own situation was, nevertheless, lost in translation.

2

Meet Isabelle and George

GRANDMOTHER ISABELLE'S PENDING ARRIVAL, be it sooner or later, would seemingly have little impact on Ann—or so Ann felt. She had scant first-hand knowledge of her maternal grandmother. She had, she had been told, seen her several times when they lived in the Midwest. Yet, she really only recalled her grandmother's more recent visit here to The Big House when her little brother had been born. Her own mother spoke rarely, and then sparingly, of her childhood and early family life. Ann had thought it was because Mother still mourned the passing of her own father and these memories were too painful. But, Ann noticed, for whatever reason, Grandmother Isabelle was also not a frequent topic of conversation nor a regular visitor.

Ann's mother wanted everyone in the household to call her mother Grandmummie—to distinguish her from her paternal counterpart who was christened Grammie—to provide the needed personal identification of each of the female forbearers. Nonetheless, Ann continued to refer to each, on those rare occasions when she spoke of her extended family, as Grandmother—no special epithets required.

Although Ann would only learn the full details later, bit-by-bit she did grow to know her maternal grandmother. Through this process, she should have learned that Grandmother Isabelle's life told almost as good a tale as Charlotte Brontë's. But, much more importantly than being just a good story, or even an impressive story, what Ann would not learn, but would absorb was the residue of Grandmother Isabelle's fundamental essence. Very probably unknown to her herself, and certainly not highlighted as honorable mention in Ann's obituary, Grandmother Isabelle had had enormous impact on the molding and shaping of the person who was to become the adult Ann.

Isabelle (namesake of her mother—her father calling his spouse "Isabelle Jane" in order not to be confused with his daughter) had been the youngest of three children, having an older brother, William, and an older sister, Anne. Her father was Irish, coming to North America in the second half of the nineteenth century at the time of the "Great Hunger," marrying a remarkable young lady from Ontario, settling in the harsh northern plains of the US to raise a family.

As a child, Isabelle had been, and throughout her life continued to be, curious, hard-working, and intelligent. She had also been, and continued to be, reserved, opinionated, and stubborn. Her mother used to joke with her—one of those jokes that wrapped up a truth with a bow—that she was rigid just like the switchman on the Rock Island and La Salle Railroad. This guy, who stayed in that small shack north of the county seat, threw the rail switch so the train either went north to Lorah or west to Atlantic. There was no third choice.

Isabelle's mother felt her daughter was exactly like that swithchman. In her daughter's eyes, there were only two choices—generally, one right and one wrong. Life was binary. There was no third choice.

Isabelle was not sure she wanted to be connected in any way to that grizzled old codger in the railway switchman's shed. But she never forgot her mother's words and, as she travelled through life, would wonder if they were really true. Was she a rigid switchman? She could not tell.

Isabelle was diligent, even dogged, in her work as long as it excited her. As soon as she considered it drudgery, she abandoned it, regardless of the price. Isabelle was loyal, completely faithful to people and ideas, as long as she felt they merited her faith. As soon as she felt they failed to warrant her fealty, she dropped them regardless the cost—often keeping a grudge for years to come.

Isabelle's father would tell his beloved daughter that she reminded him of Irish gorse, the strong plant that could thrive in the most inhospitable of places. Its sinewy branches could be bent nearly double before breaking. It produced a lovely yellow flower that had a heady aroma and could be used to make a tasty wine. It was prickly, used as a barrier, and, according to the old pagan tribes, housed witches. Its formidable spines could pierce the foot or leg of a cow, dog, or man—festering for weeks. It was one tough plant. She was one tough girl.

Isabelle was acutely aware of how she was viewed. She seemed to have no keen interest in food, clothing, or even money. Material items seemed to have no direct value, but nearly inestimable worth in terms of how they created and contributed to her personal status. This was a stark contrast to her father who spent his life in search of prosperity, always hoping to achieve real affluence to counter a family tree populated by penniless peasants.

Isabelle's father's endeavors as a merchant took them from place to place across the high plains but allowed them to enjoy a comfortable, if modest, lifestyle. His efforts provided the means for Isabelle to attend university, a singular event for young women before the turn of the century. Perhaps equally remarkable, Isabelle chose to follow a major in the Classics, a specialization that in the best of times offered limited career options.

Since before entering university, Isabelle's goal in life had been to be remarkable and be remembered. Her mother, and namesake, had been characterized as an "impressive" woman. In Isabelle's eyes, these accolades were awarded due to her mother's personality and patience, accentuated by her mother's natural beauty and the personal care she gave to appearance, even when only wearing the simplest of clothing.

Isabelle's mother, clean and laundered, had always been there for family and friends. She had always been full of energy and ready to help. She had been sympathetic. She had been generous. She had been a good wife and mother.

Her mother's attributes were laudable and perhaps truly outstanding. But Isabelle did not want to go through her life cast in this die. She did not want to be judged by outward measures. She wanted to be outstanding due to acts and deeds—real substantive accomplishments and not ethereal idiosyncrasies. She wanted to be known for her mental skill. She wanted to show that she was better, really standing out, not because of her jewelry or shoes, but because she had proven herself to be, as her own mother would have said, "One smart cookie."

Isabelle's mother would also have reminded her daughter that all our destinies are, "In God's Hands." Isabelle knew her mother had fervently believed this as she had fervently believed in *her* God.

Isabelle herself was less sure of *her* God. But, unlike her mother, she was sure that her destiny was in her own hands—deities need not apply. If she did not do it, no one would. Prayer was not the key to success, hard work was. Many prayed beside their bed every night as she had been taught as a child. Many prayed until their knees hurt. Many were still praying for their good times to come. A few worked hard—as hard as need-be. This minority of hard workers was not lifted by divine spirit but driven by an inner fire. Isabelle no longer prayed, but she was driven.

This view of her own pathway made Isabelle a formidable student, if a somber young lady. She was seen by some as overly combative and dogmatic—traits not particularly appreciated, especially for a young woman.

But, more often than not, she knew she was right and was willing to fight to prove it.

Whatever else was reflected by these attributes, they were the formula for a good student. Isabelle was certainly that, excelling in her university classes.

While at university in Lincoln, Nebraska—enduring the cold winters and hot summers in a town that was nearly a decade younger than her mother—Isabelle met George Hardy. It was not a falling-head-over-heals event—not at all. George was three years older than she. And, George was serious—very serious.

George was the eldest of seven children. He had been born in New England the same year his teenage mother married his thirty-year-old father. Despite the age difference, it had been a happy union, but George had had to assume a large portion of the household responsibilities to help his mother keep up with the long line of children that seemed, at one point, to be never-ending. George had not really had a childhood. He had metamorphosed from a little boy to the keeper of his younger brothers and sisters in the course of one summer.

The shepherding of his siblings had delayed his entry into university such that Isabelle and George were in the same class even though of different ages. This shepherding had also imparted on him a set of rather special skills that allowed him to fully concentrate on the task at hand regardless of the diversions and the accompanying cacophony. In short, he was a very good student, and this had been the real attraction for Isabelle.

They became good friends as their university studies, as well as the century, came to an end. With their new diplomas, George got a job in a bank in Lancaster, Nebraska, and Isabella obtained a position teaching high school Latin in rural Iowa. They corresponded regularly over several years until their paths once again converged, both now working in Des Moines. This opened the door to closer contacts and relations that ultimately led to wedding plans in 1905.

With two university-educated workers in the newly-formed household, they decided they could afford the luxury of buying a home, getting a mortgage on a house on Pleasant Street. The house was a twenty-year-old 900 square foot Foursquare, built when the area had been the independent town of Greenwood Park, not yet an incorporated part of the city of Des Moines. Their new North of Grant neighborhood had recently benefited from streetcar service which gave the young couple access to all parts of the city.

Married life offered what seemed like a deluge of new challenges to the couple of perfectionists still trying to adapt to living together. Cooking, eating, sleeping, saving—everything seemed to have a new complexion for young adults with new jobs and a new house to boot.

Mortgages were new banking investments at that time and George did not want to risk mixing his family finances with his work. He had a good banking job and did not want to jeopardize it in any way by borrowing from his employer. He did, nonetheless, use his contacts to arrange a loan from a competitor, Iowa Loan and Trust. This only covered forty percent of the total cost of the home and the couple had to use all their saving to be able to make the deal work. Equally challenging, the loan was only for six years, so they had to plan carefully and keep to a tight budget.

Finances were critical and for the next three years each of the newly-weds worked on their careers. George, with his character of seriousness still in high gear, climbed the corporate ladder quickly and was soon a rising star at First National Bank. Isabelle, with a fair dose of luck and finesse, managed to get an appointment teaching the Classics at Highland Park College.

These were watershed times for the budding banking industry. While there was no central bank, there was a growing number of both state and national banks, but also a noticeable number of bank failures. State-char-tered banks issued bank notes as did some private companies. The financial environment was fluid and precarious. As markets expanded and there was more of a worldview, banking pioneers such as Samuel Sachs, Marcus Gold-man, Jacob Schiff, Henry Lehman, and John Pierpont Morgan expanded their networks, offering opportunities for young men willing to work long, hard hours. George fit the ticket. He was smart and attentive with a strong work ethic—coming early or staying late were accepted as just necessary parts of getting the job done. While not an overnight success, George was pretty close. As quickly as anyone had done before him, he was named to a managerial position.

Isabelle's professional pathway, on the other hand, though charted with great care, took a detour when she became pregnant three years after they exchanged their vows. That was not supposed to happen. She was not ready for it to happen. They were not ready for it to happen. But it had happened, and they needed to adjust.

Certainly, they were both elated when she gave birth to a five-pound baby boy. Though he was in generally good health, he was what Isabelle's mother would have called puny. He looked frail with transparent skin and pale lips. He was not colicky. He did not rant and wail. He was a good baby, but he just seemed so fragile his father was initially afraid to pick him up for fear of breaking him.

The baby, named Percy in honor of Isabelle's uncle, though slight in stature, even as an infant, was gentle with a keen power of observation that foreshadowed a remarkable intelligence.

Isabelle stopped work to take care of their son. At the same time, however, calculating that a newborn equated with considerably more housework, not to mention childcare, George hired Sally to help out three days a week.

Sally was a young black mother of two from the East Side. Her husband was a driver for a local refuse company and she had been a domestic worker for seven years. All this George learned when vetting suitable candidates, wanting to be very sure his beloved family would be well-served while not being put in any sort of risk, and all the while keeping to the rather limited budget he had available, even as a newly appointed manager.

Sally turned out to be a wonder. Isabelle was delighted. While she did not really warm to her when the two were together, in true Isabelle fashion being stingy with the compliments as well as any overt signs of bonding, when she was alone with George, she bestowed all forms of accolades on the young woman who was serious and, as far as Isabelle could tell, trustworthy.

An unanticipated effect of Sally's service was that Isabelle, for the first time in her life, felt as though she had free time. One could have argued that, with an infant son, this was an illusion. Nevertheless, Isabelle grew to count so much on Sally that, on her three free days, she began scheduling time for herself.

This started with appointments at the beautician's. However, she also enquired about ladies' groups and was soon a due-paying member of DAR and Soroptimist. For the former, she was attracted by their emphasis placed on education, while for the latter, their vision of helping women reach their full potential resonated with her personal challenges.

Through the sodality provided by the organizations, again, for the first time in her life, Isabelle began being part of a wider social network. Soon she was member of a bridge club and PEO. As her social calendar began filling, she lobbied George to take Sally onboard full-time.

By the time Percy had his first birthday, Isabelle had at least three engagements a week including her regular bridge game—which she greatly relished winning. While she very much enjoyed the camaraderie offered by a markedly expanded social agenda, she was not a vain woman. She did not wear fancy nor expensive clothes—practicality and durability were key. Darks for winter, lighter colors for summer—basic, solid fabrics. She ported smallish hats, often with a short veil, and simple shoes—of good craftsmanship and a medium robust heal. She went to the beautician every fortnight, but again choose functional coiffures. She did not have manicures or pedicures, thinking these as wastes of both time and money. Her jewelry was basic as well—most often only wedding rings, pearl necklace, and a Bulova wrist watch. Other accessories were limited to a stout black leather handbag and a pair of black kidskin gloves.

Unlike, many of her cohorts, Isabelle did not preen when encircled by her peers at DAR or PEO. This was beneath her. She did not boast of her husband's job, salary, or car (they did not have). This, too, she saw as demeaning. Isabelle liked to socialize, but this was not to flaunt her "betterness". Isabelle enjoyed socializing because she enjoyed the mental challenge, the mental chess game, in which she engaged with all her companions. She took great pleasure in maneuvering the conversation, slowly directing the discourse to topics where she had an advantage, then pouncing like a cat on a mouse.

She had been raised to never discuss sex, religion, or politics. And, she adhered to this doctrine in principle. She would never launch a frontal assault on any of these taboo subjects. She would, however, often and with marvelous deftness, twist and weave the conversation to incorporate these forbidden themes, before, with amazing speed, merging all the diverse dimensions into a single barbed question that she would fling at her opponent—an opponent who most times did not even realize she was an opponent. When her opposition began spinning her mental wheels, slipping in the dangerous lexical labyrinth, failing to get her bearings to be able to craft a suitable response to this carefully crafted and baited query, Isabelle knew she had won. The taste of victory was sweet, almost a narcotic, whether on the card table or in the verbal arena.

Isabelle knew she was, as George had once remarked, "Someone who knows her onions". She was clever. She probably was even a whiz. She could easily outmaneuver people with her acute mental gymnastics. What's more, she took pleasure in doing so—not just with her girlfriends, but with George, and whomever else she might be able to corner.

Isabelle had come very far on her intellect and she was not about to let her well-honed senses dull just because she was now a mother and wife. She read the newspaper every day, listened to the radio, read magazines, and was always ready to put her mind to the test—almost any test.

It was not difficult for Isabelle to find testing grounds. She often found more than ample justification for taking up the provocation, albeit muted or tacit, and really did not need a reason to exercise her mind—what she called taking on all comers in her cerebral game of tactics and knowledge.

Isabelle had deep white, Anglo-Saxon, Protestant roots and these were strongly reflected in her beliefs and priorities. From her perspective, she had met all life had had to offer and come out a winner. This was an opportunity open to all. Only the weak, the lazy, or the unimaginative were overcome by life's burdens. If you really have the will, there was always a way. She was adamant. She was unbending. She was unswerving. She was not open to compromise as regarded her fundamental principles. Moreover, she knew she was right and she could prove it.

Isabelle had managed her busy schedule making use of the city's electric streetcar system. With a bit of supplemental promenading, she was able to get where she needed to go when she needed to be there. George, too, took the streetcar back and forth to the bank and saw no real reason to invest in a newfangled motorcar. Between trains, streetcars, and the occasional hired buggy, George felt they were always able to go where they needed with minimal fuss and expense. Ever the banker, motorcars just did not seem like a good investment.

When they were married, there were so few motorcars in Iowa that Isabelle knew nothing about what so many called the "horseless carriage". Her work until becoming a mother so occupied her time that transport was the last thing on her mind. Then, when she did begin to spread her wings, the public system was more than able to accommodate her needs. Who needed a car?

Things changed in 1915. Percy had been in school for a year. Sally was still coming every day, but not for full days. She had found another household to help out in the mornings and would reach Isabelle after lunch to assist with the cleaning and laundry and be there when Percy came home from school. Isabelle made sure all her own activities were, therefore, in the afternoon.

This seemed easy enough at first, but the realities soon began knocking at the door. Public transport was fine, but it required ample time to take delays and necessary trekking into account. It was hard for Isabelle to wait for Sally's arrival and then make an early afternoon bridge game or Soroptimist meeting when relying on streetcars operated by people, according to Isabelle, who used the sun to tell time.

Her conundrum was even worse on those days when her events went well past teatime and she would only reach the streetcar station closest to her home in the early evening—her late return making it hard for Sally to get home by streetcar in time to make dinner for her family. All in all, it was just not working out.

But, as Isabelle knew, there was always a way. If Isabelle had been one of those old Romans whose language she had so studiously studied, she would have said the gods smiled.

George had been sensitized to his wife's dilemma, sitting through many detailed descriptions of the weaknesses of streetcar travel at the dinner table. Then, to his surprise and gratitude, he came across an estate sale handled by the bank where someone needed to sell an almost new 1914 Saxon Roadster. This seemed like a solution made in heaven and George quickly did all he could to ensure he was able to procure the motorcar.

They now had a solution, or at least a solution in the making. Isabelle still had to learn how to drive. George, of course, needed to acquire the same skills, but he wisely decided that his wife should go first. Without too much delay, they were able to find someone willing and able to teach Isabelle to become a proficient driver—a necessary competency as cars were becoming the newest attraction in the state, reportedly more than 100,000 now on the state's roads.

The teacher to teach the teacher was Sam. He had worked at the Colby Motor Company in Mason City when it first started out four years earlier. But, as the company paid its employees just a little over two-bits an hour, Sam decided he could do better moving to the capital and starting a small shop to service and repair motorcars, teaching people to drive on the side.

Sam understood cars, knew them inside-out, was a good driver, and patient. However, these sterling qualities ill prepared him for Isabelle. Isabelle wanted to drive. Isabelle needed to drive. Isabelle needed to drive right away. She had not the slightest idea of what constituted a motorcar—not how it worked, how it was mastered, nor how to fathom the code of the road. She was a blank slate, but she had not the passiveness to progressively learn about cars as she had about Latin and Greek. She was in a hurry and she wanted to absorb all the necessary skills and knowledge overnight—certainly an impossible task and one that would try Sam's perseverance.

Sam and Isabelle spent many hours in the roadster—each hour feeling like three. They smashed two garbage cans, ran across three flower gardens, got stuck in the alley behind the feed store, almost hit a horse and rider, and Sam got his fingers mashed when the hood slipped from Isabelle's grip as he was showing her the basics of how a motor worked. Not to mention the smoking of the brakes, the grinding of the gears, and the screaming of that very same motor as Isabelle incorrectly undertook all the core maneuvers. Sam clenched his fists until his knuckles glowed like phosphorous, he bit his tongue until it hurt, and he closed his eyes at the most inopportune times. Yet somehow, Sam was not sure how, the moment arrived when Isabelle did know how to drive and was able to carry on without him.

Now mobile, Isabelle's routine changed yet again. She would drive to all her engagements, getting home much earlier to be able to drop Sally at home before parking the car for the day unless for some reason there was an evening outing.

Part of this change was learning about where she lived. As a traveler on public transport, she had had to know little more than the points of departure and arrival. However, as a driver, she had to navigate the entire city, learning the roads, neighborhoods, and intersections. This learning was not only geographic but also cultural—she began to see firsthand that the city was in fact a mosaic of different entities, for most of which she had had no previous knowledge. Nowhere was this more the case than in regard to Sally's East Side neighborhood.

Isabelle was well educated. From an academic perspective, she had learned more than most about the story of race, both in the country as a whole and in her new home state. She knew Iowa had been a free state during the Civil War, but this did not mean that the majority white population thought blacks were equal. It was, in her view, more of an out-of-sight-out-of-mind situation that most people simply did not want slavery in their backyard, but what others did was none of their business.

Isabelle knew that even back to Roman times, race was complicated. In Antiquity, however, while both blacks and whites were slaves, blacks and mixed-race people had access to multiple layers of society—not necessarily the case today.

In more recent times, Isabelle had studied how Iowa had had "black codes" that imposed unequal restrictions on blacks. Concurrently, from her own observations, she knew how the state had, with considerable success, courted immigrants from northern and western Europe at the end of the nineteenth century.

But the population, as she witnessed, had become more racially and culturally mixed. Immediately after the Civil War, there had been a movement of some black families into the Midwest—looking for greener pastures after emancipation. Then, as she had read, five years after the end of the war, there had been a coal boom in the state spurred on by the needs of the railroads for fuel. More blacks had come then to fill the labor requirements of the expanding mining industry.

Iowa coal mines, Isabelle remembered from recent newspaper articles, had begun to decline as there was growing competition from Illinois and

Kentucky. However, the journalists were reporting there was now a surge of immigration of southern blacks, what some were calling the "Great Migration", with rural agrarian folks attracted to the better-paying jobs of the industrialized northern and midwestern states. Some Iowans were predicting an influx of thousands of black families and some of these were greeting this news with, at the very least, trepidation.

But Iowa seemed to be a good place for all races, or so Isabelle thought. She recalled how only a little over two decades ago a man named George Washington Carver had broken the ice and become the first black student at Iowa State University. The same George Washington Carver was now a renowned researcher somewhere in Alabama. Isabelle was reminded of a piece she had read in the newly renamed *Des Moines Register* about the coal mining town of Buxton, applauding how all the races and ethnic groups worked and lived together in harmony. In fact, it was about the same time she read about the beginning of a group called the NAACP right here in Des Moines. Isabelle felt things were moving in the right direction and everyone just had to be reminded to stay in his or her own lane and everything would be fine.

While legally, politically, and culturally not the Jim Crow south, blacks in Iowa were far from being uniformly treated as whites. Some residents appeared to adhere to a separate-but-equal philosophy while others just believed the races had not been made from the same mold. Although the state had removed the ban on interracial marriage in 1851, seventeen years later a twelve-year-old black girl had been refused entry into public school. A year later the State Supreme Court ruled that separate was not equal and that schools should be integrated. Nevertheless, things change slowly, still four years later a mixed-race woman had been refused service in a whites-only dining room—the Iowa Supreme Court again intervening to declare all have a constitutional right to equal service.

In spite of everything, including not infrequently groundbreaking litigation and jurisprudence, the races often remained socially, if not legally, separated with black neighborhoods, black churches, black clubs, and black cabarets catering for the small but growing black population.

Isabelle, however, seemed unaware of any injustices. Her midwestern pedigree was solid and, for her, things were just as they had always been. She saw her views on the inalienable rights of the individual as color-blind. The seed—that when properly nourished with unwavering devotion and dedication—would sprout into a meaningful life for all individuals, white or black. It was just that each had to have realistic expectations and understand their boundaries.

Isabelle did not see injustices. She saw freedom of expression. And, she saw a landscape where there were white and black fields—never the two united. Each to their own. As it should be. As it had always been—not just since the relatively recent time of Jefferson, but since the period of Augustus. As it had been, really, forever.

Thus, when she saw Des Moines' East Side firsthand, this was a lifting of the veil—a taste of what for some could have been bitter soup. Although her own home in the North of Grant neighborhood was modest, by East Side standards it was a villa. The small garden she lamented as being nothing but a dandelion patch suddenly looked like an ornamental courtyard. Yes, conditions were seemingly not as bad as those she had heard about in the "Black Belt" ghettoes of Chicago. But her own East Side was far from ideal. The area, going from Shaw Street to Railroad Avenue on a north-south axis and from Sixth Street to Thirteenth Street, west-to-east, contained dilapidated row houses, what easterners called Bandbox or Trinity style, small and cramped. In addition to these, there were a few double houses and some isolated individual homes—nearly all the structures made of cheap materials with only the rare tiny garden and few trees. She imagined the lucky residents had cold-water indoor plumbing, most of the houses heated by coal with electricity still a rarity. Moreover, clearly only very occasional street cleaning was practiced. The place was a mess.

The first time Isabelle drove Sally home, to her neater-than-most small, almost tiny, bungalow, she recalled what one of her classmates at the University of Nebraska had said after a rowdy weekend in Chicago. Out of curiosity, and with considerable apprehension, her classmate and her companions, all white, had gone for a drink at Club De Lisa, reportedly the most well-known black night club in the city. While she had left unscathed, with her honor intact, she had commented to Isabelle that the whole place, filled with sweating black bodies, cigarettes, and booze, had a strange sweet aroma like a roasting pig. Isabelle now wondered, as she drove through the heart of the black community of Des Moines, if these houses smelled like roast pig inside? She knew intuitively that she, like her classmate in Chicago, would come and go unscathed. But in that strange emotional place that is beyond the control of logic and reason, she could feel a little prickle of fear, shockingly to her, with just a smidgen of exhilaration, at the thought of being brutally raped by a group of huge sweaty black men smelling like roast pig.

3

Meet Margaret

ISABELLE RELISHED IN HER freedom through the remainder of 1915, fine-tuning her driving and bridge skills, but not so much her interpersonal abilities. However, 1916 started out in turmoil. Within the first thirty days of the year, Austria-Hungary launched an offensive against Montenegro, German zeppelins bombed Paris, Russia battled in the Caucasus, the Ottoman Empire engaged in the Battle of Çanakkale, Poncho Villa killed a group of American mining engineers, and George and Isabella had a romantic weekend to celebrate the beginning of their second decade together. Although their relationship had been far from platonic, it would have been hard to characterize their union as one based principally on lust or even passionate romantic love. It had been first and foremost a meeting of the minds followed by the occasional, and, at times, regular coupling of the bodies. Their amorous weekend in January was the exception that set the rule and also the excitement that led to Isabelle's second pregnancy and the birth of their daughter in September.

If possible, this childbirth was even more traumatizing than the first. They were only just getting used to Percy albeit he was nearly eight and a half years old when his little sister was born. Isabelle and George had walked on eggshells for years around their son, waiting for the worst they knew was coming, but hoped it would not. They knew his frailness made him vulnerable—vulnerable to the contagious diseases crawling about the world, vulnerable to maliciousness inflicted by man, vulnerable to acts of God.

Seemingly with complete disregard to his parents' concerns, Percy insisted on being a regular child. He did all those things children do, he just did some of them differently. He was too small of stature for rigorous sports and he was too quick of mind to be held back by his classmates. He had already completed five grades of primary school and in the areas of mathematics and reading he excelled at the level of a high school student.

Percy walked to and from school. He rode his bicycle. He climbed trees. He had a stamp collection. He liked to fly his kite and enjoyed ice skating in winter. He was just a kid and after eight summers with no calamities, he had finally convinced his parents of this fact. But now they were once again turned upside-down with the arrival of his baby sister.

The fact that George and Isabelle's second child shared none of the fragility of her older sibling was perhaps of little consequence to the parents. George was tickled pink, as he liked to say, to have a healthy and robust baby girl. It was not to distract from this joy to realize he was soon to turn forty—at forty he had to have his career well in hand. He had had an enviable trajectory throughout his academic and professional careers, but he was now at the crucial tipping point. He needed one more, in his mind, obligatory promotion to get where he needed to be—to have the financial independence and security to be able to do whatever needed to be done for his family. It was, therefore, with considerable melancholy that he acknowledged to himself, and to himself alone, that he would not at this juncture be able to devote the time he would have wanted to his daughter. It simply was not possible. This made him sad, but all the more resolute to secure the family's financial future.

For Isabelle there was no pragmatic way to view this unexpected happenstance. It clearly meant her time to herself was now challenged. She knew this was not a noble condition nor one that was necessary for the benefit of the family—quite the contrary. She understood much of George's dilemma as she, too, understood all too well how necessary it was to have a secure foothold when one passed the unwelcome forty-year-threshold. With no small amount of chagrin, Isabelle realized her feelings were purely selfish. She thoroughly enjoyed her time outside the home—playing cards, jousting at mental chess, and, more and more, socializing with other well-educated and well-heeled women of her age.

Sally was still the lifeline and would continue assuming most of the household chores, keeping Percy steady on his own two feet, and now, back to full-time with the Hardy's, looking after the newborn. But this was really too much for one person and there was no way Isabelle could just drive off and leave all this to Sally—as much as she would have liked to. Her own looming forty-year-gateway notwithstanding, she so wished time would speed up and the baby, christened Margaret, would start school next month rather than years from now.

But all this self-deprecation was for naught as Margaret was only six months old when the United States entered World War I. If Isabelle had not been so absorbed in the aftermath of her childbirth and had applied the ample doses of logic for which she was so well-known, she would have realized things would probably turn out this way. War was unavoidable—at least, so many thought. As the *Register* had been recounting in such lurid detail, since the sinking of the *Lusitania* in 1915, things had not been going well with the world. The mess of the new year was surely foreshadowing the bad times to come—bad times that had now arrived for all.

The fact that much of the world had been fighting the war for almost three years was of no consequence to the residents of Pleasant Street. Isabelle had followed in the newspaper and radio accounts of the slaughter that had been ongoing in Europe and elsewhere in the world for years with hundreds of thousands having lost their lives. It was most unfortunate, but it was there not here. That damned democrat Wilson had upset the applecart, deciding "armed neutrality" was no longer possible and declaring war on Germany. He just could not leave well enough alone.

The war turned everything wrong side up. What had been known as the "progressive era", a time of organization and efficiency, became a time of at least short-term chaos as the country learned what it meant to be engaged in a world-wide battle. Everyone was called upon. Soldiers were needed at the front. Soldiers needed arms. Soldiers needed food and clothing. Soldiers needed as much support as they could be given. Many women who had been part of Isabelle's circles volunteered for a variety of activities including working in factories. There were no more bridge games, Soroptimist, DAR, or PEO meetings. Every fragment of energy was devoted to the war effort. If Isabelle had not had an infant in arms, she, too, would have been called to, or felt obliged to get more directly involved in the war effort. She began to realize that Margaret had become a decisive buffer protecting her from the full force of the war on the home front.

Percy was, of course, too young to be actively engaged. At the other end of the spectrum, George was at least not an immediate target for the military draft as conscription was focusing on men from twenty-one to thirty-one years of age.

This did not mean Isabelle got off scot-free. Sally was called to work in a local munitions factory and her husband was directed to work in supporting the Black Officer Training Camp that was being built in Des Moines. This meant Isabelle had to learn how to clean her own house, wash her family's clothes, cook, and do all the other chores which she had so happily handed over to Sally for so many years. To add to her misery, she had to also assume full responsibility for her two children—something she had never had to do before and that had never been part of her aspirations.

The war years were not easy. In Des Moines, with a large German immigrant population, there was concern of an ethnic backlash. Although Isabelle's Anglo-Saxon bloodlines undoubtedly led back to Germanic peoples, she and her family were far enough removed to slip into the Anglophile slot and not suffer any of the worries of many of her neighbors.

Fortunately, the war from America's perspective was relatively short. In just twenty months after declaring war, in November 1918, with the Armistice of Compiègne, the fighting on the Western Front ended and six months later, in June 1919, with the Treaty of Versailles, the war was over.

No one celebrated more than Isabelle. With all her heart she hoped this would signal a return to normal—normal for her being more freedom and much more help from Sally.

By Margaret's third birthday, Sally did rejoin the family—those three years a trial without much tribulation that Isabelle would not have liked to repeat. Having skipped several grades, Percy was in high school, so Sally could concentrate on the chores and on Margaret—an arrangement that pleased Isabelle no end.

Sally had been with the family for more than a decade, but throughout, Isabelle had exchanged probably less than a hundred words a week with her. She would drop her off at home on the East Side every day, the two sitting like statues in the 1919 Dodge Touring Car that George had been able to afford now that the war was over. Isabelle knew Sally had children and, of course, a husband, but all these details had been provided by George all those years ago when Sally had first started. Still, Isabelle had no earthly idea of what Sally's family life was like and she thought this was the way things should be—one must separate business and one's private life.

This lack of bonding, what some would consider a lack of empathy or, in the extreme, humanity, was not meant in meanness by Isabelle. For her, it was just the way things should be done. She greatly appreciated and, very obviously, relied upon Sally's work. She even liked Sally as a person. But you had to draw the line somewhere and Sally came to Isabelle's home to work, not for cup of tea.

The Roaring Twenties were more of a meow for Isabelle—and this was a welcome state. Before the midpoint of the decade Percy had been admitted at the young age of sixteen to the University of Chicago, seeking a bachelor's degree in Economics. Margaret was in third grade at Hubbell and Isabelle was playing bridge twice a week.

Things took a turn for the worse in 1929 when the country entered into the Great Depression as Margaret entered high school at Roosevelt High. While the rich were turned into paupers overnight, in many circumstances lives were ruined and even ended, the Hardy Family, though not unscathed, managed much better than most. Although the banking sector was hit hard, George had become an invaluable member of the senior management team and was kept on, albeit with reduced benefits.

Sally was still with the family and, as she liked to say, "Damn happy to have a job."

With quiet family celebration and gratitude, Percy had graduated *summa cum laude,* continuing, with a full scholarship, for a master's degree in economics.

With even quieter, but no less grateful, celebration, Margaret officially became Julian Müller's girlfriend. Julian, a second-generation German with roots in Dubuque, had moved to Des Moines with his family during the war. He and Margaret had met when he started at Hubbell in the fourth grade. They had been close friends ever since—the friendship blossoming to a new level when they were at Roosevelt.

All this would seem to indicate that Isabelle could maintain her accustomed lifestyle of socializing and playing cards. But this was not to be the case. While her family had been lucky, most others had faired far less well. Many of the fine ladies from DAR, PEO, and Soroptimist, who took so much pleasure in dressing in the day's finest, looking down their nose at those who could not, were no longer able to afford gasoline for their automobiles let alone the latest trappings. The large vibrant meetings where so many luscious stories had been told were reduced to a skeleton crew of those few families who had managed to keep from being drowned by the waves of economic and social pandemonium.

The ripples of the economic shock effectively put Isabelle's much-loved PEO, DAR, and Soroptimist in moth-balls—like Isabelle's favorite tweed coat with the fox collar, carefully packed-away to await better times. But on the positive side, the small group of survivors were all bridge players, and Isabelle was able to organize a rubber two or three times a week. Thus, as Sally kept the house clean and the pantry full, George fretted over the troubled financial industry, Percy studied harder than he had ever before, Margaret's infatuation with Julian grew, and Isabelle played cards.

By the time Margaret entered her senior year at Roosevelt the economy was beginning to pick up and people were feeling a little better about life in general and life in Des Moines in particular. Nevertheless, the tentacles of the Depression had touched the lives of all.

Prohibition had continued throughout the period of financial tumult, with organized crime being ever more visible in Des Moines and increasingly touching the lives of many. This led to social unease that sat very uncomfortably on shoulders already fatigued by the weight of the Depression years. Politically, the Republicans steered Iowa's policies with anti-immigration and pro-union legislation accompanied by opposition to unemployment assistance and public works.

Then, much to Isabelle's chagrin, the dreaded Democrats had taken control when that detested liberal Franklin Delano Roosevelt had moved into the White House making Isabelle wish Margaret was at any other school—the name of her high school a searing reminder, far too often, of the horrible consequences that she knew would be wrought on the country by the despicable FDR.

Regardless of the trepidation regarding Mr. Roosevelt's leadership, life in Des Moines continued and in summer of 1934, fully in the grip of the New Deal, Margaret graduated from Roosevelt, a year after her now, dearest chum, Julian.

The commentaries were mixed in regard to Julian's post-Roosevelt-High endeavors. He had entered college at a local Des Moines school. Some said this was to be closer to Margaret. Others said it was because he had to help his father after classes and on weekends. Whatever the reason, Julian was still around and sitting in the audience with a great smile on his face when Margaret received her diploma. The two spent a steamy summer in the hot and humid atmosphere of Des Moines, often talking about getting married and starting a family—discussions that Margaret did not share with her family.

Unexpectedly, seemingly without any advance notice to her best friend nor her family, Margaret decided to go to Iowa State in Ames, thirty-five miles due north of Des Moines. Her argument to Julian was that she had been accepted into an excellent liberal arts program and was so close it was almost like she had never left their old neighborhood. This did little to mollify Julian's concern that even across town was too far away.

For all the drama from the young couple, Isabelle was nonchalant about the whole issue. As a well-educated female, still rather an oddity in some circles, even in the post-war years, she very much encouraged Margaret to continue her studies. Where she went and what she did were really of minor consequence to Isabelle. It was more the journey than the destination that mattered. She believed in stretching the limits, the direction of stretch depending on the individual. Isabelle did not believe in predestination. In fact, her belief in self-expression was very much in concert with her views on her own evolution, but quite tangential, even at odds, with her view of the world. Indeed, while in principle she believed everyone should be able to exhibit self-expression as she had, she believed, as well, that there were inherent limits of this expression that were engrained in one's environment. She would never dare say "class" or "caste", but in reality, she believed each individual operated in a sphere that was controlled by outside forces, be they for better or worse—some endowed by nature with more opportune circumstances than others. As an example, her much loathed FDR was, as she very reluctantly admitted to herself, free to express himself, indeed, *needed* to express himself, within the limitations of his office—which were very grand. Nonetheless, the innate restrictions of the Democratic Party's collective mind (and naturally restricted built-in human potential) inhibited tremendously the meaningfulness of Mr. Roosevelt's self-expression. She had no doubt that Mr. Osborn's son, who delivered the morning paper, as the product of a thoughtful Republican family, had more to offer in terms of self-expression than that terrible man currently sitting in the White House.

Margaret did make it home from Ames almost every weekend. Sally kept her room spotless and, if one did not know better, it was easy to think the occupant of the sunny and bright bedroom was a full-time resident.

Margaret and Julian would spend most of the weekend together, but Margaret would make sure to have at least one meal with her parents. Isabelle was not sure what the youngsters did during their time together, and to large extent, she did not want to know. It was enough for her to see her daughter. To see she was healthy, in good state of mind, and, according to all reports, doing fine in her studies. Isabelle was very appreciative of the meal Margaret set aside for her family.

The years had weighted heavily on George. His normal vigor seemed to be waning as he got closer to his sixtieth year. Although Isabelle hardly mentioned it, she knew her husband had worked ever so hard to keep his family afloat—not just afloat, but perhaps a little bit ahead of many who had been so affected by the war and the Depression.

George loved their daughter with a passion that often made Isabelle wince—her own relationship with her husband was defined by many things, but not by passion. The times father and daughter spent together during her weekend visits were the bright points of George's week. In many ways this affection was reciprocated and frequently Isabelle was unsure if Margaret was really coming home to see George or to see Julian.

Isabelle was, therefore, surprised when Margaret announced at the end of her sophomore year that she planned to transfer to the University of Colorado. This decision was, from Margaret's perspective, cloaked in the need to expand her intellectual and cultural horizons as she had spent her whole life fenced in Warren, Polk, and Story counties of Iowa.

However, Isabelle had heard over the bridge table, or more exactly over a cup of tea after an especially thrilling rubber, that her daughter may have had some sort of parallel life. Margaret had matured into a beautiful and charming young woman. It may have been too naive to assume she would live a convent-like life when on campus at State. Margaret was, after all, a member of Kappa Kappa Gamma sorority. She had lots of classmates—men and women. She attended social events.

Isabelle had no idea if her daughter was celibate and felt it was none of her business. For years it had seemed as a foregone conclusion that Margaret would marry Julian. What, when, and how they did what they did were their responsibility.

Things appeared to be changing. The over-the-tea-cup chat had indicated Margaret had developed a close friendship with one of the school's first-string football players. The teller-of-tales who had tattled on Margaret's on-campus social calendar seemed to think the footballer and her daughter were spending more and more time together. As almost a postscript, the prattler had mentioned she had heard the star athlete was changing schools, having been offered a really good deal at the University of Colorado. Was this related to Margaret's current plans to transfer?

George and Julian were shattered by the news. The former seemed to have a bit of a spark go out of his eyes, while the latter appeared to enter into a shell of rigidity, his chin always thrust out as if looking for a fight.

Isabelle had a blander outlook on the situation. Although she suspected it was a pretext, she agreed that widening one's horizons was always a good thing. Margaret had seen little of the world. A move from the plains to the foothills of the Rockies could be a good thing. Attending a second university could also be broadening—new ideas, new approaches. The more experiences Margaret could absorb along the road to her college degree, the better.

When the time for new student orientation came around, Isabelle had Sally help Margaret pack up her things and get to the train station for the fourteen-hour trip west. Her daughter was, for the first time, far enough away to really be considered as gone. She now joined her older brother as a member of the household *in absentia*.

George seemed to become melancholic on the weekends. Julian was just gone.

Isabelle tried to perk up George by arranging picnics, concerts, or even contract bridge with husband and wife teams. Sadly, George hated cards, was very selective about his concerts, and could only endure so many picnics regardless of how much he liked the principle. In the end, Isabelle gave up and only managed to arrange for more bridge games for herself to keep out of the house and out of George's way.

It was Easter of her junior year when Margaret came home for the holiday and without preamble announced she was once more changing schools, this time returning to Iowa and attending Grinnell. This was announced in a matter of fact way, neither Isabelle nor George knowing if Margaret assumed her parents would pay for another about-face. There was no discussion of academia and definitely no reference to any football player. It was simply a fact. She had already made the preparations and next fall would be much closer—only fifty-five miles away to the east on the road to Iowa City. There was also no mention made as to whether or not this next chapter would include regular weekends in Des Moines.

Sally, once again, was instrumental in Margaret's academic maneuvering. She met the train and helped get Margaret's affairs home and stowed in the attic. Margaret then spent her time doting on her father, visiting family, and renewing old friendships. She did reconnect with Julian, who had left school after his sophomore year to work full-time for his father. The two had several evenings together as well as Saturday afternoons when Julian was free. Then, just a few weeks after arriving, it was time to go. Sally helped Margaret one more time get her items down from the attic that smelled of dust, mothballs, and peanuts. The two ladies carefully stowed the cargo in George's car for the drive to Grinnell.

Sally and George accompanied Margaret to her dorm room in George's 1935 Chrysler Airflow. Once they had carried Margaret's boxes and cases up to the second-floor room, they met her roommate, Alice, a girl from the little town of Poplar Bluff in the southeast of Missouri. When George recounted their day to Isabelle, she had a smile, telling George, "Alice must have thought Sally was Margaret's personal hand servant."

Isabelle, always the intellectual, recalled that the slave plantations of southern Missouri were actively farmed until only about seventy years ago, a period short enough for strong feelings to survive. She wondered how her daughter, somewhat of a closet liberal, would fare if Alice turned out to be an ardent supporter of the long-lost Confederacy. Truly, Isabelle mulled, a possibility for another valuable learning experience.

In the absence of sororities and with the uncertainties as to how she would bond with her new roommate, it might have seemed that Margaret could have found campus life a bit dull, resuming her old habit of weekending in Des Moines. This was certainly the outcome for which George prayed. Isabelle had no idea as to the status of her daughter's relationship with Julian. Secretly, she, too, hoped Margaret would restart her regular visits home and pick back up with Julian—talking about marriage and family.

All these thoughts aside, Margaret apparently adapted very well to her new school and her new roommate, as she was seldom to be seen in Des Moines. She would come home for holidays and even showed up unannounced a few times to try and bring her father out of a slump after Isabelle had given her a call and chided her for abandoning those who cared for her so deeply.

In May Isabelle and George received a formal invitation to Margaret's graduation ceremonies and by July Sally had helped Margaret, yet again, get settled in her old room in the family home. In less than a month after resettling in her old familiar surroundings, Margaret got a job working full-time at Younkers Department Store.

For Isabelle, albeit this was not the situation for which she was searching, nor was it a situation that seemed durable, it did represent momentary stability. Each morning, before Isabelle rose, George left for the bank in his car, Margaret took the streetcar to Younkers, and Sally showed up. Isabelle was free to do what she wanted, when she wanted, and where she wanted. Things could have been worse.

Margaret would sometimes join her parents for dinner—often the meal having been prepared in advance by Sally. Other times, Isabelle would not see her daughter for several days. But she accepted this as just the normal part of having an adult child living at home. Her daughter was a woman who could and should manage her own life. That she was back living at home was an accommodation while she made the transition from university life to a career or a family, or both.

George might spend several hours in his study on weekends, but he did spend time with Isabelle, the two going for a walk, a movie, or out for dinner. If Margaret was around, she might join her parents. If she was not at home, Isabelle hoped she was with Julian, but had no idea of the sort of social life her daughter led.

This routine, at times feeling like strangers sharing the same quarters, continued through the Christmas holidays when Margaret was working a lot of overtime as shoppers were becoming more and more numerous with the departure of the Depression. Isabelle was happy that Margaret decided to spend Christmas Day with her father as he would have been downcast if he had not shared this special day with his special girl.

George continued to put in long hours, returning home with more of a hunched back and darker circles under his eyes. When he came up the steps, he shuffled as though carrying a heavy weight. Isabelle was worried, but he assured her that everything was fine.

Just before Easter, on a Thursday night when Margaret had not come home for dinner, George had gotten up from the table to clear away the dishes from a tasty pot roast prepared by Sally when, halfway to the kitchen, he crumpled to the floor. He never saw or felt Isabelle rushing to his side.

There was complete shock. Isabelle did not know how to get in touch with Margaret, so she called Percy. Her son had totally immersed himself in his Chicago life, studying hard and finishing well in his master's program, then, following his father's lead, getting a good job at Mutual Federal Bank. He had not been home for several years but wrote his mother long letters every week. Isabelle looked forward to the arrival of these missives and felt she was living his life vicariously with him. Now it was she contacting him with very grim tidings. Upon hearing of the death of his father, he was unquestionably shaken, but regained his composure quickly and promised to be in Des Moines by the next train.

Percy now *en route* and awaiting Margaret's return, Isabelle's shock and pain spun in her mind like a fiery pinwheel. It had always been George and Isabelle. What was it now?

She thought of her cousin who had also lost her life-long companion; realizing now how incompletely she had understood the gut-wrenching grief—the life-changing sorrow. She wished Mabel were there, so she called.

Mabel lived in Des Moines, but the two typically had little contact. Mabel, from the Canadian branch of the family, had come to Iowa when she married the now deceased Francis. Her husband had been a long-time resident of the River Woods neighborhood, working as an accountant for a property management firm that oversaw many of the apartment complexes in the area.

Long before becoming a Hawkeye, Mabel had gone to teachers' college and been trained as a pedagogue for primary pupils—a job she first held in the hamlet of Platte, South Dakota, about the time Isabelle was giving birth to Percy. Mabel was five years Isabelle's junior.

After two years in Platte, Mabel had just started teaching at the Rose-bud Indian Reservation when, on a weekend trip to Sioux Falls, she met Francis who had been there to attend a meeting of the American Institute of Certified Public Accountants. The chance encounter at a local restaurant had led to Francis abandoning his meeting for a movie and a walk in McK-ennan Park. The two kept in regular contact and two years later Francis traveled to Rosebud to ask for Mabel's hand. They had married then and there, with Mabel artfully interweaving parts of several Sioux ceremonies into their nuptials. At the end of the school year Mabel moved to Des Moines and took a teaching assignment at River Woods Elementary School—she was twenty-eight, it was 1912.

After twenty-five years of teaching, Mabel retired to take care of Francis who was in failing health. The couple had had no children and Francis required nearly continuous assistance. Three years later, her much-loved husband died. Mabel remained in their home, regularly tutoring seventh graders to help them better prepare for high school.

Although Isabelle welcomed Mabel's arrival in Des Moines, she immediately felt they moved in different circles. Isabelle would have angrily denied any accusation of snootiness, but she did feel the honest truth was that different people had different strengths, different likes and dislikes—she and George just happened to be part of a new economic and intellectual gentry. Nevertheless, Isabelle would send Mabel a Christmas card and try to call at least once a year. She and George had gone to Francis' funeral, but Isabelle felt they had little in common and probably looked at life through very different lenses.

Now circumstances had joined their paths more closely. Isabelle needed someone—someone with whom to grieve, someone on whose shoulder to cry. Sally was with her, as always. Loyal and considerate Sally was at Isabelle's side as soon as she heard of George's passing. But Isabelle needed more.

Despite the hour, to Isabelle's surprise, Mabel assured her that she would be right over.

Mabel had found a wide-eyed, stoic Isabelle sitting on the couch next to a teary-eyed Sally—both rocking as if to a rhythm only they heard. The usual take-charge manner of Isabelle had vanished. Her domineering spirit had wilted. She looked old and frail next to the stout form of Sally.

It was now Mabel who took control. She had Sally make tea for the three of them. She made sure all the important calls had been made. She then sat with the other two staring at the front door waiting for Margaret.

It was after midnight when a smiling Margaret sashayed through the entrance to be greeted by unexpected and unwelcome lights and the stares of three older women—the pain in their eyes a sure omen that her evening was ending on a much more somber note than that on which it had started.

Only Mabel could find the words to tell Margaret.

Margaret collapsed on the floor and wailed. Margaret wailed and wailed and wailed.

The three ladies sat on the couch and watched as though engrossed in a Japanese Kabuki dance. Exhausted by her contortions, Margaret lay in a heap and hyperventilated. The spectators seemed to time their respiration with the painfully deep breaths of the agonized girl on the floor.

By sunrise the household had entered into that state of numbness that follows a catastrophe. Mabel made coffee. Sally went to the train station to collect Percy. Isabelle stared out the window while her daughter was comatose on the living room couch.

There was slight consternation when Sally retuned not just with Percy, but also with an attractive young lady of slight build and with light brunette hair setting off hazel eyes. After embracing his mother, sister, and his heretofore unknown second cousin, Percy introduced the newcomer as Helen, his betrothed.

The announcement of Percy's plans for marriage under any other condition would have been met with great glee from Isabelle and probably a staider acceptance from Margaret, who had a view of her older brother more as an icon than a human being.

Margaret was sufficiently younger than her brother that she could not even claim to be following in his wake. Her youth had been untouched by his. It could almost have been described as two detached and unrelated individuals growing up in the same family. Yet, while Percy had not been a physical presence during Margaret's childhood, he had been a spiritual resident of her home who had been her loadstone and, in some ways, her mentor. He had made a great success of all things he encountered. He was smart. He was kind. He had accomplished the difficult with aplomb.

While Percy set the goalposts for Margaret, he was not in truth a flesh and blood occupant of her youth. He was more like that favorite teddy bear to which a child ascribes all manner of powers and wisdom. He was an essence and he was now home for the most terrible of reasons.

As if sleepwalking, the family went through the routine of saying their goodbyes to George. Isabelle, ever the pragmatist, overcame her shock, accepted the inevitability that awaited all, and secretly, in the darkest part of the night, said adieu to her husband, thanking him for being there for her throughout the years. Her eyes were dry, her mind clear, but her heart filled with a heavy sadness—a melancholy more relating to her future than the should-be-felt emptiness after the loss of a lifetime partner and lover.

Isabelle was not religious. She had nevertheless agreed with her children that there should be a church funeral, but more for the reputation of the family than the feeling that God had anything to do with the event. It was the one certainty for them all. That damn liberal Clarence Darrow had gone just a few months earlier. Death took the good and the bad. George was one of the good ones, but there was no escape.

Her children, however, were not as stern about death, the passing of their father, and the role of God. They believed in God. They believed in a caring and loving God. In the abstract, they understood death was part of life. But they felt robbed. They felt their dearly beloved father had been stolen. He had not suffered from a dreadful illness. He had not died on a battlefield. He had not succumbed to some horrific accident. He had simply stood up from his dinner table and died. How could a caring and loving God allow such a wonderful man to be taken so? His family needed him. His children needed him. Where was the justice? They were lost and Isabelle could think of no way to get them back on track, to get them to understand that things just happened. There was no understanding. There was no right and wrong. Things just happened.

Each grieving in their own way. Each adjusting to the loss in their own way. Each looking forward to a different and changed life. They sat about the house like passengers at a bus station, seemingly indifferent to their fellow voyagers, absorbed in their own worlds.

Only Sally tried to keep them together. She buzzed about them like a bee pollinating flowers. She brought cups of tea and pats on the back, she shared memories and wiped away tears. And then the bus came, and they were gone.

Percy and Helen retuned to Chicago. Margaret immured herself in her room. Isabelle left looking for a card game.

Isabelle found cards not to be enough, but to be a good start. She found, as she had hoped, a certain impersonality to the match, almost a reversion to the more basic instincts of purely winning. If one chose well, and Isabelle did, there would be minimal discussion combined with worthy opponents.

Cards were certainly better than her lady's groups. Here all the ladies fawned over her—condolences, regrets, and sympathies. None of these welcomed by Isabelle. She avoided her groups and their members.

Outwardly, even to Sally and Margaret, she maintained an indomitable and dispassionate appearance. Inwardly she was torn apart. She knew she needed to do something. With her nearly atheist beliefs, religious comfort seemed out of the question. She turned again to Mabel. There just seemed nowhere else to go.

After George's funeral, Isabelle had thanked Mabel for her most-appreciated help, gave her a hug, pressed on her a big dish of Spanish rice brought over by a neighbor, and said goodbye. Isabelle had really thought she would return to her old ways and send Mabel a card next Christmas and maybe a phone call at Thanksgiving. But for a second time she needed her cousin and was frustrated with herself for admitting this fact.

Margaret had slowly emerged from her room like a butterfly from a chrysalis—equally damp and riffled looking. She did not communicate much to her mother. She did not eat much at home. But she did go back to her job at Younkers.

Isabelle was on her own. A condition that was new to her.

One day she was heading to a rubber across town at the Wakonda Club, the in place to be seen these days. After crossing the Des Moines and Raccoon Rivers, heading south on Ninth, she found herself turning left on Park, not right to go to the club. Almost as if chauffeured by another, she drove in the opposite direction of her original destination, ending up parking in front of Mabel's house in River Woods.

She almost left, embarrassed to be knocking at the door, coming unannounced to a home where she had never been before. But when Mabel opened the door and greeted Isabelle with a wide smile and an embrace, Isabelle was somehow thankful that whatever spirits had guided her had led her to her cousin.

Isabelle entered a small and tidy home, the living room filled with bric-a-brac and with lots and lots of black and white photos on the walls. Mabel followed Isabelle's gaze to the pictures and led her on a guided tour of members of Francis' and her families, including a sepia snapshot of Mabel's mother, Louise, in a great Canadian snowdrift with a beautiful girl looking slightly older than Louise. Mabel identified this second girl as Isabelle Jane, Louise's sister and Isabelle's mother.

This was the first photograph Isabelle had seen of her mother. There were few photos ever taken and Isabelle was not one to keep mementos. But now, seeing the two happy girls wrapped in a blanket of snow, she wished she had had more keepsakes to preserve her family's spirit in one way or another.

Mabel did all she could to make Isabelle feel at home. After a cup of tea and some chat about life in general, the tension in Isabelle seemed to abate like a bullfrog after a good croak. Although she was still unsure in her own mind how to deal with Mabel, she felt more at ease than she had in weeks.

Slowly and deftly Mabel directed the conversation and the cousins were soon talking about coping with the loss of a spouse and how to connect with long-lost siblings. Mabel was able to extract from Isabelle the fact that she had been basically *incommunicado* with her older brother and sister. Brother William probably still lived in Minneapolis where he had married a local socialite who wanted nothing to do with her in-laws. She claimed, Isabelle had no clue if it were true, to be a direct descendent of John H. Stevens, one of the founders of the city. More importantly perhaps, and certainly more relevant to her own lifestyle, William's wife's father was a key actor on the important Minneapolis Grain Exchange. In short, she wanted nothing to do with her husband's boorish Iowa farmhands and this suited Isabelle all too well.

Sister Anne was a different story. She and Isabelle had been very close in their childhoods and remained in regular contact. It was, in this case, a question of geography and not sociology that kept them apart. Anne had married a professor from Florida State University. He had been several years her senior and after fifteen years of campus living, the childless couple retired to the western side of the state, buying an orange grove near Sarasota. As with Mabel and Isabelle, Anne had lost her husband a few years ago, but still lived in their big southern-plantation-style home with a live-in helper named Violet.

As they conversed, a thought materialized in Mabel's mind. Here were three widows still in good health and with at least modest means. They should get together. She shared her reflections with Isabelle who, against the odds, was tempted.

All in all, the visit went well, the cousins agreeing to have lunch in a few days to continue their discussion.

Isabelle was feeling more positive when she returned home to find Sally ironing clothes in the laundry room. Even though she had strong emotional ties to this woman who had been by her side for so long, she rarely showed any affection. However, today she told Sally to knock-off early. Isabelle said, moreover, that like in days gone by, she would drive her home, so she could have more time with her family. Sally was happily surprised, maybe even stunned, but far too wise to let this opportunity pass.

When Isabelle retuned home again after dropping off Sally, she found Margaret sitting in the living room. This, in and of itself was unusual over recent days, as her daughter had chosen to be cloistered in her bedroom when in the house. Margaret's demeanor gave no hint as to what was in store. She was neither smiling nor frowning. Indeed, she looked almost as spurious as the girl in the Blue Bonnet ads.

Isabelle sat in the big Morris chair that had been George's favored venue for reading the evening paper, fixed her daughter in her gaze, and sternly enquired how things were going at work. Margaret retuned her mother's gaze, nearly a glare, and in a voice that sounded like it was coming from outer space, announced she and Julian were getting married in June.

On the surface this was great news to Isabelle. She had always liked Julian, thinking he would be a good match for her daughter—and even a good catch as he was a hardworking and intelligent young man. Yet, this disclosure literally falling from the sky was a bit disconcerting and Isabelle was too wary to show too much support until the full picture was more clearly visible.

Isabelle was never privy to the inner workings of her daughter's mind—all the more so when she had made the decision to marry Julian. Yes, marriage was a two-way proposition, but Isabelle knew Julian had been seeking this outcome for years; he would have needed no convincing to walk to the alter with Margaret—the sooner the better for him.

Knowing all the details or not, Isabelle felt this was the best move for all concerned and set about encouraging Margaret to prepare a memorable event and not just the slipshod ceremony she appeared willing to accept.

George's death hung like a pall over everything, including the pending marriage. Margaret, who should have been happy about her upcoming wedding, could scarcely bring herself to discuss the event with her mother, even though she knew all too well the responsibility for organizing the service rested with her family—even if the head of this family was just recently deceased.

All Margaret could think of, once she had grappled with the larger fact of getting married, was how could she get married when her father was not there to walk her down the aisle?

With Isabelle's intervention, Margaret finally agreed that Percy could give her away. After all, she loved her big brother dearly and he reminded her a great deal of their father.

Little by little, things fell into place and on a hot June Saturday, blessed with a fresh breeze, Julian and Margaret wed in the Lutheran Church on Ingersoll Avenue. The reception was held on the church grounds at Waverley Hall. Everything went well. Margaret was splendid in along white gown.

Julian, with his brothers beside him, was gallant and charming. Percy was duly paternal. Percy's wife, Helen, seated next to Isabelle, exuded pride in her new husband. Isabelle sat through the ritual thinking she, and those seated around her, should be blotting tears seeping from her eyes, but, dry-eyed, she was only feeling a sense of gratitude that things were going smoothly, and her daughter would soon be a wife.

Margaret and Julian had taken a short honeymoon to Koekuk, Iowa, on the Mississippi, where they indicated they had enjoyed seeing the river's locks and dam as well as attending a play at the Grand Theater. But within a fortnight Julian was back putting in long hours with his father at the lumberyard and Margaret was at Younkers.

Isabelle's world was adapting to a new cadence. She began a new routine with no husband nor daughter in the house. Sally still came and kept Isabelle clean and well-fed.

Isabelle was basically able to do as she wished as she had inherited everything from George, including being recipient of pension funds and insurance payments. But her old habits were still an important part of her customs and she was again a regular at PEO, DAR, and Soroptimist, as well as, at the card table. However, Mabel was a new piece on her chess board, and she arranged to see her much more frequently as she found she truthfully enjoyed her cousin's company.

Autumn came with a flourish of color and Isabelle began making plans with Mabel for the new year. They often spoke of Anne in Sarasota, deciding it was time to stop talking and start doing—beginning with going to Florida after the first of the year when the weather was miserable in Iowa and they could appreciate, maximally, the more southern climes.

However, before Halloween arrived, it became clear the world may not support the two ladies' plans. Japan had invaded Canton while Hitler had taken Sudetenland from Czechoslovakia. That damn Mr. Roosevelt had his hands full and it seemed like the world was going to erupt with the ashes falling on Des Moines.

The world did reel under multiple forces, but the United States managed a nearly impossible balancing act, showing to its people that there was still a reasonable semblance of order and no reason for concern.

In early February 1939 Isabelle and Mabel took the train south, passing nearly a month in the Florida warmth, spending long hours talking with Anne, playing cards, reminiscing, and discussing how everything was in disarray. Violet proved to be an exceptional cook with a keen understanding of southern cuisine. The ladies enjoyed their leisure, while Violet took care of their needs.

One evening after a stand-out dinner, Isabelle felt a tweak in her brain to ask Anne a question that in proper social circles of those days would likely be considered as improper: how did she handle her help? Isabelle had observed Anne's relationship with Violet and it somehow seemed more serene and even efficient than her relationship with Sally. When the races were so fundamentally different—mentally, socially, culturally different—how did Anne manage to have such a poised household?

Anne immediately understood the question and was ready with an answer, although she was really not sure if her sister would be able to understand it.

Although from the same unbending high-plains stock, while Isabelle had spent her adult life in the Midwest, Anne had spent hers in the South. It was true she was not and never could be a real southerner. Her elocution and lexicon were wrong—had she been a real southerner, others would have said she talked funny. Her habits and customs were different. She did not give homage to the Stars-n-Bars. But through osmosis, in many ways, she had become an adopted southerner.

In her adopted lifestyle she had had what might be considered as full-frontal contact with black people. Every day, throughout the day she was in their company in one way or another. This proximity had almost incongruously led to a different sort of understanding.

She still believed in separate but equal. However, to her, this was not just hyperbole from a white person who felt embarrassed that her race was frequently better off than her neighbor's. She absolutely believed in the two dimensions: black people should lead their separate lives, but they should, in truth, be equal.

She had consoled Violet when her mother had died. She had celebrated with her when her first child was born. She had waited in anxious anticipation with her when her husband had had a serious operation. She and Violet had shared much more of their lives than just housework. There was still no question about who was boss, but there was also something else—some added humanity in the relationship.

Isabelle listened intently to Anne's analysis, but as Anne had feared, she understood little. She interpreted the discourse as meaning she, Isabelle, needed to be more paternalistic. This was, of course, the opposite of Anne's hypothesis.

Isabelle and Mabel returned to Des Moines thinking how wonderful life in Florida must be without the biting cold of winter—the snow, the slush, the ice. They were so attracted to the warmth of both the climate and Anne's household that they decided to make a repeat journey just before Thanksgiving—celebrating this event with Anne, surrounded by her orange grove.

4

Meet Isabelle's Bradley

THROUGH THE IOWA SPRING and summer Isabelle took care of all the loose ends that were surfacing after George's departure while she allowed herself to be consumed by her social calendar, seeing Margaret and Julian only once a month for dinner and an update as to their goings-on. She and Mabel took the train to Chicago to spend the Fourth of July with Percy and Helen who had a new daughter, Barbara, named after Helen's great-aunt. Then, with considerable anticipation, in November they were back in Sarasota.

Anne had been waiting for her cohorts with a surprise, or more correctly, an idea that could develop into a surprise, or at least a pleasant time. When her sister and cousin had got settled in their rooms, after Violet served a stiff bourbon to each, Anne asked if, given their newfound fondness of warm temperatures, they had ever thought of going to visit Hawaii.

Anne had done her homework. The Matson Line offered all that was necessary. The *SS Lurline* sailed from San Francisco to Honolulu. Once there, Matson had built the Royal Hawaiian Hotel where they could stay right on the beach and enjoy a true paradise that would put Sarasota to shame.

Isabelle and Mabel took the bait like an amber jack in Sarasota Bay. What a wonderful idea! They should, no they must do it.

The ladies shared more than ancestry. They shared individualistic and determined personalities that, once committed, were unwavering. At this point in time, all were determined they should spend next Valentine's Day in Honolulu.

Accordingly, they met in San Francisco in late January to begin their adventure. The passage was most agreeable and in the process of meeting fellow passengers, Isabelle happened to meet another Hawkeye. Bradley Baker was a business man, originally from Iowa City, who had followed his business to Des Moines, living there for the past decade. After the recent death of his wife, he had decided to take a break from, what had so far been, an almost workaholic existence and see parts of the world he had only previously read about in books.

Bradley had a grown daughter, Dorothy, a year younger than Margaret, who was a lawyer and, like Isabelle's brother, living in Minneapolis—one of those little quirks of life the Fates so enjoyed constructing along our by-ways. She was married, her husband Lawrence a reporter for the *Minneapolis Daily Star*. They had no children, each concentrating completely on a demanding career.

Bradley enjoyed a stout toddy on the deck, seeing this as the best elixir for driving off any cool breezes that might threaten his high spirits—the expulsion of any menacing wraiths sometimes requiring multiple doses. He quickly procured willing support from Isabelle in his efforts to evict dispiritedness. The two would often sit on the leeward side of the ship and talk about nothing in particular. This almost out-of-character low-key behavior from Isabelle was seen as quite remarkable by Anne and Mabel who found a challenging rubber nearly every day and missed Isabelle's keen acumen at the cards.

Isabelle found Bradley much more relaxed than George. Perhaps this was because he was, for the first time in his life, making a concerted effort to relax. Perhaps this was because Bradley was five years older than George. Or, perhaps this was because, like Isabelle, Bradley had lost a spouse and now saw his remaining years through a different lens. But most probably, this was simply because everyone is different—but she liked Bradley's differences.

Not surprisingly, upon arrival in Honolulu, Bradley, too, was staying at the Royal Hawaiian and their relationship continued, even flourished with the soothing seas of Waikiki. Isabelle did do sight-seeing with Mabel and Anne, but she spent a good deal of her time walking and talking with Bradley or sitting on the lanai and having some sort of tall tropical drink that really tickled the cerebellum and taunted the cerebrum.

One afternoon she and Bradley were sipping their third multicolored mixture when Isabelle stared deeply into her glass topped by a small variegated paper parasol, anchored to the glass's rim with a chunk of pineapple, and then looked around the hotel's terrace. She pivoted, asking Bradley to do the same. His pale blue eyes swept the veranda, showing bemusement, not knowing the object of this scrutiny. When he had taken it all in and was again staring at Isabelle, she remarked how the drink was a swirl of color—red, yellow, orange, and green. She then noted the terrace was the same, "Look, the yellow-skinned Chinamen," she assumed, "the ginger-skinned Polynesians, a few tawny colored individuals with broad noses and kinky hair, and even a rare Negro." All of these she contrasted with the pale and pointy features of the tourists being served by this panoply of humanity. She surprised Bradley by concluding that all this pageant of races and ethnicities was there in the middle of the Pacific Ocean to cater to the needs and desires of this impermanent group of European descent.

Bradley asked Isabelle if she were following events in Europe. Indeed, back home in Iowa there were new émigrés from Germany—hundreds of thousands, mostly Jewish, Germans coming to America over the past several years. Antisemitism was rampant in Europe. The "winter war" was raging. From Spain to Poland people were being mistreated due to their race or ethnicity. Bradley wondered if Isabelle did not think things were better here with this hopefully equipoised but cluttered hodgepodge of origins and customs than with the Third Reich where one group was seen, indeed forcefully imposed, as superior.

For the first time since they had met, Isabelle held Bradley in a stark gaze, her head even trembled a bit as she wanted to say something but felt it was best unsaid, at least for the moment. This was a brief peek to another Isabelle who had extremely strong feelings and did not like these being questioned or twisted around. In her mind it was crystal clear, like the waters of Waikiki, who was paying and who was doing the work here in paradise and why these arrangements were as they were. Nonetheless, she did like Bradley and it was not the time nor the place to discuss profound beliefs as to the nature of the world and its occupants.

Isabelle and her entourage, now including Bradley, had an enjoyable three weeks in Hawaii, then an even more enjoyable three months telling all their comrades about their wonderful and exotic vacation.

When the *SS Lurline* docked in San Francisco after five days at sea, Bradley said his goodbyes to the three ladies as he was spending another ten days with a friend in Sausalito, across the bay. He gave Isabelle an extra snug hug, promising to call her as soon as he was back in Des Moines.

The ladies took the Chicago and North Western Railway's modern *City of San Francisco* to Chicago, departing Oakland, arriving in Central Station forty hours later, almost as long as the sea voyage to Honolulu. Even though the journey was long, the premium service kept the discomforts to a minimum and the club car was well used by all.

They had booked three rooms in the Palmer House and, by pre-arrangement, spent a day getting rested before meeting with Percy and his family. They had an excellent dinner at the Lockwood Restaurant in the hotel, happy to see the Chicago-based Hardy Family, congratulating Helen on her obvious pregnancy. The next day, they went to the Hardy house for dinner, then the following day Anne took a train to Tampa while Isabelle and Mabel boarded the Rock Island train to Des Moines.

Isabelle warmly embraced Mabel when they reached their destination, then each went her own way. Isabelle was most contented to note, as she opened her front door and entered her tidy home, that Sally had kept all dust-free and in perfect order. There was even the welcoming smell from the mingling scents of Pine-sol and Minwax that reminded her of walking down the corridors of Hubbell during parent-teacher visitation—it was as if she were returning home from her card game and not over a month of travel.

Given her practical attire and frugal habits, Isabelle traveled without much fanfare or baggage. She managed with one large striped tweed suitcase which was rather heavy, but she could handle it when she must, as she now had to, to get it from the porch where the taxi driver had kindly left it. She would let Sally manhandle it upstairs as she needed nothing from inside and the few little gifts for Sally's children could be removed at Sally's next visit, which she guessed was the next day.

After a good night's sleep, Isabelle decided she needed to check in with Margaret. She knew her daughter was totally engrossed in the business of becoming a wife and, hopefully in the not too distant future, a mother. She and Julian had already decided, as they had informed Isabelle, they would build a new home on 67th Street. Once they had moved in, Margaret would quit her job at Younkers to concentrate on building a home for the children they hoped would soon be on the way.

However, Isabelle had to first deal with settling back in. She needed groceries and Sally was coming soon.

After all these years, Sally had her own key and entered as though she were visiting her mother-in-law's home. By the time Isabelle went downstairs, she was pushing the carpet sweeper over the entry hall where bits of debris had been tracked in with Isabelle's arrival.

Isabelle smiled at Sally, it was an honest and caring smile. Sally knew this. Isabelle then thanked her for her efforts during her absence. Sally knew this was sincere, but it was delivered in that off-handed, distracted way that had taken Sally so many years to accept, never to like. It may have been a latent mannerism, but it was an affectation that, to the outsider, would seem to be totally deficient as a thank you for even the smallest favor—not to mention all the real devotion Sally had always shown to her work. But definitely, by now Sally knew how things were done in Isabelle's world.

Sally's people kept many proverbs from the bad days in the South. One of these was "you can't bend a dry fish". Isabelle was a dry fish. Sally accepted this with no malice.

Isabelle asked Sally to make her a cup of coffee. She then got a pad and pencil and, sitting on the sofa, made a list of things Sally would have to buy to restock the larder.

Isabelle then called Margaret at work. They agreed Margaret would stop by her mother's home on the way back to the rental that was her temporary residence. Margaret arrived a little before six, Isabelle had a pot of tea and plate of cookies ready and waiting. As they sipped their cups of strong Fortnum and Mason's loose leaf, their favorite, Margaret effused about married life, how wonderful Julian was, and how all her expectations were being exceeded.

Isabelle took great pains to show the proper degree of enthusiasm and encouragement. She was still uncertain what had precipitated this marriage, suspecting that George's death had been the catalyst pushing Margaret in a direction of which she was unsure and which she had, at least subconsciously, resisted for years. But, the pragmatist in Isabelle celebrated that motive was less important than the outcome and, if they were truly happy together, she could ask for no more. She had always liked Julian, even though she herself felt that his family did not really reciprocate this affection.

Julian's father was a strict German and his mother, also, very Germanic, if less severe in her outlook on life. With four children, the family was larger than most and a challenge to guide through the rigors of the Depression and World War.

Isabelle understood we do not choose our in-laws nor our parents. She deemed she had been luckier than most on both accounts. So, she gave her daughter her most motherly smile, squeezed her hand, and said how happy she was for her.

After a few more sips of tea and some aimless chitchat, Isabelle mentioned to her daughter that she had had a splendid time in Hawaii—seeing Margaret as apparently being too slow in getting around to this topic. Between descriptions of the wonderful climate and gorgeous beaches, she let it slip into her narration that she had met a nice man with whom she had shared much of her time.

Margaret's pupils constricted, and she immediately had a vision in her mind of her mother in bed with some old man, naked except for a straw hat and a flowery bandana. Her own invented image made her shudder with near nausea and anger at the same time.

Her mother was her father's wife and that was that. She emphatically told her mother so, spilling her tea in the process.

Isabelle's relationship with Bradley had so far been totally intellectual and social, not physical and, she, equally emphatically, told this to her disquieted daughter.

Isabelle tried to change course, pivoting back to Julian and how the fact that he had to assume the duties, at least temporarily, of traveling salesman for his father's products could not be easy for the newlyweds. However, Margaret, most stubbornly (a family trait) stuck to the topic of her mother's social life, reiterating the inviolate obligation for absolute fidelity. She was even going to go further, but decided to follow her mother's lead and, at least for the moment, move on to less contentious subjects.

This more and more typified Isabelle and Margaret's relationship as they interacted more as two independent adults and less as mother-daughter. Often it was like skating on Gray's Lake. There were welcome smooth spots where you could go very fast. Yet, there were rough spots where you had to slow down. And, there were spots where the ice had buckled and shattered under stress, refreezing into an uneven and unknown consistency—here you had to proceed with extreme caution.

Margaret felt she had been destined to be a wife and mother—focusing all her efforts on these endeavors, leaving only a few scraps of time and energy for her own mother. Isabelle realized full well her girl-child's priorities, knowing these were practically diametrically opposed to her own. Isabelle had but a fraction of the maternal instinct of her daughter, as Margaret would have been the first to attest. She also had only a scintilla of the domestic skills, or more correctly, the love of the domestic skills, that presented itself in Margaret. The two were very, very different.

Isabelle had not been home long before she began planning her next adventure. She invited Mabel to lunch at the Wakonda Club where she steered the conversation to the great time the two ladies had had when they visited Anne. Shouldn't they do it again, soon?

In the end, Mabel took no convincing—she was as ready as Isabelle to shed the dreariness of a nearly house-bound life in Des Moines for what she romantically saw as a life on the road. They agreed to meet at Isabelle's to call Anne and set things in motion.

Isabelle had not heard from Bradley for some time, but with his stopover in Sausalito, she thought this was to be expected. Moreover, while she would never ever have admitted it to Margaret or anyone else, she was uncertain in her own mind as to how to handle the Bradly matter.

She did have a strong affection for the gentleman, and he was indeed a gentleman with a style and manners that underscored an affinity to érudition, decorum, and a manly sort of étiquette. She enjoyed talking with him and sensed in him, as in George, the mental acuity that would allow her to engage in all varieties of mental gymnastics to see who would win a tacit game of king of the hill. But—and it was a big but— did she want to intimately share her life with anyone else?

In moments of clear-eyed self-appraisal, she knew she was not really the domestic type—if such a type existed—she doubted it. She had never put her husband and children centermost. She had and did love them all. And, she loved them all deeply. But this was her love, her affection in a more abstract form that needed space—that needed to be at arm's length to be able to maneuver, to be able to breath. Margaret and Percy knew. George had known. Mentally, spiritually, and, equally importantly, physically, she needed to be able to feel the expansiveness of living.

She liked people in her own way. She thoroughly enjoyed chatting with people across the bridge table. She enjoyed challenging others at a cocktail party with a well-bodied screwdriver aperitif in her hand. She enjoyed debates with the co-members of PEO, DAR, and Soroptimist. She could even find some pleasure in the banal and pointless jabber that could spontaneously arise with a neighbor, someone at the grocery store, or a fellow client of the Post Office. But when all was said and done, she was her own best friend.

Where would, where could, Bradly fit in? Did she want him to fit in? What would be the price to pay? In reviewing the situation, she once again realized it all focused on her and her wishes and her lifestyle—this fact all the more reason that she needed to move forward with caution.

Her introspections provided no solutions. Hence, as had frequently been her strategy, she played another hand and would take the results as they came up. She took a note card of good quality linen paper with iris on the front, the purply-blue a color she thought reminiscent of Bradley and Hawaii and jotted a few carefully selected words—hoping he had had a safe and trouble-free trip back to Des Moines, providing her phone number, which he already had, on the bottom next to her spidery signature.

She and Mabel had already contacted Anne and were preparing for a trip south the coming month when she got a call from Bradly. She was not surprised.

After some crisp small talk, when Bradley confirmed all had gone well and he was once again comfortably situated in his home, he asked Isabelle if she would have lunch with him the next day downtown at the Savery Hotel.

Isabelle happily accepted, her creeping doubts for the moment at bay. They exchanged a few more pleasantries about the weather and how well Governor Wilson was doing, then rang-off with a renewed promise to see each other the next day. Isabelle sat next to her phone, now in the cradle, thinking of Bradley alone in his big 1912 Craftsman Bungalow on 7th Street. He had proudly shown her pictures in Honolulu. It was the home where he and his wife were going to spend their golden years. It had been the apex of *their* lives—the monument to *their* happiness. Bradley was very proud of this house—*their* house. Would there even be a place there for Isabelle? Would she want to take up that place? Would she think, could she think of leaving her own home?

At the Savery, Isabelle and Bradley enjoyed a leisurely lunch with an excellent bottle of cabernet sauvignon chosen by Bradley. They started with an analysis of the world's situation, each considering himself or herself a wise and steady observer of global politics, which had totally gone to hell, due, in no small measure, to that imbecile in the White House—Franklin Delano Roosevelt. Dunkirk had nearly been a terrible catastrophe. Vichy France was now in Hitler's pocket as his troops occupied the Channel Islands and His Highness, FDR, did nothing—not a damn thing—each excusing the other's vulgarity between sips of the excellent full-bodied red wine.

By the time Isabelle's *coq au vin* and Bradley's rump-steak arrived, they had managed to shift gears to local issues—the dedication of the Field House and the drowning of a child in the Raccoon River. They agilely leapt from topic to topic—be they large or small. All this seemed to be like a ballet with the dancers pirouetting, doing a *plié* or an *assemblé*, moving across the floor but never reaching the center.

This frustrated Isabelle. She had little patience for, what she considered, pussyfooting around. If there was something to say, say it and be done with it. In a moment of lucidity, she concluded they were too close to their roots here—be those roots people or structures. They needed more neutral ground, much as it had been in Honolulu. They needed a clean slate to be able to be themselves; to be able to look at each other as a discrete entity without all the local baggage. They were going to get nowhere at the Savery. It was time for dessert.

Over her *banane flambé* and Bradley's *crème caramel* she stopped the dance and perfunctorily stated she and Mabel would be going to Florida next month. This complete drop of syntax took Bradley a bit aback, but he regained his composure quickly, congratulating Isabelle on her plans, supporting the trip as a good way to have a change of climate and keep family ties strong. Truly typical of Bradley, sterling attempts at correctness.

Over coffee they talked once again about the world at large: the Dutch surrender, the Belgium cease fire, the Western Desert Campaign, and how Booker T. Washington ever ended up on a US postage stamp. Cups drained, Bradley announced he had an afternoon appointment with his solicitor. Luncheon over, the two stood, had a somewhat tepid hug, and left the lobby by different doors.

The Bradley matter still in suspense, Isabelle concentrated on all the necessary preparations for her trip south. Five weeks later, having arranged everything with Sally and Margaret to ensure her affairs and her home would be well looked after during her absence, Isabelle and Mabel boarded the *Des Moines Rocket* to Chicago. There were another two nights in the Palmer House while they had a nice visit with Percy and his family that was just long enough. They then took the *Dixie Flyer* south to Jacksonville where they connected to Tampa and took a bus the last sixty miles to Sarasota and Anne's welcome embrace.

It was like entering another universe. This was not Des Moines. The ladies knew from their previous visit that Anne had a lovely and spacious home—kind of a tropical plantation with a veranda around three sides. The airy living and dining areas were cooled by breezes that entered from a series of French doors, while all four bedrooms also opened on the veranda to catch the breeze that was scented with a mixture of oranges and the sea. As before, Violet had made up a room for each of them and they felt as though they were in a luxurious five-star hotel—even better than they had experienced Honolulu.

After refreshing themselves, they took seats on the veranda where Violet had laid out trays of fresh fruit, tea, and biscuits. After their refreshment and updating each other as to the latest events in their lives, they shuffled their chairs into a kind of circle around the coffee table and began three-handed Canasta. This was to become their main pastime during the stay of the two northern ladies. Each of the three players was a serious contestant who hated to lose, so games were high energy, often accompanied by displays of frustration or anxiety—Isabelle's periodic eruptions surprising both her compatriots.

When they were not concentrating on their cards on the veranda, they were quietly reading from Anne's extensive library, walking along the pathways that led to nearby orange groves, or traveling to local attractions in Anne's 1938 Ford Coupe. The ladies were very much kindred spirits and soon they established a routine that had just the right amount of togetherness and separation to ensure no heightened tension and that maintained interest of each in the others.

They were just beginning their third week when Isabelle received a letter from Bradley. He sent his warmest wishes, informing Isabelle that he would be traveling to Tucson in a fortnight, asking her to join him there.

She considered discussing this invitation with her chums but foresaw a uniformly positive view. In their eyes, and perhaps hers, she was a widow too young, too intelligent, too energetic to spend the remainder of her life as a spinster. She needed male companionship. But did she?

Her extended family here present around the Canasta table would see this as a huge opportunity. Bradly was charming. He was highly educated. He was at the very least not poor. This was not an event upon which to scoff—this was a chance upon which to pounce.

These arguments notwithstanding, both Mabel and Anne were still single women today, many years after the deaths of their spouses. How easy it can be to advise others when perhaps one should follow one's own words?

Thus, between tasty meals prepared by Violet, challenging card games, afternoon promenades, and calming reading, Isabelle played mental volleyball—bouncing the ball across the net.

She sensed this was a pivotal point. She still heard her daughter's admonitions—she was George's wife. She still felt a hole in her stomach when she silently spoke his name. She still was swept by regret that she had not shown George her emotions more unabashedly. She still lamented she had not better reciprocated the love her husband had lavished on her—not been a better wife. Alas, pragmatic as always, what was done could not be undone—sad but true. But Bradley was still "undone".

At the end, she did as she so often did when trying to cope with difficult decisions—she threw her hat in the wind. She carefully crafted a reply to Bradley on plain white notepaper. She thanked him for his letter. She informed him that she would be leaving Florida in three weeks, plans to which no one but she was privy at that point in time, and would be happy to reroute her return trip to pass through Tucson. She continued, since he was more knowledgeable about such matters, could he advise the best train route from Tampa as well as make a booking at a suitable hotel in Tucson—these details he could advise by return letter or telegram if the time was short.

She sealed the letter and in so doing, for the time being, closed the open matter of Bradley. What would happen would happen. It was time for tea and Canasta. When she told the girls, as she surmised, they were enthusiastic—a golden year's romance for Isabelle was more than they could have hoped for—again, great support for doing what, perhaps, they themselves should do. Regardless, Mabel and Anne offered Isabelle their heart-felt approval for her plans, reading far more between the lines, and already assuming that this would lead much further than Isabelle herself thought.

They continued their routine, waiting to see if Bradley would quickly confirm the arrangements as requested.

They did not have to wait long, as within ten days they had a letter from Tucson, not with the itinerary, but with the tickets as well as a confirmation for a room at the Hotel Congress.

Mabel decided the Florida climate agreed with her and, with the eager encouragement of Anne, declared she would not be returning north when Isabelle left, but staying in the Sunshine State for the foreseeable future.

On the appointed day, Anne and Mabel accompanied Isabelle to Tampa and waved to her from the platform until the train looked like a mere spot on the distant rails.

Bradley met her in Tucson, the hot dry heat a major contrast to the hot humid conditions of the Gulf Coast. After a maybe too brief embrace, he put her bags in the trunk while she got in the passenger seat of his blue 1939 Hudson. They drove the short distance to the hotel while Bradley told her the story of the 1934 fire that destroyed the hotel but led to the capture of John Dillinger.

At Isabelle's insistence, Bradley agreed to let her rest until the following day even though he had already prepared for an evening out on the town. They agreed he would come to collect her at eleven the next morning, and they would lunch together in his garden. This seemed most prudent to Isabelle who wanted to limit her interactions with this still largely unknown man to congenial daytime activities and not potentially more troublesome nocturnal amusements or intimacies.

As promised, at eleven sharp, Bradley called up from the reception desk. They drove to a residential district named, as Bradley proudly proclaimed, Sunnyside, on Highland Street, just south of Broadway and not far from the Country Club. His home was Spanish style, a red tile roof and white plaster walls, surrounded on all sides by small but well-kept gardens set off by verdant lawns that would make the nearby golf course jealous.

They sat in the shade on colorful canvas chairs, sipping gin and tonics after a quick tour of the house which Isabelle found to be clean and functional, but lacking any lived-in feeling—probably readily explainable, since Bradley's main residence was still in Des Moines. The drinks were deliciously tart thanks to the succulent limes. Isabelle relished their freshness while Bradley gave her a ten-minute lesson in local history going back to the Hohokam Indians, then to the Spanish occupation, the Gadsden Purchase of 1854 which made Tucson part of the United States followed by the arrival of the Southern Pacific and lots of Chinese workers in 1880. In 1912, Arizona became the forty-eighth state. Fast forwarding to today, this led to a city of 37,000 with a mixture of Latinos, Indians, and Asians, with whom the majority Anglo Saxons now shared the ancient plain surrounded by the Santa Catalina, Tortolita, Santa Rita, Rincon, and Tucson Mountains.

Isabelle's curiosity was piqued by the apparent racial mix as described by Bradley. Of course, Des Moines had all these racial groups as well as African Americans (at least in her private thoughts, Isabelle insisted on re-ferring to African Americans as "Negros"). Of course, as she had learned when helping Margaret with her homework, Des Moines had been located on former lands of various tribes of the Sioux—the Ioway Group part of the original Siouan People. The state had received displaced Indians from many tribes including the Chippewa. And, indeed, Isabelle supposed, in addition to Indians, there were most likely Latinos and Chinese people (silently, Isa-belle thought of them as "Mexicans and Chinamen") all about town. But the truth was she never really thought about them. She never really saw anyone except white people. She did not do this by intent. She did not, she thought, shy away from other races. But, with the exception of Sally and Violet, she just did not encounter people of other races very often. The porters on the train and the maids in the hotels were black, but these were almost unseen faces. Quite simply, her social niche was fully occupied by principal play-ers who were white, Anglo Saxon, Protestants. Strangely, it was almost as though she had just come to this realization at this point in time.

What was perhaps most interesting was that for Isabelle this realiza-tion was not a value judgement, not an eye-opener, not a critique. This was simply an observation. This was a mental note of the type she would make if she saw the salad fork was in the wrong place when the table was set, if a man's tie was poorly tied, if a woman's slip showed. An observation by someone who was a keen observer.

As their ice cubes rattled in their glasses and the story of Tucson con-cluded, Bradley took Isabelle's hand, helped her out of the hammocky chair and guided her back into the house where he seated her at the table and then disappeared into the kitchen to bring several bowls and platters of food to the center of the already-set table.

As he prepared to serve the plates, he informed Isabelle that he imag-ined this was rather a larger meal than that to which she was accustomed at mid-day. As it was, in fact, already after noon, exceptionally he had opted to follow the Canadian custom of having supper—a heavier but less formal meal, often in the later afternoon. He had some grilled trout on a bed of saffron rice. Next to this was a bowl of creamy garlicky mashed cauliflower. The fair was completed by a platter of *crudités* including carrots, celery, green peppers, olives, and broccoli. Finally, there was a small precut loaf of rosemary bread.

Bradley served Isabelle a large potion and took an equal share for himself. As he tucked in, he elaborated how he thought after a hearty meal they could go for a promenade in Randolph Park.

Isabelle found the food tasty and well-seasoned. She was, however, put off by the large portions; much more than the modest-size portions she preferred. She mostly ate around the edges and thought of her future as Bradley moved on to the topic of the world's future, Mr. Churchill's decision to fight the Germans, and the sinking of the *SS Arandora Star*.

They had a delicious selection of fruit for dessert, accompanied by a good port. They did then drive to the park for a walk; they enjoyed the fresh air, commenting on the flora and fauna as well as world politics, never missing an opportunity to revile the works of the evil FDR. When they reached the inflection point and began the return leg, Isabelle announced preemptively she was still a bit fatigued from her travels and would appreciate returning early to her room.

When she was safely back in her room, Isabelle exhaled deeply. She did not know why. Was she more conformable alone than in Bradley's company? Did she feel safe from temptation? Did she feel safer in her own thoughts without being challenged by another?

Isabelle had turned sixty the year after George died. While still physically and mentally strong, she was no longer middle aged by any estimation. She was joining the elderly team and, as such, wondered what in the hell she was doing going out and looking for adventures and relationships with other men.

Isabelle continued to question her relationship with Bradley. But in true Isabelle fashion, she was able to push this to a back recess of her mind and concentrate on seeing the sites of a part of the country which was all new and unfamiliar to her. She convinced Bradley to organize their time so that their efforts could be focused on seeing the natural beauty of the area. They took a series of picnics to Willow Canyon. They went to the Tucson Mountains and enjoyed the saguaro that reminded her of so many scarecrows in an Iowa corn field. They went to Kitt Peak, the highest point of the Quinlan Mountains, where they had the rare chance of seeing a puma. They even crossed the border into Nogales, enjoying Mexican beer and scenery.

The days were full and soon she had spent three weeks in the Grand Canyon State without seeing the Grand Canyon, but having seen, or so she felt, almost everything else there was to see. Moreover, summer was drawing to a close and it was time for her to get home to Des Moines to prepare her house and herself for the wintry time to come.

She asked Bradley to make her bookings for a quick trip north to Iowa. Then, with her tickets in hand, they had one final leisurely dinner at the Hotel Congress on the eve of her departure.

Things were nearly derailed as she became apoplectic about her nemesis FDR instituting military conscription—the draft. Bradley was unsure if her ire was provoked more by the president or by the act of conscription. In either or both cases, his views did not coincide completely with Isabelle's. Fortunately, each pulled back from the precipice before their last supper turned into political histrionics—each fueling the other.

While basically on the same side of the row concerning the country's role in the war, there were important issues separating their opinions. Recognizing this, they seemed to intuitively know they needed to change direction to lower the energy level of their last evening together. Opting for more calming subjects, they followed Mark Twain's advice that one can always talk about the weather, switching topics to the seasonal cooling of temperatures and projections for a cold winter combined with a severe influenza epidemic that was foreseen for parts of the country.

Over a fragrant snifter of Courvoisier, Bradley and Isabelle toasted their future—Bradley hoping this was the beginning of a new relationship. After a quick hug and peck on the cheek, Isabelle went up to her room where she mulled over this possibility. A new relationship. Uncertainty coiled within her and she almost felt as though she were again pregnant—not a thought that pleased her.

Within two days, the dry and somehow elegant desert expanses of Arizona had been replaced with the rolling hills and growing hustle of Iowa as farms were beginning to harvest their corn. She turned the key on her front door, stepping across the threshold and expecting to be embraced by the fond aromas of Pine-sol and Minwax. However, to her shock, the air smelled stale like one of those Hopi houses they had visited when she and Bradley had traveled to the north, missing the Grand Canyon, but passing through the Indian reservation and spending the night on the road in the strange Mormon community of Pine. That musty odor was fine for the Indians, but not for her home. This was unacceptable.

She left her suitcase in the hallway and went up to her room for a bath and change of clothes. While she could not say the house was truly dirty, it was certainly not clean and definitely not clean to her standards which Sally knew all too well. She insisted on spic-and-span even if she herself did not adhere to the highest of standards in her personal habits.

The bath was soothing. She decided to deal with the matters at hand tomorrow and go to bed early tonight. No one had known she was coming home today. She revered spontaneity. Her life was hers and, to the extent she could, she would maintain control. This included going where she wanted, when she wanted. What would be the Bradley effect? She fell asleep thinking more of Bradley than Sally.

She was having a cup of coffee and only a cup of coffee when Sally arrived. The cupboard and fridge were bare—no stores put in for her arrival. The fact that she had not announced her coming was no excuse. She expected preparedness.

Sally saw Isabelle standing by the kitchen table when she entered with her own key by the back door. She could almost feel the storm clouds over her employer's head. Nonetheless, she tried to sidestep the pending bout by heartily wishing Isabelle a warm "welcome back" while extending her hope that all had gone well.

This fell on deaf ears and Isabelle's glare was enough to shrivel stronger souls than Sally's. Isabelle unleashed a torrent of accusations, grousing on and on, but carefully choosing her biting words so as never to be vulgar in her attack.

It was some time before Sally could get a word in and, by that time, she had been so chastised and felt so maligned that she was unsure if she even wanted to say anything. But her sense of correctness overcame her resentment and she attempted to explain the situation for which a person with whom she had had nearly a life-long relationship should have shown much more patience and tolerance.

As she clearly explained, of course she knew the state in which her employer expected her home to kept during any absence. Of course, she knew that her employer could come home at any time, as she had demonstrated many times before. Of course, she knew her employer was always fatigued by difficult journeys and anticipated relaxing in her home with its accustomed cleanliness, with its cupboards full, and it being ready to be lived in as though its owner had never left. Of course, she knew all this. Of course, she would have complied with these expectations if it had been possible. She sincerely regretted it, but it simply was not possible.

Sally further explained, although she sensed Isabelle was already at the limit of her listening time, that her sister's brother-in-law had had a serious accident. Her sister had to help out and that meant she herself needed to help her sibling with her own family. Thus, Sally had agreed, as it was summer vacation, to take care of her sister's two children. Who could have imagined that these children along with her own would all come down with the measles? Who would have thought? But it happened, and it took all Sally's time and energy to deal with all the sick children. She was sorry, but that was what had happened. It was not out of negligence, but due to serious health issues.

Isabelle acknowledged the end of Sally's tale with an exhaled *humpf*, turned her back to fill her coffee cup, and asked in the most stringent of tones what Sally was preparing for her breakfast.

Sally had tolerated all of Isabelle's foibles for years. This was nearly the breaking point. This arrogant and rude old lady who had lost her husband, driven her children away, and was totally unappreciative of all the things people did for her—this lady was not a very nice person. Sally deserved better. But she knew these were not good times. War was just over the horizon and she needed this job badly. So, she swallowed hard, counted to ten, put on a forced obsequious smile, and asked Isabelle what she would like her to buy at the grocery store, so she could have a good breakfast—whispering "OK Boss" under her breath as she went out the door.

Unbeknownst to Isabelle, this was a pivotal moment that under other circumstances would have been much more of a life changer. Quite simply, if she had lost Sally, she would have had a difficult time getting on. She unquestionably would not have been able to keep to her indulgent schedule to which she was accustomed. Geopolitics and local economics had prevailed, and Isabelle went about her daily routine as though nothing had happened. She was back to her card games and meetings, her home once again smelling of Pine-sol and Minwax.

At PEO, DAR, Soroptimist, and around the card table Isabelle would complain about how hard it was to get good help these days. She would drop subtle crumbs about her trips to Florida and Arizona, highlighting, as winter approached, how much she had enjoyed the sun and the warmth. She would avoid political confrontations unless she was completely sure of the terrain, at which time she would lambast the government with great glee and an impressive vocabulary.

Soon after, in her mind, sorting out Sally, she got in touch with Margaret as she had even kept her daughter in the dark about her comings and goings. Margaret stopped by for tea and confirmed that she and Julian were fine. That seemed adequate for Isabelle. She provided only the scantest outline about her travels and asked even less about Margaret's adventures during her absence.

She called Mabel's house only to have no one pick up, so she assumed her chum was still with Anne. For a fleeting moment she thought about picking up her suitcase which was still in the hallway, because Sally for some reason had not managed to get it upstairs, and going right back to Sarasota.

This would be fun, she thought. But she decided she needed to stay put for a while as she tried to chart her course—a course which was still very unclear to her.

Isabelle was not someone to lie awake at night worrying about life's caprices or even her own destiny. She did not spend hours deep in thought, though she was more than capable of very analytical thoughts. She assigned to each topic a priority and devoted suitable energy to that topic based on its ranking.

The list of topics in her mind was considerable, ranging from that idiot in the White House to her daughter's future. But right now, the top billing was Bradley. It took no keen observer to see that he was looking for a new partner in his life. He, as she, had been married a long time and was accustomed to thinking in terms of "we" and not "me". Isabelle was still largely a "me" person.

Yet, she longed for George. Not solely or even essentially in a biological way, but in a spiritual fashion. Living as one for decades changes your very substance. There is real synergy, symbiosis. They finished each other's sentences, knew each other's most private proclivities, knew the taste and smell one of the other. Time had stitched them together.

She relished being free to do as she wished. But, with George at her side, she had still done as she had wished. A mate, if it is the right mate, does not mean shackles, does not mean a loss of freedom or individuality. She could not bear to lose these things. But with Bradley she thought perhaps they would remain intact while she would again be part of a greater whole. But she was unsure.

She knew she had to decide. She innately understood there was an urgency in Bradley that she could fulfill, but if she chose not to, he would go elsewhere. Pragmatic as always, she made her decision—or part of her decision. She would stay in Des Moines for Christmas and do all she could to celebrate the holiday with Margaret and Julian. She would then arrange to observe the new year with Percy and his family. She would see if Mabel had come home and if she could join her for the two festivities. If Bradley had come back to town, she would make sure to visit him during the holidays. If he stayed in Arizona, she would maintain a good correspondence and propose they get together before the end of January. There it was, by this deadline she would make her decision. She would see how her family reacted and judge how to weigh their inputs, but she herself would decide by the end of January.

Most things fell into place as Isabelle had planned. Mabel came back after Thanksgiving and was happy to have the opportunity to share Christmas and New Year's with her cousin. Isabelle's children could not refuse their mother and plans were put in place as foreseen for the two holidays. Her normal Des Moines routine filled the gaps and at least once a week, on a quiet evening, she would craft a special letter to Bradley after she learned he planned on staying in warmer climates throughout the coming months. Each of these missives received a prompt and seemingly warm, and even charming reply. Bradley was impatiently awaiting Isabelle's visit in January. He had already booked her room at the Congress.

The exception to these as-anticipated results was Isabelle's relationship with Sally. Sally was as efficient and diligent as always but gone was the exuberance and warm personality. It was replaced by a business-like manner and matter-of-factness. Sally realized that years and years of being together had not built any meaningful bridges. On the surface, she remained the black maid, beholding in all ways to her *patronne*. But she now realized the singular trials and tribulations she had shared with her employer were meaningless. She had not shared these moments, she now understood, as a close confident, but as an employee—a servile employee who may see all, but who should say little and feel nothing. It was simply a job, full stop.

Isabelle could be quite insensitive in relation to subjects where she had a strong opinion, or where she felt she was absolutely right. In other words, in most situations.

Nevertheless, she was, for better or worse, close enough to Sally in her psyche that she knew things had changed, probably irreversibly. She accepted this fact academically. Sally had been wrong.

But, as much as she tried, she could not really come to grips with this complete breakdown of a relationship in which she had so actively participated for so many years. There had been many occasions when she and Sally had had a rough patch—just as happens with anyone with whom you are in continuous close contact— just like she had from time to time with George, but this was different.

One evening, after writing Bradley, she stayed at the secretary she had been given by George's parents for a while longer and penned a letter to Anne asking about how she dealt with the household help. Referring to their discussions on this subject during her first visit to Sarasota, how did Anne ensure good service and respect? How did she walk that thin line between discipline and encouragement? How did she handle a potentially strong-willed woman working in her home? How did Anne deal with a black maid?

Before Isabelle could receive guidance from Anne, before she could fix a date for her Tucson visit with Bradley, before she could buy Christmas presents for her children and grandchildren, before any of these things, the world changed. On December seventh, Pearl Harbor was bombed. The United States was at war. Isabelle's life, along with the lives of millions of others, had changed.

There were no family celebrations of Christmas or New Year's. There was no January trip to Arizona. There was war. Julian and Margaret were brought into the war effort, he in making munitions and she in making other supplies for battle. As a banker, considered as an essential person, Percy's life was the least affected. Julian's two brothers and sister entered the armed forces. Helen's three cousins did the same. No one was untouched. Isabelle's riddle regarding Bradley remained unsolved but was no longer the centerpiece of her cerebral smorgasbord. The world was at war.

Life in Des Moines revolved around the war. The holidays passed almost unnoticed. The new year brought the Battle of Bataan, the Japanese capture of Kuala Lumpur, and the first American troops in Europe.

There was talk of rationing, but so far Isabelle, approaching her sixty-third birthday, had been spared too many serious complications, only having to adjust her day-to-day activities to those of Mr. Roosevelt—this fact filling her with rancor. Her meetings were now a thing of the past, as only the most elderly members had any time that was not fully devoted to the war effort. She was able to rustle-up a card game or two each week with those antediluvian card players who were as addicted as she. She also spent progressively more time with Mabel, often the two just reading the paper or listening to the radio since, although not physically engaged, they certainly had more than a passing interest in the affairs of a world threatened by the Germans and the Japanese along with their cohort of perverts.

When MacArthur left Corregidor, Isabelle and Mabel thought the end was in sight. Even in the middle of the Great Plains of North America they were not safe from the hoards that were set on destroying white Christian civilization. Then of course, from what they read, Hitler for his part was equally set on establishing a society of elitist whites, even if maybe not Christians.

The world was in tatters. She could not help thinking of those years four decades ago on the cold northern plains where there was a fire in her soul—excitement, anticipation, and optimism driving a young woman, an outstanding scholar, a unique student of ancient languages—to do more, and to do better. Those were heady years when her mind burned for knowledge and her body for George. Today, in the rearview mirror, those years looked implausible. They looked like something that had never happened. They looked like fiction—a story she might have read in *Readers' Digest*—but, not the story of her life. She realized the embers of those fires of youth had quenched a long time ago. What was left?

She now saw what mankind was capable of doing to mankind. The crumbling of the world was only one of the more outlandish signs. The New Deal politics of those responsible had set things in motion—had set the stage for catastrophe. The leadership's lack of discipline and control had aggravated an already bad situation. Liberals were blatantly embracing the uneducated and the unenlightened—the lazy and the soiled. Of course, all were citizens of one country. Of course, all were equal under the law. But, as those waging the war against America were so vividly demonstrating, all were not equivalent socially, culturally, or morally. There was, in both domestic and international affairs, a moral, a cultural, and a social high-ground. There was right and wrong. There was correct and incorrect. There was a natural order to things. In this order, moreover, there were those who had the primary role to set standards and propriety, while as well, there were those who assumed a secondary role to follow the rectitudes laid-out by the decision-makers. This was a delicate balance that, when disrupted, led to chaos, disorder, a complete loss of civility, and world pandemonium. This led to world war.

If Isabelle had had the time to really devote the mental energy to the subject she would have liked to have had, she would have been even more despondent. As it was, she was only frantic. Too much was happening, too fast, both at home, and in the world at large.

All was in motion. She felt she was on a Ferris wheel, and it was time to get off (she hated Ferris wheels).

Margaret had come by on Sunday to inform her mother she was pregnant. Yes, it was wartime. Yes, she and Julian were working ten to twelve hours a day. But life goes on and she was going to have a baby—Isabelle was again going to be a grandmother.

She was still digesting the news of her daughter's soon to arrive child, when she had another visitor. Bradley. As a septuagenarian, he had little to do with the war other than follow the news. This fact notwithstanding, the commotion of the war had kept him separated from Isabelle, albeit the two communicated regularly with increasingly long and florid letters.

He had come back to Des Moines to try and simplify his life in a time of complexity. With Fort Des Moines being used now as a training center for the Woman's Army Corps, he had used some of his many contacts to get in touch with people involved with this training. In short, he had managed to arrange to sell his house to one of the main actors in this endeavor. Thus, with all the uncertainties swirling around, he would concentrate his life in Tucson where he could not avoid the war but would be in a warmer climate as he maintained his role as a spectator in the ongoing drama and horror of combat.

He was in town to settle the sale but had even a more important and pressing matter to settle. Over his cup of coffee with Isabelle, he just blurted it out—he had come to marry her. Thus, as the Battle of Midway raged, during the month of June renowned for its marriages, Bradley asked Isabelle to be his wife.

The waves of uncertainty crashed into Isabelle. This was not how it should have gone. This was a known entity. This was an issue she had analyzed. She had had a plan. She had needed time to assess, time to weigh the options, weigh the pros and cons. But, like so many things these days, all her plans were for naught. She had nothing to do except say, "Yes" or "No".

She said, "Yes". But, as always, there was a codicil. Isabelle had conditions. They would only marry when she had secured Margaret's blessing. This she would do as soon as possible, and they should try to wed in the coming month. However, they would stay in her house in Des Moines until Margaret had her baby and until Isabelle was sure that mother and child were in good health. Then, and only then, they would move to Tucson and he would promise to take her to see the Grand Canyon soon after their arrival.

Bradley was ecstatic.

Isabelle was contemplative.

She continued thinking forward, her brain now in high gear. She too would need to dispose of her fond old home in Des Moines. However, she had no insider information or old friends to count upon to be able to seal a deal at a time of war. So, as she explained to Bradley, she would arrange with Mabel. She would put the house up for rent. Mabel would oversee the rental and share in half the rent. Isabelle would continue to pay Sally and have her look after the house on a reduced basis. Then, with Sally's now freer house-keeping schedule, Isabelle would convince Mabel to take her long-time caretaker on to help her at her own home while ensuring the rental was in good shape until such a time as it could be sold.

Isabelle liked planning, she liked organizing, she liked having control of the situation. And, Isabelle liked having her plans followed—most often, followed to the letter by others if not by herself.

Her misgivings about the here and now were, at least partially, if perhaps temporarily, allayed and she felt good in the pit of her stomach that she had a sound, solid, detailed plan to move forward. This was good. Bradley, Margaret, Mabel, and Sally were all integral parts of this plan and they all had to do as she saw fit. Her major task was to ensure they all, indeed, saw the wisdom in her arrangements and agreed without too much resistance. This was her present task.

As she had envisioned, Margaret and Sally were the most difficult to bring on-board. Margaret still, and in all likelihood forever, believed her mother's one and only husband was, and should be, her father. She maintained her opposition to a second marriage, but ultimately had to accept that her mother's life was her mother's to live. Having expressed her clear and emphatic position (more precisely, her opposition), Margaret needed to get on with her own life that was all too soon to change significantly with the arrival of their first child. So, she did not really accept, but she agreed to disagree and move on.

Sally was a different story. The glue that had held her steadfast to Isabelle for years and years had come unstuck. She now saw Isabelle through different, she believed, clearer eyes. She felt she was manipulated and taken advantage of. She felt she had made many, far too many, sacrifices of her own life, of her family's life, so that Isabelle and her family could do as they wished—these forfeits never repaid, never acknowledged. Her continued relationships with Isabelle were, therefore, not a choice, but a reflection of the difficult times and the few options a black woman in her position could have.

With this as a backdrop, to now have Isabelle tell Sally how she had organized her life for the coming years, this was just unacceptable. It was not that she found fault with the plan itself. It was that the way it was presented, really imposed, was just not right. She was indigent. But, like Margaret, in the end, she saw that it was a suitable arrangement for the circumstances, especially given the difficult political climate. She begrudgingly acquiesced, but without a smile on her face.

Hence, Isabelle relished in her victory of sorts, remarking silently to herself that it seemed far greater than those the stumbling political leaders were encountering on The Front those days. She then carefully crafted a letter to Percy, informing him of her decisions and the changes in her life, without asking for his inputs.

As the US Navy and Marines prepared for the Guadalcanal Campaign, Isabelle and Bradley wed in a civil ceremony attended by their children with their spouses, Mabel, and Sally—the latter deciding that regardless of her righteous umbrage and Isabelle's hubris, she must attend.

Isabelle was uncomfortable about inviting any of the old friends she and George had cultivated over the years and Anne certainly would not leave Sarasota for a wedding. She had asked Bradley about inviting any members of his family in addition to his daughter Dorothy, whom she met for the first time at the time of the ceremony. However, Bradley had rather defensively insisted there was no one close by. This stimulated the flutter of a few butterfly wings in her stomach as she realized how little she really knew about him, his past life, his family, and his deeds. Be that as it may, the decision had been taken, the action taken, there was only one avenue open: move forward.

The venerable newlyweds set up home in Isabelle's house that trapped so many memories. It felt strange to have Bradley in George's place in the bed, in his seat at the table. It seemed strange to have his clothes in the closet, to find his hair in the sink, and his socks on the floor. But Isabelle accepted this all as the new now. This had been her choice. She had to admit she enjoyed having a man around the house, having someone with whom to have a good discussion, having someone with whom to appreciate a good meal, a good song, or a good joke.

Slowly the two melded. Isabelle was not sure she loved Bradley, but she was comfortable around him. And, she was truly not sure she had loved George. She was not sure she knew what love was. She thought she loved Margaret, her own flesh and blood in the truest sense. But even there, they were so different—fundamentally made of different stuff. While she accepted love as a concept much flaunted by all, she began to doubt that it really existed in any true condition. People were basically beings that looked out for their own self-interests first and foremost. Was this reality compatible with love? She did not know. Her own life had not shed any insight on this topic. It was something upon which she could contemplate for days to come. But to what end? She filed this away with many of her other unanswered questions in that part of her brain where she kept all her pending files. It was time to get on with life.

After the Second Battle of El Alamein, but before Thanksgiving, Margaret gave birth to a healthy baby girl. After considerable debate, from which

Isabelle completely excused herself, Margaret and Julian agreed on naming their daughter Ann—mostly in honor of her great-aunt but dropping the "e" in deference to Julian's wishes.

Despite the continuing mobilization and the establishment of rationing, Margaret was able to stay at home and take care of her new daughter—finding all necessary to make her welcome and keep her healthy and safe during her first weeks and months.

Bradley and Isabelle spent Christmas with the new family then managed to get to Chicago to pass New Year's with Percy and his family. Celebrations were muted. Gasoline rationing had been instigated. American convoys crossing the North Atlantic were under heavy attack. The madness continued. There was little festive spirit.

As both the Battle of Stalingrad and the Iowa winter came to a close, Bradley and Isabelle prepared their move. Bradley again raised the option of selling Isabelle's home. However, even considering the precariousness of the day, with a good prospect for a rental under Mabel's vigilante eyes, they reconfirmed their agreement not to sell the house for the moment. There was the war. There were Margaret's uncertain plans. There were life's vagaries. For the immediate, Margaret would help Mabel look after her childhood residence. They would jointly decide its destiny at some point in the future.

Sally agreed to oversee the packing and shipment of Isabelle's effects to Tucson. Mabel agreed to accompany the couple to Sarasota to formally present the new brother-in-law to Anne. All was at the ready.

Bags were packed, goodbyes said, and within a fortnight Isabelle and her companions were enjoying the breeze on Anne's veranda. Isabelle took satisfying note that Bradley and Anne seemed to have hit it off with none of the initial reservations she had seen from some of her old bridge and PEO mates in Des Moines. They spent three weeks enjoying the tranquility of the Gulf before heading west to the desert. They arrived, by design, in Tucson at the same time as Isabelle's affairs. She was, accordingly, able to start straight away getting the cold and impersonal Spanish-style home transformed to her liking—into something more lived-in, perhaps even with a little charm if not warmth.

5

Welcome to Tucson

ONCE ORDER HAD BEEN established, and these things do not happen quickly, it was time to establish a new routine. There was no PEO, DAR, or Soroptimist. There was no Sally. And, most of the domestic duties fell on Isabelle. While Bradly had better than average culinary skills, he tended to appreciate cleanliness from afar. Although always prim and neat, he had little experience in such basic tasks as laundry, ironing, dusting, or polishing silver. Isabelle found herself saddled with most of these unpleasantries and, for the first time in a long time, was needing to spend more time at home than away.

Ever the intellectual, she opted to look through rose-colored glasses, seeing this new homey phase of her life as a welcome opportunity to grow her mind. She had always said, "A day you don't learn something is a wasted day". Once her chores were completed, she devoted hours a day to reading—the paper, books, magazines. She wanted to learn—albeit she wanted to learn what she wanted to learn, not perhaps what was on the broader table of knowledge.

She also saw strengthening her mind as strengthening her skills at her beloved cards. She was able to ferret out bridge games like a Bluetick hound—soon sitting at the card table at least twice a week.

Bradley would occasionally join her for a rubber, though he much preferred listening to a baseball game on the radio where he could loudly praise or insult the teams in the privacy of his living room. He, too, spent long hours reading as well as making regular trips to town to visit old friends over a cup of coffee or, better still, a single malt.

He initially invited Isabelle to come with him on these visits, but she rarely wanted to accompany him to new haunts or to connect with his old comrades—male or female. While she could be personally engaging and was, one-on-one, most frequently her old candid self with him, she seemed to withdraw from other social contact unless it was across the card table.

Bradley had worried that picking up roots from Des Moines after all the years would be a difficult task for his bride. She had, after all, spent most of her adult life in this community where she knew many, was considered as an icon by some. Bradly found his concerns to be ill-founded. Isabelle transitioned seamlessly. She appeared to have no difficulty closing the door on her Des Moines years and opening a new door on her Arizona future.

In fact, Isabelle had no problems leaving Des Moines. She had come to realize she had had few real friends, even if she had had many acquaintances. There had honestly been only a small handful of people who even cared if she left or stayed. This had come as a surprise to her. When she had made the decision to accept Bradley's offer and its implicit move south, she had imagined the outcry from all those she considered as close friends from PEO, DAR, Soroptimist, the Country Club, and all about town. All those old friends who had come to express their congratulations at Margaret's wedding and their condolences at George's funeral—where were they? Vanished. When she was a widow moving away, no one cared. So be it. She accepted this, reinforcing her belief about the natural fickleness and selfishness of people, her good self, of course, exempted.

It was late summer, very hot and dry, when Isabelle felt she had become situated to her satisfaction in her new home and new neighborhood. She was becoming accustomed to new ways, new places, new faces. She began to feel optimistic for her own future and that of the country. After all, the Germans had lost the Battle of Kursk while the allies had invaded Sicily. Things were looking up.

Bradley was less optimistic—not about the war, but about his wife. He knew her well enough to know she always needed a challenge—a really good challenge. She did not handle monotony nor drudgery well. If she were not working on some mental puzzle, she would be unhappy. And, she would be irritable, even venomous. He worried reading and cards were not adequate distractions. She needed more.

He decided they needed to travel. He had taken Isabelle to the Grand Canyon, as promised, as soon as they had come to Tucson. But since that rather brief sojourn, they had been stuck in place in the city they called "The Old Pueblo." It was not a good time to cross international borders, so a return trip into Mexico seemed ill-advised. He concluded a good option would be a trip to New York. They could see plays, walk the byways of Manhattan, and get a real taste of current affairs in the city considered by many as the center of the universe. With this in mind, he made the arrangements.

They indeed had a most pleasant time experiencing early autumn in New York. It was many things. It was a remarkable change of pace and scenery. It was a palpable demonstration of the real impacts of the war on all segments of the country. It was art. It was gastronomy. It was the human condition. It was a different realm. The trip appeared, to Bradley's satisfaction, to mollify some Isabelle's need for distractions. She knew, as did her husband, that she required challenges. Nevertheless, she appreciated with greater lucidity that there was a right time and a right place. New York convinced her that Tucson was her place at this time. What it lacked in intellectual stimulation it more than made up for in spiritual peace and respite.

However, when they returned to the desert, after the Battles of Berlin and Tarawa, Bradley was ready, even anxious, to see what, his age notwithstanding, he could do for the war effort. Isabelle worked hard to cool his ardor. She convinced him that, given the ongoing rationing of everything from fuel to beans, the best thing the two of them could do was simply get out of the way.

Bradley was hard to put down. He thought he could volunteer at Tucson's Davis-Monthan Army Air Field which was home to the 355th Fighter Wing. Isabelle's patience was evaporating when she reminded him more adamantly of his age. He gave in to her insistence to the extent he no longer openly talked about somehow doing something somewhere to help out. But, as they sat in the garden each morning reading the paper, he perused the pages, hoping to find something that an old man could do to help his country at this threatening time.

On Boxing Day, after a quiet Christmas of just the two of them, they were enjoying the *Tucson Daily Citizen*, reading, among other things about the sinking of the German battleship *Scharnhorst* by the *HMS Duke of York*. They were having a cup of chicory due to the rationing, gratefully accentuated by slices of delicious *stollën* baked by Julian's mother and sent by Margaret in her Christmas package (wrapped in old newsprint).

They talked a bit about how, unlike some of German origin, Margaret had been lucky that Julian's family had not been subject to the same sort of treatment that was being dealt the Japanese across the country. It was so fortunate Margaret and little Ann had escaped any internment camps.

In character with Isabelle's bimodal perspective on the world, she felt the Japanese in particular, and possibly Asians in general, were an inherent threat—putting them in camps likely the prudent choice. In fact, putting radical Nazi-loving Germans away somewhere was not a bad idea. But how did you know a good fellow from a bad seed? Isabelle did not know. She only knew that her family were unquestionably on the good side of the ledger with Julian's siblings all serving in the heat of battle. This fine family should not suffer any ethnic bigotry—they were true blue.

On this note, Bradley remarked to Isabelle he had just seen in the paper a reference to the 364th Infantry Regiment that had been involved in those terrible racial revolts of Thanksgiving last year, those American street battles where more than a dozen had lost their lives and that many referred to as "The Phoenix Massacre" since the troops had come from Camp Papago Park near that city. After these most regrettable events, according to the *Citizen*, the African American soldiers had been transferred to a military base in Mississippi where they had created more problems. Now it seemed they had again been moved to military complexes in the Aleutians.

Isabelle replied with one of her now well-known *humpf's*, followed by a rather brief exposé.

"I don't see why, with all these disciplinary issues, Negros are even allowed in the service," Isabelle said. "there has to be a better place for them, I am sure." She went on to blame FDR, saying it was probably that nincompoop in the White House's gift to those people, some sort of allowance to compensate the poor unknowing souls for their manipulation as political pawns by an unconscionable Chief Executive. As always, if they had known their limitations and stayed in their own place, they would now not be sharing some frozen rock with the equally ill-fit Eskimos. All these tribal people encountering great difficulties as they moved away from the niches God had created for them.

Bradley was more surprised by his wife's reference to God than by her views on the head of state, which he shared, or by her opinions about the races. Regarding this latter topic, he knew he did not share his wife's perspective—he viewed the peoples of the world through a much different lens. Nevertheless, he did not want to ignite flames on their still new and fragile hearth. Bradley truly believed in the old axiom, "Slow and steady wins the race." He really felt he could help his wife see issues through his lens if he was patient and presented the topic to her a little bit at a time—allowing her to digest the core of the matter and come to a conclusion herself. He was sure she would ultimately come closer to his own point of view.

Bradly was learning that "slow and steady" was much slower than it was steady. Obviously, it was a learning process, but it was taking a long time—especially for someone who was so smart and well educated. The weeks and months passed, and the old ways persisted.

And there was the war. It too persisted.

The new year came with almost no notice. The bombing of Berlin accelerated as did the fighting in Anzio. The war was seemingly approaching its zenith and a frustrated Bradley read about these battles in the *Citizen* while sitting in the shade of his garden in joyously colorful chairs and feeling more like his wife's obedient hound than a contributing noncombatant. But no word was said, cross or otherwise. The winter temperatures were reaching the mid-sixties, the air was fresh and dry, and the garden felt as though it could have been a sealed-off part of the globe—a private courtyard in Castillo de Vélez-Blanco in Andalucía or the royal ornamental gardens of Mardin Castle, Mesopotamia.

The garden seemed to become the center of their universe. Through the eyes of the *Citizen* they were voyeurs through the hedge to the big outside macrocosm that was at war and suffering other pains of nature and humanity. While in far-off places, Japan launched the Ichigo Offensive in China while Germany lost the battle of Sevastopol and the eruption of Mount Vesuvius went almost unnoticed except to the families who lost loved ones and had to flee their homes. News closer to home seemed no more benevolent nor judicious.

While American troops fought distant enemies, home-front folk continued to wage their own culture wars. Eight decades after the Emancipation Proclamation, racial wars continued. One day after the eighty-first anniversary of the Proclamation, a fifteen-year-old black boy was lynched by three white men in Florida because he had sent a love letter to the daughter of one of the men.

A bit later, two weeks before Easter, six white men murdered a black minister in Mississippi because they had heard there was oil on the land he owned. After the minister's death, his family fled, abandoning their land. No one was ever held accountable for the minister's death.

Two weeks after Easter, in South Carolina, a fourteen-year-old black boy was on trial in an all-white courthouse for the murder of two white girls. He was convicted in ten minutes by an all-white jury and executed two months later.

These events just added to the long list of racial tribulations taking place across the country. When protesting racial inequities in the administration of an agricultural development program, a black man in Missouri was arrested for ostensibly assaulting a white woman and then lynched by a mob after having been shot by a police officer. White workers at a Detroit automobile factory producing military hardware went on strike when a black worker got a promotion. White workers at a Texas shipyard attacked black communities when a white woman alleged she had been accosted by a black man.

Bradley read all these stories in the *Citizen*. While internally he marveled how people, in principle under very real threats of being occupied by foreign powers determined to control the world and them with it, could have the stamina to continue to fight another racial or cultural fight at the same time, he did not share these thoughts with Isabelle. He would give her a quick summary as he knew she did not read these types of articles. She inevitably acknowledged his sharing with a muffled *humpf* and continued her own reading focusing on the status of the war and the travesties, in her mind, of the outrageous president.

One day while reading in the garden, Bradly came across mention of a new book just published by the Swedish Nobel-laureate Gunnar Myrdal entitled *An American Dilemma: The Negro Problem and Modern Democracy*. Bradley zoomed in on "the Negro problem". According to the reviewer, the problem was a result of whites' dislike of blacks and their use of the relatively low socioeconomic status of African Americans as justification for this prejudice. Bradley saw the author describing a deep-seated bigotry that was kind of "They're poor because that's their place" assertion. Apparently, the solution to white oppression was the economic advancement of black communities which would then negate the basic premises upon which the whites' dogma was based.

When he summarily informed Isabelle, as usual, of the new book, this seemed to exceptionally catch her attention. While generally disinterested in journalistic recountings that she considered as overly dramatic and sometimes even fiction, ever the academic, a scholarly work by a world-renowned economist was worthy of her own intellectual consideration. Thus, to Bradley's surprise, she engaged him in an hour-long discussion about the purported content of this new work.

Isabelle was still uncomfortable with the topic of race and still smarting in ways she poorly understood after her acrimonious encounters with Sally. She accepted the world—her world—as a mixed bag, a hodgepodge of peoples with different ethnicities, religions, politics, priorities, and skin colors. A stew of humanity going back to ancient times. Yet, as much as she accepted the world was this heterogeneous pot, she believed the pot was not truly heterogeneous with random order throughout its space. She believed the different segments or populations composing the pot's contents were, rather, structured in an ordered fashion with those most able to contribute meaningfully to the advancement of society having more prestigious, more powerful, more important positions than those who lived in the margins. In her order of things, white, Anglo-Saxon Protestants were the nucleus of the stew—the social and economic cement that allowed mankind to move forward, be it ever so slowly.

Thus, as Isabelle digested the fact that an esteemed international thinker had analyzed the question of race in her country, she realized her own musings were part and parcel of a more relevant conversation. She then decided on the spot that she and Bradley should go back to Sarasota and see Anne where they could have a *tête-à-tête* about race in America and how they, as the aging intelligentsia, should advise their offspring, should they ever choose to listen to the wisdom of their forebears.

Bradley was getting used to the increasing frequency of Isabelle's spur-of-the-moment actions, or proposed actions. While the idea of a change of venue had great appeal to him, and he was fond of Anne, enjoying Sarasota, he had serious reservations that a trio of old fogies would be able to agree on anything, let alone solve any problems—be these problems ever so in need of solving. Moreover, with the whole the country focused completely on the war, as it should well be, he was uncertain they could manage to get a sleeper compartment on the train for the more than 2,000-mile trip. But it was worth the try as, at this point, anything was better than more days in the garden with the *Citizen*.

Bradley succeeded and within three weeks they had made arrangements with Anne and were in a comfortable car on an eastward-bound train. As they crossed Texas, Bradley proudly presented to Isabelle his "*petit Cadeau*," as he called it. He knew Isabelle's thirst for knowledge, not just anything anyhow, but pieces of information that fit into the puzzle upon which her brain was working. And, she was always working on one or more puzzles.

Bradley recalled how most of their recent thoughts about racial issues had been catalyzed by the "The Phoenix Massacre," but he had been digging in the Tucson Public Library and discovered there had been a very similar event in Texas—the state they were now traversing. He had intentionally saved this juicy bit for this part of the journey, as someone might keep a sandwich in his bag for sustenance during a long trip. This local color tale was his gift.

In 1917, sometime ago, but a time they both could well remember Bradley was sure, during WWI, the government was building a new military camp in Texas—Camp Loggan, near Houston. The Army had sent the third Battalion of the all-black twenty-fourth United States Infantry Regiment to guard the new camp site. When two white police officers attacked black soldiers, the barracks emptied as the troops wanted vengeance. By the time calm was re-established, there were twenty deaths involving people on both sides along with several innocent bystanders, including notably a captain in the Illinois National Guard. Before the file was closed, "justice" was delivered: nineteen of the third Battalion were executed and forty-one imprisoned for life. So, deliberated Bradley, a quarter of a century later a very similar event takes place in Arizona. Does history repeat itself? What would their favorite Nobel-laureate Mr. Myrdal say?

Isabelle listened intensively to Bradley's saga. She somehow managed to overlay what she considered as Sally's negligence at housekeeping with military race riots and came to the conclusion that people of African origin were not the same as other normal people and should not be expected to behave normally since for them normal was different. It was sad but true and the unfortunate events were not really a result of hate or even unbridled emotion, but rather of politicians who did not really understand the circumstances and did not know how to deal with those who were culturally and ethnically different—Democrats were responsible.

Bradley did not quickly impose on Isabelle's thoughts, nor interject his own. Their trip was long and there was ample time for these thoughts to germinate and develop roots of their own accord. As the country approached the midpoint of the twentieth century, rail travel was fluid, companies being purchased by competitors, routes changing. This unpredictability was aggravated by the war which obviously took precedence—trains transporting troops and *matériel* often rightfully sidelining passenger trains.

In addition to the uncertainties of wartime travel, their itinerary was particularly long, challenging their patience while testing their relationship to be at even closer quarters for even longer periods of time. They took the Southern Pacific's *Sunset Limited* from Tucson to New Orleans. At the Crescent City they changed to the train of the same name. They disembarked in Atlanta taking the *South Wind* to Jacksonville where they finally connected with the *Seaboard Air Line* for the last leg to Sarasota. All in, scheduled and unscheduled stops, transit and travel times, unforeseen delays, the voyage from the Sonoran Desert to the southern end of Tampa Bay required four and a half taxing days.

The soft bed, the breeze on the veranda, and Violet's good cooking were all welcome remedies to overcome their fatigue. Soon the couple was comfortably settled in Anne's cheerful home and a new routine formed where Isabelle and Bradley would take their morning coffee in the solitude of a quiet corner of the veranda—sipping, chatting, and reading the *Sarasota Herald-Tribune*. Bradley would often chuckle out loud when reading the *Our Boarding House* cartoon and drum his fingers irritably as he scanned the *City Tourist and Trailer Park News* section. By mid-morning, spruced up for the day, they would see what special activities Anne and Isabelle could dream up for the trio.

Sarasota offered a number of possibilities. There could be a minor league baseball game at Payne Park, the site of spring training for the Boston Red Sox. While it was now early summer and, in principal, high season, the Sox were away and in a hiatus as their star player, Ted Williams, had entered the military a year earlier. This fact reminded Bradley that he, regardless of his efforts, lame as they may have been, was far from any military action, even if there was a bombing range across the bay at Longboat Key.

The Keys themselves were also good options for an outing. Lido Key offered the Lido Beach Casino while all the Keys offered pristine Gulf-shore beaches, now nearly abandoned during wartime. Longboat Key still had the remnants of a once flourishing truck farming industry and beautiful fruits and vegetables could be found by the discerning customer. If they preferred to eat on the spot, there was delicious clam chowder at Roberts' Inn on Siesta Key.

Then, nearly everywhere to be seen were references to the town's best-known residents, the Ringlings. Like Isabelle and Bradley, the seven Ringling brothers had Iowa roots. Their claim to fame was the *Ringling Brothers Barnum & Bailey Circus*—the Greatest Show on Earth—that they had purchased in 1907—the circus going back to 1875 when it was called *P.T. Barnum's Great Traveling Museum, Menagerie, Caravan, and Hippodrome*. In 1927, the sole surviving brother, John, decided to establish permanent winter quarters for the circus in Sarasota. John then started The John and Mable Ringling Museum of Art. He also built a thirty-room mansion in town, constructed the John Ringling Causeway to connect Lido Key to the mainland, set up bathhouses on this Key, founded Ringling and Oil Field Railway, made an unsuccessful effort to build a Ritz-Carlton Hotel on Longboat Key, as well as being the chief operative in a wide variety of real estate and other investments. John, who had at one time been one of the wealthiest men in the world, had died eight years earlier, nearly a pauper. But, destitute or affluent, the Ringling Family had left an indelible mark on Sarasota for which Isabelle and Bradley were grateful—this imprint offering new things to see and new things to learn for those with only a fleeting knowledge of things so fanciful as a circus.

As Isabelle had shown repeatedly through her competitiveness at cards, she had a very aggressive and cerebral view of leisure. A circus *per se*, where people crammed together to watch crazy people do crazy things, was not her view of time well spent. The history of the circus, going back to before the birth of Christ to the Circus Maximus—with her own intellectual specialties focusing on the ancient world—was a topic of interest. This interest flowed in a winding channel all the way to a keen interest in Sarasota and the area's, to Isabelle's eye, fascinating history that embraced the bay, the keys, and a variety of cultural groups starting almost four-hundred and fifty years ago. Not quite ancient history, but interesting nonetheless.

Before leaving Tucson, Isabelle, too, had gone to the library. She had visited the well-run and well-stocked Carnegie Free Library to ferret out Sarasota's biography. There was a lot of material to digest. But in a nutshell, as she recounted to Bradley when they were in any of the interminable train cars that took them to the Sunshine State, she had learned that the Seminole, who she had thought to be the original people of the area, were, in fact, the result of a variety of immigrants from different, more northern tribes fleeing any of a variety of disturbances in Georgia and the Carolinas in the early eighteenth century. Those indigenous tribes displaced by these newcomers either died from diseases introduced by their Spanish Overlords or were relocated to Cuba when Spain traded Florida with Great Britain for Cuba in 1763. Then, as Isabelle wove her tale, through ethnogenesis, a subject of personal interests to her, the melding of the immigrant peoples formed the Seminole.

It was barely a hundred years ago that these people, in their turn, had been pushed into deeper, more inhospitable parts of the hinterland and the area opened to the white man. In fact, it was just less than one hundred years ago that Florida had become a state. And, as she looked about the town of Sarasota, she marveled to Bradley, reminding him of their discussions on the train, how much these early white men had been able to do, right up to John Ringling.

Bradley had done some research as well. After all, one of the main reasons for undertaking the long journey was to discuss the interesting topic of race with Anne. Bradly knew full well that this reason for the impromptu travel was pure pretext—Isabelle just had an itch that needed scratching. She could only take so much of one thing at one time and she had had her fill of the garden in Tucson. Nevertheless, this fact notwithstanding, the topic of race was officially out there to be picked up, even though it was not often found in their discussions, most frequently being a subject hidden behind a curtain that remained drawn. Thus, albeit he was uncertain as to his wife's real disposition, Bradley was determined to take advantage of this opportunity to fully pull back the curtain and expose the enigma, in his mind, that was race in the 1940s.

Bradley had already filled Isabelle in on numerous acts he considered to be racial atrocities. He now decided to try and focus on race today in Florida to be able to add fuel to what he hoped would be lively discussions with Anne. He had read about the Rosewood Massacre, only a score of years ago, just south of the Suwannee River, when a white mob had razed the mostly-black small town of Rosewood, reportedly killing eight black people and losing two of their own in the process—all this to exact vengeance for a white lady from the nearby mostly-white town of Sumner who claimed, with no substantiation, she had been raped by a black man. Then, as Bradley had read, just last year, not far from the state line with Alabama, a black man had been forcibly taken from jail and lynched.

These were but a few of the examples of racially-instilled violence Bradly had flagged. There was, however, he now knew, a more insidious and pervasive racial problem, like those they had seen in Arizona, that related to blacks in the military. There were reports that "colored" soldiers at MacDill Field, not far from Tampa, were mistreated. There were even proponents of the related fast-spreading rumor that "Negro" military, due to inherent racism, actually sided with the enemy. Less than a year ago, J. Edgar Hoover himself had submitted a report to the White House about un-American activities of black communities, examining to some degree the political, social, and economic conditions of the day that may have promoted racial unrest. In regard to Florida, Bradley's subject *du jour*, the FBI had found that African Americans in the cities they examined were dissatisfied due to the conditions of life in general, but not because, at a time of war, they supported the country's enemies, as some would try to have all believe. There seemed to be no subversion. There did appear to be a lot of racism—this fact borne out by the miscegenation statute passed by the state of Florida that very year that made it illegal for whites and blacks to intermarry (really to interbreed).

Bradley felt he had plenty of fuel for the discussions he hoped to catalyze. Yet, he wanted neither to disrupt their enjoyable touristy outings nor to precipitate ill feelings against anyone, including himself. He knew that if he prompted this exchange, it would not be spontaneous and not have the results he hoped for—these being an expansion of Isabelle's ever-so-sharp mind in the area of race relations and the need for racial tolerance. He knew, as well, Isabelle often presented herself as intolerant, even dogmatic in a very erudite way. But, although he felt he was beginning to get to know his wife rather well, he was truly uncertain as to the depth of these feelings—was she profoundly, even defiantly intolerant, or was this an affectation. Was his spouse a bigot?

As the *Herald-Tribune* replaced the *Daily Citizen,* Bradley's days were filled with all variety of pastimes from fishing in the bay to catching an act at the A. B. Edward's Theater to basking in a *chaise lounge* on the white sands of Longboat Key. Each day he perused the news and collected new items in his mental portfolio to use in the pending family deliberations on race.

In the meantime, there was a small slice of the subject playing out in front of him—the interactions between Violet and Anne. Isabelle had told him of her discussions with her sister some five years earlier, when Anne had so clearly described how she saw the racial mix in her community and in her home. Bradley remembered how Isabelle had thought that Anne had managed to establish a more poised household in Sarasota than she had in Des Moines.

Bradley suspected Isabelle did not know of his interest in race—his perhaps almost hidden sensitivities about race. Isabelle knew Bradley was an Iowan who had been raised in a small town outside of Des Moines, but she really knew little about Bradley's childhood, his parents or grandparents; the subject had simply never come up.

Bradley had indeed been born in 1871 in Lucas, Iowa, a little less than fifty miles south of Des Moines. The town of Lucas had been born only five years before Bradley himself was born—born when the Burlington and Missouri River Railroad Company built a station at this site. The town was not incorporated until Bradley was sixteen years old and by that time it had become an expanding coal mining community with a growing number of mines and miners.

Before the platting of the town, the residents of what was to become Lucas County had been rough and ready settlers keeping ahead of starvation and abject poverty by raising a variety of plant and animal crops. Bradley's grandfather had been born in Missouri, his own parents among the earliest settlers at the end of the eighteenth century. As his grandfather had entered adulthood, he decided to leave the family compound and travel north up the Chariton River. After much wandering, he built his home near what was to become Lucas. In addition to farming and raising a few animals, he earned some income trading with the local Indian tribes. He developed particularly close relationships with a young Ioway man about his own age, Eltun-qui-he, and, through him, met his new friend's younger sister, Kish-tah-che-un, with whom he instantly fell in love. While she slowly reciprocated his feelings, for the rest of the Ioway family it had not been an easy relationship, nor were the arrangements facilitated by the times. But the inevitable outcome was that Bradley's grandmother was an Ioway, a Chewerean Sioux.

The Ioway had moved south from the Great Lakes, becoming skilled hunters of the bison. However, as was sadly often the case, they had suffered terribly through their relationships with the white man. Smallpox, introduced by the new masters, killed virtually half the tribe and, in 1836, through a variety of ill-understood treaties, many of the survivors, including many of those living around Lucas, were relocated to Brown County in Kansas.

Had the tribe not suffered so from these upheavals, it would have been highly doubtful that anyone would have accepted an intermarriage between the beautiful young Ioway maiden Kish-tah-che-un and an upstart Missouri-bred farmer. But, in the insecurities of the time, the girl's family saw relative stability in the white man's ways, even though they abhorred these to the root of their being. Hence, as the lesser of two evils, the marriage was blessed and now Bradley had a direct linage to the Ioway—his grandmother Kris, a full member of the group the Dakota Sioux called, for no apparent reason, "the sleepy ones".

While Bradley was keenly aware of his ancestral linage—and felt great empathy overlain by a sense of injustice for the travails of all the native peoples who were the original caretakers of the country—to his deep regret, he had not been close to his grandmother. His own parents had built their home just six miles away from his grandparent's farm and, while six miles was not very far, it was enough of a barrier to force a youngster to keep his visits to his grandparents to a minimum with the exception of organized festivities like Christmas and Easter.

He, of course, knew his grandmother—knew her cooking, knew her smell, knew her sense of humor. But he really did not know her. He did not know what it meant to her to be an Ioway—what it meant to her to be an Ioway married to a white man. He did not know how she saw the plight of the Native Americans as their way of life continued to be assailed from all sides.

His one salient memory, the one bronzed souvenir he carried with him to this very day, went back to his thirteenth year—the Fourth of July, to be exact, of the summer just before he entered high school. His grandparents had come to his house for Independence Day celebrations—fried chicken, sparklers, and cherry bombs. After the meal, served in the garden, his grandmother joined the other family members in the kitchen, leaving him alone with his grandfather. Bradley remembered their conversation as though it had taken place this very day.

"Well son," his grandfather had intoned, "You've done pretty well for yourself."

Grandfather was not one given to small talk nor idle flattery and Bradley was nonplussed.

"What'd ya mean Grandpap?"

"Gosh, my boy, you've already gone further in school than your Grandma or me."

"Well, I'm no fan of school, so I figure you both turned out pretty well without having to go through all the suffering of Mr. Gaylord's seventh grade class."

"Don't knock school, young man, it'll stand you in good stead."

"Well, if it's so great, why didn't you two go?"

"We should have and now regret we didn't." His grandfather inhaled. "But things were different in our day."

"Different?"

"Well, for me it was just simple pigheadedness. If I hadn't been a such a hurry to see where the Chariton came from, I would have got the schooling I really needed."

"And Grandma?"

"My boy, that's a different story. You know she's an Indian. And, since she's been with me, she's been an Indian without a tribe. This land is all hers, but no one cares. She and all her brethren are seen as animals. People call her 'heathen' to her face. They would never allow her in a school with white kids. She's the smartest person I know, but most folks would rather fall in a mud-puddle than give her a smiling 'hello.'" His grandfather let the phrase hang as they were rejoined by the others from the kitchen bringing big slices of chocolate cake to be enjoyed before the lighting of the fireworks.

His grandfather had never had another chance to talk about the difficulties they had faced as a mixed-race couple. But Bradly could still clearly see the pain in the old man's eyes when he referred to the love of his life as a heathen. Bradley could feel the despair the man felt, having seen how badly one human can treat another.

He had always thought he would really get to know grandmother Kris when he was old enough to understand politics, understand men. But in 1888, with Des Moines a booming city where many were making their fortune, like his grandfather chasing the Chariton, he left Lucas and never returned, never getting a chance to have those long in-depth discussions with his grandmother. He only managed to be there for her funeral, to cry at her graveside.

He had gone to Des Moines to make his fortune. However, he found himself to be but one of the many looking for riches. He also found that, if one was going to succeed, one needed to stand out. He was one of hundreds, maybe thousands, of bumpkins trying to race away from the farm and catch the twentieth century

He found plenty of odd jobs and learned what it was to work very hard for very little. He learned how tough it could be away from the farm, away from family. He decided he must make a break and make himself stand out. He thought of his grandfather's advice on schooling. After three years of being somebody else's worker, he managed to gain admittance into the brand-new University of Chicago. It took him a long time—partially due to the newness of the university and partially due to the financial uncertainties of his own life. But, in the last year of the century he graduated with a degree in business. It then took him another two years to find a good position on the Chicago Product Exchange. With perseverance, he worked his way up the corporate ladder and after a decade in the trenches with the Chicago entrepreneurial class, he felt he had enough personal solvency to ask his companion of several years for her hand in marriage.

He and Cathleen bought a nice bungalow in the new Austin neighborhood and prepared to spend their lives in the Windy City. They worked hard side by side to build a solid foundation for their future. By this time, it had been more than a decade since Bradley had returned to Iowa—there just was no time.

Three years after their marriage, Bradley got word that his grandmother had died. Uncertain how an urbanite like Cathleen would handle rural Iowa and that part of his family tree that had Indian roots, he convinced her she needed to stay in Chicago to oversee some unforeseen repairs to their house while he made the quick trip to Lucas to represent them both at the funeral.

As he took the train south to Des Moines, he regretted immensely his subterfuge. Why should he be ashamed of his background? Why should he have so little confidence in his wife to think these issues would adversely affect her? It had been the wrong move.

He had been so disgusted with himself, for both his treatment his wife and his neglect of his grandmother, that he decided he must embrace his history and should move his family back to Des Moines.

In 1914, he got a loan from Lincoln Savings Bank to start a transportation company in Des Moines, Baker Hauling, moving produce from the farms to the city. A year later, their daughter, Dorothy, was born to inaugurate their new home on Seventh Street.

Bradley did well. He diversified. He expanded. Cathleen became his compass and talisman. She was his confidante in business deals. She was the manager and overseer of their house and the principal guardian of their daughter. Then, when Dorothy was a junior at Drake University, Cathleen contracted pneumonia and before Bradley knew what had happened, she had died.

Father and daughter were nearly destroyed by the loss. Dorothy wanted to drop out of school to take care of her father. But Bradley told her she owed it not only to her mother, but to the memory of her great grandparents, especially Grandma Kris, to stay in school and, if possible, continue on to law school as she had planned.

Dorothy had stayed in school and was, now, soon to be a partner in a prestigious law firm in Minneapolis. Bradley, until he met Isabelle, had redoubled his efforts in multiplying his businesses and enlarging his wealth. But, in quiet moments, particularly when on his second Bourbon highball, he would become keenly aware that it was really the regrets over the lack of education on the part of his grandparents that had driven him, often under very difficult circumstances, to forge ahead with his own studies and to insist that his daughter do the same. In many ways, it was due to the impossibilities of Grandma Kris receiving the education she wanted that had pushed Dorothy and himself to the point where they were today—to the successes they, each in their own way, had accomplished.

In these peaceful moments, he would wonder what his life would have been like if his grandparents had been more educated. If Grandma Kris had not be ostracized and demeaned, what would he have become?

This brought his rumination back to the present—back to the threads that linked the bigotry that had confronted his grandmother every day of her adult life with the nearly daily battles with prejudice he witnessed, while good people were, at the same time, dying on the battlefields of Europe and the Pacific to defend these very same personal freedoms—freedoms that incorrigible people in this country ignored continuously.

It was soon the Fourth of July in Sarasota. Much of the gaiety was overshadowed by the unknowns of war. From their armchair observation posts, to Isabelle and Bradley it seemed as though there were pitched battles being fought everywhere—in Finland, France, on the High Seas, and in Burma the two sides tore at each other. It was impossible to tell who was winning and who was losing. There just seemed to be more carnage after more carnage.

All this was in the wake, not a month earlier, of the invasion of Normandy, Operation Neptune and the overarching Operation Overlord, that had been in all the papers and on the radio. A massive movement of troops onto the continent involving nearly 7,000 vessels. Many called this the turning point of the war. But, when the president had come on the radio to address the American people, Isabelle could only mutter, "damn Democrats" and turned the set off.

With the war as a constant backdrop, their routine was never the same, but always the same. When the trio met up during the latter part of the morning, they decided if there would be an outing and, if so, if it would be a full day affair. Most of their excursions were limited to the afternoon after a good game of Canasta and an even better lunch, made all the more salivating with Violet's special mixture of herbs and spices.

On days with longer outings, like a fishing cruise, a trek in Myakka River State Park (Bradley never having the courage to tell Isabelle the park had been established by FDRs Civilian Conservation Corps), or a jaunt through Tampa or St. Petersburg, they would forego the cards and the delicious midday meal—generally supping in a local restaurant selected by Anne.

While their arrival in Sarasota had chiefly been a result of Isabelle's impulsiveness, these local forays seemed to be in the hands of the gods—the god's handiwork interpreted on a regular basis by Isabelle and Anne. The two women obviously shared a strong affection, and sometimes even the same choices in sites to see. It was not really a magnetic attraction of opposite personalities attracting each other. But it was a joining of very different spirits and temperaments who, through time, seemed to have forged steadfast, nearly unshakable bonds—bonds that had not always been there, that had not been an automatic result of sisterhood.

Bradley sensed these bonds were frequently strengthened by silence. Isabelle was very outspoken about her views—especially her political opinions, not that she was short of opinions on everything from knitting to astronomy. Anne, conversely, kept her potentially more controversial thoughts to herself. She had undoubtedly been more open, more effusive, when engaged with her professor husband. However now, with her hardline and often intolerant sister, she found reserve the best tactic. In truth, she was so tight-lipped about her views on many topics that Bradley had to confess he was not really sure where his sister-in-law stood on lots of current issues.

Tactical silence apart, the two sisters were simply very divergent.

Anne was effusive, warm, and caring. Isabelle was stoic, cerebral, and standoffish. When they would walk along the beach, if they found a whelk or spotted a fiddler crab, Anne would marvel at the intimacies of nature, while Isabelle would wonder about the origins of their Latin names. When they saw small children walking home from school, Anne would wonder if they were getting three meals a day, while Isabelle would ask herself if they had really learned something that day. When they were passing by and saw the crew of men leaving Jones Chemicals at the change of shifts, Anne hoped they were going home to a welcoming family and Isabelle hoped they had met their daily quota. However, idiosyncratic differences and sisterly bonds were gone when the two faced each other over a game of Canasta—then it was no mercy, no lurking intellectualism, no charity. It was pure, and it was simple—to the winner the spoils.

The cards, the weather, the common love of seeing what tomorrow would offer, and the fundamental oneness of family merged into an ambience that was both positive and compelling. The two aging ladies clearly loved each other and, each in her own way, loved Bradley. So, there it was, as the war raged, they sensed they had some sort of utopian bubble they were reluctant to burst. The weeks flowed into months and they continued to enjoy all there was to enjoy.

One sunny morning as Bradley and Isabelle emerged from their room, they found Anne comforting a sobbing Violet. They felt ill at ease and were in the process of going out for a walk to leave the two old comrades together when Anne indicated they should take seats on the veranda next to them. As Violet sobbed, Anne explained her younger brother had been one of the Tuskegee Airmen, part of the 332nd Fighter Group. After the invasion of Italy and the liberation of Naples in October 1943, the Group had been stationed at an airfield one hundred miles to the northeast of the City of the Sun. The fighters were escorting heavy bombers on raids into Germany, Austria, and Poland. Her brother had been shot down escorting a formation deep into German territory.

As the waves of anguish receded, Violet said she would have to travel home to make sure her family knew of the young airman's death and then to assist with whatever arrangements were to be made. There was no body. He had been shot down behind enemy lines and, according to accounts, his plane had vaporized. She had no idea what her family would do, but she knew she had to be with them when they decided.

Violet's childhood home, still home to her parents, was De Funiak Springs, Florida, a town like Lucas, Iowa, founded by a railroad—this time the Pensacola and Atlantic Railroad. The family had moved south from Luverne, Alabama, about seventy-five miles to the north. De Funiak Springs, an academic community with both a well-respected high school and college, was considered as a relatively safe port in an area being crisscrossed by violent racial storms.

Violet still had a lot of family in and around Luverne—family that, even before the loss of her brother, had already suffered extensively. Violet's cousin Fred was a laborer at Andrew's Peanut Farm. Fred's son Bobby had been a good student all the way through high school and had gone on to Atlanta to get a good job as a timekeeper at a major agricultural supply company. Four years earlier, Bobby, twenty-six, had come back to Luverne to introduce his fiancé to his family. When Bobby was walking down the sidewalk while he waited for his fiancé to get her hair done, he happened to meet a police officer whom he greeted. Unbelievably, the officer exploded, yelling, "any niggra that greets me better greet me with Mister!" This citified farmer had no call to disregard required local traditions.

The officer knocked Bobby to the ground and then dragged him to the jailhouse. While the officer was opening the cell door to throw Bobby inside, Bobby bolted, running down the street away from the jail. The officer quickly hailed a handful of white men loitering about, chasing Bobby into farmland outside town. A week later, Bobby's body, riddled with gunshots, was found in Patsaliga Creek.

Violet had gone back to De Funiak Springs to join her parents and travel up to Luverne for Bobby's funeral. There was never an inquiry into Bobby's death and the family was advised, if they wanted to avoid future problems, not to ask any questions. What was done, was done.

Now the family had lost another young man in his prime—albeit, in the eyes of most, under much more honorable circumstances (not that Bobby merited any dishonor). Violet would again go back to De Funiak Springs to join her parents in mourning, this time someone closer to home.

As Violet composed herself, and Anne wiped away the tracks of the tears scarring her face, she advised her employer and concurrently her friend that she would travel north the day after next, using the interim to make sure the house and its inhabitants were in good shape to be able to weather her absence.

Violet and Anne had been together for nearly thirty years—Violet coming to work for Anne and her husband when they first moved to Sarasota from Tallahassee—a move applauded by Anne to finally get her free of what she considered to be the myopic conservative stronghold that she found Leon County to be. While moving only a little over 300 miles away, Anne felt as though she had entered into a whole new, less encumbered world.

Anne's husband, Albert, fully supported the relocation as he found his academic interests more in the nature of feeding his own intellect than trying diligently, if often futilely, to expand the thought processes of young men and women who were seen as the future of the country, but whom he found more often than not to be frivolous souls more interested in tasting the fruits of life than in understanding from where they came.

Albert loved Anne deeply. He regretted each day in Tallahassee when he saw how much of an outsider his wife was. Once he received tenure and had established a professional reputation, he and Anne began planning their departure where she could express her thoughts more openly while he could indulge in his favorite pastimes of fishing, reading, and writing scholarly works. Sarasota was the perfect spot for their needs.

When Violet had started taking charge of their household, she had been a married woman with her own household to manage—a husband and a son to shepherd. However, soon after Albert passed away in 1933, Violet's own husband Willie was stricken by a severe case of influenza and died after a valiant effort to overcome the disease. A year later, Violet's son, Sam, finished his studies and got a job as an electrician at the General Electric plant in Schenectady, New York.

It made complete sense to Anne and Violet that Violet should move into Anne's big house rather than continue to be burdened with the maintenance of her own home. Thus, the two ladies had been cohabiting as employee and employer since 1934. Over the ensuing decade they had developed a very special relationship where there was still deference, but also a high degree of mutual respect.

They also established synergistic roles. Violet ran the day-to-day activities of the household—cleaning, cooking, and overseeing a part-time gardener. Anne took care of any bureaucratic or administrative issues or obstacles like taxes, problematic utilities, or even the occasional trespasser.

Violet was on the job all the time—all the time except when the Church called. She was an active and devoted member of the Bethlehem Baptiste Church. As she had done when her husband was still alive, she went to Bible study every Wednesday night and to services every Sunday. She also volunteered to help decorate and undecorate the church for various religious celebrations as well as help serve meals at the periodic church potlucks.

It was her unbinding faith that kept her going over the days after the news of her brother's death. She cleaned the house thoroughly, changed all the linen, made a big casserole, wrote out instructions for the gardener, stocked the pantry, packed her small brown cardboard suitcase, and went to the bus station after hugging each of her housemates and leaving a few unharnessed tears on the stoop.

As Violet walked out of the yard, the trio standing on the veranda all felt pangs of disquiet. Anne felt a great sadness for her friend and anxiety that she would make it home and back to Sarasota without any major problems. After all, she, too, was no longer a young woman. Bradley empathized with Violet's loss, admiring her courage. Isabelle felt a sort of detached sorrow over the death of Violet's brother—not quite as abstract as the melancholy one feels when one sees a dead dog in the road, especially since the young man had died in the height of battle, but still a grief more in principle than in practice. Her overshadowing emotion was the image of her older sister hugging Violet and wiping away her tears. The deep devotion was obvious. But Violet was black. *Could*—should— *a white lady, like her sister, love a Negro?*

If Bradley had been able to read his wife's thoughts, he would have leapt at the opportunity to open the discussion of race for which he was (he thought) so well prepared. However, he assumed the prevailing feelings of all were those of mourning at the loss of, from all reports, a fine young man who had given his all for his country.

Violet had done her usual impeccable job and the trio was nearly able to carry on as usual—the house clean, the larder well-supplied, and good food on the table. However, it was as though a counterbalance had been taken off the scale. The air was different.

Bradley sensed the change in the energy, noticing how the sisters seemed to be less magnetically connected. Perhaps this was because Isabelle moderated her normal extremely acerbic style when she was in the presence of her older sister and Violet. Bradley knew his wife calculated very carefully. Undoubtedly, in deference to the subservient role she saw for household staff and the need for the "*patronne*", her big sister, to constantly be in the position of unchallenged authority, she felt random sharp attacks from a junior sister could, in Isabelle's view, erode the necessary disciplined juxtaposition needed to be maintained at all costs.

The ardent sororal nexus that permeated all but the most competitive card game seemed to be weakening. Each appeared to allow more of her natural personality to show—personalities that had been diametric from birth. The unveiling process was slow but insidious. It reached its climax as

Isabelle was losing badly to Anne at Canasta, Bradley almost insignificant in terms of how the cards were deftly played.

Isabelle was already in a foul mood as her nemesis, FDR, had, as a true confirmation of the Democratic Party's insanity, as if this were needed, been nominated at the Party's Convention for a third term. *A THIRD TERM! Damnation! What folly! What lunacy!* Then to be losing badly to her sister at Canasta! Life was just not fair.

Isabelle drummed her fingers against the table, then hammered a fist into the surface shouting, "Damn!"

Bradley and Anne inhaled deeply as if in concert.

"Damn! Damn him! Damn that man! Damn FDR!" Isabelle repeated, with even more intensity.

Bradly and Anne sat immobile, uncertain of what to do or say. Such an outburst was, honestly, not completely out of character for Isabelle, but, for such a controlled lady, a true rarity. They had no idea what to expect, sitting wide-eyed, nearly gaping.

Isabelle fixed her fiery eyes on her older sister, "And you! You're just as bad! Have you forgotten all you were brought-up to respect? Have you forgotten your heritage? Your culture?"

Anne hemmed and hawed, taken completely aback.

"It's all because of that damn liberal Albert—you never should have married him!"

Anne did not want to let an attack on her beloved husband go by un-challenged, but she had no clue of what Isabelle spoke and, sadly, knew not how to insert a rejoinder.

"It was shameful! Rubbish!" continued Isabelle, showing no signs of losing steam for her tirade, "How do you think I felt? How do you think poor ol' Bradley felt?"

At this point, Anne could mutter, "What?"

"What indeed! You and that Negress! We saw you hugging her, almost caressing her. When my George died, did you hug or caress me? Look what you did—and with a black woman! What would our parents say?"

Anne and Bradley stared at each other—incredulous, both embar-rassed for the other. Bradley felt the issue with Violet was just the spark that lit the smoldering flame of Isabelle's total frustration with the world as a whole: the war, politics, the new generation. He truly felt his wife was not simply this completely rattled over the fact that her older sister had com-forted her long-time black companion over the loss of her brother—albeit, she was certainly uncomfortable with this display of honest emotion. This was the rupturing of an abscess that had been festering for a long time. This was an interweaving of many factors, all of which were antithetical to Isabelle's view on life.

For Bradley, this outburst was also the unwelcome confirmation that his hopes for an objective discussion about race, a subject that in many ways had led them to this very card table, were likely dashed. Isabelle was uncovering deep-seated biases that, unfortunately, could not be redressed by objective intellectual discussion. He feared these were imprinted on her very soul and knew all the facts and figures he had so assiduously collected over the past months would now be lost in the cobwebs of an unopened file in the back of his brain.

As Bradley refocused on the drama at the card table, Isabelle expounded, "New Deal, more like the road to perdition. That man has taken us to the abyss! Total numskull! A cripple like Hephaestus. Like Hephaestus, he should be thrown out into the deepest reaches of the sea. We teeter on the verge. Like Boreas, he will bring a frigid wind that will blow us over the edge. He has doomed our country!"

Bradly excused himself, though no one noticed, going to the sideboard to get three snifters of brandy. Isabelle seemed to be preparing for her next onslaught and, perhaps, there would be a wee break when he could get her to take a bit of cognac and let her nerves relax.

Bradley succeeded in coaxing Isabelle to take a couple of healthy swallows of the amber liquid, at which time she seemed to get a better grip on herself, if not her seat. She would, of course, never apologize. She had, of course, only reiterated the truths as she saw them—the issues they all knew all too well. But she would, for the tranquility of the household, take things down a level or two and get back to the game at hand—even if she did lose.

Later that afternoon, there were several losses to chalk-up on an imaginary score board Bradly had now set up to replace his mental folder on racial incidents. Isabelle did lose her game of Canasta. Anne lost some of her equanimity. Bradly lost the, perhaps always, illusional chance of digging deeply into racial issues with his wife and sister-in-law.

They returned to being a trio, but somehow not the indomitable threesome of yesterday, but a more cautious triad that was keenly aware of the differences between them and the necessity of leaving most of these in the shadows if they were to be able to maintain a convivial family circle.

Bradley recalled Isabelle frequently telling him how her mother so often cautioned, "three's a difficult number." This seemed to be becoming the case in Sarasota.

The demeanor of the household was heightened after a lull lasting several weeks when the national joy at the liberation of Paris by the allies seeped into the house—Isabelle, Anne, and Bradley all finding great jubilation in the event and happiness in sharing it with the others. The war, in fact, combined with more mundane topics like the weather or the state of the roads, was about as contentious a subject as the three could now broach without fears of reverting to the anguish of high-temperature subjects that could catch fire from one moment to the next, upsetting once again, and perhaps regretfully for good, the delicate balance of personalities that had to be kept in check if the two sisters were to continue to stay under one roof.

Isabelle's tantrum had burned all their fingers. But, as all now took more care of what and how they spoke, it was soon moved into the category of unpleasant memories. Anne was even able to make light of the event, reminding her sister that their mother had always said that ladies avoided talking about sex, religion, and politics. She had been a wise woman, their mother.

In early September, the allies liberated Brussels and Violet came back to Sarasota. She was a bit more taciturn than usual, it had been a difficult trip, but she quickly immersed herself in her work—the task of getting every-thing back in good shape rather daunting as the trio had long exhausted her pre-departure preparations. It probably would not classify as a mess, but close—the pantry was nearly bare, the house enveloped in dust and pollen, and the kitchen resembled an army bivouac. Neither of the sisters were at all domestic—another of their ill-recognized common denominators—and Bradley had obviously finally decided he could not overcome and joined the disarray.

By mid-month, as the allies prepared to expand out from Brussels in the ill-fated Operation Market Garden, Isabelle announced over coffee and junket served with fresh strawberries, after a lunch of a refreshingly spicy chicken salad, she and Bradley had decided to return to Tucson early the next month to be at their residence to be able to vote. Isabelle could not help but add that she was grief-stricken that undoubtedly that disastrous FDR would be reelected for an *illegal* third term by the irresponsible, corrupt, pro-Communist Democrats. Nonetheless, she could not be at peace with herself if she did not at least cast her own vote for Wendell Willkie.

Three weeks later, they had managed to make all the travel arrange-ments and repeated the long trek back to the now welcome high elevation, dry climes on the banks of the Santa Cruz River. As a parting gift, Anne had given Isabelle a satchel full of carefully selected books—books filled with tales of anthropology, ancient lands, ancient languages, and ancient religions—nothing in the collection about current politics, social issues, or economic challenges.

Thus, as the train sang along the west-bound tracks, Isabelle read while Bradley stared out the windows, watching the universe fly by, thinking of this world and her problems. He now wistfully realized, in all objectivity, it had been a mirage. It had been doomed before it had started. He had had the illusion that his wife would have been able to engage her big sister, and possibly he himself, in honest in-depth discussions about the world's future—be these about race, railways, or rainbows. This could never, would never happen.

The two ladies saw this world through totally different prisms.

Yet, this reality aside, it would have been nice, from his perspective, if, given Anne's interracial lifestyle, the two sisters could have talked more—just by chance, maybe Anne putting a small crack in Isabelle's wall of intolerance. But they were now going back to their home, the wall solidly in place, no cracks in sight. It was frustrating. Bradley was aware that his own thoughts, feelings, and beliefs were much closer to his sister-in-law's than his wife's. Nevertheless, he loved Isabelle, probably because of, and not in spite of, her various foibles—or what he saw as foibles (she would certainly hotly contest this point, he knew).

After the seemingly endless trip, they once again found themselves, following more than three months of absence, opening the door of their home. While a bit musty and dusty (Bradley wondering what it would have been like to close-up a house in Sarasota for more than a hundred days), it was fine, and it was home. Open windows and clean sheets did wonders, and soon they were back in the garden with the *Citizen*.

Not long after General Mac Arthur returned to the Philippines and Charles de Gaulle took control of the French government, it was time to vote and, as Isabelle had known well in advance, yet to her chagrin, FDR was still president—still at the helm swinging his wrecking ball. Bradley dared not vocalize his thoughts that FDR had not done too badly. Over and beyond the war effort, Bradly now supported more of the president's actions as, in retirement, he had more time to educate himself on the intricacies of managing a country as complex as the United States. He felt the establishment of more national wildlife refuges, forests, and parks was excellent. He particularly liked the bases for the Civilian Conservation Corps. But it was FDRs proposal for a Second Bill of Rights, guaranteeing, among others, that all had access to food, clothing, housing, education, and health care, that pleased Bradley the most. He felt this was insightful, humanistic, and necessary. Of course, none of these issues would be discussed with his dear wife. Life was too short. Tranquility was best maintained by not rocking the boat.

Seemingly in the blink of an eye, the year was over. Christmas and New Year's had come and gone, each celebrated in the relative anonymity of their garden. The war stormed. The allies' advance from Paris to the Rhine crossed the Siegfried Line.

FDR was inaugurated to a fourth term (Isabelle was rabid) and soon thereafter attended the Yalta Conference with Churchill and Stalin to discuss the fate of a post-war Europe. Afterwards, on his return travels the president met with the heads of state from Ethiopia, Egypt, and Saudi Arabia before finally getting back to brief Congress in early March. Within six weeks, to the shock of all, including Isabelle, FDR was dead.

Isabelle was certainly glad to be rid of her antagonist, although she had no hopes that Harry Truman was any better. She did, nevertheless, to her own surprise, feel sympathy for Eleanor Roosevelt at the pain, as she herself had experienced, of losing a husband. Politics aside, Eleanor, five years her junior, tweaked Isabelle's intellectual curiosity. She was bemused that the First Lady's first name was Anna, while she liked to be called Eleanor. She was attracted to the fact that Eleanor was a niece of Teddy Roosevelt. She was uncertain whether she liked the fact that Eleanor had married her fifth cousin. But she was infatuated by the talk that, although the First Lady had had six children, she had told confidents she was not maternal—a situation with which Isabelle could well empathize. And, from the more prurient perspective, Isabelle was, as were many, titillated by the rumors of possible relationships with such famous ladies as Amelia Earhart. The question whispered by some: "Was the First Lady a lesbian?"

Isabelle found the First Lady offered so much more than the terrible policies and infidelities of her husband. She was still not a fan. Yet, she was somehow a distant, but keen observer.

Life without FDR was a carbon-copy of life with the old man. But somehow things seemed to be operating at lightning speed. Just days after the president's death, the Battle of Berlin began. In less than three weeks, the Axis powers in Europe surrendered, Mussolini was executed, and Hitler committed suicide.

Isabelle and Bradley felt as though they were at the cinema—conceivably a cinema whirling on a merry-go-round. Of course, the cinema had always had newsreels about the war. They had seen with their own eyes the battlefields and the destruction. But there was another war story being acted out—day in and day out, everyone was living on a war footing. People lived their own version of the war in their living rooms. Whether rationing, war-related work, or just gut-wrenching fear, everyone was experiencing the battles—the wins and the losses. For months this personal war theater, even for old folks like them, had been going on at a slow and steady pace. Now it had accelerated unbelievably.

May eighth, 1945, became the day that commemorated the European victory—V-E Day. The fast pace got faster. By July, Germany had been divided between Allied forces and the Philippines had been declared liberated. At that time, Japan seemed to open some doors for peace in the Pacific. But the war there carried on and the loss of life continued. When Japan refused to accept the Potsdam Declaration and surrender, on August sixth and ninth President Truman gave the go-ahead to drop atomic bombs on Japan. On August fourteenth the Japanese Emperor accepted the Potsdam Declaration and surrendered. The surrender was announced across the globe the following day, but only formally signed in Tokyo Bay abroad the *USS Missouri* on September second—thereafter called V-J Day.

Within weeks, in the shadow of the A-bomb's mushroom cloud, it was as though the pages of war had been turned—or perhaps for some the book never existed. Tales but a few months old now seemed to have taken place years ago.

There was a focus on a bright future—on a new (and good) world order. On October twenty-fourth, the United Nations and the International Court of Justice were founded. It was a moment to concentrate on reconciliation and peace.

Strangely, from Isabelle and Bradley's vantage points as ardent onlookers sequestered in the garden, nearly at that same moment, the rhythm of world disorder changed, but did not stop. After years of worldwide war, there were now dozens of less-visible national skirmishes—violent and not. Instead of peace, the waves of dissent seemed to be moving across the globe. Brazil, Indonesia, Mongolia, India, Azerbaijan, Greece, among others, were apparently encountering challenges to a peaceful transition to a post-world-war world. It was hard to understand. It was chaotic. It troubled Isabelle and Bradley. Then, on December twenty-first, Isabelle's disquiet was magnified many times when one of her touchstones, General George Patton, died as a result of injuries received during an accident when his Cadillac Series Seventy hit a two-and-a-half ton GM truck in Rhineland-Palatinate, Germany. He was sixty years old—only a year younger than Eleanor Roosevelt.

Patton had been a vocal opponent of the Democratic presidents. He had reportedly accused the culpable administrations of mismanagement, of being pro-Russian. There were rumors, lots of rumors. Patton had secrets. He was coming home at the end of the war, some said, to tell all. He was popular. He strenuously opposed the Democrats, or so it seemed. Many felt he was a threat. Many said the accident was no accident. All this fit perfectly with Isabelle's views. She had counted on this general to come home and restore some sanity. Now he, too, was gone. The chance to right wrongs was gone. As the year neared its end, the insanity continued.

Then another holiday season had passed, and it was again a new year— the first official non-war year in a long time. Isabelle and Bradley felt they had somehow been in the isolation ward during the war years—sitting in the bleachers for the most part, limiting their presence to Tucson and Sarasota, not visiting their family in Minneapolis, Chicago, or Des Moines— keeping in touch only my mail. A harsh outside observer would probably have criticized the couple for blatant abandonment of their family during a time of crisis. This critic might, Isabelle knew, have some justification. They could have, and maybe should have, kept in closer contact. However, in their own defense, but hopefully dispassionately and not in rationalization, they knew their children's families were fine and that their children were, in their own ways, completely involved in the war effort. Their visits and the travel these would have required could well have been more of a burden than a benefit. Hence, for better or worse, Isabelle and Bradley had been standoffish.

But, the war was over, and it was time to see children and grandchildren. While the French war in Indochina was brewing and the Iran Crisis was unravelling, it was still too cold in the northern latitudes for Isabelle and Bradley to undertake trips to reunite with their children. They could plan, however. So, they sent letters to all, trying to identify the best times after Easter when they could come north for a visit. Finally, after considerable back-and-forth, they had an itinerary in place to travel at the end of April, going first to Minneapolis, then to Chicago, ending up in Des Moines. Their visits in the first two cities would be short, only a few days. They would stay longer in their former hometown, seeing not only Margaret and her family but also Mabel along with sundry friends and acquaintances. Their timetable got them back to Tucson by the end of June so that they spent the hottest months in the dry desert air and not the stifling humidity of the Midwest.

Isabelle had mixed emotions about their planned pilgrimage. She fundamentally believed, "you can never go home". She might argue that she was even unsure of where her real home actually was. But, in practical terms, she believed that when the sun set on a day, that day was gone—forever. There were, of course, no do-overs in life. There was also no going back for a look-see. Returning to points of the past would only lead, in all likelihood, to angst and self-doubt.

In the face of these facts, Isabelle also believed the conventional wisdom of parents being the critical shapers of a child's youth was only partially true. Unquestionably, there were formative years in the early stages of all lives when a plant, a pony, or a child could be trained. These adjustments, if successful, were lifelong.

However, as she herself knew all too well, the demands of life were not only surviving youth—they were also surviving life. While early childhood years were crucial, early adult years were no less compelling. When a young adult was facing marriage, a career, taxes, and poor health, who offered guidance? Who provided the training? In the natural course of affairs, it was the older members of the group, those who had already passed these obstacles, who helped the younger members maneuver the terrain.

She recalled visiting one of George's friends at his farm, years ago. Like all farms, the place was full of machinery, tools, chemicals, and all manner of contraptions. Many of these common bits and pieces of farming could be harmful to the well-being of a dog—the animal being impaled, poisoned, run-over, or maimed.

Nevertheless, as was generally the case for country dwellers, the farmer had an old dog—a mangy, old, yellow thing, but that was not the point. His neighbor had just given him a young puppy. While she and George were visiting, she spied the old dog leading the pup around the barn and outbuildings. The farmer said the old hand was showing the newcomer the lay of the land.

People needed this too.

Isabelle had been ten years old when her own father had died, and twenty-eight when her mother passed away. How she wished they were still around. How she lamented that, as she had passed through young adulthood, she could not rely on her parents' wisdom to help her make the right decisions and take the right actions. How she missed their firm hand guiding her.

She was not sure she was much of a guide herself. She was not sure she had much real-life wisdom to share. She felt she was not very good at problem-solving. And, her own life was certainly not a sterling example to emulate. Yet, all these facts notwithstanding, she wanted her children, their children, to at least have to opportunity to benefit from their parents' presence as they struggled down the pathways of adulthood—an opportunity she sadly never had had.

Over the five months since they had reestablished their home in Tucson, Isabelle had decided she needed to do something more than oversee the household and read in the garden. After all, it was the ennui of endless days in the garden that had pushed her to propose a trip to Sarasota so that Bradley could engage her sister in his interminable concerns over man's inhumanity to man. Avoiding judging her decision, she was acutely aware that uninterrupted hours and days of idleness could lead to problems. Hence, she was determined to find a new avocation that would provide more structure in her life and hopefully encourage Bradley to do the same.

Isabelle decided to take up painting. She sensed she had an inherent talent for transforming three dimensions into two—she wanted to get serious about it.

Bradley turned out to be her most fervent supporter—suggesting she first take some classes. But this was not her style. Painting, after all, could be no more intimidating than ancient languages she had studied, so she simply bought the necessary supplies and set up her easel. In no time she had turned one of the spare rooms into a studio and was painting no less than three hours a day. She found she enjoyed seeing her projects advance and materialize. Painting would never compete with cards, but she enjoyed it.

Bradley wanted to follow her lead and considered painting himself, or perhaps pottery, or even weaving. But all these were nonstarters. He needed something that took him outside and away from the house, to a fresh new environment where he would not be overloaded with his ruminations. He had seen in the *Citizen* where Ben Hogan was playing at the El Rio Golf Course and decided if it was good enough for Ben, it was good enough for him, in spite of the fact he had never played golf a day in his life. .

Like his wife, he went out and bought his supplies. But, unlike his wife, he took his new supplies to the course and procured top-notch instruction on how to play a game he had heretofore considered an ensemble of stupid gestures as men who should know better chased a little ball around a manicured garden.

To his great surprise, once he had the basics in hand, he found he liked the game and began going to the course at least four times a week.

He and Isabelle were now less claustrophobic to each other. They spent fewer hours together and during this time had more things to talk about— the latest painting, the most recent golf game, or even the price of chicken as he was doing more shopping for them when he came back from the golf course.

In fact, their new avocations were absorbing so much of their time that they found they no longer had enough left over to take adequate care of the house. After considerable analysis and discussion as to how to best proceed, they put an ad in the *Citizen* for a full-time housekeeper—but not a live-in. Among the many applicants, they chose Maria, a fifty-six-year-old widow who had come across the border from Mexico with her parents when she was five years old. She had managed to finish high school and immediately married Emilio, a worker on a cotton farm. They had had two children— one had died of measles and the other was now working at a filling station in Phoenix. Emilio had died in a farm accident in 1938. Maria had spent the last fifteen years keeping the house of a retired New York banker who had recently passed away. She had good references. She needed the job. They needed a housekeeper. The deal was done.

Isabelle was most relieved to be freed from her least favorite task: housework (taking care of small children a very close second). However, she was resolved not to make the same mistake, as she saw it, she had made with Sally. Maria was an employee. She was not a friend, confidante, or chum. She was not going to become a Violet. Isabelle did not want to know where she lived or how she got to and from work. Isabelle wanted Maria to show up at nine-thirty sharp and to be out of the house by teatime unless there were extenuating circumstances. That was it—clear, with no personal strings attached

As Maria had grown up and been schooled in Tucson, her English was very good. Nonetheless, she still spoke fluent Spanish, the language of her childhood. Maria would automatically revert to Spanish when she had occasion to encounter someone she suspected of having Hispanic roots. This included Isabelle and Bradley's part-time gardener Julio as well as the occasional tradesperson who came to the door.

When Isabelle heard Maria speaking Spanish, she did not like it. Although she knew better, she always felt Maria must be talking about her behind her back. Then her intellectual self would intervene and scold her gut-reaction self. She was, after all, a student of ancient languages. She knew, or should have known, about communication. She knew people enjoyed speaking their mother tongue, regardless of how much of a polyglot they were. She understood some people often felt they were only really able to express themselves when speaking in the language of their youth. Yet, even with all these intellectual garnishes, Isabelle hated Maria speaking Spanish. She hated it, but she used all her willpower to not intervene and refuse this behavior. While she did not want to bond with Maria—was fearful of bonding with Maria—she also did not want to antagonize the woman in whose hands she had entrusted her home. So, she fumed like a kettle nearing the boil whenever she heard melodic Spanish words echo from the garden or the stoop. She then fumed more because she had caught herself fuming.

For his part, Bradley was just happy he no longer had to stop at the grocery store on the way back from the golf course and that he no longer had to mop the floor when he tracked in dirt from the eighteenth tee. He found Maria to be efficient and amicable. Most importantly, he noted with satisfaction that Maria had established a tenuous relationship with his wife, nonetheless based on some level of mutual respect and tolerance. He was a bit surprised Isabelle had adapted so quickly to having a Latina in the family circle—but necessity, or the perception of necessity, can push people to do many things they normally would find onerous. He wondered if Isabelle ever thought of the difficulties facing the Latino communities in Arizona. However, he knew better than to ask and now filed away these queries in his unopened mental folder, realizing all too well how far astray his preoccupation with these issues had led him some months earlier. He decided to concentrate on his golf swing.

No one was more surprised than Maria that in a remarkably short period of time, she became a fixture in their household. She could, of course, sense Isabelle's not-all-that-well-concealed feelings. She could feel Isabelle bristle when Spanish filtered through the house. But Maria had finely-honed people skills and quickly knew when to apply flattery and when to only smile demurely.

They had a working arrangement.

Maria even invited Isabelle and Bradley to Easter Mass at her church. While Maria was totally unaware of the dangerous ground she was treading, Bradley was once again startled at the mini drama that must have been playing out in his wife's mind. Isabelle had been invited to a ceremony at a Catholic Church, and not just any Catholic Church, but one principally for foreigners, foreigners who spoke another language, services that were probably in another language. Normally, Isabelle would (literally) never have been caught dead in such a surrounding. Her Christian foundations were queasy at best—completely and absolutely excluding those heretic Catholics. And then there was the whole question of immigrants—strangers from strange lands, strangers of color. Yet, even with all this prejudicial baggage, Isabelle did somehow manage to decline Maria's kind offer with aplomb and not the sneer that Bradley could have anticipated.

For Bradley and Isabelle, at Easter, there were no religious observances nor even painted eggs. There was only a period of relaxation and reading in the garden followed by a good beef roast with spinach and sautéed potatoes with peach pie for dessert. Over coffee, Isabelle remarked to Bradley how strange different customs can be. Margaret's mother-in-law decorated Easter eggs—really only egg shells as she blew out all the stuff inside—with sequins, ribbons, and seashells and then hung these on a dead branch she had put in the center of the dining room table, calling it an "Easter egg tree." This was so strange—so nearly idolatrous for people who claimed to be so religious.

Margaret's in-laws so often seemed so strange in regard to Isabelle's outlook on life in general and festivities in particular. It seemed people invested far too much in antiquated traditional festivities when there was so much else that was left undone. She wondered if her daughter had embraced what Isabelle so frequently saw as the pagan practices of the hordes—the hypocrisies of the many. She hoped Margaret was alright.

Within a few days, in fact, Isabelle was beginning the awaited trip that would take her to her daughter, allowing her to see first-hand if her dear girl child was really doing as well as her letters indicated—and, if that granddaughter was really growing as quickly as reported.

Then they were off.

The first stop was Minneapolis. Isabelle had a pleasant enough, and more importantly, a brief enough visit with Bradley's daughter Dorothy and her husband Lawrence. They were polite and erudite. While she had met Dorothy before, this was the first time they had really had any time together and the first time she had met her husband. The childless couple, now middle aged, lived comfortably enough, but definitely not luxuriously. They each had good careers, both having been promoted in their respective ventures to near the top of the ladder. But, as was clear from their discussions of their work, each saw himself or herself as a vehicle for helping the disadvantaged and the vulnerable. In short, they were purebred liberals. If Isabelle had asked, and she would never ever do so, they were unquestionably the type of folks that had admired FDR and thoroughly supported that imbecile Truman. They were not Isabelle's kind of folks—few were.

Bradley noted Isabelle's discomfort, but chose to ignore it. He dearly loved his daughter, regretting their relationship had become more detached due to time and space. It saddened him she had no children, but he was delighted to see how successful she had become and how she had focused her energies on those who could benefit most from her skills.

He also had a real fondness for Lawrence. His son-in-law clearly, deeply, and honestly loved his daughter—they were lucky. Moreover, Lawrence was sharp. He was a damn good reporter and Bradley knew enough newspapers intimately to know when someone was on the top of their game—Lawrence was at the summit. He was also, unbeknownst to Bradley, a golfer, so the two took in two rounds during the visit—this only building stronger ties between them.

They could not have visited Minneapolis, of course, without calling on William. They had not involved Isabelle's big brother in the planning when they were putting their itinerary in place—this was really a trip to reconnect with children. They had, however, written William to inform him they would be in town, suggesting they all go out for a drink at the bar in the Foshay Towers, the tallest building in the city and rumored to be the tallest building between the Mississippi and the Pacific Ocean.

True to form, the suggested *rendezvous* had been no off-the-cuff thought by Isabelle. It was a well-thought-out tactic to prick William's wife who was always haughty, espousing only the biggest and the best. Betty was the spawn of those *nouveaux rich* who had so benefited from the bad government of Democrats since well before the war—even if they did not share much of the lamentable Democrats' tragic view of the cosmos.

Isabelle saw her sister-in-law as one of those unfortunate individuals who thought money could compensate for a lack of real culture and intellect. In short, Isabelle thought she was a sorry case—certainly not someone with whom she would want to spend any time, even though she still loved her brother very much—or thought she did. Thus, if she did have to suffer the indignity of sharing a table with her unfortunate sister-in-law, let it be in the tallest building in the city. If Betty's family was so grand, why had they not built this skyscraper?

Bradley and Isabelle had intentionally postponed the drink with William and Betty until the eve of their departure—there would be no double feature. They arranged to be seated at a corner table before the illustrious couple arrived.

At the appointed time, actually at a quarter of an hour after the appointed time, much to Isabelle's consternation, they spied the august couple crossing the room to meet them.

"My God," Isabelle whispered in Bradley's ear, "she's wearing mink in late spring, of all things! And, look at that necklace!"

They all hugged each other then took their places to await the waiter for ordering drinks.

"Sooo sorry." Betty nearly oozed. "We're an itsy-bitsy late. It's that big new Cadillac Series Sixty-two convertible William bought me, bright red, cute as a bug's ear, you should see it. But, it's just so huge. I have such a time trying to park it, and here around the Tower there are so few spaces big enough. It's almost more than little ol' me can handle."

Isabelle swallowed hard to keep from saying what she wanted. What was a tired old lady like her doing in a red convertible? William bought it? Sure, with her money. With her daddy's money. She'd never worked a day in her life and William had done pitifully little, although he always put on a good pretext. She realized she was holding her breath. She exhaled and said, "Oh, it must be a beautiful car. You folks in these big open spaces do have a different life, having to have these great big machines to move about. I'm sure it can be quite a job. We've always tried to live where we can get by using public transport—imagine that."

Betty did not even seem to realize Isabelle's toying with the truth. She rearranged her mink collar so her gold and pearl necklace was more clearly visible, pinching William on the cheek, asking, "Snookims, what should we drink?"

"I'll have a gimlet."

"Peachy, I'll have a gin fizz. Sister Isabelle, what do you and your hubby want, we're paying?"

"Oh, how nice. We'll have two double scotch on the rocks—easy on the rocks."

The liveried waiter came and took the order with a slight bow. Betty ruffled her mink collar. William seemed like he needed to go to the bathroom. Bradley was watching intently a spot on the ceiling on the other side of the ornate room.

The drinks were served with fanfare and Betty picked up the discourse, as if on script.

"I just begged sweet William to do all he could to convince you to stay another few days in our terrific city. The day after tomorrow is the really, really big *soirée* for the Women's League—just anyone who's anyone will be there to help raise money to help out all those who don't seem to be able to get by—so sad."

"Sad indeed," intoned Isabelle.

"These poor people," Betty continued, "if they just had a bit more drive, they probably wouldn't need the lifting hand from the League; but we do what we can."

While, under other circumstances, Isabelle would have bolstered Betty's argument about the, purported, needy really being folks who just needed initiative, at the same time having a good rant at the soft-hearted but dim-witted Democrats, given the present company and her antipathy toward her sister-in-law, she antithetically found herself on the other side of the discussion. To keep face, she tried to deflect.

"You never know what others are going through," she offered, meekly.

This brought Bradley's eyes back into focus. On this subject, he could not miss a chance to pitch-in. "Yes. In truth, we know so little of how hard life can be for so many." Then, deciding to get in his wife's good graces, he added, "Even for people like us—just ordinary folk—not the pillars of society you two are—even we are so fortunate to be able to escape the day-to-day challenges confronting a large number of very vulnerable people living right in our own neighborhoods."

William sensed the conversation was teetering and could go in any of several undesirable directions. He decided it was time to get back on track.

"Well, even if you guys can't stay for the gala, we're so happy the weather cooperated with you for this short, almost hasty," he could not help himself from adding, "visit. At this time of the year, you never know what Minnesota is going to serve up. But we're sure the nice weather facilitated the visit with Bradford's family."

"Bradley," Isabelle nearly snorted.

"Ah, Bradford." William seemed not to notice his sister's remark. "I've heard really good things about that daughter of yours—one top-tier law-yer—and that from a woman. Amazing."

"Bradley." Isabelle tried again, with a bit more venom. She was starting to shift the weight on her hips like she was going to leap across the table at her brother.

"Thanks, Bill," Bradley quickly replied, hoping he could keep his spouse in her seat, "she's a fine girl. We're proud of her and her husband."

"Hmm," inserted William, not sure if he wanted to challenge the 'Bill' or go at the son-in-law. Deciding on the latter, he continued with a smile, "guess he writes OK, but you know, that unscrupulous *Daily Star* is really a left-wing, liberal mouthpiece for unkempt folks coming into the state, even coming from overseas after the war. These crude uninvited newcomers want to turn everything upside-down. They challenge everything the established families with deep roots do, saying we all need to be 'progressive.'"

Bradley knew better than to open that door. He drained his glass, let his ice cubes twirl nosily around the empty tumbler, eyed Betty, and said, "How about another round on us?"

Isabelle exhaled visibly. She was battling with herself as to how far to carry this unpleasant discussion with these unpleasant people, even though one of them was her brother. She eminently enjoyed sparring with people but liked sparring with her equals. Under different conditions, she believed William could still hold up his end. But Betty was a lost cause. Isabelle could destroy her in minutes, but at what cost?

Isabelle fervently believed in *laissez-faire* economics. She believed there were, there always had been, and there always would be, people who had more than others—people who worked harder, were smarter, were more innovative. This was as it should be. But this did not apply to people who were on easy street simply because of who their father was—people born to riches. That was a European concept. That was British. That was dumb luck—not initiative and smarts.

While she bore her brother no real ill will, she knew, and he should have known, that he had put his coin in the slot machine and hit a jackpot—that was pure luck. This was what it was. However, the kismet that bathed their days in old family wealth and standing gave neither of them license to talk about what was right or wrong. They could, should, only marvel at how luck manifests herself—most frequently in the most baffling of ways. They should simply be grateful the gods had chosen to place them high on this heap of sugar beet farmers, loggers, and iron workers. They needed perspective.

Gratefully, the drinks came. The conversation swirled around the banal like water, anxious to get out of the drain. Soon all family obligations had been met, embraces were exchanged, each couple going its own way—as it had been and would continue to be.

The next morning, they had brunch with Dorothy and Lawrence before going to the station. Given the theatrics of last night, Isabelle was warmed by the real bonds that existed between Bradley and his daughter—bonds that seemed to be building with Lawrence as well. While Isabelle could never think of these two professional young people as blood relatives—not real family—she did appreciate their smarts and their skills. For her, that was a lot.

Then, too soon for Bradley, and just in time for Isabelle, they were on the train to Chicago. Percy and Helen met them at the station. Barbara, nicknamed Barbie, was in school, in second grade. The baby, Charles, named after Percy's Uncle Charles, called Chuck by one and all, was in the caring hands of a good Norwegian nanny.

Percy and Helen dropped Isabelle and Bradley at the Palmer House to get settled and rest until evening when they would come by and take them to their home for dinner and a chance to meet Chuck for the first time.

As they aired their clothes from their suitcases, Isabelle remarked to Bradley that Percy looked well, but that Helen appeared frail. Isabelle knew Percy was now well up in the hierarchy of Mutual Federal and assumed they had household staff to do most of the chores, they certainly had a Norwegian nanny. Accordingly, it seemed unlikely it was work that was fatiguing Helen—maybe she was ill?

Bradley cautioned against making too many suppositions; he warned Isabelle, as he was wont to do, about her over-active imagination. All too soon they would be sitting in her daughter-in-law's living room with a stout toddy. This would be a good time to assess Helen's health. They just needed a little patience.

As foretold by Bradley, within hours they were seated on comfortable settee, sipping a tasty highball, and marveling over how much Barbie had grown and how much Chuck looked like his dad. Over her glass, Isabelle inspected Helen from her well-coiffed permanent to her shiny patent leather pumps. She seemed fine. She showed great affection for her whole family and took the presentation of the evening meal in hand competently, even though it was probably the hands of others who had done the preparation.

Isabelle truly marveled at her grandchildren. She felt a stab of regret at seeing her grandson only when he was already three years old. She was indeed negligent. But, what could she have done? What could she do? Life was what it was. She lived in Tucson. More to the point, she had neither the energy nor the empathy to devote to a three-year-old. Raising her own two children, even if in a rather offhanded way, was about all she could hope to have done. Of course, she could love her grandchildren and she did.

As with Dorothy, their visit with Percy was short—some would say almost perfunctory, given the long gap in seeing their offspring and their families. They justified the brevity by underscoring Percy's big responsibilities as a major actor in the Chicago banking arena and Helen's total involvement with two small children, one basically still a baby.

Going south to Des Moines, Isabelle and Bradley took the *Rocket* to the Rock Island Depot. Margaret, with a four-year-old Ann in tow, met the train, hugged Isabelle, shook Bradley's hand, then escorted the Red Cap struggling with the trolley loaded with luggage to her car, and drove them to the Savory Hotel where she had reserved a spacious and quiet room on the ninth floor.

As with so much regarding her mother, Margaret did not know much of the details of her visit other than, as communicated earlier in the year, she and Bradley were coming to reconnect with family. In Margaret's rather incredulous view of her mother's carryings-on, she was unclear as to what "reconnect" meant. Isabelle had never been the warm and cuddly parent she had seen from a distance in other households—the warm and cuddly parent she hoped she was. Margaret had always thought of her mother as a mother sparrow. When the chicks were ready, she pushed them out of the nest—fly or fall.

Margaret momentarily chuckled to herself at the thought of her mother as a mother sparrow. Her mother would not like the comparison—not one whit. Isabelle was not a big woman—not tall nor big-boned. She was, to the contrary, and unlike Margaret's in-laws, slight of frame. She had a rather narrow face with narrow-set eyes and a pronounced nose below a high forehead that was often in the shadow of a hat—frequently, a hat with a partial veil. Isabelle wearing her hat and cocking her head as she was prone to do when preparing a tart reply could well be seen as the mirror image of a mother sparrow. And now the mother sparrow had come back to the old nest.

Pushing that amusing thought to the back of her mind, Margaret realized she was uncertain about how to proceed. What were her mother's and Bradley's plans? Did they themselves know? What of accommodation for the remainder of her mother's (she felt no obligation for Bradley) still-to-be well-defined visit? Should she encourage her to continue at the Savory? This seemed both aloof and an unnecessary expense.

Their old family home was there, but sadly empty (and doleful, Margaret thought), awaiting a decision as to its future. Margaret did not relish having Bradley and Isabelle stay at Sixty-seventh Street, in the cramped guest room of, as she thought of it, "The house Julian built". She loved her mother, but there were limits. Isabelle was, like a spicy Asian curry, best savored in small doses.

Yet, what were the options? Mabel was well aware of the visitation but had offered no lodging. None of her card-playing or sororal comrades had proven to have much lasting camaraderie—none even proposing a cup of tea with Isabelle when Margaret had phoned a hand-full to let them know their old crony—or so she had thought—was coming back to Des Moines for a brief stay.

She had, therefore, decided she needed to figure out what was best for her mother—a task to which she was unaccustomed and with which she was uncomfortable. Nonetheless, she unilaterally decided, in spite of appearance or cost, the best option was the Savory.

That first evening, over a home-cooked dinner of Swiss steak with potatoes and carrots accompanied by tapioca for dessert, Margaret presented the housing arrangements. Since Isabelle uttered no protestations, Margaret assumed she had chosen well. Still, her mother had not been forthcoming with any details of her stay in her old hometown.

Later, as Margaret drove home with Ann from the hotel, after insuring their visitors were well settled in their comfortable quarters, she realized she did not, definitely did not, think of Bradley and Isabelle as her parents. Her father was dead. Isabelle was her mother, but she was like someone with a split personality. There was the Isabelle of Isabelle and George and there was the Isabelle of Isabelle and Bradley—the former was her mother and was gone just like her father.

Margaret was a traditionalist. As such, she owed some form of allegiance to her family—all her family. Thus, she owed some deference to Isabelle as the woman who had born and raised her. When all was considered, she figured she had not come out too badly. She was content with her present situation—a situation for which in some ways her mother had groomed her, although her mother was probably the least domestic woman she knew and she, herself, totally enjoyed her domestic duties. She loved her husband. She loved her daughter. She loved her home. She loved her city. For much of this life and these loves, in one way or another, she had her mother to thank.

Thus, despite her differences with her mother's lifestyle and priorities, she was grateful for her mother being instrumental in getting her to where she was—in helping, even if somewhat in the abstract, in achieving her current happy state. She imagined, if it was all boiled down, she did not feel the same deep abiding love for her mother she felt for her husband and her daughter. She felt, nonetheless, a responsibility to respect and protect her mother. Maybe that was enough?

Isabelle was surprised at how happy she was to be back in Des Moines. While living there, she had always thought of the city as a *blasé,* nondescript agglomeration of brick and mortar that was almost like a wart on the landscape. The city seemed unrefined, vulgar, uninspired. She was astonished to find she now saw the city as attractive, energetic, welcoming. Who said you can never go home? Maybe the secret was to go home, but to stay in a nice hotel?

While enjoying a hearty breakfast in the tastily furbished Savory dining room, back in the state whose motto was, "Our liberties we prize and our rights we will maintain," Bradley lightly teased his wife, asking if her rights were maintained. Then, after one last cup of, really quite delicious, coffee, Margaret and Ann picked them up and gave them of tour of town to see how things had changed during and after the war. They ended up at Margaret and Julian's for a light lunch and then lots of chitchat.

Margaret filled the visitors in on all the good news. Julian was back working with his father now that his wartime job had ended. Margaret, too, was now able to devote full time to her family and home. Although Julian worked long hours, basically being his father's right-hand-man, they were enjoying life, playing some tennis, going on picnics, and even occasionally going out on the town with some of their old friends—these nights-out greeted with delight by Margaret. She loved to dance—she loved to dance with Julian. Julian loved that Margaret was happy much more than he loved dancing.

Bradley and Isabelle provided the skimpiest of recitals about their goings-on since moving to Tucson. Margaret knew in general about their time in Sarasota and both Isabelle and Bradley sensed that Margaret was very much an out-of-sight-out-of-mind person. Margaret had made her feelings about Bradley clear before her mother remarried. There was no need to re-plow old ground. But there was also no need to overpower the afternoon with unwanted details. Isabelle quickly steered the conversation to a blow-by-blow narration of Ann's past few years—a topic all could agree was of the utmost importance.

The next day there was the unavoidable and unenviable dinner with Julian's parents. Isabelle had known Julian's mother, Martha, for years. But this long-time connection had not made the heart any fonder. They just did not see the world the same way.

Martha was the exact opposite of Isabelle. She was more like the grand-parent envisioned in the now hundred-year-old poem, "*The New-England Boy's Song about Thanksgiving Day*". Margaret could easily see people going over the river that through the woods to visit Martha. She was not sure they would go that far for Isabelle. Martha was stocky, just short of rotund. She had thick white hair, a plump, smiley, wrinkled face with a round button nose. She seemed to always be laughing. She seemed to always be cooking. She loved to bake, enticing her family with breads, cookies, and cakes filled with sweetness and flavor. She loved her home and filled each nook with cherished bric-a-brac and glassware, souvenirs she meticulously dusted and cleaned. Not only was she a happy housewife, but to Isabelle's horror, she was totally apolitical. Martha had no clue as to who did what in the running of the country, and she could care less. She deferred on this subject completely to her husband.

Margaret thought ofttimes of how much of a contrast there was between Martha and her husband Robert. While both guarded their mannerisms from the old country, Robert was not a blithe homemaker as his spouse, he was a methodical and sedulous entrepreneur who viewed life with military precision and discipline. Margaret felt he would have probably found his niche as a member of Hitler's third Fallschirmjaeger Division during the Battle of the Bulge—not a very complementary thought for her father-in-law.

Isabelle was unaware of Margaret's thoughts as her daughter would never dream of sharing such a demeaning image with her mother, feeling she would tarnish herself and others. In truth, Isabelle was unaware of most of her daughter's inner feelings.

Margaret intently loved her husband. She deeply loved her mother-in-law. She really loved all her in-laws. This was a deep attraction where she honestly felt more a part of their family than the family into which she had been born. Nevertheless, this chemistry could not dampen the fact that she felt her father-in-law's strict, and, more often than not, implacable views of life inside and outside the family, were more resonate with Kaiser Wilhelm's Empire of the nineteenth century than with mid-America of the twentieth century. Perhaps not surprisingly, on this point, mother and daughter were of more similar views then either knew.

Isabelle thought in the abstract Julian's family was nice enough. She did have a real fondness for her son-in-law (like her fondness for a good red wine) and really nothing against his family. During the war, she would certainly have reacted vociferously if Julian's family had been interned just for being German as so many families were imprisoned for just being Japanese.

As all Americans, except indigenous peoples, came from "foreign" stock, with notable exceptions, Isabelle did not, as a general rule, hold people with overseas roots responsible for the reprehensible actions of these countries, and their allies, during the war. But, although not responsible for the terrible bloodshed, people could not pull away from their own roots—they could not change centuries of history that had molded their very culture and shaped their thoughts. No one could. We were all the products of the forge of time that hammered us into what were and bent us to do its bidding.

Julian and his family, be they innocent of the recent carnage, were German to their toes—they could not help it. They were what they were just as she was what she was. German obstinance and dogma were a part of their essence in the same way her more delicate French and Irish cultural roots were a part of hers. Their essence reacted unavoidably from the gut and hers from the brain. She knew American society was a stew of many ingredients—but each kept its own character, even when cooked with so many contrasting flavors. Alas, brought back from her abstruse musings, she donned her mask of the stoic intellectual and, almost as a detached observer, tried hard not to insult anyone or tear down any bridges while dining with her daughter's in-laws whom she knew were so important in her daughter's life.

Then, individual idiosyncrasies aside, the inescapable evening welding the two families together, if ever so briefly, came and went without major pitfalls. Each had approached it like going to the dentist—something that was unpleasant, but unavoidable. It was over.

The next day, Isabelle took Margaret and Ann shopping, buying a few items for them that she hoped would be souvenirs of their time together. At Younkers, Margaret found a delightful dress for Ann and a nice blouse for herself. Isabelle then found a few pieces of turquoise jewelry that reminded her of Tucson. She bought a nice necklace for her daughter and a smaller replica for her granddaughter. After shopping they went to the soda fountain where Ann had a banana split, Margaret had a vanilla shake, and Isabelle kept them company while drinking a chocolate malt.

The pleasant day was topped off with a dinner, now incorporating the men, at a new Italian restaurant, Noah's Ark. They had a genial meal, Ann full of superlatives for her spaghetti with meatballs, followed by a big bowl of spumoni ice cream.

The next day, in an attempt to make the visit really memorable, or perhaps in an attempt to make what might be seen as her negligence less remarkable, Isabelle had arranged for them all to travel to Amana, a little over a hundred miles to the east of De Moines. Isabelle felt a visit to Amana would add depth to the German roots of her daughter's family.

As Isabelle had studied some years previously, Amana, or the Amana Colonies, were the home of a group of people of German origin who still spoke the German language. They had fled Germany under conditions not too different from the pilgrims. They had disagreed with the teachings of the all-powerful Lutheran Church, being followers of Pietism. After years of being unable to practice their faith as they wished, they had decided to move to America, establishing the Ebenezer Society in 1843 near Buffalo, New York. When the original settlers outgrew their land, in 1855 they moved to Iowa, to a large tract they procured near the Iowa River, where they ultimately established seven villages. The Society governed these villages, trading with what was considered as the "outside world." They had their own communal enterprises such as farms, sawmills, and cotton mills, there were also village specialists such as barbers, butchers, tailors, and even doctors. However, their economy was badly affected by the Depression—they needed to overhaul their fiscal arrangements. Thus, in 1931, they created the for-profit Amana Corporation, a diversified portfolio including, as of 1934, the Electric Equipment Company that worked in the booming field of refrigeration. Their economy improved, and the community thrived, while demonstrating an alternative lifestyle with strong Germanic influences. They had chosen an alternative lifestyle. They had demonstrated ingenuity. It was an interesting subject, Isabelle felt, for Ann's continuing education.

They had a good trip east in Julian's car, Isabelle and Ann playing zip white horse while Margaret read, and Julian appeared to be far away in his thoughts. They arrived at the Homestead Hotel where they would spend the night and had a light lunch, dropping off their cases before continuing to visit the colony. They visited a few of the colony shops, saw the homes and the fields. But most of the educating came from Isabelle as she shared her catalogue of history regarding the Germans who had formed what some called the Community of True Inspiration. That evening they had dinner at the Ox Yoke Inn that had opened a few years earlier and was already renowned for its fine German cuisine.

The next morning, they took their time getting back on the road west, stopping off for a picnic (packed by the Ox Yoke folk that morning) at a particularly shady cemetery they passed. Isabelle had always enjoyed visiting random cemeteries, walking among the tombstones, enthralled by the variety of people who had passed through the graveyard's portals. Margaret had always thought this to be a macabre practice. But the food in the hamper was delicious, the day was sunny, and Ann enjoyed playing hide-and-seek behind the headstones with her dad. So, Margaret said nothing and soon they were back on the road.

By the time Isabelle and Bradley were dropped back at their Des Moines hotel, everyone was tired—tired of moving about, tired of being extra polite, tired of weighing words and expressions, tired of thinking too much and not being spontaneous enough. It was a good time to begin withdrawal.

Even though Margaret was unable to rekindle old fires with any of her mother's old consorts (a subject she had recounted only superficially to her mother), Isabelle still felt she needed to reach out. She must still have, she thought, a few friends. After all, she had spent much of her life in this very city. There had to be some remnants of this other life. Her previous misgivings notwithstanding, there had to be some of the old group still around— still wanting a rubber, still wanting to rehash the good old days. She needed to contact her old friends (to see if they were really "old friends").

Isabelle was also eager to see Mabel—a reunification she had put on hold until the link with Margaret and her family had been solidified. She only hoped this protracted renewal would not be poorly seen by Mabel, who she counted as one of her dearest friends as well as her cousin.

Accordingly, Isabelle and Bradley refocused. They sincerely thanked Ann's family for everything, promising to arrange to have a cup of coffee before they left town.

As they changed gears, they noted, to their satisfaction, they were scoring three-out-of-three—they had successfully engaged with all three of their children without major mishaps. They had accomplished a major part of their objective. While the longer-term results were still pending, they had done all they could to rekindle their relationships with their offspring.

Isabelle often equated her family relationships, those at least for her nuclear family, with sailing ships. Not those big winged clippers that traversed the world's oceans. Small replicas, at best, tinkered together with bits of kindling, newspaper, and straw. During those seemingly careless days of her youth, when great thunderstorms would roar across the summer northern plains, the cloudbursts created hundreds of tiny rivulets as the sky's deluge drained into parched fields. She and Anne would find whatever bits and pieces were available and each would make her own craft, sailing this down her own channel—each sister very meticulous about, and protective of her vessel and her waters—a chunk of wood with a paper sail held on high by broom straws, pushed by a muddy surge. To Isabelle, this seemed to depict her family, each with his or her own vessel, sailing their own, often turbid waters.

6

Wakonda Friends

ISABELLE CALLED MABEL TO find a good time for the long-time buddies and cousins to get together. Mabel said she had a surprise for Isabelle, inviting her with Bradley for tea the following day. This arranged, Isabelle and Bradley found themselves with a day to themselves, family-free. They decided to go to the Wakonda Club where Bradley could enjoy the links and Isabelle would certainly find a number of her old friends around the card tables in the great room that overlooked the fifth green.

Bradley called around and happily found a threesome he could join, arranging to rent clubs at the clubhouse. Isabelle made no such arrangements knowing that on any given day there would be more than a few people with whom she had passed many hours concentrating on hand after hand of bridge. Thus, as Bradley strolled to find his mates on the first tee, Isabelle scurried inside to see who was competing with whom over the card table.

She found three tables of ladies immersed in their cards, all of whom she knew at least to say, "hello" to in passing. Therefore, Isabelle seeing herself as the wayfarer come home, expansively greeted the covey of card players.

One by one, they looked up over their hands, holding their cards tight to their chests as they offered muted salutations:

"Isabelle, you're back, how was Chicago?"

"Isabelle, how's George—oops, sorry, so sorry . . ."

"Isabelle, heard your son-in-law couldn't get in the army—is he OK?"

"Isabelle, someone said Margaret had lost her baby?"

"Isabelle, didn't I hear you're divorced now?"

"Isabelle, someone said you'd been in hospital, you OK now?"

Isabelle was infuriated. She hoped she had not reddened in rage. She staidly walked from table to table, progressively fixing each lady in her gaze, as she shook their limp hands ever so lightly, addressing the ensemble, "My dear friends, so good to see you all. Also, good to see you all looking so well and prosperous. My husband and I were just driving by, passing through Des Moines for the first time in just years. We've been up in Chicago to celebrate my son's promotion as a senior manager at Mutual Federal. He may be transferred to New York, so we wanted to see him before he gets to The City and gets so important even his dear parents can't get an appointment. Oh, it's so, so good to see ya'll still keeping at the cards in defiance of the years; means those eyes and memories are still kind of sharp, huh? Gosh girls, you're so dear, but I've got to run, our driver is waiting as we want to make it to Omaha tonight; my husband just has to get back to Houston immediately—those ol' oil companies just can't get by without the boss around. So, if any of you dears are ever down our way, do stop by, we'll fill your tank."

All chuckled and Isabelle evaporated, head high, back straight. But, before she had escaped, she heard one of her erstwhile colleagues, maybe even someone she had once considered a friend, exclaim, to the apparent joy of others, "Ol' 'little red' kind of sashays like a Bantam hen, doesn't she?"

Isabelle went to the garden on the east side of the building where she could not be seen by those inside. Sitting at one of the tables discretely placed about among the flowers, each with a wide parasol that partially concealed the occupant, she ordered a double whisky on the rocks. She briefly got up and asked the guys at the pro shop to let her husband know where she was seated, before ordering a second stout drink.

She sipped her second drink more slowly and remembered she had heard her mother, Isabelle Jane, refer to friendship as the rarest of all gems. She had cautioned her family, there are many who claim friendship, but ever so few who earn it. A true friend, she underscored, was seldom found. If one could reach the zenith of her life, her mother had added, with three true friends, one had been a remarkable success. Oh, Isabelle thought, so true.

This group, so enthralled by the cards, still thought of her as 'Little Red'. How infantile! What a sign of their obviously limited intellect and imagination. She was so glad to be rid of them.

This epithet had nothing to do with the color red. Isabelle's complexion was actually a bit tawny and her hair, once dark chocolate was now, to her great dissatisfaction, kind of a mousy grey—but certainly not now, not ever, red. The red, Isabelle knew, referred to the *Little Red Hen* from the children's story. Isabelle's bird-like features did perhaps provoke some, seeing her sharp and smallish appearance, to think of her as resembling a rather scrawny hen. Yet, Isabelle thought, the reference was less about her countenance and more about her essence.

If Isabelle were honest, she might, with some pride, see herself as the industrious and clever red hen who had been forced to endure lazy, noisy, and otherwise irritating individuals in the course of making something of her life—something of importance—something many of the others could never hope to achieve. Being like the hard-working, and ultimately successful hen was not in and of itself a slight. But it was, nonetheless, infuriating to see how quickly and easily the others, her peers, or so they thought, quickly jumped to categorize and judge people when they knew so little of substance—knew so little of the real truth. People were so easily misled. People so easily misled themselves.

Her introspection was interrupted with the arrival of Bradley, smiling happily after an obviously good game. He enveloped her in his gaze, giving her a peck on the cheek.

"Finished second, not too bad. Nice sun. Nice course. Nice day. How about lunch?"

"Back at the hotel."

"But dear, they've a great chicken salad here."

"I've about had it with chickens. Let's get to the hotel, have a bite and I'll call Mabel to see when we can pop by her place or even go out for dinner even though we've a date for tomorrow—I'd be nice to see a friendly face today."

Bradley had known from the beginning he was but an advisor in the course of his and their lives, a chancellor to the monarch. Isabelle had the wheel firmly and unwaveringly in her hands, and it was there it would steadfastly stay. He may have been the boatswain, but she was, without any doubt, the captain.

He could see she was upset, but also knew this was one of those upsets into which one dared not delve. Isabelle needed to sort whatever it was out internally before she vented. His tactic was to occupy her with something pleasant so that the internal rumination would take place in the background, hopefully not resulting in a full-scale eruption. He knew tea with Mabel was on the calendar for tomorrow, but as Isabelle was already talking about changing their schedule, so he thought maybe he could propose a more significant change that would help his wife shift her mood.

"How about this," he started tentatively, testing the waters, "rather than going to Mabel's for tea, let's see if she can accompany us on an outing."

The *humpf* was noncommittal.

Bradley knew that, while his spouse's preferred cuisine was relatively bland staple midwestern cooking of meat and potatoes, with the regular addition of wholesome vegetables and the much-appreciated inclusion of a well-prepared sweet for dessert, she did occasionally enjoy an epicurean experience, either exploring *entrées* from other lands, or carefully sampling the latest popular items of food fare. Albeit she was no fan of the extremely popular hamburger sandwich that had appeared everywhere since the turn of the century, from time to time she did enjoy experimentation—perhaps this was one such time.

"Why don't we drive up to Marshalltown tomorrow? One of the guys in our foursome was telling us about a new place there called Taylor's Maid-Rite Hamburger Shop. He says this is the just the ticket to see what all the fuss is about with the hamburger. You could see how you like it?"

"Ahhh hmmm *humpf.*"

"We can call Mabel as soon as we get back to the hotel. I'm sure she'd love to reconnoiter this café."

There was only silence from across the table, with the intermittent clinking of the ice cubes as Isabelle's second drink was now finished.

"Better still, let's invite Mabel to dine with us this evening at the hotel. We can make all the arrangements together."

"Ummm," Isabelle replied. A reaction Bradley interpreted in the positive. He then offered his wife his hand to help her up and took her arm to escort her to the car.

When they got to their room, Bradley went to his grip and took out a long leather zippered bag that contained a fifth of scotch. He poured each of them a stiff shot and, as they savored the burn, he watched Isabelle exhale slowly as she regained at least part of her equanimity. After a few moments of silence, she got out of the brocade chair and sat on the bed as she picked up the receiver and gave the front desk Mabel's number.

The call went through quickly, Isabelle soon apologizing to her cousin about being so disruptive as to propose amending their schedule. Disruption aside, Isabelle felt they should try and get together this very evening—she and Bradley inviting Mabel for dinner at the hotel.

Mabel's halting reply highlighted the fact that this was surely an unanticipated call, and obviously in some ways an unwelcomed change of plans. She explained to her cousin that, as previously indicated, she had a surprise for her, and she had made all the necessary arrangements for this surprise to be ready tomorrow—these suggested late adjustments probably making revision of the overall lineup troublesome. Yet, all that notwithstanding, she understood (meaning she understood Isabelle more than she understood the circumstances) and would be happy to come to the hotel for dinner that evening—adding, just for emphasis, flexibility being one of the advantages of being an elderly and unattached lady.

They had a good meal after a very heart-felt embrace, the two ladies not having seen each other for many months. They made small talk about getting settled in Tucson, visiting with Anne, and traveling by train. Knowing Isabelle had been back to her old haunts at the Wakonda Club, over dessert, Mabel innocently asked how the card game had gone at the club.

Isabelle visibly bristled and simply said that those ladies were horrid.

Bradley deftly changed the topic, asking Mabel about the surprise she had in store for them, while apologizing for any confusion their sometimes, tangled planning might have caused.

Mabel was a bit evasive, so Bradley changed tack and asked her if, even though they had initially planned on having tea together on the morrow, would she instead accompany them to Marshalltown. He filled in some of the blanks by describing how his golf partner had said this was *the* place to go for the best hamburger sandwich and, since they were not all that keen on this new faddish food, he and Isabelle thought it would be best to get the best if they were to judge if it were worthy for consumption.

Mabel had come prepared. Although she had had no idea of what was in store over dinner, she was reasonably confident Bradley and Isabelle would completely change the arrangements for the next day. Foreseeing this inevitability, she had already taken the necessary measures to postpone her own plan by one full day. She then agreed to accompany her cousin and her husband to Marshalltown with the proviso that they would, indeed, have tea at Mabel's house the day after.

The tough work of planning done, they ordered coffee and cognac, sitting completely at ease around the table, chatting about the meaningless subjects really good friends can talk about in complete spontaneity and candor, no worries about misinterpretation or inadvertently hurting someone's feelings—Isabelle and Bradley smoking, Mabel just enjoying the fact that she was once again reunited with her much-loved cousin.

As the cigarette smoke swirled above their table and the golden cognac warmed their innards, Mabel mentally crossed a boundary she rarely approached, asking, "What if?". Mabel was typically unflappable and resigned—these qualities coming from an almost fatalistic view of life. She knew the good came all mixed up with the bad and pretty much accepted each day as it came—she saw no real alternative. Even so, at times, very infrequently, she freed her mind to ask, "What if?".

She really liked her cousin. She realized full well Isabelle was a flawed individual—but so were they all. She realized Isabelle could be a bully. She could be insensitive and even vicious. She could also be kind and thoughtful—even loving.

Mabel admired Isabelle's intellect. She appreciated her cousin's sense of humor. She envied her explorer and damn-it-full-speed-ahead attitude. But mostly, she accepted, she cherished Isabelle's camaraderie. Life alone was difficult. Isabelle helped. And, she now wondered, what if she had become close to Isabelle years earlier? How would an even bigger dose of her cousin have affected her life?

Best just relish the present and not idly contemplate what-if's. Mabel took a large swallow of cognac and looked at her watch—it was time to go.

The next day they got an early start to their day traveling to the northeast. Marshalltown was about sixty miles away. They went to the coal town of Altoona, with over 600 residents, a fair-sized community for rural Iowa. They skirted Melbourne; the town, with about four-fifths the population of its bigger brother to the south, was nearly destroyed by fire in 1903. As planned, they arrived in the County Seat of Marshall County, Marshalltown, late in the morning, having some spare time to take in the city of over 19,000 before procuring their gastronomic objective: the best hamburger.

Marshalltown, named after the country's fourth Supreme Court Chief Justice who had been born almost 200 years earlier, not in Iowa but in another agrarian community of Germantown in what is today the state of Virginia, was emblematic of the more citified areas of the rural Midwest—a combination of well-established farming and more recent industrial growth following the war.

Their destination, Taylor's, proved to be as unimposing as any place of its kind could be. Isabelle remarked to Mabel that it would be truly dumbfounding if such a common establishment could produce anything but the most common of food. They felt a bit out of place taking their seats in a booth with red vinyl benches and then ordering what was largely considered as the day's choice for kids, three hamburger sandwiches. Isabelle fidgeted awaiting the lunch, feeling very much as though the whole of Marshalltown was observing her through the big plate glass window behind which they were seated—the whole town waiting to see how she would react to the hamburger.

When it came, she found it as unimposing as the café itself. It was, in fact, nothing more than a round piece of bread—a roll—with some meat, tomato, lettuce, pickle, and onion inside. It tasted much as she had thought it should. It was just maybe acceptable, but not anything worthy of praise—maybe two stars (out of five). The major impact of the meal was the difficulty she and her companions seemed to have in eating it with civility. The consumer pretty much had to just take big mouthfuls, chomping away with some of the filling oozing out onto the hands or falling on the table—quite a Philistine way to eat—not something to be repeated any time in the near future.

Bradley secretly was bemused at Isabelle's antics with the hamburger. He agreed with her that it was really nothing all that special and very difficult to eat. Nevertheless, he had proposed this adventure to give his wife a change of venue and the hamburger had fully accomplished this objective. The discussion never touched on any of the painful or soul-searching topics with which Isabelle was so often preoccupied. There was a fruit-salad of discussion for dessert—a retake of John Marshall's court, an examination of the growing use of refrigeration and its impact on Iowa industries, a lament for the decline of the railroads, and, of course, a now objective assessment of the role of the hamburger in American diets. Bradley considered the trip a success.

After a post-lunch walk about the city center, they drove south by more secondary roads, going to Haverhill where they visited the old Mathew Edel Blacksmith Shop and marveled at how quickly technology changed. They then cut across to the atrophying berg of Van Cleve, nearly moribund since the railroad left town. From here they rejoined the main road south, back to Altoona and thence to Des Moines.

They were all tired by the time they dropped Mabel off at her house. No one noticed the old, now sky blue, once yellow school bus parked down the street.

The next day Bradley spent the morning with his newspapers while Isabelle, once she had scoped-out the headlines, spent her morning writing letters to their children—a mixture of thank-yous, lifestyle guidelines, and political warnings that only Isabelle could deliver. They had a light lunch and were at Mabel's for tea by four o'clock sharp that afternoon. No one again seemed to see the blue bus parked on the street, a testament to that old adage about being too big to be noticed. But they were surprised when they entered Mabel's living room to find a couple about their age already seated. The gentleman looked somehow familiar to Isabelle, but she could not recall if she knew him and, if so, when and where.

Mabel, grinning ear to ear, proudly announced her surprise: this was their cousin Justin and his wife Gwen. The clouds lifted a bit and Isabelle vaguely remembered meeting Cousin Justin in her early childhood. However, they had not seen each other for a lifetime and had been in no contact at all over the years.

Mabel set the stage by announcing that the blue bus on the street was, in fact, the home on wheels for Justin and Gwen—an old school bus the two had converted themselves into living quarters with both sleeping and cooking facilities as well as a cramped but functional toilet. It was quite a feat of engineering and this led into the recounting of how Justin was indeed a rather well-known engineer.

Justin was, as he explained himself, a chemical engineer. He had advanced degrees from the University of Minnesota and had been recruited by the government to work in Los Alamos on the Manhattan Project during the war. He had been part of the team that had developed the first atomic bomb. Before, during, and just after the war, he had spent, by his calculations, over 60,000 hours (Isabelle quickly calculated, over twenty years—spoof!) working on chemical reactions that could produce energy, as in a bomb. His work had been pivotal in the major discoveries that had allowed the work to actually culminate in the bomb. But he was now out and ecstatic to be done with the laboratory, the government, the unending hours, and the even more unending stress.

Their children grown, he and Gwen had moved from New Mexico to southern California where they still had a small home. In their driveway they had rebuilt the interior of a retired Blue Bird school bus, repainting it in honor of its namesake. They then put their home in mothballs and decided to drive about and see the world—most days just heading out with no particular destination in mind. After thousands of miles and scores of memorable experiences, they decided they should set a course to contact the family members they knew, to try and rebuild bonds, and share wisdom. In this way, they had arrived at Mabel's stoop, completely unannounced—but welcomed with a fond embrace and a warm smile.

Isabelle was surprised, yet again, when Sally appeared from the kitchen to serve tea and biscuits. Isabelle stood up and gave Sally a big hug after she had put the tray on the coffee table, but there was a kind of coolness in the embrace from both sides.

Over cups of the refreshing tea, Mabel pushed Justin to tell tales—tales of Los Alamos, tales of California, and tales of the road. Justin resisted Mabel's prodding initially, reticent to talk about the war and unsure of his audience when talking about the United States. But Mabel's persistent nudging finally pressured Justin over whatever barriers he imagined, and he spoke at great length, if not in precise detail, about the lives he and Gwen had been leading and their views of post-war America.

Isabelle initially concentrated on each word because she was frankly interested in both the speaker and the discussion. But Justin's droning monotone soon deflected her ever-active brain—a brain that was often, she thought, like an octopus's tentacle. It was always moving, always probing, always looking for a loose leaf to turn over, always looking for a weak spot to prick, always looking for a new door to open. In this way, her mind spun almost uncontrollably around like a pinwheel—sending off sparks and colored lights as it sought a new rock to look under. Justin had galvanized her thoughts, directed her energies to her country, and how it could or should be viewed. But he could not hold her attention.

Somehow her deliberations jumped out of an imaginary blue bus and landed on a book she had read some years ago—the 1902 work by Yone Noguchi, *The American Diary of a Japanese Girl.* This was the view of the country through the eyes of a young foreigner—a sardonic examination of many of America's ways through the filter of a very different culture. In some inexplicable way, she felt this approximated her position as she saw the country, but, in her case, through the eyes of a sixty-seven-year-old with twenty-twenty vision—or at least twenty-twenty mental acuity.

Bradley watched his wife out of the corner of his eye. He knew her sharp-edged mind had already reached speeds that had far overtaken Justin's conversation. She had a fixed smile and an almost blank stare as her head slowly bobbed as if in rhythm with the cadence of Justin's speech. But inside that aging skull, she was far away. Something Justin had said had triggered another series of thoughts and analyses that now fully occupied Isabelle's neurons. He had seen this act repeated so many times as he recited the news to her in the garden in Tucson—one moment she was there and another she was gone. Not gone psychologically but gone to fight her own mental battles that had been brought about by Bradley's orations concerning politics, race, religion, golf, horse racing, or even the weather.

Justin was just wrapping up his story, describing how, before reaching Des Moines, they had travelled to Hot Springs, Arkansas, which had been flooded by soldiers for redeployment just after the war, but was returning to a more typical focus on spas and gambling, the Hotel Arkansas Casino one of the many big gambling joints that made this town known for bathing, now also known for giving guests in its casinos a bath, as they left all but their drawers with the gangsters that ran much of the community. Justin smiled at his little joke and then closed by describing how much they liked seeing the Ozarks before they got to Iowa.

Justin sipped his now cold tea and seemed to be considering if his bladder could support still another cup. Thankfully, Mabel saved him, declaring it was now well past teatime and they should make plans as to how to keep in closer contact in the future. Family was family. Family was important.

Isabelle refocused and chimed in to Bradley's surprise. She said she had been planning on talking with Mabel and Bradley about organizing a visit to Anne's in Sarasota—she was sure Anne would welcome the visit. Why not all plan on meeting in Florida to celebrate next Easter all together?

This received full support. It kept the family joints well oiled. It brought Anne into the circle. Most importantly, it was far enough in the future so as not to conflict with anyone's immediate plans—but not so far in the future that it seemed like it might never happen.

Sally cleared the dishes. The invitees shared a few more moments of small talk. Then Justin and Gwen said they had to take their bus to the filling station to get it checked over as they hoped to be back on the road tomorrow. Bradley and Isabelle offered a little white lie that they had to get back to the hotel as they were expecting a visit by Margaret. Mabel concluded all was well, noting she had to get Sally going on the evening meal before her helper made her own way home. It was over. It had been a success.

Isabelle lay awake in bed—Bradley snoring not so quietly next to her. She wondered what it would be like to sleep in a blue bus—not just tonight, but many, many nights. To each his (or her) own, she supposed, but not really—if we left each to their own devices, what would we have? We'd have a mess—probably a new New Deal and a damn FDR replica. Yes. We needed to be open-minded—but how open?

She and Bradley had done the rounds. They had seen the family—even some folks like Justin and Gwen who they had had no idea they were going to see. They had tried to be polite and correct (even, in some way, to that damn Wakonda gaggle). They (she) had tried to be patient and understanding. It was a job and they had done it. They had spent the past days and weeks reinforcing bridges—building family bonds. Like Mabel had said, "Family was important".

But, how far did you go for family? Were there limits? What about addressing misdirection? What about when they were wrong? What about when you knew better, when you were cleverer, when you were just smarter? What about then? Family's fine. Family's even great. Family was love. She thought, she hoped, she, at her age, knew love. Love or like, she was not sure? She had loved her parents. She had, indeed still loved George. She loved her children. She loved her siblings and cousins. She thought she loved Bradley. But maybe she also loved lemon meringue pie. Where did the boundaries of love fall with regard to the boundaries of right and wrong? What was the limit between good sense and nonsense?

She had fought her way through university. She had fought her way to be recognized as a capable intellectual—not an intelligent woman (as women go), but an intelligent person. She had fought to keep things together when her husband died. She continued to fight to keep her mind sharp—her wits honed. At the end of the day, did it not all boil down to one thing—you, yourself?

She had seen how flimsy friendships were. Did she really have any true friends? Probably not. Were family ties really that much stronger. Should they be that much stronger? After all, family members have as many foibles as those would-be friends.

She knew she and Bradley got along because he respected her space and her intellect. She knew he disagreed with her on many things. But he did not challenge her. He did not try to convert her. He treated her with tact and even caution.

She and George had had quite different views on life too—especially as they aged and saw the world through different optics. But George was fully occupied with his work. What spare time he had, he divided among his children and his spouse. This meant there really was little one-on-one time—few occasions when it was just the two of them hashing out this or that. And, when they did have to settle key issues, these were matters like the mortgage, insurance, doctors, or a new stove—items that affected the day-to-day lives of their family, not abstract discussions about who was treated fairly by society.

She knew two thousand years ago Anaximander had proposed a model for the universe, later expanded by Plato and Aristotle and called by some the Ptolemaic System, where the Earth was the center of all. Was there a corollary? Was self the center of all? Were not those with the greatest capabilities the leaders—those less well-endowed the followers? Was not she the gist of those groups with which she participated—be they family or otherwise? Would it not be not living up to her potential to go down to the lowest common denominator? Were not those with the clearest introspection able to see the highest common denominator? Was her role not to build her family up with her abilities and not settle for second place—mediocrity?

Isabelle remembered her studies. She recalled how Veritas, the Roman goddess of truth, daughter of Saturn, was said to have hidden in a well because the truth was so slippery. Did she seek Veritas, or was she Veritas? Deep thoughts, crazy thoughts for the dark of night. The ancient scholars, Origen and Augustine, had written about predestination long, long ago. If they were right, all Isabelle's anguish was for naught. She was but a pawn, having no control over her moves, having no say in her relationships. It mattered not whether one put family bonds above the interests of society. It mattered naught if one felt a calling to a higher good. Nothing mattered other than that that was predetermined to matter.

But, in spite of her Christian upbringing and her purported following of Christian teachings and ethics, and in spite of those occasional Sundays when she found herself in church, not to mention her regular rantings against the Catholic Church, she was at heart an agnostic. As such, predestination was not part of her presumptions about humans and human nature. She believed, she had to believe, that each and every person was the author of their own successes or failures—success requiring guts and savvy, failures resulting from an inability to satisfactorily meet life's challenges—a result of individual, societal, cultural, or even ethnic imperfection. Or, was it so?

The shadows crept across the ceiling and Isabelle wondered.

Isabelle knew well the caprice of time. It was like one of those wooden tops with which her brother William used to play. You wound the string tightly, gave it a great pull, and the top spun about, following a seemingly invisible pathway—first straight and steady, then, as time ran out, wobbly and foundering.

Time appeared to Isabelle as an eddy, those cyclonic currents she had seen along the Mississippi, where the great river exerted powerful forces with the strength of Achelous, the Greek river god, that bent nature to its will. Time swooshed over her—time and place often becoming a blur.

She and Bradley had a few more days in Des Moines—time for a final round of golf for him, time for final cups of tea with Mabel for her. They had a pleasant lunch with Margaret and Ann, going to the Des Moines Botanical Center afterwards for a stroll among all variety of wondrous plants. On their last night, they had an early dinner with Margaret's whole family and then went to the Paramount Theater to see *The Lost Weekend*, the Billy Wilder film with Ray Milland that had won the Oscar that year for Best Picture. The alcoholic theme of the film was really not very appropriate for Ann, but, fortunately, she slept though most of the feature.

In rapid succession, Isabelle was back on a train, then back in her home in Tucson seeing if Maria had kept all shipshape, then back in the garden reading the *Citizen*. It was then the Fourth of July and somehow the world seemed to spin off its axis and it was then almost Easter and they were preparing to go to Anne's. The new year had started with much news ranging from the death of Al Capone, the abolishment of the German State of Prussia, and the growing concerns for something called the Cold War. Bradley kept Isabelle briefed on the state of affairs as she spent more and more time on her painting. Then they were off for Sarasota and the much-anticipated reunion.

The gathering at Anne's went relatively well. There were no bombastic events or impulsive eruptions. This was not because that potential did not exist. Bradley and Anne were often holding their breath, awaiting Isabelle's reaction to something Justin or Gwen had said—some socialistic, Democrat, Catholic, liberal, FDR-favoring, ignoramus drivel. Although Justin and Gwen were not nearly as extreme as Isabelle might have categorized them, their thoughts and priorities were far from hers by any measure. Yet, she seemed to give them a pass. She made no feverish assaults, not even snide remarks. When Justin would say something good about social programs or empathize with the situation of so many disadvantaged trying to climb out of poverty, Anne and Bradley would look at each other and grit their teeth. But Isabelle remained inexplicably calm—limiting her inputs to the occasional mild *humpf.*

In fact, Isabelle was not being particularly polite or reserved out of respect for her hostess's domicile—she was not keeping her own counsel out of respect for family's feelings. She simply did not give a damn about the conversations. In Des Moines she had heard enough from Justin and Gwen to make a good appraisal. She had already put them in a cubbyhole under that heading where she put poor, hapless folk who were not really worth the energy to try to educate.

As others were enthralled, or at least interested in Justin and Gwen's tales of Los Alamos, California, and being American vagabonds, Isabelle was planning her year—weighing options, thinking of what she wanted to do after they left Anne's.

There was one potentially problematic moment when the full troop was enjoying a toddy on the veranda. With no forewarning, and for no apparent reason, Anne recounted to Mabel how Isabelle, evidently triggered by her old nemesis FDR, had really raved during her last visit—had had a nearly vehement conniption fit. Mabel, out of curiosity or just to needle her cousin, had wanted to revisit the matter. Fortunately, Anne was able to dissuade her, and the subject was never brought up again. Nevertheless, Violet, who was serving the drinks, did hear enough to ask her employer and friend for the full details later that evening. Anne was able to gloss-over the most repugnant parts of Isabelle's tirade. Still, Violet heard more than enough to rethink her views of this aging pullet from the northern plains. Violet had known Isabelle to be unpredictable, potentially inflammable. Someone to be handled with care—especially when discussing delicate issues (to Isabelle) like the poor, the needy, or the mistreated. Violet now knew the two lived in different worlds.

As the family reunion wrapped up, Bradley surprised all by suggesting they meet again in a year, this time in Hawaii. He spoke lavishly of how he had had the good luck to meet Isabelle on a trip to Hawaii, how thankful he was for this serendipity, and how he thought they should all celebrate together. While he and Isabelle still had some time to go to reach their silver jubilee, Bradley gallantly declared he already thought of their upcoming anniversary as being enshrined in precious metals—a moment due serious joy and appreciation—a moment to celebrate with family in Hawaii.

Everyone congratulated Isabelle and Bradley on their lasting and loving marriage as well as thanking Bradley for the idea of having another gathering next year. However, all also said life was too much in flux to be able to plan so far ahead for an event that had significant logistic and financial implications. But the plan was left on the table for consideration.

Justin and Gwen were the first to depart in their blue bus—uncertain of their destination, just heading north. A few days later Mabel, Isabelle, and Bradley headed off in the same direction, but with a clearer destination: Atlanta, to visit the Emory University Museum. The museum had a top collection of ancient art that had been calling to Isabelle for some time—now being a good excuse to spend a few days appreciating the rarities while trying to explain to Mabel and Bradley why these articles were, in fact, of such great importance.

After listening to her cousin's two-day history lesson, Mabel was happy to continue to Des Moines while Isabelle and Bradley started the westbound leg to Tucson.

When they were once again alone, Anne and Violet sat side by side on the veranda, thoroughly enjoying a cool glass of minty tea.

The Sarasota plantation house resumed its familiar cadence—two old ladies, one white, one black, enjoying each other's company.

Familiarity reigned too in Tucson. As they were now accustomed, Isabelle and Bradley found their home ready to welcome them, clean and well-stocked thanks to Maria's admirable efforts—efforts overtly unnoticed by Isabelle, she acting as though this was only to be expected, but softly applauded by Bradley as he slipped Maria a crisp hundred-dollar bill when she left.

There were times, like these, when Isabelle had been so indifferent, probably rude, and then left her husband to take a bath, that Bradley wondered if he was being honest with himself when he expounded upon how fortunate he was to have found Isabelle and taken her as his wife. Was this completely true? Try as he would to come to an answer, he could not.

It was not physical love, as this was rather rare, and detached when it did occur. It was not having a super trophy wife on his arm. Isabelle had a certain amount of inner charisma (when she wanted to show it), but she was far from dazzling. It was not her attentiveness, looking after her husband,

and her home. Her regard for all things domestic was minimal at best. It was not wealth. She was comfortable, but he had far more resources than she. So, what was it?

He guessed it was her mind and the fact that she kept him from solitude. She was smart—very smart. While she could often be bullheaded, she had a quick, analytical brain, and was well-educated. She could, when she chose, engage him in the most stimulating of conversations. And, in so doing, kept him from being alone. He had less family than she and had chosen, for better or worse, to live far away from those he did have. No, when all was said and done, she did help him survive. She was demanding. She required, at times, supreme patience. But, yes, he concluded, it was worth it.

Life flowed on. Isabelle was unsure if the year had really unrolled as she had imagined it would when musing in Sarasota, but it took its own shape and was soon at its midpoint. She painted. She found a new bridge club, but also found card players in Tuscan to be much less rapacious than her old crowd in Des Moines. Bradley played golf. They sat in the garden and read the papers, discussing the goings-on, questioning the state of the world. Maria kept the house sparkling, but she and Isabelle passed almost as though they did not know one another. In general, Maria knew her routine by heart. If there were special tasks, Isabelle would advise of these when she saw her first thing in the morning when she came for her first cup of coffee—Maria made an excellent cup—but there would be little discourse thereafter, although Bradley was always adding a kind and friendly word.

From the garden, one could hear Isabelle moan—the world was a mess. Truman was worried about the Cold War and created the CIA (people should worry about Truman). There was a terrible hurricane in Florida (Anne was fine). The Muslim state of Pakistan was formed after the Partition of India (why were there Muslims anyway?). Princess Elisabeth announced her engagement to Lieutenant Philip Mountbatten (was not our country founded by those running from the monarchy?). As usual, Bradley tried to put a different slant on the news—recalling to Isabelle how a young black man had recently been lynched in Pickens County, South Carolina, how the state of Arkansas had just passed a statute on miscegenation as well as put in place a poll tax affecting black voters, while the United States Supreme Court had ruled that all-white juries were unconstitutional.

Isabelle reacted to most of Bradley's disclosers with a mild *humpf*. At one point, however, she did interject that that idiot Truman had attended some sort of meeting, something called the NAACP—so if he was involved, it could not be good.

Good or bad, and there were good days and bad, the days ran one after the other like milk cows following each other into the barn in the evening. The painting, the cards, the garden debates formed a rhythm that was only broken occasionally by trips to nearby cities, mostly to visit museums. Isabelle particularly liked the Museum of Anthropology of the University of New Mexico in Albuquerque, this linking back to one of her favorite subjects—the past. Although this past was the past of the New World, and she preferred the past of the Old World, she enjoyed any ancient history. This also led her to the Heard Museum of American Indian Art and History in Phoenix.

Typical of her often-paradoxical behavior, she had no remorse over the loss of Indian cultures and peoples, seeing it natural that the "heathen" give way to the civilized. Yet, she showed great respect, almost reverence, for these same cultures—fascinated by what they did, how they did it, and why they did it. She would sew mental tapestries linking patterns in Indian societies with those of the Greeks and Romans. She would study their tools, their farming methods, and their ways of governance. All this was in the abstract. She could somehow appreciate sophistication, even in simplicity, while still supporting the concept of "the chosen" attempting to annihilate what others might consider the innocent. For Isabelle, the intellectual and the pragmatic could be completely contradictory; on different opposing but parallel plains.

Then, soon after Burma had obtained independence from the United Kingdom and Mahatma Gandhi had begun his protest fast to the death against violence, Isabelle intended to begin work on their trip to Hawaii. But, as she knew all too well, nothing was as predictable as unpredictability. Shortly after the new year that she and Bradley celebrated quietly, New Year's being signs of aging as opposed to reasons for rejoicing, she received a call from Margaret. Isabelle could tell her daughter was very upset. They, Margaret's family, were moving west—being transferred really. It was tragic.

Grandpa Robert, as she now apparently called her father-in-law, and his partners, apparently, could not get enough raw material to keep their company running smoothly. The post-war boom was putting stress on the supply of many items, including lumber. Lots and lots of former GIs were building homes and having families. It was a great time to be in business if you could stay in business, and they could only stay in business if they got more lumber. The solution was to send Julian to Oregon to find, buy, and run a sawmill. Of all the harebrained ideas, Margaret could think of nothing more squirrelly. Nevertheless, one did not argue with, one did not even discuss with Grandpa Robert. It was decided, it was done. They were going west—and soon.

Isabelle did not respond well to emotive situations—she thought of herself as someone who operated from the brain and not the heart or the gut—operating dispassionately and sensibly. She was unsure of what Margaret really wanted as well as of how to react, regardless of her daughter's expectations. Isabelle understood Margaret loved Des Moines. It was her home. She had her friends and her memories. She lived in a home built by her beloved husband. She walked the same streets she had walked as little girl. She was conformable. She was secure.

Yet, Isabelle was sure that Margaret would find, as she herself had found at the Wakonda Club, that those upon whom Margaret counted, those she considered as real friends, were in fact imposters—halfhearted acquaintances at best, more probably defamers if the truth were known.

Isabelle was also not surprised at the quixotic behavior of Robert. He was a realist. He had grown up making hard decisions and was able to make these without any prejudice for his family—even if these choices were perhaps at times impractical.

To Isabelle, the circumstances were clear and the conclusion clearer: take your darling family and go west. Some battles were worth fighting, others were not.

However, Isabelle said none of this to her daughter. She commiserated with her over the shocking changes being imposed on her and her little family. She sympathized with her over having to leave Des Moines as she, Isabelle, had also had to do. She consoled her over the difficulties in pulling up roots and starting a new life as she, Isabelle, had also had to do. She expressed sorrow. She expressed consternation. She even expressed anger. Then she hung up, wishing her daughter a *bon voyage*.

Isabelle confirmed to herself that she could do nothing about her daughter, about Des Moines, or about the West. But she could plan a trip to Hawaii and, if her daughter was already settled in the West, she could see her on this jaunt to the islands.

As Ceylon attained independence, Isabelle was in full swing, contacting family, travel agents, and hoteliers to determine who would be accompanying them to Honolulu, how they would get there, and where they would stay once they arrived.

Her coordination efforts met with mixed success. After long delays, not being truly sure how to contact the ever-on-the-move couple, she got a letter from Justin and Gwen saying they were heading for Maine and would not be able to fit a trip to the Pacific into their busy schedule that year. Anne, much easier to get a hold of, equally decided to forego the trip. She professed it was because she had some real estate affairs requiring her attention, but Isabelle wondered if it were not her health.

Unlike with Mabel, who so far had neither confirmed nor cancelled her travel plans, Isabelle did not talk in any depth about health issues with her big sister. Over the years, she had seen Anne having increasing difficulty in getting around as freely as she would like. She walked with a cane. She had to be helped out of some chairs by Violet. She seemed to favor her right side when she sat. Nonetheless, all in all, for an aging matron, Isabelle thought Anne was doing quite well. She would have to ask Violet.

While she was confronted with fewer travelers, she was also finding exciting options for the travel itself. She decided they should leave Honolulu after a few days and take an inter-island vessel to Hilo. She had been able to arrange rooms at the prestigious Shipman House Bed and Breakfast where Jack London had stayed. She had also done research on the fifty-foot-high tsunami that had hit the Big Island two years earlier (confident it would not repeat itself during their visit) as well as the increasing activity from Kīlauea Volcano. She had found they could visit the Hawaiian Volcano Observatory and peer right into the volcanos—looking hell straight in the eye.

In the end, for reasons never fully grasped by Isabelle, Mabel bowed-out of the outing as well. It was, therefore, only with Bradley that she was able to look into the fire and brimstone that was the lava and gas of an active volcano. She felt like she had been able to peek into the kingdom of Hades—wondering what fate was in store for them all.

Yet, beyond ponderous questions like whether their future would be overseen by Hades or his sister, Demeter who presided over a fertile Earth, they had a wonderful trip—great accommodation, delicious meals, splendid sites, and, even more rare, nice people.

As it was just the two of them, they followed a much more flexible schedule, staying in the islands much longer than they might have if they had been part of a larger group. They enjoyed all the tropical paradise had to offer. Bradley managed to get in some golf and swimming. They both enjoyed many walks along many beaches. The weather was marvelous. Bradley's complexion soon rivaled a polished antique cherry Chippendale chiffonier. Isabelle's coloring, from the tip of her pointed nose to the peaks of her small ears, regardless of where she was or what she did, remained a slightly smudged tallow color.

Spring was over when they returned to Tucson. As always, Maria had the house in order. Isabelle was able to pick up where she left off in her studio while Bradley did the same on the greens.

They had been back six weeks when Isabelle got a call she had often feared might be coming. Bradley had collapsed on the golf course and was in hospital. She rushed to his side then tore after the doctors to get the real story. He had had a heart attack. It was severe, but he had a good chance of recovery. Full recovery, however, would require a long period of recuperation. It was probable he would have to limit his activities, alcohol consumption, and rich diet from here on.

Isabelle called her daughter to let her know about Bradley's health. Margaret was polite but reserved, almost subliminally letting Isabelle know once again that Bradley was not her father. Margaret did take the opportunity to inform her mother that they were packing up to head out west. Julian had recently made a preliminary trip to Oregon. He had managed to make many of the preparations for them to minimize the pain of the move (Margaret emphasizing "pain").

The company had bought an old mill that had once been a complete village. Also, among many other things, there was a house (decrepit or strong, who knew?) ready and waiting for them when they arrived. They planned on spending the Fourth with Julian's family then heading out to their new life—to the unknown.

Margaret's annotation of "the unknown" elicited a completely different reaction from her mother than she had imagined. For a brief moment, just a split second, Isabelle's mind darted away, seeing herself as a researcher in a laboratory, staring intently at a small black box with no visible sign of entry—the unknown. It lit her imagination. It transported her. She had to forcibly bring herself back to her conversation with her daughter.

Taking care to cast no aspersions, Isabelle assured her offspring, who had seemingly not inherited her mother's curiosity and embrace (at least intellectually) of the exotic, that the West was absolutely beautiful, historic, and just as well supplied with potable water and electricity as Des Moines. The trip there would, in her view, be a memorable event and they should make sure to stop and show all the spectacular attractions to Ann. When Bradley regained his strength and Margaret's little family was well-settled, they would plan an outing to come and visit.

That was that—the fork in the road. Des Moines was now a stopover and not a hub. Osmosis was drawing the family in different directions. Such was the way of things. Isabelle needed to get back to her painting and cards—and Bradley, of course.

Maria proved to be an able nurse and before Thanksgiving Bradley was able to go out for golf, limiting himself to nine holes. This was good for Bradley, as the month was a total disaster for Isabelle. That loathsome lummox Truman had, in a squeaker, defeated her beloved Dewey. According to the papers, the able challenger lost by less than five percent; Democratic robbery. Isabelle mourned for days.

When the feast of Thanksgiving came, they celebrated with Dorothy and Lawrence who had come to see how their father was getting-on. It was tense. First, the Minneapolis couple was delighted with the election results—eager to expound on how Mr. Truman would carry even further all the vital policies of the great FDR. Thereafter, Bradley had to quietly intercept the liberal youngsters, warning them, to keep the peace and his own blood pressure down as the doctors required, it would be necessary to avoid any further political discourse—deflecting as necessary if the subject was opened by others.

Then, while Dorothy and Lawrence demonstrated they were disciplined and able to steer clear of potentially bombastic topics as well as avoid the snares Isabelle carefully buried within the conversations, they insisted on opening the subject of Bradley's mortality. They asserted that a severe coronary for a seventy-seven-year-old man who had been a *bon vivant* was a sober alert, if not omen. It was time, well past time, to get his affairs in order. No one, his daughter emphasized, was wishing for anything other than many more years of good health, good times, and good golf. But, of course, one never knew. Had, indeed, this been more dire, been the end, then what turmoil the family would be in trying to sort out all the various concerns. Bradley really needed to take things in hand.

Isabelle, nerves already pulled to the breaking point, would have none of Dorothy's talk. This was not the time. This was definitely, absolutely not the time. It was Thanksgiving. It was the time for turkey, stuffing, mashed potatoes, and bread sauce. It was a time of being thankful that Bradley, her father, was still able to take his seat at the table and enjoy the repast. It was not, need she repeat, *definitely not*, a time for supposition, fearmongering, and planting misgivings.

All seemed to let out a sigh of relief when Dorothy and Lawrence headed home on Sunday morning. Bradley was happy they had come and appreciated the fact that they cared. Isabelle was still grieving for Thomas Dewey.

By contrast, the holidays were quiet and uneventful. With the new year, the Indo-Pakistani War ended, Truman (the "lamebrain" from Isabelle's seat) was inaugurated, and Ben-Gurion became the first elected Prime Minister of Israel. Bradley seemed to be in fine form. Margaret was also fine. She had sent a Christmas card saying they were excited about having their first Christmas "Out West" where they had been able to go and hunt their own tree, go greening to select the most aromatic of boughs to decorate the house, and where, they were happy to report, like in Des Moines, they could go ice skating.

For her own inauguration of the new year, Isabelle started her largest canvas, a desert scene with saguaro cacti in the foreground and the Catalina Mountains in the background—a softly colored tableau in buff, umber, ecru, and muted greens.

While the temperature was climbing to reach the summer highs, Isabelle finished her desertscape, Bradley was up to eighteen-holes, twice a week, *Nineteen Eighty-Four* was published, a monkey was the first primate in space, Ranier III became the Prince of Monaco, and, as Bradley so studiously reminded Isabelle, Kansas passed a statute permitting racial segregation, although a federal court required University of Kentucky to admit black students to some of its schools, at the same time Texas coal mines required toilets separated by race, and Georgia put in place a voters test targeting, according to reports, black voters.

By the time another solar cycle had been accomplished, the People's Republic of China was proclaimed. Although the Chinese civil war was in its twenty-second year, Chiang Kai-shek and his followers had fled from the Chinese mainland to Taiwan. Closer to home, a World War II vet killed thirteen neighbors in New Jersey and the first cowboy western aired on television. Isabelle and Bradley had hoped to take a long trip, possibly to Cuba to see the Tropicana Night Club and try their luck at La Habana Gran Casino National. But this was not to be. While Bradley was regaining his energy, he was still not ready to go too far from home, his soft bed, or the faithful ministrations of Maria.

The new year arrived with Isabelle in a particularly bad humor. Over the holidays, Maria had requested two weeks off to visit family near Yuma. Isabelle had been ready to categorically refuse, although this was the first substantive time off Maria had requested since she had started working for them. Bradley understood the importance of the festivities to Maria. She had, in confidence, explained to him that family from Mexico were planning on slipping across the border and they would have a real family fiesta, assembling many, many members of her large extended family for the first time in nearly twenty years. Bradley knew she had to attend and did all he could to finally win, if begrudgingly, Isabelle's approval.

But this meant that Isabelle, not only, had to do all the despised housework, take care of their meals, and cater to her husband's needs, but it was also the holidays. While they had nothing special planned and did very little in terms of decorating the house or bringing in special festive supplies, there were always people dropping in to wish them "Merry Christmas and

Happy New Year". Heretofore, Maria had been able to run interference for these most often annoying disturbances—now Isabelle would have to do this herself.

Those merrymakers who had crossed their threshold were not impressed by Isabelle's astringent mien and did not dally. Thus, the impositions on Isabelle's time and patience were minimal beyond the day-to-day responsibilities of the household—responsibilities she personally felt she had long outgrown. But she supported the indignities well, Bradley doing all he could to help with the chores and minimize his own demands on her efforts. Then Maria was back, the new decade was off and running, and Isabelle started a new canvas.

All the news was about the Cold War and spies and such. Alger Hiss and Klaus Fuchs were on the front page, making Isabelle think she should always be looking over her shoulder to see who was watching. People were talking about civil defense and you could hear reverberations of the mantra, "better dead than red". Isabelle had known that FDR sitting down with that devil Stalin would lead to no good and now current events were, once again, proving her right.

Spring was leading to summer, not long after King Leopold III announced he was handing over to his son Baudouin, that muttonhead Truman announced he was going to war in Korea. War! Hadn't they just ended a war?

Isabelle was ruffled by the stupidity of people, as well as the supreme stupidity of politicians. Then, to add insult to injury, Bradley had to keep adding his silly footnotes. As he persisted in noting to her, things were often upside-down. The stupidity of people was not just war. While the Supreme Court had ruled that institutions of higher education could not treat people of different races differently, and the Court had also declared there could no longer be racial segregation in railroad dining cars, two-thirds of the states had some sort of anti-miscegenation laws on the books, and a district court had concluded that segregation in Washington, D.C. schools was legal. No wonder people like Josephine Baker were still living in France and making a lot of noise about how abhorrent the racial situation in America was.

Isabelle was not sure how Bradley could be so concerned about human nature and not really fearful that the treacherous Reds were threatening their very existence. But any counterattack she was planning on her husband's nearly intolerable social liberalism was cut short by the news that Margaret was pregnant.

7

Meet Walter

Joyous, Margaret called her mother, telling her she was expecting to have a baby in mid to late September. She and Julian were beside themselves—this was what they had been wanting for so long. They had begun talking to Ann about how she would soon have a new little brother or sister. She seemed disinterested, at times almost hostile. Still, her parents were sure she would come around.

Isabelle began instantly putting in place a plan. She wanted to be with her daughter when she had her second child, as she had been when she had had her first. Margaret was almost thirty-four. Not old, certainly not too old to be having a baby. But still, she was almost thirty-four. She told Margaret that she and Bradley would put a trip on their calendar to be out west in the fall when the baby came. It would be wonderful.

In point of fact, there really was not all that much time for Isabelle and Bradley to put their plans into action. They decided to go to Los Angeles and then up the coast. But then Bradley got a call from Dorothy, checking on his health. She maintained, nearly with legal flourish, her father should come first to Minneapolis. She was determined to see how her father was doing with her own eyes. She advised she had excellent contacts at the much-acclaimed Northwestern Hospital and, if her father was not in good shape, she would ship him off to this facility in an instant.

As often, Isabelle reacted badly to what she saw as inappropriate impositions by her stepdaughter. To Isabelle, Dorothy's stipulations were an insult to Isabelle's ability to adequately take care of her husband, as well as a ploy to convince Bradley that she, Dorothy, was his one true chaperon in this life. A chaperone who honestly and profoundly cared about him, unlike his wife, who was willing to jeopardize his health by forcing him to make a transcontinental trip before he was fully fit, just to witness the birth of a baby who was not even from his direct lineage.

Isabelle was tempted to make the harshest reply to Dorothy, demanding they maintain their travel plans via Los Angles and unquestionably not acquiesce to this unreasonable command from Minneapolis. However, Bradley soothed her ruffled feathers, assuring her that, while he was in the best of hands and once again in excellent health, it was prudent to keep strong ties with Dorothy as family was still the bedrock of all. He knew his wife was aware that their Dorothy had a tendency to over react and this was just her bringing her legal practice into her family affairs—especially since the couple had no children to shape and guide. Isabelle should not read more into this than it was—simply a daughter's concern for her father's health. They could easily re-route themselves via a northern passage that would still get them out west in plenty of time for Margaret's scheduled delivery in mid-September.

Accordingly, the changes taking them to Minneapolis were made, reminding them that the only certain thing was uncertainty.

They had scheduled a week with Dorothy. Too long for Isabelle, but at one point Bradley had been considering a fortnight, so a week it was. Then, after all this, they got a telegram just after arriving in Minneapolis that the doctors thought Margaret would deliver early. Margaret had had several miscarriages and these changes raised the specter that all was not well.

Isabelle put aside any flexibility or diplomacy and simply declared they would be leaving Minneapolis as soon as they could get confirmed connections west. It did, much to Isabelle's regret, take them a painful two days to get their onward travel confirmed. This was at least a small block of time for Dorothy to verify that her father was in fact alive and kicking. This observation notwithstanding, Dorothy still tried to insist her father see specialists before they left town. But the rush to Margaret's side made this impractical and Isabelle carried the day as they waved goodbye to Dorothy and Lawrence barely forty-eight hours after saying hello.

They arrived on the Southern Pacific's *Shasta Daylight*, Julian standing on the platform as the liveried Pullman porter helped Isabelle down the steep step from the sleeper car. He greeted them with a forced and tired smile. Margaret was home but staying in bed for several days. She had had their baby two weeks early—a boy, a little, tiny boy. The baby was still in the hospital, in an incubator—but, he would be home soon.

The station Red Cap, a bit more tousled than his counterparts on the train crew, got their bags in the back of Julian's 1948 Ford Woody. Julian drove them through a dingy industrial area, down a main street that could be anywhere USA, across a few low hills covered with sage brush and juniper, and then on to the compact community that circumscribed the sawmill Julian had come to manage. To one side of the mill was the lake and to the other, a cluster of houses, ranging from very small to very big, with a grocery store, barbershop, and dancehall on the periphery of the residential neighborhood. Julian drove down a lane, turned and crossed the railroad tracks that serviced the mill, entered an open chain-link fence, pulling-up in front of the biggest house in the village—an impressive, if not aesthetically-pleasing, box-like affair of two floors topped by two large chimneys. Surrounding the residence was a variety of outbuildings including a barn, storeroom, gazebo, and even a small fishpond.

Isabelle was not prepared for the grandeur of her daughter's home, but she was even less prepared for the bustle that was visible with four cars parked around the circular drive and a number of people seemly milling about.

Julian noted his mother-in-law's puzzlement, and explained the stars had somehow aligned and, after almost two years of seeing no old friends or family, they now were truly inundated with visitors—visitors who were most welcome, even cherished, but who all seemed to come at the same time—the same time his son had also chosen to arrive. Things were hectic.

Isabelle's bemusement changed little, and Julian expanded. His own aunt, his mother's big sister, Beatrice, had come up from Southern California. By pure happenstance, his sister, Annabelle, with her husband Hal, had shown up while on a long voyage traversing the Pacific Northwest. And, to add to the crowd, Isabelle would be happy to note that Justin and Gwen had pulled in the other day—their blue bus parked on the other side of the house.

Julian accompanied his mother-in-law and her husband up the few stairs to the wide front porch, whereupon the front door opened, not to reveal Margaret as Isabelle had imagined, but a tall and stately, already-grey-haired lady whom Isabelle instantly recognized as the adult version of the little girl with pigtails and a faded blue poplin dress of years ago. Although she could not have remembered the name if Julian had not just mentioned it, she knew immediately this was Annabelle—the little tag-along following her big brother those years ago on Pleasant Street in Des Moines.

Annabelle warmly embraced both Isabelle and Bradley, shepherding them into the living room while her older brother brought in the luggage. Walking with a smooth, straight gait that Isabelle admired, knowing her own was far from this regal, Annabelle guided them into the parlor where the other visitors were seated. Introductions were made for Beatrice and Hal, the only travelers the Tucson couple had not already met.

When all were seated, Annabelle served the newcomers coffee as she explained Margaret was resting upstairs. Just as Isabelle had added her milk and sugar, Julian arrived saying their bags were all upstairs in the guest bedroom. He would take them up to freshen up once they had finished their coffee. Isabelle stiffened a bit as she felt her time was already being laid out by others. Bradley sensed the minuscule changed and squeezed his wife's hand. They then enjoyed their coffee over small talk of where Justin and Gwen had been, how were the rains in Southern California, and how Hal liked working for Drake University.

Thankfully for Isabelle, who tolerated, at best, only small doses of chit-chat, Julian soon came to accompany them to their room. They ascended a wide staircase, at the top turning to the right, Julian indicating he thought they might like to greet Margaret before going to their own room.

They entered a large master bedroom with an equally large fireplace and large walk-in closets accentuated by a large bathroom. However, the main attraction of the room was the annexed sunny and bright sewing room where Margaret was seated on a daybed. As they passed the threshold and took the one step down to this cozy spot, Margaret rose with obvious difficulty, embracing her mother sincerely, if a bit coolly. She then offered Bradley her hand before reclining again on the grey and red brocade bedspread.

Julian moved to sit on the hassock beside his wife as Margaret welcomed her mother, briefed her ever-so succinctly about the birth, saying that little Walter—they would call him Walt—would be home in a few days and they would have his bassinet set up here in the lovely sewing room.

At the pronunciation "Walter," Isabelle's eyebrows peaked—a sign, her daughter knew all too well, of stupefaction, bewilderment that could turn into aggravation that could, sometimes, turn nasty. She tried to intercede to avoid any unpleasantries.

"Walter was the name of Julian's uncle—not really much of an uncle, as he died at the age of two years old. But, since we had had so much difficulty in having this tiny baby, we wanted to honor this other little boy who did not manage to stay on this earth very long."

Isabelle was little satisfied. A baby boy named Walt. *Ridiculous!* She was sure her mother's husband, Westley, would have been a far, far better role model than a dead baby. Then, she had read in the paper the other day on the train that the top boy's names for 1950 were James and Michael— what was wrong with James or Michael? Walter! But she did not want to further alienate her daughter at this point by picking a losing fight over her grandson's name.

She swallowed hard, inhaling deeply, declaring she and Bradley were anxious to see the little guy once he was snug in his bed in the sewing room—little Walt. In the meantime, grabbing Bradley's arm, they needed to get to their room and change out of their traveling clothes.

Julian quickly escorted them down the hall to a large bedroom that looked over the veranda at the back of the house. As he wished them well, Julian said they would all be meeting for a drink on that very veranda in about three hours. In the meantime, he said they could rest while he went to pick up Ann at school—he knew Ann would be excited to see them once she got home.

Isabelle and Bradley went downstairs about an hour before the scheduled *aperitif*, finding Ann and Annabelle chatting quietly in the solarium. Isabelle had visions of Ann looking up, seeing her, and running gleefully across the room yelling, "Grandmummie, Grandmummie, Grandmummie!".

Ann did look up. It was unclear if there was any recognition in her hooded eyes. She quickly averted her glance and continued, almost without a break in her tempo, with her discussion with her aunt. Annabelle, witnessing the exchanges, took center stage and, as a kind of ring master, presented Ann to her maternal grandparents as though she had never seen them before.

With the formalities completed, Isabelle attempted to join into the conversation, gleaning that the topic was how boring Ann felt second grade was—already being displeased after less than a month of classes. However, Ann maintained her focus on her aunt, scarcely acknowledging the presence of the others.

The potential tension was broken with Julian coming in with his own aunt, inviting all to step outside to the back veranda. Here, under the lattice roof, nearly a dozen stout slatted green wooden chairs with heavy cotton cushions where arranged in a semicircle, looking out to the garden beyond the nearby cottonwood tree where, Isabelle noticed, Julian had built an extravagant treehouse for Ann.

Hal joined them as Julian announced with a big smile that Margaret would be joining them as she was feeling much stronger—undoubtedly, he joked, due to the arrival of her mother. Isabelle, uncertain how to interpret this last comment, tried unsuccessfully to put on a smile.

Justin and Gwen ambled onto the veranda from the backyard from where they had evidently been strolling. As Julian was in the process of confirming that all those assembled would be satisfied with a mint julep—professing he was noted for being a virtuoso at the concocting of this delicious potion—a rather more-than-middle-aged, big-boned woman entered with a tray of peanuts and pretzels. Julian interrupted himself to present to his in-laws, their wonderful helper Zelda. Zelda's husband, he added, worked in the mill—the couple occupying the small house on the property, on the other side of the vegetable garden.

Isabelle noted her son-in-law, perhaps a bit intimidated by his new status and accommodation, was uncomfortable, unlike she herself, in calling the household staff lodging what it honestly was: "the quarters". Julian might paint it a different color, call it "the small house", but it was originally the dwelling for those who served the master and Julian, with Margaret at his side, was now the master.

Isabelle turned her attention to Zelda. She thought this sinewy woman looked like something out of the *Wizard of Oz*—she smirked to herself, realizing she was glad her son-in-law had introduced this lady, because if she ran into her in the night, she would be afraid she might have seen an apparition.

As Julian disappeared to the kitchen to prepare his specialty, Annabelle took up the conversation, pointing out how the semi-arid conditions made the late afternoon air feel rather cool, certainly compared to Des Moines, even with the temperatures in the eighties. Justin chimed in that the dryness was visible on the surrounding hills, which were brown and barren, although people told him the backsides of many of these bluffs were heavily wooded— the nearby sawmill under Julian's care a testament to the forest resources that were undoubtedly abundant, in contrast to the parched view seen on much of the nearby lands.

Isabelle could pick up just the slightest pungent scent of the lake as the breeze strengthened and the temperature seemed drop—the conditions on the veranda becoming even more enjoyable. Indeed, there were surely stark comparisons with Des Moines and even Tucson or Sarasota—but did not these people have something better to talk about? This pointless banter was a waste of time. She hoped Julian would bring the refreshments soon. She knew him to be a mixologist who did not serve watered-down drinks. His libations were always strong enough to tickle the cerebrum of the most hardened drinker—drinks of the sort, as George used to say, that would put hair on your chest. Not that she wanted any hair on her chest, but she would not mind a massage to her neurons to help tolerate the incessant babble that inevitably was the centerpiece of such uninspired family get-togethers.

As if reading her mind, Julian appeared with a big tray containing eleven sweating aluminum tumblers. Placing the tray on a corner table, he served each of the guests a drink, leaving three on the tray, announcing that Margaret would be coming down any minute now. Additionally, his younger brother Steve and his sister-in-law Christine, who lived across the street, would also be coming as soon as they got their children settled. Their young son Tim was just a year older than the newcomer Walt and his big sister Sara would take care of him while the parents were across the street at this family gala.

Almost beaming, Julian then held up a small eight-inch dowel, a mini pestle, stained with years of use, announcing that this was his "magic muddling stick"—the secret to a truly good mint julep being that the potion be properly muddled in well-chilled tumblers. He hoped they all enjoyed their drinks—there was more in the kitchen.

Isabelle recalled vaguely somewhere hearing a julep was a fine drink meant to be sipped—she gulped. She needed some rapid numbing to comfort her brain which was currently painfully awash with the silly blah, blah, blah coming from a group of people who really had nothing to say to each other.

With surprising rapidity, she drained her tumbler and slipped it onto the tray, exchanging for a full container. Catching Julian's eye, she made her first contribution to the repartee.

"Julian, dear, please get our dear Margaret another fresh drink. I've stolen hers as you've done such a splendid job of blending with your magic muddler."

As Julian obediently scurried away to the kitchen, Isabelle felt a welcome tingle of nerves as a big swallow of the delicious liquid hit her stomach. It was working.

She was only half way through her second tumbler when her daughter made her appearance, as if scripted, followed by a youngish couple Isabelle assumed to be Steve and Christine, although she had only seen Steve a few times as very much a youngster in Des Moines, and she had never met Christine.

Their almost choreographed entry somehow reminded her tickled brain of high school physics when she had tried to help Percy with his homework. She herself was far from scientific, and poor Percy had no aptitude in this area whatsoever, despite his generally sterling academic performance. They had been studying vectors and how two forces coming in the same direction can be additive. She thought of the people coming together through the veranda door as being an additive force. She smiled to herself. She imagined the people awkwardly straddling galloping vector arrows, trying to align their forces to make a difference and failing miserably. Ride those arrows!

Again, as if prompted, Julian appeared just in time to give his wife a perspiring tumbler and then make all the necessary introductions before seating the new arrivals. Julian was a good host.

The prattle continued unabated. The only good point being there was no discussion of work or sawmills. There was a lot of chitchat about how wonderful, even glowing, Margaret looked—how great it was they had a baby boy, how child birth was always so miraculous, how babies were a gift from God—but a helluva lot of work—and on it went. Isabelle tuned out the chatter and tried to remember what grade Percy had received in physics.

She had just convinced her son-in-law to mix another one of his wonderful drinks when Christine, who had basically been sitting quietly next to Steve who himself had contributed very little, commented, as just an off-hand remark during a slump in the twaddle.

"Isn't it a shame, all the death and destruction in Korea. What a terrible situation! Not long ago, those North Koreans killed hundreds of people at the Seoul hospital and then just the other day there was the massacre of American troops at something called Hill 303. It is so sad. We just had a war—a terrible war. And now this."

"Sad, indeed," Gwen joined in, "it is a dangerous world we live in. Dear Margaret, your little boy is coming into a world that is not the world we knew. It's the Cold War. It's a mess. Churchill, what a wonderful man, is even talking about a new super army that will involve all of Europe—Canada and the United States, too. There's so much going on. Things are changing so fast. And this war is killing so many. It is really sad."

A little spark grazed Isabelle's brain and she felt she must break her stoicism and interject the truth.

"Sad, yes. But all the fault of that damned Truman. It's his war. We wouldn't be in any of this mess it that dunce Roosevelt hadn't been such a milk toast. If he'd stood up to all those others, we'd be in a much better place today. And then the old dolt, that numbskull, goes and drops dead and we get FDR II. It is simply horrid."

Bradley had tried to grab his spouse's arm before she launched her attack, to avert the inevitable. But he was too late. The rocket had taken off.

Isabelle felt she needed to emphasize the point, as these people had no real clue about what was happening.

"If we continue to be faint-hearted," she continued, "to think only of those who, through their own lack of gumption, show weakness, we will fail." For some reason, the idea of Percy failing physics briefly flashed in her mind. "If we continue to be bleeding-hearts who take the world's problems on our shoulders, we will see all that we have worked for evaporate in a Democrat-inspired haze."

Bradley thought Isabelle had stopped, but she was just taking air.

"If we continue to open our doors to any and every Tom, Dick, and Harry who wants to come here from some other place where things just aren't very good today—well, we'll find ourselves, as we already do, in place where things aren't very good. As long as we help freeloaders, punish those with initiative, and are led by dopes, we are destined to slide downhill. One day we will look to those who pushed us down this hill and see them for what they truly have been—crooks and incompetents. Rubbish! Damn then all."

Everyone took a big mouthful of their julep.

"Well mother," Margaret said, trying to divert the growing torrent, "there are always difficult times. You and Daddy went through so much and I am sure at times it seems like all was for naught—but look how it has all worked out."

"My dear," Isabelle, her eyebrows severely peaked, almost sneered, irritatingly unsure of to whom her daughter was referring when she said 'Daddy.' "We are not they."

"Excuse me, Mrs. Baker," Christine retorted, "I don't think we should generalize."

"That's right," Gwen inserted, and Isabelle thought they were like the Bobbsey Twins, equally nonsensical.

"There's always two sides to every story," Gwen continued, "isn't that so, Justin."

Justin obviously did not want to get drawn into the debate, but did manage a muffled, "These are truly trying times."

Annabelle thought she might be able to redirect things to calmer waters. "Personally, I can certainly say, having been there, that war is terrible. We should never go there casually, without real justification. But sometimes it cannot be avoided. When it is inevitable, when it comes as much as we may wish it would not, we must support our leaders and our troops. And, as our leaders and our troops, we support those who need, who depend on us. We need to help others as we too have been helped."

Isabelle glared and contributed only a *humpf.*

Beatrice thought maybe she could get things back to where they were when she had arrived.

"Mrs. Baker, my dear, when folks get as old as we are, we have seen so much, and it is easy to lose faith—to become a pessimist—to doubt. But I am sure you'll agree, things have a way of working out."

"Yes mother, Aunt Beatrice is right," Margaret said. "We can do nothing about Washington here on the lakeshore. But we can enjoy the night, enjoy the company, and be happy we have a chance to be here to celebrate little Walt."

"Margaret, as you know so well," Isabelle started, "we all can and should be vigilant, doing our . . ."

"As your mother was saying," Bradley boldly interrupted, "we can all do our part to make tonight memorable and to wish the new mother all the best. Join me in a toast."

All raised their tumblers, Isabelle drained hers.

Margaret then donned her hostess cap, announcing they were going to have a cookout. Everyone was advised to pick up their tumbler and move through the house, out to the front yard where Julian, with his own two hands, had built a terrific barbecue. With Zelda's able help, they had put together a great heap of a variety of shish kebabs. Everyone should pick their choice from the pile and cook it themselves to their personal taste, as Julian's new barbecue was so immense it could handle everyone's food at once.

Under her breath as she stood, Christine whispered to Steve, "Everyone having their own choice and preparing things the way they think best and not the way others think is best—now that's a novel idea."

Isabelle was looking for a refill and the barb, if that was its intent, went unheard.

Once Isabelle had procured a new beverage, which was indeed as yummy as her son-in-law had promised, she moved to the front yard, mischievously wondering abstractly what else her daughter would consider as "immense".

The move from the back to the front of the house was an unexpected stroke of genius. It successfully broke the conversation—everyone now concentrating on what to eat and how to cook it. Once the guests had their shish kababs on their plate, they served themselves salad from the nearby table—potato, tossed, cucumber and onion, or Jell-o with pineapple and cottage cheese. Then each had to find a way to balance the overflowing plate and the long skewer in such a way that the meal could actually be consumed. With no organized seating, this meant that small groups formed around suitable outcroppings that could accommodate the eaters.

One cluster, by no accident, included Margaret along with her mother and Bradley.

Margaret was mortified, dropping her mask.

"Mother! You simply must behave. You are welcome to your own thoughts and convictions—but so are others. We're here to celebrate little Walt's arrival—not to fight for the New Deal or the Fair Deal."

"Now Margaret," Bradley said, as his stepdaughter skewered him with her fierce eyes, "you know your mother just cares a lot."

He might have continued, but Margaret had no patience and wanted the matter closed once and for all.

"Intentions are not my concern!" she emphasized, "Everyone here is a valued and loved member of our family. We are newcomers in a strange place. We want and need and enjoy ALL our family. My mother will not split us apart or set us one against another because she hates Democrats or Catholics! Understand well. This is the beginning and the end. No more!"

Isabelle was honestly stunned by her daughter's vehemence. She could only stare into space and then concentrate intently on her shish kabob. Meticulously, she removed each morsel daintily with her fingertips, plopping them in ladylike fashion in her mouth, and chewing thoroughly. She pretended she was eating alone in a bus station waiting room. All that was missing was a white linen handkerchief to elegantly wipe the corners of her mouth.

Contrary to her mother, Margaret ran the skewer through her teeth and pulled off several chunks which she half-swallowed, half-chewed—almost choking. She then gave the couple her broadest smile and, not looking back, sashayed to the other side of the yard where Steve and Christine were eating with Beatrice and Julian.

Isabelle finished her shish kabob and then her salads—looking Bradley square in the eyes, she could only manage a *humpf*, before walking off herself, in the other direction, into the now dark recesses of the large yard.

After the meal, people drifted off in their own directions, Isabelle and Bradley deciding to make an early night of it, cloistered quickly but unabashedly in their room.

It was perhaps an exaggeration to say it had been a bruising evening, after all, Isabelle had a reputation to live up to, but it had not been really congenial. If nothing else, if no long-term discord, Isabelle had made her mark. What was the impact on her, now that she was in a more calming environment where she could look back over the past few hours?

Bradley poked around the edges, fearing the repercussions of a frontal attack, trying to see how wounded, if at all, his wife felt.

There did not seem to be a clear diagnosis. She seemed upset and did not want to talk about the evening's discussions. But she still seemed to have a rather cheerful outlook on their visit and their travels. Bradley, as so often the case, was a bit befuddled. He decided the best thing was a good night's sleep so, before drifting off, to decompress, they talked about the news, about the Bloody Gulch Massacre in Korea when scores of American GIs lost their lives— Bradley wondering if America could keep the world safe and Isabelle stressing she would rather be dead than red. Soon there was the smooth tempo of two almost harmonious snores coming from the guest room.

If one of Isabelle's old friends, the Greek goddess Eirene, the goddess of peace, and also, by the way, the patroness of prosperity, had been watching over Isabelle the whole evening, she would have rejoiced. The wheezes wrapped in sleep were the first signs that her charge Isabelle had found peace that day. By extrapolation, these were also the first moments when Bradley could find some much-needed serenity. If Isabelle had thought she were sleeping in Eirene's shadow, she certainly would not have missed the chance to remind the goddess not to forget the prosperity while she watched over her.

The next day, when Isabelle and Bradley came down for breakfast at the kitchen table, they found Margaret, Beatrice, Annabelle, and Hal huddled around their coffee mugs—apparently Julian was at the mill, Ann at school, and Gwen and Justin were, as usual, who knew where. Isabelle and Bradley served themselves from the big stainless-steel percolator on the counter. As they placed their stoneware mugs on the white Formica table, those already seated in the vinyl and steel tubing chairs squirmed uncomfortably.

Margaret decided to confront the unease head-on.

"Don't worry. Mother never starts the day with a rant," she chuckled.

The tension was broken. The small talk continued about how well the vegetable garden had done this year and the apple trees across the street in the orchard were loaded. By the way, Mr. Perelli, who ran the local grocery, had a new visitor, too. His niece had come all the way from Italy.

Isabelle watched the steam rise from her mug. Bradley watched Isabelle. The others had shifted gears and were speculating on whether or not this winter would be a record-setter.

Margaret excused herself and with amazing speed had a breakfast of scrambled eggs, toast, and melon, with orange juice, on the placemats in front of each of her guests. Over the tasty meal, the diners, for reasons Isabelle could not fathom, took their aimless chatter in an unexpected direction—the Rose Parade in Pasadena. They weighed, to the smallest detail, this year's event. Paul G. Hoffman, who had been the president of Studebaker and then administered the Marshall Plan in Europe after the war, had been the Grand Marshall and he had been grand indeed. Isabelle wondered who cared?

After breakfast, Isabelle and Bradley slipped into the solarium where Isabelle wanted to sit quietly in the sun. As his wife tried to warm herself from outside in, Bradley applauded her self-control over breakfast, while everyone one just babbled on about nothing at all of importance.

He had just finished heaping praise on his spouse when he looked up to find Margaret standing in the doorway. She took a seat across from them, saying she had some good news and an exciting possibility for them.

Now that she, Margaret, was back on her feet, she had to concentrate on getting the house in order as little Walt would be coming home in a week or less. Everything needed to be scrubbed and polished. Beatrice and

Annabelle had offered to help Zelda and herself. And, while many hands make light work, too many hands make a mess. Justin and Gwen were taking their bus to visit Crater Lake. Then, for her parents, she had wonderful news.

While the house was all disarrayed, she had arranged for her parents to have a quiet and relaxing time at a favored nearby site called Lake of the Woods. Here many of the better-off families (translated as the ruling aristocracy, Isabelle knew) had cabins where they would go when the valley got too hot, to enjoy themselves with fishing, swimming, and water skiing. Tom and Carol, Walt's Godparents, were one such family. They had generously offered a car and their cabin at the lake to her parents—a rare chance to really stay in the forest, seeing how beautiful and fresh it was at the end of summer.

Isabelle was immediately on edge when her daughter had repeatedly used the term *parents*, knowing Margaret never had, and never would, consider Bradley as her father. She clearly was using all the tools in her box to try and get her mother out of the way. Well, why not let her have her little success? She deserved it. After all, it was far better than sitting amongst these people and listening to the absolute rubbish they spouted.

Margaret added a footnote that she hoped would seal the deal. In less than ten days, as her mother knew perfectly well, she would celebrate her thirty-fourth birthday. Julian was organizing a little family get-together. Gwen and Justin would be coming back for the festivity and she wanted to make sure that her parents (that word again, Isabelle thought) would be here to share in the celebration.

Isabelle suspected her daughter knew that she and Bradley had tickets on the train south just two days after the upcoming thirty-fourth birthday celebration. Margaret had mapped out their entire stay. Well, why not? Without even consulting Bradley, not even looking keenly at his expression to see how he was thinking, Isabelle quickly thanked her daughter for making such terrific plans for them. It would take no time at all to get their things together. If Tom and Carol's car were available tomorrow, they could head up to the lake *posthaste*.

Margaret excused herself to get back to cleaning the kitchen and then preparing for sanitizing the house. Isabelle was reminded of what they said the Pharaohs declared when making an order: so let it be written, so let it be done. She and Bradley were being packed off to the lake. So be it.

Fortunately, there were a lot of books in Margaret's house and Isabelle filled a box with those that tweaked her fancy. She and Bradley packed their bags and the next morning Julian delivered a forest green (appropriate,

Isabelle thought) 1949 Chrysler New Yorker for his in-laws to use as they went off on their jaunt to the lake.

It was not far, and they had good directions. By mid-afternoon they were sitting on a conformable, if a bit worn, settee in a log-cabin that was quite well outfitted. But Isabelle was already beside herself, finding herself in the darkness of a virgin forest where the sun never really shone. By contrast to the warm and bright afternoons at Margaret's, here it seemed like, at this early hour, night was ready to fall. Isabelle had Bradley build a big fire in the stone fireplace before they dug into the pantry for its offerings for the evening meal.

There was a general store about two miles away that offered anything else they might require. They really had, Isabelle knew, all they needed. And, this might be a wonderful spot for hard-working executives to relax over a weekend or for young kids to play during summer vacation. But it was not a great place for an old couple who already spent most of their time together without, what some might say, contact with the real world.

Isabelle decided her charge was to read all the books in the box. Thus, she spent her days with her nose in a book; sometimes in a lounge chair on the dock, sometimes in the settee, sometimes on the hearth, sometimes on the floor, sometimes on the bed, even sometimes on the toilet—and she was mighty happy that this rustic retreat had indoor plumbing.

Bradley encouraged Isabelle—challenging her to finish all the books— warning her, however, that her bookish appetite was greater than the number of hours in a day. There was only so much time when someone could read—she would never finish them all. He then divided his own time between cooking, taking naps, and fishing off the dock.

The days passed. Isabelle had to admit it was not all that unpleasant. Soon it was time to get in the New Yorker and head back to Margaret's— making sure to stop somewhere in town to get her a birthday present.

As they came back into town, they parked near the Baldwin Hotel to see what type of shops might be available for a suitable present for Margaret. Isabelle was extremely surprised to find a small boutique just two blocks from the hotel that had the most amazing selection of items; oriental carpets, brass tables, wooden chests, strange knives, and, of keen interest to Isabelle, an amazing selection of small marble statuary, probably imported from Greece and Italy, but truly surprising to find in a backwater western mill town.

When she saw the depiction of Penelope, she knew she had found not just a suitable gift, the perfect gift. Penelope was seen as the goddess of faithfulness, patience, and feminine virtue. This was ideal.

She did not consult with Bradley, nor did he expect her to—he only paid the bill. As it turned out, it was much harder to get the little statue gift wrapped than it was to find the right gift. But this too was finally resolved. Reasonably gratified, Bradley and Isabelle pulled up in the circular drive on the eve of Margaret's birthday, satisfied with themselves and the results of their labors.

The house was in a hubbub, organizing Margaret's birthday party that was combined with little Walt's coming out party, as he was no longer so weak as to need an incubator and hospital care. He was home—his blue bassinet safely installed in the sewing room where his parents could monitor his every breath.

The party itself was undoubtedly considered as a success by Julian and Margaret. All the family, visiting and resident, were present as were Tom and Carol and several key people from the mill office, the local Congregational minister and his wife, a local doctor and his wife, a local rancher and his wife, and two other families that operated sawmills in the county. There were, quite simply, a lot of people, nearly none of whom Isabelle knew.

She and Bradley found a hidden corner and, sipping their hardy bourbon highballs, made true to Julian's reputation, they commented amongst themselves about the guests, their clothes, their mannerisms, and their probable views of current affairs—it was all great fun.

Margaret seemed more than happy that her mother was effectively out of sight and making no ruckus. She left her in Bradley's care while she played the polished hostess and while little Walt slept in the now dark solarium, oblivious of the world around him and the strange people that populated it.

As the party was on a Friday, it went late, all a bit the worse for wear thanks to Julian's well-stocked and well-used bar. The next day everyone staying at The Big House arose with cobwebs in their head—everyone at least except Ann and Walt.

They had one final day to recover, absorb the bouquet of Margaret and her family, and suffer through absurd prattle—while honestly marveling at how well Margaret had adapted to a place she, as she herself proclaimed, still did not really like. Then, the next morning, after a good breakfast and an unsentimental goodbye to the other guests and Zelda, Isabelle and Bradley got into the Woody with Julian, Margaret, and Ann. They got to the station well in advance of the arrival of the southbound train and had a final coffee and final worthless chitchat (in Isabelle's view) before the train arrived and they got their seats for the relatively short trip to San Francisco, where they were spending a few nights. This time the goodbyes on the platform were emotional, even teary, with the little family waving from the side of the tracks until the train disappeared out of sight.

Julian released a great sigh, as though he had been holding his breath for days.

"That's that," he said, as he gave Margaret a great big hug and then the two of them wrapped Ann tightly in their arms. For her part, Ann was completely unsure of what had happened, but she enjoyed the attention.

Several miles down the track, Bradley let out almost a snort, and squeezed Isabelle's forearm.

"How about a hand of rummy, old girl?"

Back at the mill village, Christine gave Steve a peck on the cheek. "Boy, aren't we glad our kids don't have Mrs. Baker as a grandmother?"

Isabelle and Bradley had an enjoyable time in San Francisco—maybe a great time. After the high level of stress and frustration at Margaret's, each experiencing these distresses for separate reasons, their, albeit, short time in the City by The Bay seemed like a pressure valve had been released. They walked through China Town—visited the H. M. de Young Memorial Museum and the San Francisco Museum of Art. They ate with relish lunches at Original Joe's, Eddie Rickenbacker's, Tadic Grill, and Swan Oyster Depot (although Isabelle avoided the oysters, to Bradley's mock disgust), savoring dinners at Shadows, Cliff House, The Old Clam House, and Omar Khayyam's, and drinks at the Top of the Mark with more cocktails across the Bay in Sausalito. Bradley's old friend in this charming bay-side community took them for a picnic north into the Napa Valley.

They saw several movies, Isabelle's favorite, the film that had come out that very year, *King Solomon's Mines* with Stewart Granger and Deborah Kerr. Isabelle had thought the movie was about one of her special subjects; the ancient world, specifically Solomon, the son of David and King of Israel before the birth of Christ. Isabelle was surprised to find the movie's story being about colonial Africa; a quest across East Africa that showed many fascinating aspects of the countryside and the people of this land overseen by Britain. She noted from the credits, the film was based on a book written by Sir H. Rider Haggard in the 1880s. She marveled afterwards to Bradley how the United Kingdom had been able to amass an empire that started in the beginning of the nineteenth century and only now was beginning to unravel as pieces peeled away, starting with the independence of India nearly three years ago. Were not, she wondered to her husband, things better when human evolution was guided by the wisdom of the Empire?

When they boarded the sleeper car for the long trek back to Tucson, they felt that a good time had been had by all.

The trip home was uneventful, even the homecoming itself, as Maria had done an exceptional job of keeping all polished and ready for the boss. By Halloween they were back in their old routine. Dorothy had suggested, somewhere, Isabelle thought, between an order and request, that she come to spend Thanksgiving with her father—saying it was to help them start the season of this new decade. But really, Isabelle knew, it was to see how Bradley's health was holding up while trying to inveigle her way deeper into her father's psyche. Isabelle was against the idea from the start, strongly against it. She felt Dorothy was best taken in small doses and from a distance. Nonetheless, she realized she had to walk softly so as not to push her husband too hard—his possible reaction doing exactly what his wife did not want, just to show he was (he thought) the boss.

Isabelle had a flash of genius and booked rooms at the El Chorro lodge and restaurant in Paradise Valley, near Phoenix, for the twenty-second through the twenty-fifth November. She then told Bradley she had won a Thanksgiving Vacation in a lottery organized by her bridge club. The girls had all anted up for a really special prize and, lo and behold, Isabelle had won!

Most unfortunately, they had to let Dorothy know that they would be out of town on Thanksgiving and they would have to postpone her visit until the new year.

The reasons for the vacation notwithstanding, they had a very enjoyable stay at El Chorro. The management had really outdone themselves in the preparation of their Thanksgiving dinner, a combination of traditional American and Mexican fare, as Isabelle most flatteringly commented to Bradley. Bradley had thought for a moment of saying, "Mexicans are Americans, too." But decided this discussion would likely lead down an avenue that would, at the very least, put a damper on their pleasant sortie.

For her Christmas present, Bradley greatly surprised Isabelle with a trip to Hawaii. They had so many fond memories of the islands that he had booked another trip for the end of February. Isabelle was ecstatic.

Although the world was in no better shape in the new year, with the Second Battle of Seoul underway, the United States starting testing nuclear bombs in Nevada, and even long-standing parts of the British Empire like the Gold Coast lobbying for independence, it was a wonderful time to go to Honolulu. Bradley had really outdone himself and booked a room in the Lahaina Inn, right near the port and bay front of this old whaling town on Maui.

Even though the whaling history of Hawaii was only a hundred years old—not ancient like Isabelle's subject of choice—she did enjoy preparing for the trip by reading up on the history of whaling in the Pacific. She particularly enjoyed reading about the riots when whalers attacked missionaries, blaming them for an edict by traditional rulers prohibiting, as had previously been the custom, young local women from going out to the whalers to entertain the crew. *Tropical fruits*, she thought secretly, *ripe and ready, but kept from the table.* If these people had had the correct long view on things, they would have understood that the oldest profession was part of the fabric of all societies; part of one group using another, as it had always been through history. Isabelle noted, yet once again, how people are so often off target—all enthralled about one thing that is of only small importance, while they blindly march ahead not seeing the issues that are truly the fulcrums that allow societies to be moved.

Romantically, granting that romance at their age had a wholly different connotation, they spent Valentine's Day on the beaches of Lahaina. But romance was pushed back to the benches, as Isabelle was content to enjoy the sun, thinking of all those cold and miserable Februaries spent in the Midwest, while Bradley somehow got his wires crossed and was stuck in thoughts about being on a tropical island beach. These reflections somehow led him to contemplation about all the young men who had died on similar beautiful beaches across the Pacific during the war. Would he have braved the odds at the battles Iwo Jima, Guadalcanal, Okinawa, Midway, or in any of the scores of bloodbaths that occurred so recently in these tropical paradises?

Fortunately, neither Bradley's introspection nor Isabelle's circumspection put a real damper on their holiday. This was, in fact, one of the rare occasions when Isabelle could say she really had fun.

Isabelle truly enjoyed what she considered as the carefreeness of being a tourist. While she was far from the diehard housekeeper at home, when traveling, she did feel a responsibility to maintain a certain degree of order and propriety in her home-away-from-home—even if much of the actual work involved doing what was, in fact, supposed to have been done by others. With not so much as a minor outcry, she would make the bed after she and Bradley had risen and even use a soiled towel to perfunctorily dust or wipe out the bathtub.

Similarly, at home, she felt a responsibility to oversee Bradley's and her own health—doctors' visits, good food, vitamins, exercise, and all that. Yet, as a tourist, she felt almost liberated from these responsibilities. While they tried to exercise some self-control and were certainly more active than in those days sequestered in their Tucson garden, their diet was definitely expanded, both in terms of quantity and variety. They even, shockingly, skipped vitamins on several days. In spite of all, they remained in good form—chipper, as Isabelle would say.

Equally appealing, as a temporary visitor, a wayfarer, she was able to say pretty much anything she wanted to pretty much anybody she wanted— the chances of meeting up again with those involved in these chance en- counters so minimal that her modest aplomb could also be less controlling. Truly, it was all liberating.

Despite her high spirits as she and Bradley walked barefoot along the wave line or ate plates of delicious mahi mahi, it was soon over, by St. Pat- rick's Day they were back in the deserts of Tucson. Within two weeks, it was as though they had never left.

Over the years, they had witnessed a rapid growth of Tucson—many cold-landers like themselves seeking the dry warmth of the desert during the otherwise cold and unwelcoming months of winter and early spring in more northern climes. The newspaper said the town would soon reach 50,000. This was a quarter the size of Des Moines, and they had wanted to live in the calm serenity of a small town—not experience the growth of a getaway for New Yorkers and Chicagoans.

As that idiot, in Isabelle's educated view, Truman waged war, not only with Korea, but with that most honorable hero Douglas Mac Arthur (a sad event where the General clearly saw the real greater red threat that Truman, in his myopia, refused to accept), Isabelle and Bradley found themselves in their old routine of golf and painting.

They would still have their newspaper-reading combines in the gar- den. Just as the battle between Truman and Mac Arthur was reaching its crest, Bradley came to his garden station with an air of melancholy. As his anti-Truman sentiments were much milder than hers, Isabelle enquired as to the source of this unhappiness obviously generated by some story in the paper.

He explained that a sheriff in Florida had shot two black men who apparently had been unlawfully convicted of rape, their convictions over- turned by the Supreme Court. They had been in the sheriff's custody for the first trial, and he was transporting them from the penitentiary to undergo their new court-ordered trial when, according to the sheriff, they aggressed him and he had no recourse but to shoot the two handcuffed prisoners. In reporting the event, the journalists had provided some of the history, stating there had initially been four black men accused of raping a white woman—in addition to the two shot by the sheriff, one had been lynched before going to trial, and the other, a sixteen-year-old boy, was already serv- ing a life sentence. Bradley was incensed.

Amazingly, Isabelle's reaction was a total surprise to Bradley: she suggested they should plan a trip to Florida. They had not seen Anne for quite a while, and it was well in order to see about another train ride to Sarasota. She would contact Mabel to see if she could meet them there. It was time to get the old team together.

Bradley adjusted. He pivoted in his wife's direction, leaving his ill feelings about resolving racial problems in the background. He agreed it would be nice to see Anne again, suggesting they wait until autumn before going to the more humid Florida surroundings. This would allow them to enjoy the dry desert breezes over the summer months while giving Isabelle ample time to make all the arrangements to ensure that Anne was ready, and that Mabel could join them.

This presented Isabelle exactly what she needed (as Bradley knew) to add that extra spark to her daily pace. A plan to prepare—arrangements to make. She immediately set about the task, this a perfect complement to her day of painting, perching in the garden with her [their] papers, and guiding Maria, who remained largely an enigma in Isabelle's eyes.

Isabelle had established some level of personal relationship with Sally. After all, Sally was an American, even though she was black. Sally was an Iowan, even if her roots maybe still touched a far-off land. Sally had grown up speaking English, even if it was of a poor quality. She had known where Sally lived, what her family was like, what church she attended, and which was her favorite baseball team.

But Maria? Maria was essentially a foreigner who spoke a foreign language as her mother- and preferred-tongue. Isabelle had never been to her home or seen her family. She assumed Maria did not follow baseball because she was fundamentally not an American. She knew Maria was Catholic because all those people were Catholic—but she had no idea of where or how often she went to mass. As long as there was a stern hand as oversight, Maria did a good job. That was all Isabelle knew. That was enough.

Summer came into full stride as Isabelle fine-tuned their travel arrangements. They still shared their newspapers in the garden, often over a refreshing gin and tonic, noting the reports from the Great Flood of '51 that ravaged parts of the Midwest, the testing of an atomic bomb at Enewetok Atoll, and even the trial of those damnable traitorous Reds, Julius and Ethel Rosenberg. And in Korea, Isabelle's fair-haired Mac Arthur, who, with guts and resolve, had been ready to use the very same atomic bomb against the

Red Plague, was replaced by that nitwit in the White House with a General Ridgeway who, according to common, Isabelle thought, *very common*, press releases, had catalyzed the troops and they very ably met the Chinese Spring Offensive. After the battles of Imjin and Soyang Rivers and of Kapyong, the Reds were pushed back to north of the thirty-eighth parallel. This reinvigorated American military seemed to bring pause to the Northern aggressors, and the door for an armistice was opened. But, while the top representatives sat around the table, the soldiers continued to die in assaults that did not stop just because the talks had started. The clashes of Bloody Ridge, Punchbowl, and Heartbreak Ridge took lives, as resolution seemed as evasive as always.

Their garden remained their sanctuary where they would lay bare the bones of mankind's travails, somehow protected by layers of leafy vegetation, feeling they were invisible to the rest of the world, examining their environment as an astronomer might examine the cosmos through his telescope—with cool, detached objectivity, or so they felt.

Summer's end was in sight and within a fortnight they would get on the train east, destination Sarasota—both Anne and Mabel awaiting their arrival. Then, their analysis of current affairs would shift from the garden to Anne's veranda.

But, for the moment, they enjoyed their courtyard dissection of the news.

Isabelle smirked as she sipped her drink, reading in the *Citizen* that that day, September eighth, in San Francisco, forty-eight nations had signed a peace treaty with Japan—over six years after victory had been proclaimed. She remarked to Bradley how this was testament to the fact that politicians, chief among them that despicable Truman, dragged everything out for as long as they could to justify their presence. At least in this case, unlike more recently in Korea, hostilities had ended while the politicians went about their lackadaisical and often pointless tasks. They were certainly paid far too much to do far too little. They should be paid based on their intellect. That would be a solution. If that would happen, Roosevelt would have been paid two cents a month while a generous public might give Truman a nickel.

Bradley was detached. He offered nearly no rebuffing of Isabelle's emotive and, he quietly felt, frequently groundless tirades. Indeed, it was he and not she who replied to the topic of presidential pay with a pithy *humpf.*

He was literally off his game and he did not know why. He had not been on the links for over a week, finding himself embarrassed that he felt more comfortable sunning himself like a tabby than chasing his ball across the manicured course. He felt old. It was not pleasant, but it was unavoidable.

He no longer had the stamina to dive deeply into the *Citizen's* articles to try and find the hidden bits that really told the story. He did not have the energy to enter into gentlemanly debate with his wife over the sad, or otherwise, state of affairs of this great country. A warm seat and a cool drink seemed to be the most he could hope for. He was not weak, or as Isabelle might say, "puny", he thought, he was just tired. He would feel better when he was sleeping awash in the Florida air perfumed with oranges. He would get rested then.

But for now, there was no time to dawdle as Isabelle was at full speed ahead to get everything in order, bags packed, house prepared, Maria briefed, tickets purchased, and then getting settled in her sleeper for the nearly hypnotic ride serenaded by the song of the rails.

By the Autumnal Equinox, Isabelle and Bradley had regained their guest room at Anne's. They had received affectionate, even exuberant welcomes from Anne and Mabel with a slightly more-staid greeting by Violet. They soon adopted their typical cadence; initially days were spent on the veranda enjoying toddies and exchanging tales, then days spent touring various sites around the bay and inland, to marvel at the changes taking place in the land of Juan Ponce de León (Isabelle particularly awed by the changes one could scarcely imagine in the more than 430 years since de León's reported visit—this verging on ancient history), finally days spent in a kind of equilibrium state where each divided his or her time between quite personal time and more communal activities.

Bradley, heretofore the main impetus behind the evening happy hour as well as many of the outings to such places as the Ringling Estate or Roberts Bay, assumed a more subdued role. He was happy to sit in for a hand of Canasta or help clear the table, but he seemed more preoccupied and less adventurous. Most importantly to his housemates, he seemed, atypically, considerably less willing to engage Isabelle in debates on the hot topics of the day. Without his buffer, after a few stout cocktails, Isabelle was unfettered in her staunch and often colorful attacks on many of the changes in today's society.

Still, in spite of Isabelle's increasingly frequent outbursts and Bradley's impassivity, it could easily be said that all thoroughly enjoyed their time together. Cards, walks, meals, drinks—the days were full, and, between scorned politicians and misunderstood family members, there was never a shortage of tales to spin.

As winter announced her coming to northern regions, Sarasota became a harbor of warm delight—the fall temperatures at least ten degrees above the generally pleasant Tucson. They all spent a fun Halloween, playing a game of charades at which Isabelle excelled. As Thanksgiving approached,

Anne decided, with Violet's help, to put on a royal feast with all the fixings. They would stuff and roast a turkey, prepare homemade cranberry sauce, bake a pumpkin pie, and serve it all up with Brussels sprouts, mashed potatoes, and gravy. Isabelle, a reluctant participant in the kitchen, even agreed to make their mother's famous, if often unappreciated, bread sauce as an additional garnish to the resplendent menu.

By the week of the celebration itself, the house was full of delicious aromas that made all the residents wish they could partake of the gastronomy immediately. But the preparations continued. Anne wanted all to be perfect.

On the eve of the festivity, Isabelle awoke to delectable fragrances—the fresh waft from the garden coming through the open door to the veranda mixing with the bouquet of Violet's pumpkin pie baking in the oven and Anne's fresh coffee, undoubtedly waiting for the house guests on the kitchen counter. Bradley was on his side, sleeping away, she thought, oblivious to the pending pleasures to the senses the day offered. Isabelle reached over and shook his shoulder. It was like trying to move a log—rigid, not pliable, not astir.

Bradley was dead.

Isabelle screamed.

The three ladies rushed in, realizing immediately what had happened, shepherding Isabelle into the living room—Violet quietly calling for an ambulance, just in case.

Sadly, there was no reprieve. Bradley Baker had passed at the age of eighty.

8

After Bradley

As the reality set in, Isabelle set about dealing with the loss of her husband in her typical business-like way. She notified Dorothy and then Margaret. She contacted Bradley's lawyer, who was in Des Moines, learning that, a bit of a surprise to her, her spouse had wanted to be buried in that city where he had spent so much of his life.

Isabelle organized with local undertaker to make the necessary arrangements for the body to be sent to Des Moines by train, she would, of course, accompany her husband. She then set a date for the funeral as well as a time and place to meet with the lawyer for a reading of the will.

It was early December when she and Mabel boarded the train north— Bradley's casket in the baggage car. They were met in Des Moines by miserable weather and long faces. Dorothy and Lawrence were already there as were Percy and Helen. Margaret had said she could not travel with the baby and extended her condolences over the phone and in a lengthy letter she crafted for her mother.

The funeral itself as well as the graveside ceremonies were all accomplished with a minimum of confusion or hassle. Aside from the children, Mabel, and Sally, there were few in town still alive who had known Bradley Baker. His obituary was eight lines in the *Register,* starting almost with a disclaimer: One-time Des Moines resident. With little fanfare, Bradley Baker was laid to rest.

The same cannot be said after meeting with the lawyer. Dorothy, as Bradley's only living blood relative, expected to receive significant mention in her father's testament as well as in the distribution of his rather large estate. To her utter shock, her father had left everything, every single thing, to

Isabelle. Dorothy was speechless after the reading, fleeing the room in tears, Lawrence at her shirttails, returning immediately to Minneapolis without saying goodbye to anyone—particularly not to her stepmother.

Isabelle accepted her inheritance with equanimity.

Later that week, at the Wakonda Club, the lawyer's wife recounted to her chums how a fortune, ill-gained through the whiskey trade with Canada during prohibition, of some old big-time Des Moines businessman, had been stolen by his second wife out in Arizona, shunning the real family, and creating quite a stir.

Isabelle never spoke to anyone, even her daughter, about Bradley's inheritance. No one knew if she had had to play her cards adroitly or, if simply, the gods Tyche and Fortuna had smiled upon her.

Whatever road had been taken to reach the current situation, Isabelle lost no time in adjusting her life as a now spouseless aging female. After all the formalities, she had a dinner with Percy and Helen before they headed back to Chicago. She took Sally to lunch and spent several afternoons with Mabel. She did not visit her in-laws, much to Margaret's chagrin, but did take one last pass through the Wakonda Club herself to, in her mind, throw sand in the faces of the uppity ladies who spent their days there.

Tying up all these loose ends required staying in Des Moines until after the new year. Never very religious nor festive, Isabelle had always been indifferent about the Christmas holiday season. The real heart-felt sorrow she experienced at Bradley's totally unexpected death put even a greater dampening on her desire to do anything that remotely resembled celebration. She was both relieved and content to leave the city called the Hartford of the West and get back to Tucson.

Once home, she set in motion the next phase of her plan—a course of action upon which she had decided while still in Sarasota—promptly, after Bradley's passing. Everyone had cautioned her about making precipitous decision. She needed to be patient. She needed to let go of the pain. She needed to think clearly. She needed to make decisions slowly.

She was having none of this. She thought it might have been good advice for others, but it was not for her. She nearly immediately saw the course that lay ahead for her and she was in a hurry to get on with it, to put her past behind her, and to recreate, yet again, her life in the way she wanted.

She invited her acquaintances from Tucson to a lavish tea arranged by Maria. Over a redolent pekoe accompanied by delectable pastries, she announced her departure from the city to parts unknown—she saw no need to share her plans with people with whom she had shared so little of anything else. She felt she had no true friends here—really, no real friends anywhere if you discounted family—immediate and extended.

There was nothing keeping her in Arizona. She packed up her things. She sent some basics to Anne's so that she would have a base there. She then got a team of able-bodied movers to put everything else, from her painting studio to her under-used kitchen, in great packing drums that she put on the train west to Margaret's attention. It was only after the load of her personal effects was on its way that she called her daughter to inform her of the arrival at The Big House in about ten days of all her mother's affairs.

With no small degree of remorse, bundling her memories in her mind as she had her trappings in the packing drums, she contacted Pueblo Real Estate and put the house on the market. She sat silently in the garden with one last gin and tonic as the agent hammered in the "for sale" sign near the sidewalk in the front yard.

Isabelle then gave Maria a languid hug, picked up her old striped tweed suitcase, and got on the train to go back to Sarasota.

At Anne's, Isabelle spent a month wandering—a sleepwalker. She wandered about the house and garden at all hours while she mentally wandered about the recesses of her brain, trying desperately to objectively, unemotionally evaluate her place and time in, what some called, the Golden Years. She saw little gold, thinking of this period—keeping with the metallic metaphor— more as lead-lined: heavy, pulling one down, toxic.

She missed Bradley horribly. She was not sure if she loved Bradley—if she had ever loved Bradley. But he had been the center of her comfort zone for years. He unabashedly challenged her, he educated her, he made her laugh (although not often), and he made one helluva a cocktail.

She supposed she loved her children. After all, children were what one did. People got married and had children. But her children were no longer children. They were adults and they had gone their own ways—perhaps ways Isabelle herself would not have chosen—but she could accept this. They were there, they were her lydian stone, her guide, to take her to one of the many realties within which she lived. But they were not, and probably had never been, a critical part of her life—Bradley had been, though.

Somehow, through supreme stupidity or denial, she had ludicrously thought she and Bradley would live and play together for years to come and then, in some ill-conceived way, just be gone—together. Now you see them, now you don't. *Abracadabra alakazam.*

It was not to be so.

She accepted the facts. She did not cry—she almost never cried. She lamented her own stupidity for not preparing earlier for this inevitability. She was angry that she and Bradley had not discussed this unavoidable happenstance. She was sad Bradley was no longer at her side. Yet, most of all, she was afraid. For the first time in her life, she was nearly completely alone.

Of course, she was not alone. She had children, she had Anne, she had Mabel. She had had her brother, but he had died a year ago and she had not even gone to the funeral. She was not truly alone. There were many people who were completely alone. She was not. Nonetheless, this fact notwithstanding, she felt, deep down in her soul, totally alone for the first time.

After a month of disquiet and too much thought, she decided she needed to redefine her life. She needed to make herself over. She needed to construct a "new" Isabelle.

She was free of attachments. She had money. She had time. The new her would emerge from the chrysalis. But, not as a beautiful butterfly. She was far too self-conscious, all too aware of her lack of beauty by most standards. She would not be a splashy butterfly, but a humble grey moth—a run-of-the-mill moth miller. Common, unobtrusive, not liked by many, yet still able to fly.

And, she decided to do just that.

In her search for paths to follow, she had begun making regular visits to the Sarasota Bay Country Club to join the aristocratic crust in a rubber. Over the generation the Club had been in operation, it had established a reputation among many as *the place* to be. While Isabelle felt no affinity with the highborn, who considered themselves the blue-blooded gentry, all others simple interlopers, she did occasionally see value in their company. They could go places and meet people. They could open doors that would normally be closed to her. They could be a springboard if properly played.

As always, Isabelle was good at her game.

At the club, on a pleasant early spring afternoon, she found her bridge partner, reportedly an heiress of the John Hamilton Gillespie Family, and herself seated across from another grey-haired dame who claimed to be a cousin of the well-known, wealthy, and deceased Owen Burns, and her partner, a rather suave mature, to be kind, gentleman to whom she was introduced as Captain Scott. Isabelle's' shrewd card skills made her team the dramatic winners, in the process, illuminating a snapshot of Captain Scott's biography.

Captain Scott came from a New England seafaring family. He had gone to sea at a young age and worked his way up—above average intellect and energy, Isabelle remarked, undoubtedly greasing the skids for his advancement. By the beginning of the war, he had become the captain of a freighter running between New York and La Havre. As such, he had played a key role, as had so much of the merchant marine, in the Battle of the Atlantic. He had been part of the ill-fated Convoy HX229 which had been attacked by scores of German U-boats; twenty-two allied ships and 372 sailors lost. Now, however, Captain Scott had changed lanes. He still often had the pulsating deck of a ship under his feet, but he was no longer in command, no longer even a member of the crew. He now used his extensive knowledge of the world's ports to organize tours for small groups of elite tourists, going by luxury liner to some of the globe's most exotic places.

This tantalized Isabelle like few other things ever had.

She immediately set about gently infusing herself with the captain—using as much sedate charisma as she could muster under the circumstances. She invited him for cocktails to Anne's. She and Anne arranged an outing with him to Anna Maria Island. They even invited him to dinner to enjoy Violet's finest gumbo.

This was not seduction in the truest sense. Isabelle had had two husbands—that was more than enough. She was honest with herself about her age, her appetites, and her abilities. Marriage was definitely, unequivocally, not in her future. But she was convinced, travel could and should be. And, Captain Scott was, she felt, her ticket.

Isabelle found the good captain not one to be entrapped by some form of exaggerated emotional guise, but someone with whom one could build a relationship that should, through good business, benefit both parties. Isabelle could easily pay for her world travels, but she realized she needed a capable steward like Captain Scott to conduct the voyage and direct the voyagers.

Isabelle hoped Anne would be her travel mate, but Anne, with a helping hand from Violet, was completely content to watch Sarasota grow around her. Anne had, she herself believed, seen enough of the world; even the part she could watch closely from her veranda often seeming to be overwhelming.

Isabelle then thought of Mabel. The weather in Des Moines was still unpredictable and cool with spring more of a hope than a reality, so Isabelle had little difficulty of convincing her good friend to come down to Sarasota to enjoy a few weeks of lovely weather with Anne.

Mabel had not even unpacked her bag before Isabelle steered her to the Club and an elegant high tea service, which they shared with Captain Scott. Isabelle let the Captain expound upon the Mediterranean Voyage he had in mind—sailing from New York to Gibraltar and working their way around the north shore—Málaga, Barcelona, Marseille, Florence, Rome, Naples, Athens, and Nicosia—coming back via Palermo and Lisbon. It would be wonderful.

Mabel was stunned, but enthusiastic. Isabelle was enthralled. As Captain Scott described the destinations, her mind went back to her studies of the ancient world, realizing she was about to set foot in lands she had only read about. She was going to be able to see with her own eyes what only her imaginations had viewed. This would indeed be wonderful.

So it was. With little further ado, it was agreed. Captain Scott would identify four or five other passengers to join them—a small group of six or seven being cost effective for all concerned. Mabel would go back to Des Moines to get ready. The two ladies would meet the good captain in six weeks in New York—ready for a journey that would last two or three months, revealing many of the marvels of the ancient world as well as the splendor of today.

The voyage exceeded Isabelle's expectations. It was superb. Shipboard life was comfortable, her co-travelers generally of her ilk—educated, conservative, well-off, but not too ridiculously rich, hailing from middle America, and keeping largely to themselves. When in port, they had equally comfortable accommodation in three or four-star hotels accented by delicious meals in little out-of-the-way restaurants known to the captain. Onshore, they would sometimes go on outings as the whole group, getting into a rented Volkswagen bus that howled mightily going up hills leading to the hinterland. Other times, they would break into small groups, going off in different directions, using hired transport appropriate for their number.

Isabelle came prepared with a small trunk of carefully selected and cherished books describing the histories of her destinations. The tomes, covering the Greek and Roman empires, were easy to select—mirroring her area of academic specialization. It was like going back to visit old friends—really, Isabelle thought, far more pleasant than going back to visit old acquaintances, one dare not say friends, in Des Moines.

She selected works from the Greek historians Herodotus, Thucydides, Dionysius, Plutarch, and Arrian as well as those of the famous writers, Homer, Sophocles, and Euripides. She added selections from across the Ionian Sea including the great Roman historians Ovid, Horace, and Vergil—accompanied by the writers Livy, Sallust, and Tacitus.

As her adventure was starting in Gibraltar, she also needed to have literary backstops for her sojourn through the old Moorish lands called Al-Andalus. Flowing across the Straights of Gibraltar from Africa, the dark-skinned Moors had conquered the Iberian Peninsula, extending to Sicily, Malta, as well as parts of Italy and France. She knew the Moors—the *Maures* as the Romans called them—occupied these areas from 711 to 1492 when European Christians finally pushed them back onto the African Continent.

The crowning result of the long Christian-Muslim battle was called the *Reconquista*—the reconquest—the Christian's retaking of Spain and other European lands from the Islamist intruders. Unfortunately, finding historical records and writings of that period was considerably more difficult than accumulating her readings for Rome and Greece.

Rome had, Isabelle was aware, ventured into northwest Africa before the birth of Jesus. Thus, some of the history of Moors was recorded by Romans such as Silius Italicus. Isabelle found that King Alfonso of Spain had also contributed to the history of this period, as had the Muslim authors Ali ibn al-Athir and Ibn Abd al-Hakam. Eventually, she was able to amass a sufficient body of history to feel comfortable she could interpret well what she was to see—putting it in the proper historical perspective.

Isabelle did her literary homework in preparation for the journey at the Strozier and Goldstein libraries at Florida State University. Anne still had contacts on campus and friends in Tallahassee, so she was able to use the weeks leading up to her departure from New York to accumulate as much knowledge as possible.

As she had known in advance, it was the Moors who took most of her time. In the process of getting solid documentary works of the Moors' European colonization—it was, in truth, a colonization of Europe by Africa, ironic in the context of present-day geopolitics—she realized the Moors were ethnically a diverse group, reportedly including people from as far south as present-day Sénégal and Nigeria. As she moved through her research, she also came to realize that there were at least notations that a marked number of European nobility, artists, poets, and composers of the sixteenth to the nineteenth centuries, were reported to be "mulattos"—observers of the time attributing this "mixed blood" to the lingering influence of the Moor's presence.

Isabelle's throat tightened a bit as she read about the racial conundrums—these from Europe covering 800 years—significantly longer than the United State's ongoing uncertainties as to how to deal with different skin colors. Isabelle thought Bradley would have loved this discussion. She did miss him.

Isabelle's chest of books endowed upon her the mantle as historian for their little group of pilgrims. She took up the mantle begrudgingly. She had no desire to spoon-feed her co-travelers. She was here to enjoy herself, not educate others. But the captain was insistent, and Mabel was convincing, so she agreed to impart on her clique of voyagers basic background information in the hopes this would expand their appreciation of what they were seeing and where they were walking. This instruction most often took the form of a gathering around a table in a bar or café on quiet evenings when her co-excursionists plied her with wine while she spun tales about their locale, attempting to avoid mundane academic detail—trying to emphasize why these ancient stories and places had an impact on today.

Isabelle was uncomfortable in her role as part-time educator. She had not signed on for this. She hated teaching. But, in the end, it was a very sympathetic group with a great thirst for not only alcohol, but also knowledge. It was alright.

By the time the group reached Florence, they had established a kind of equilibrium—almost like an extended family, Isabelle thought. Though, she was the first to admit she was a poor judge of how well an extended family worked.

In truth, perhaps, she concluded, as she dug deeper into the grey corners of social analysis, their group was not functioning as a typical extended family, whatever that might be, but more as her own rather protracted family. Percy and Margaret had, and always had had, their own separate lives with only sporadic, frequently superficial, contact with their parents. Bradley had had a very similar relationship with Dorothy. This embracing-at-arms-length kinship was probably a good descriptor of the links within the touring group.

As would be expected, she and Mabel had a very close, almost sororal, rapport. The two ladies also felt a strong alliance with Captain Scott. However, with the other globetrotters—a Chevrolet dealer and his wife from Fort Wayne, a semi-retired ophthalmologist and his real-estate-dealing wife from Dayton, and, a recently widowed, and out-to-pasture, as Isabelle saw it, Presbyterian cleric from Grand Rapids—there was kind of a standoffish affiliation. The other five, as Isabelle and Mabel called them, were, as with a family, partners, willing, or otherwise. They most often shared the same lodging and meals, commiserated over the same debacles, were rained upon by the same storms, and offered a helping, even if fretful, hand to one another.

It was mid-August, Isabelle sat in her deck chair, scribbling notes after a thoroughly enjoyable visit to Palermo, as she felt the deep throb of the ship and the sea as they slowly plowed through a low swell *en route* to Lisbon. They were past their starting point, through the Pillars of Hercules, and on to the culmination of their circle through the Mediterranean. The journey had been memorable. She wondered why she and Bradley had not embarked on such an adventure years before. But she was not one to dwell upon the *should have's*. It had been a good decision to put her confidence in Captain Scott and follow him to the furthest reaches of the globe's largest inland sea.

Onward and upward.

A month later, a few days before her daughter's thirty-sixth birthday, Isabelle descended the gangway of the Cunard Line's *Caronia*, walked down Pier Ninety-two on the Hudson River, exiting in Manhattan from the New York Port Authority's Passenger Terminal with Mabel—already ready for the second act in the theater of her worldly exploits.

But it was now time to deal with the present before planning the future—albeit, the future was not that far off. Mabel had to spend some time in Des Moines to address many more pending issues than she would have liked. Isabelle decided to accompany her, spend a few days poking around her old haunts; then going up to Chicago to see Percy for a few days before swinging out west to see how Margaret and baby Walt were doing before returning across the breadth of the country to regain her bed at Anne's. From her Sarasota base, she would plan the next phase necessary to fulfill the demands of her new-found wanderlust.

Isabelle's loop through her past worked out just about as she had expected.

Much of Des Moines had changed to the point she no longer recognized the city. She made no specific efforts to reconnect with her old crowd. She visited the Wakonda Club one afternoon and did play a hand of bridge, but with people she met for the first time—her old crew seemingly long gone. Mabel had a tea party, inviting those long-time comrades who may have considered themselves as Isabelle's friends (regardless of how Isabelle had seen the relationship). Only a few managed to attend—most unavailable or dead. Over the full-bodied Earl Grey and the homemade oatmeal-raisin cookies, those who shared Mabel's living room shared very little else. It was clear that their lives had taken completely different paths—those still at home too jealous or indifferent to even ask Mabel and Isabelle about their voyage, although all apparently knew all too well of the ladies' adventures through an amazingly active scuttlebutt labyrinth that targeted Hawkeyes, past and present.

This was all of no surprise to Isabelle. As was so often said, and Isabelle again recalled, "You can't go back." And, she did not want to. She had turned the page.

Then, on to Chicago—Percy and his family were fine. Percy was busy, busy, busy. Helen was flustered with high cost of living in a high-end neighborhood of Chicago, unhappy with the schools, the roads, the public transport, the crime, and the weather.

Moving westward, Margaret was hot and cold. She was happy to see her mother, did not want her mother's visit to stress out her husband who was spending ten hours a day in the mill trying to get things up to snuff, was worried about the social skills of Ann, and the overall health of Walter, and very definitely did not want to talk about Bradley. Whereas Percy and Helen had simply not had time to listen to Isabelle's recounting of her wonderful Mediterranean trip, when Ann was at school, Walt taking a nap, and Julian was at work, Margaret was stuck, for better or worse. Whether out of a feeling of filial obligation, or out of real interest, Margaret herself was unsure of her true motives, she did sit with her mother in the solarium with cups of coffee and the exceptional cigarette and listen to Isabelle effusively describe her voyage from beginning to end.

When all was said and done, Margaret was happy for her mother. She herself had no desire to travel—already coming from Iowa out west was more than enough for her for a lifetime. For Margaret, if her family was healthy and happy, she could ask for no more. But she saw a fire in her mother's eyes, for the first time in many, many years. She listened, she hoped attentively, as her mother described how thrilled she had been to set foot on foreign lands, places she had previously only studied. She sat, respectful and quiet, as her mother declared how she had also thoroughly enjoyed the preparations for the travels; the research and collection of her little trunk of books, even the dealings with the travel agents, cruise lines, and hotels.

Over several days, interspersed with the rapid-fire day-to-day work of a young mother with a toddler as well as the duties of the household supervisor, over many cups of coffee and really only a few cigarettes, mother and daughter sat in the warmth and brightness of the solarium, reliving, more for the benefit of the traveler than the spectator, the marvels of seeing sites and hearing sounds that echoed over more than two thousand years. Isabelle enjoyed seeing the present, but she was in awe of the past. The accomplishments of those ancient civilizations were stunning—it was even more amazing to be able to touch what remained up to today. Those long-past times had been wondrous times—Isabelle's studies had been authenticated and justified. How many of today's artifacts, she wondered, would be available to the casual traveler in two thousand more years?

Tales told, family embraced, Isabelle was soon on the train east. She was appreciative of the time she had been able to spend with her daughter. She had scarcely seen her son-in-law; her granddaughter too was largely absent—whether at school or sheltered by choice in her room with her books and dolls. Ironically, despite Margaret's significant duties, Isabelle was able to see more of, talk more with her daughter than she had in years. Baby Walt was really the only competitor for her time—needing a warm bottle, a hot bath, or a fresh diaper.

Isabelle was heading to the great hub of Chicago from where, without calling on Percy, she connected with a southbound train that would ultimately get her back to Anne. By the time she had reached Anne's, she had a new plan well sketched in her mind. They would embark on an around-the-world tour. It would be wondrous! She would work with Captain Scott and they would imagine a terrific itinerary that would carry them around the globe.

Isabelle dove head first into her project of the moment. She had just seen much of the north side of the Mediterranean, so logically she should start at what had been left out—the south side. She wanted to add some adventure, using her favorite films as benchmarks. The 1942 Bogart-Bergman film *Casablanca* was not only dramatically excellent, but it enticed her to visit the city much as her infatuation with *King Solomon's Mines* made it a foregone conclusion that she would make it to East Africa.

Isabelle sat with Anne at the dining room table, the *Encyclopedia Britannica Atlas* open between them, charting routes through the lands of Arabs and Berbers, the Masai and the Kikuyu, Hindus and Buddhists, the Lua and the Kachin, the Tamil and the Mahuri—inspired yet again at the diversity that occupied their planet.

Starting at Casablanca, hoping it was as beguiling as portrayed by Bogie's character, Rick, they mapped a passage including Tunis, Tripoli, Alexandria with a sojourn up-river to Cairo, Mombasa with a ride on the rails to the interior and Nairobi, Bombay, Ceylon, Burma, Siam, Hong Kong, Taipei, Tokyo, and continuing by sea on to New York via Honolulu and the Panama Canal. It was not exactly the trail of Phileas Fogg in Jules Verne's 1873 adventure novel *Le tour de monde en quatre-vingts jours*, but it was awfully close.

Once she had outlined her thoughts, Isabelle set about locating Captain Scott. He was a regular in Sarasota, but she did not know where else he stayed nor when he planned to be in town. He was the quintessential wayfarer. His permanent address was in New York City, a town house in Hell's Kitchen—a neighborhood known for its proximity to the port and its reported affinity for post-prohibition organized crime. The town house was the residence of his Liverpudlian uncle on his mother's side. Contrary to first impressions of his surname, the captain was not a Highlander, but was the product of lowland English gentry with deep roots. He was always on the move, either shepherding a group of excursionists, preparing for a voyage, or recovering from one.

Isabelle wrote to him in Manhattan, saying she was seriously planning a new jaunt, and asking could he kindly get in touch.

He replied with a phone call to Anne's, saying he would be in Sarasota in a week's time and would enjoy meeting Isabelle, and Anne if available, for lunch at the Club.

Sitting in the quiet elegance of the Sarasota Bay Country Club, it was an easy sell to hook the captain on a rerun of the nearly-Fogg expedition. It was ambitious. It was, in some ways, risky. It was long. But, as the captain summed up, it would be, "One helluva of a time."

It was almost Christmas. Captain Scott said, with luck, they could hope for sailing after Easter. There was a lot to do.

That year, Easter came just after April Fool's. Toward the end of the month, later than they had hoped—on the day that Watson and Crick published their pioneering work explaining their discovery of DNA, a little over a month after Nikita Khrushchev was named First Secretary of the Soviet Communist Party, two months, more or less, after transgender actress, Christine Jorgensen returned to the United States after sex-change surgery, as the Korean War dragged on with no armistice, as witnessed by the ongoing Battle of Hill Eerie, and only a fortnight after Jomo Kenyatta was imprisoned for fanning the flames of independence—Isabelle met Captain Scott on the deck of the *Georgic*, ready for a second transatlantic voyage. She was, to her great relief, accompanied by Mabel. Her cousin, and dearest friend, had vacillated. Did she really want to embark on a foray that could last six months or more? Could she afford it? Could her septuagenarian body handle such an engagement? But, in the end, she was as excited about going as Isabelle.

Captain Scott explained to the ladies that already onboard were two young couples; not seventy-somethings like the three of them, but mere puppies in their mid-sixties. The Andersons were a great couple; Mr. Anderson had recently retired after years working for the city of Rapid City, South Dakota. The Meriweathers were great folk too, just a little reserved. He had had a stationary store in Fayetteville, Arkansas, for years; the store was now run by their son. Mrs. Meriweather had been a high school teacher in the city up to her retirement. All told, Captain Scott assured his, by now, lady friends, it was a good group setting off on a wonderful once-in-a-lifetime around-the-world adventure.

Captain Scott's projections proved true and the journey unrolled before them like a well-written book, Isabelle anxious to turn every page. Whereas the voyage on the north side had more-or-less kept them in European cultures and peoples, the passage on the south side was totally distinct.

From the onset, it was different cultures and peoples. Casablanca, and of course Morocco, were Muslim. The people mostly of varying shades like old shoe leather, but quite un-European in their appearances and actions—although, as Isabelle remarked to her group, the impact of European culture was ubiquitous. Then, like fertilizer slowly moving up the roots of an Iowa corn plant, the excursionists moved eastward into progressively more, as Isabelle saw it, authentic cultures and peoples. Cultures whose actions were far removed from what might be considered as European norms. People, getting darker and darker, wearing stranger and stranger garb, speaking more and more fantastic languages; the people were wholly un-European. It was intriguing, at times almost titillating, and at times daunting. But it was always as though she were looking through a prism. Even though she was physically among these peoples and in these cultures, she felt she witnessed them from afar.

By the time she found herself seated on the train from Mombasa to Nairobi, she was beginning to feel overwhelmed as to how diverse, almost chaotic, the world was. While the first-class car was filled with a lot of white colonists, she was, in general, awash in a sea of black faces, wearing never before seen garments, speaking languages she had never heard, eating never before tasted (nor after, Isabelle assured herself) foods—and, all looking, indeed staring, at her. It was wondrous. It was intimidating. It was all she had hoped for.

As they moved further eastward, as though following Fogg's balloon, the skin tones and the language tones changed; the foods, the clothes, and the buildings mutated. But it was all as strange as it was wonderful.

This was an odyssey, much like, Isabelle imagined, Ulysses' fabled journey of that name when he traveled home after the fall of Troy—his journey greatly affected by the advice of others—Isabelle seeing this as her epic voyage after the loss of Bradley—also influenced by others, as well as by factors beyond her control. Often, in alien settings, whether the North African Desert or the inner-city throngs of Bombay, she felt she was moved by the waves of humanity of which she was a voluntary member, if an inarticulate observer.

Her membership, however, Isabelle thought was that of an emeritus witness. She, and perhaps she alone (at the very least, she among a few), had seen and was able to look at humanity from detached altitudes—raised to these lofty levels by her rare powers of reason, her fine education, and having lived a perspicacious life whose passages had led her to a plenitude of people—the good and the bad.

Isabelle thought of herself as Egeria, the female pilgrim of the fourth century. She smiled inwardly as she saw how appropriate the link to Egeria was—this also being the name of the ancient Roman water nymph who was a valued counselor, appreciated for her wisdom and prophecy. This comparison, in turn, bought a smirk to her face as she thought of the painting, *The nymph Egeria dictating the laws of Rome to Numa Pompilius*, by the recently departed Spanish painter Ulpiano Checa. While she hoped she shared the wisdom, she knew all too well her body in no way reflected that attributed to the nymph.

She then recalled one of Bradley's favorite lines to punctuate his thoughts, "Who gives a damn?"

As in their first travels, sometimes Isabelle and Mabel would strike out on their own, sometimes they would seek the company of Captain Scott, and other times the whole squad would navigate together.

The Andersons and Meriweathers proved to be pleasant enough. Each in their own way, they seemed most motivated to have new and unique experiences—likely, Isabelle guessed, experiences they could polish and embellish when recounting to neighbors and family over cocktails, at Elks' meeting, or a barbecue. This, perhaps shallow rationale aside, the two couples endured the inevitable travails with poise and respected the privacy and individuality of the other members of their team.

By the time Captain Scott escorted the crew through customs in Siam, they really were a cohesive group—getting along well together through a strategic mixture of encouraging both quality communal effort and personal time throughout their nomadic days. Normally a group only moves ahead at a speed equal to the speed of its slowest member. In this case, however, the group moved ahead at a quicker pace, the dawdlers or those feeling out-of-sorts pushing themselves in order not to frustrate their colleagues.

The world they visited was intoxicating, but in turmoil. They did not stop in Algeria, sailing by since the climate was very unstable as local groups tried to shed French colonial rule. Kenya, with the start of the Mau-Mau Uprising, was only slightly more stable. While India had been independent for seven years and Ceylon along with Burma free of colonial control for six years, these countries were still in transition periods that led to considerable flux—both in their politics and in their tourist industries.

With all that was changing and metamorphosing around her, Isabelle felt she was witnessing the world while sliding down a knife's edge, seeing glimpses of both past and present with clouds offering imperfect views of what could be the future. She felt on the cusp—she wished she were sharing this, in some ways revival, with Bradley.

Bradley's absence was all the more poignant when, belatedly, she got news of finally an agreed-to armistice for Korea. According to reports in the *Herald Tribune*, this was still not a peace treaty—the warring parties were still in talks. The Korean Peninsula had been split since 1948—a by-product of the Cold War and inane Democratic politics. From 1950 to 1953 the United States had flushed this distant land with American blood. According to the paper, a total of over 36,000 killed and more than 92,000 wounded. All this loss and still the egregious parties, the losers, refused to formally capitulate. And the leaders, the Democrats, just blithely went ahead leaving this Red abscess in the country's side.

And, at what a price?

True enough, there was now, at long last, a much-needed Republican in the White House. Eisenhower was surely the kind of man one wanted as a leader—he was a tried and proven commander. But he had to try and reset the clock after years and years of Democratic shenanigans and mismanagement. It was no small task and it would take him months if not years to get things back on the right track. These were difficult days.

Isabelle thought back to the old days when wars were quick and simple. She remembered, before she had been born, that where Margaret was now living, there had been an Indian uprising over eighty years ago: the Modoc Indian War. She recollected, in the garden in Tucson, reading in the *Atlantic Monthly* that this insignificant war had resulted in about fifty deaths and eighty wounded. Now that is the way wars should be fought, she thought—keeping the thought to herself as Mabel was far too liberal and close-minded to be able to have a real discussion about war and peace or politics and sanity. She missed Bradley.

Their journey continued. At times she thought of it like those black-and-white news films they showed in the movie theaters during WWII—the real war. She could hear the whirling and clicking of the projector and see the flickering of the images, many scratched or out of focus—but still incredibly important. Her days and her voyage were flickering by.

Two days after Columbus Day, when Isabelle and Mabel once again walked down Pier Ninety-two, the rust and golden fall leaves presented such a splendid tableau that Isabelle briefly wished she were back in her Tucson studio, putting what she was seeing on canvas. But as quickly as her sea legs left her, she was ready for something, yet unsure what.

Almost on a whim, but with more consistency, she decided—she and Mabel should immediately go to the Adirondacks to savor the Northeastern Autumn, digest their just-finished around-the-world thriller, and get some much-needed rest in a calm and serene environment. Mabel agreed, more because she was afraid of what was awaiting her in Des Moines after such a long absence than out of a love for fall foliage or a need to relax in bucolic upstate New York.

The two elderly compatriots, irrespective of their motives, enjoyed the near reclusion of the Adirondacks. After all the hustle and bustle of traveling combined with the chaos of a world changing faster than it could adopt and adapt, the almost doleful stillness was cathartic; slowing their momentum, internalizing their thoughts, bringing the here and now into clearer focus. They spent a fortnight, looking for, and finding a certain harmony that seemed to revitalize them, giving each the stamina necessary to move ahead and look for new challenges. Albeit, these now seemed anticlimactic after the fascination and hardships of circumnavigating the globe—witnessing never before seen places, experiencing never-imagined scenes, thinking heretofore undreamt-of thoughts.

After their respite, they traveled together as far as Cleveland, Mabel continuing west to Chicago and on to Des Moines while Isabelle headed south to Pittsburg and onward to Sarasota. It was nearly All-hallows Eve when Isabelle rejoined her sister and then spent the next seventy-two hours regaling her with detailed tales of travel to parts of the world that the erudite Anne only recognized as obscure references, never places her own sister would visit.

For anyone three-quarters of a century old, a world tour would be considered as a harrowing accomplishment—not to mention someone who went to the what many would see as the outskirts of civilization. Yet, Isabelle was not especially fatigued. She was certainly not exhausted. More than feeling drained, she felt saddened that the trip was over. New and exciting events day after day had been a terrific boost—prompting her to get up early, be active all day, and even go to bed late. It was as though she had been a perpetual motion machine that was now in neutral—its wheels still spinning but going nowhere. She found herself back in the routine of the aging. Not only did each day offer monotony rather than adventure, but there was no reason to get up early—no special reason not to take a nap. She could sit on the veranda all day, enjoy Violet's excellent cooking, and go on as though she had nary a worry in the world—and in that routine, she reasoned, there were, in fact, few worries other than not waking up one day.

She did endure a period of quiescence while she took care of her chores in the refuge of Anne's most pleasant abode. She wrote letters to family and friends—those few people she still considered as friends, that is. She wrote to her solicitor, her banker, and her broker. She made appointments, much to her distaste, with a dentist and an internist. She even went shopping, not because she enjoyed it or wanted to dress in fashion, but simply because the journey had been tough on her clothes. In point of fact, she hated shopping for necessities (for unique mementoes, it was OK) and had special ill feelings for buying clothes. She felt every adult should be able to get a suitable wardrobe once that would last them a lifetime—anything more was either waste or preening, or both—each a severe misdeed in Isabelle's eyes. Nonetheless, her thinking on attire aside, her clothing had been washed all too often by overly energetic launderers using severe scrubbing methods and old-fashioned lye soaps. As a result, many of her garments were literally threadbare.

Regardless of the long list of to-do's, with the new year, she had all her affairs in order, had filled-in all her family, had refreshed her wardrobe, and even had a clean bill of health from the doctor and the dentist. It was time to seriously plan the next step, which she was sure would involve traveling somewhere to do somethings exciting—something someone, anyone, needed to do before they turned eighty.

Isabelle decided the only cure for her frustration was to take another world cruise. She immediately devoted her energies to scrutinizing options, identifying "must see" places, and looking into how one got from here to there. It was a repeat performance of her preparations for her just-finished expedition, but, more challenging as there were now places she had seen and would not want to see again—she was turning into a real-world traveler, having to carefully select new destinations.

Anne supported her little sister, but with no small dose of trepidation. Isabelle was, she knew, in amazingly good health for someone her age. She had low blood pressure and good lungs—perhaps a testament to taking good care of herself—but, also a benefit of longevity in the family as she herself was doing well in her advanced years. All this notwithstanding, one could not and should not discount the impact of over seven decades of hard living. For example, she knew her sister's knee bothered her—she had been shot accidentally by a neighbor with his pellet gun over sixty years ago and the old wound was now making itself felt, especially in cold weather. And this was just an example. Who knew how well she was actually doing? She was not a complainer and she would certainly not confide in anyone, not even her sister, if she thought she had serious health problems.

Nevertheless, Anne knew Isabelle would do what she wanted regardless of the positions of others—it was simply best to be supportive.

And, as Anne also knew she would, Isabelle devoted herself totally to planning what she saw as her last (maybe) hurrah.

Isabelle saw Captain Scott from time to time when he was in town—mostly at The Club. She had apprised him of her plans. He was guardedly encouraging, not being put off by the dreams of an old lady. He had seen Isabelle in action for too long, in too many varied and difficult circumstances, to discount her ability to once again encircle the globe.

Isabelle's plans were beginning to take form. Unlike previous trips, she was planning on flying Pan Am's Rainbow Service to London, crossing the channel to Paris and boarding the Orient Express to Istanbul. They would then continue through Turkey to Ankara, ending in the port of Antalya where they would take a steamer to Beirut and then on to Haifa, traveling inland to Jerusalem, continuing south to the port of Eilat which had come into prominence during the Arab-Israeli War of 1948. They would sail down the Red Sea to Jeddah, visit Mecca before continuing around the Arab Peninsula to the Shah's Iran and the port of Bander-e Abbas. From the coast, they would travel overland to the foot of Mount Kuh-e Rahmat to the unique ruins of the ancient palaces of Persepolis. These splendid structures had been started by Darius in 518 B.C.—the construction continued by his son Xerxes, and his grandson Artaxerxes. They would then cross the Arabian Sea to the Indian Ocean, sailing to the British Protectorate of the Sultanate of Maldives for a short break before continuing eastward to Java, the Philippines, and finally the Gilbert Islands before, as previously, ending in Honolulu.

This was a true marriage of the two previous voyages, while visiting completely new places. The first voyage had been rather conservative, focusing greatly on the historical value of the ports of call—especially their places in ancient history in regard to the Roman and Greek Empires. The second voyage had been an exploration, visiting exotic sites, relishing in the planet's diversity. Now, Isabelle had sewn these together into a tapestry that was a mix of both the historic and the exotic. Her nerves were already on edge in anticipation when, just after Ascension Day, she shared her itinerary with Captain Scott over tea at the Club.

The captain was more than a little impressed with Isabelle's work. It would be a long and complex itinerary, but one few had had the imagination to concoct. Her excitement was contagious, and he began to think of the practicalities to be addressed before one could realistically think of embarking on such an ambitious journey.

He and Isabelle had been going back and forth on the minutia built into the route—this one much more elaborate than Mr. Fogg's. There were so many pieces. He was not sure they all fit—regardless of all the hard work Isabelle had put into shaping them.

It was just after the Fourth of July, they were engrossed in timetables and accommodation, with only mild expectations of being able to depart before winter, when everything fell apart. Isabelle received a call from Helen. Percy had died. One day, just like so many others, he was getting ready to go to the bank when he just fell over. The ambulance crew pronounced him dead when they arrived. He was forty-six years old—so much for thoughts about longevity in the family.

Isabelle, with Anne at her side, went immediately to Des Moines where they picked up Mabel and went directly to Chicago where they had rooms at the Palmer House. It had been just sixteen years ago that she and Mabel had come to Chicago to celebrate the Fourth with Percy and Helen, just after George's death—in their wildest imagination, they had never thought they would be back because of a death in the young family. Percy was an up-and-comer. He was full of life and full of promise. Now, he was gone.

Margaret, adoring sister, joined the ladies at the Palmer House—Julian staying back to oversee familial and professional responsibilities. It was a dismal time. It was filled with melancholy, weeping, and fond memories that were all the more outraged because of the youthfulness of the departed.

Margaret was dumbstruck. She was barely coherent between sobs. Anne and Mabel shed their tears and then were somber, as much for the unfortunate present and for the inevitable future. Isabelle remained dry-eyed throughout. She had a hollowness—a great weight that tried to crush her heart—but she would not whimper. The forces that had taken George and Bradley, had now snatched Percy, would not beat her. The forces would come, of course, but they would come on her terms, not theirs. She would not let them.

For all that, Isabelle knew all too well, felt all too well, the truth of aging. Nenia Dea, the Roman funeral goddess, waited for all.

Isabelle, Anne, and Mabel were, at the end, all companions with death. They had all come to grips with the reality that it was part of their future, maybe their very near future. But a young man, with a young family, who had not even reached fifty, this was just wrong. They knew life was not fair, but this was ludicrous. Dare one talk about the sanctity of life, about God's Love? This was not a group that solemnly celebrated a man's life. This was a group full of anger that wept bitter, irreconcilable tears. To the end, Isabel refusing to accept the droplets that streaked her cheeks.

Five days later, when the four women left a crestfallen Helen with two children on the platform as the train pulled out for Des Moines, the anger was still palpable.

Margaret accompanied the three older women to visit her in-laws in Des Moines before returning west. Isabelle still kept Julian's family at arm's length, so she and her daughter said goodbye at the train station—she and Anne spending one night with Mabel before going on to Sarasota.

It was the latter part of August before Isabelle was able to come to some sort of partial acceptance of Percy's death and, as she liked to say, "Pull up her boot straps," and get on with life. For her, getting on with life meant getting on with her planned excursion.

Labor Day was late that year, September sixth, and it was only after this holiday that Captain Scott was due back in town, after a brief stint in New York. But once Isabelle was able to get him seated in front of her, she set the hook, laying out a meticulous program leading up to their target departure for Istanbul before Palm Sunday—204 days to make all the arrangements and get on the plane for London. She was committed.

To the supreme consternation of all, especially Captain Scott, they were able to maintain the schedule sketched out by Isabelle. Six weeks after President Eisenhower sent military advisors to Vietnam and a day after April Fools', some wondering who the fools were, Isabelle, Mabel, and Captain Scott met at Idlewild Airport. Here the captain introduced the two ladies to their new traveling companions. There was Theodora—a widow ten years Isabelle's junior, an heiress to fortune from a large sporting goods manufacturer, a wearer of floppy feathery hats, and someone who liked to be called "Teddy". There were the Simpsons, ranchers from Wyoming whose children now ran the ranch while they gallivanted about. Finally, there was Seth, a widower of about Isabelle's age who had spent his whole life establishing and managing an upscale jewelry store in Manhattan. He had done very well and just sold his business for a small fortune, part of which he was investing in this trip.

There seemed to be no immediate electric shocks of antipathy among the travelers, so Captain Scott patted himself once again on the back for having assembled the right people for the job at hand.

They had a good flight, Isabelle and Mabel's first long distance passage by air, landing in London the day after they left New York. They spent a few days in the city before crossing the channel. During this time, Prime Minster Churchill resigned his office at the age of eighty. This touched a spot too close for comfort for Isabelle, who secretly was always a bit unsure her health would hold out during these sometimes-tough travels. But she reassured herself, this was no time for second thoughts.

Nine weeks later, as they sailed down the Red Sea, Isabelle thought back to those few days in London and was thankful she had managed to carry on, as the journey so far had been, at the very least, challenging. But the sites and experiences were up to par with her earlier cruises and the group was also equally tolerable. Tedious Teddy, as Isabelle thought of her, proved to be a real talker, entering too often into one's private space, but basically an alright kind of person. Seth was as stalwart a traveler as he must have been a businessman—never complaining, always upbeat. The Simpsons were stoic, almost as one envisioned ranchers to be in a good Western—like

Gary Cooper in *High Noon*, the smash hit for which he won an Oscar two years earlier. They were there, they seemed to always be there. They said little—never moaned, but also rarely openly admired places or peoples.

Regardless of the impressions of her mates, Isabelle continued to be spellbound by one fantastic event or place after another. She found herself in places she had never dreamed she could ever be. She found herself experiencing situations she never could have imagined. She was, once again, bewitched by the journey. When, just a week after another Labor Day, she finally walked down the gangplank in Honolulu with a spring in her step, she was ready to start all over again.

Mabel said if she did, she would do it alone.

Airplanes were now an accepted part of their routine, so Mabel and Isabelle flew to Chicago to pay Helen a visit and see how all the family was doing, now over a year after Percy's death. As was becoming their habit, Isabelle then accompanied Mabel to Des Moines, spent a few days in old familiar places before heading back to Anne and Sarasota.

From Anne's perspective, this was a rerun of Isabelle's last return. Her sister was intense, almost jumpy, as she recounted the many unbelievable places they had seen, people they had met, food they had eaten, and sounds they had heard. She retold events in unequivocal, and colorful, detail—savoring each moment. She then fell into the doldrums as the inevitability that it was over sunk in. She was back. She was in Sarasota. There was no train to catch, no bag to pack, no porter to tip, no taxi to hail, no hotel to find. There was only Violet's good cooking, good weather, and quiet—none of which assuaged the void that Isabelle was now feeling almost painfully.

The world continued to behave in its frenetic ways—over recent months an El Al flight from Vienna to Tel Aviv was shot down with all on-board lost, there were anti-French riots in Morocco and Algeria, and a massive hurricane had just hit Mexico. But Isabelle seemed jaded by the very topics that had so recently stirred her blood. She was nearly in a stupor.

Anne was concerned, but uncertain as to the actual problem. She had heard and read of people who were high on adrenaline, people whose nerves were stretched to the breaking point by war, misfortune, or great excitement. People who had done heroic, superhuman things in the heat of the moment—things they could never have accomplished under normal circumstances. Was this Isabelle's problem? Had she kept herself hyped-up on adrenaline and taut traveler's nerves to make it through the journey? Had she overcome the apparent disadvantages of age by sheer force of will? Was she now physically recovering from months of terrific stress? Or, was she simply still wanting to feel the world move beneath her feet? She asked their long-time doctor, Dr. Harvey, but he had no clue as to the real cause of Isabelle's frump—if she were indeed in a frump. His best advice was lots of sleep, good food, and serenity. At least, Anne thought, this prescription would be easy to fill at her house.

Nonetheless, Anne continued to worry. Isabelle continued to stare into space. Violet continued to clean and cook.

A distraction was needed. Anne began plans for an elegantly simple Thanksgiving, hoping this would bring her sister into the present from whatever far-off place she continued to visit in her mind. But before Anne had bought the turkey, she came home from the Club with good news, she hoped, and bad news, she was sure—racial segregation on interstate trains and buses had been banned, and a war in Vietnam had started. Anne gave Isabelle the newspapers with the stories, but her sister left them untouched on her bedside table. The cosmos, Anne concluded, whether at home or abroad, was unfathomable.

By the end of 1955, if Isabelle had been following the papers, as had been her usual passion, she would have concluded that one of Bradley's hot topics, race and racism, was still more than alive and well. While trains and busses had been desegregated, and the Supreme Court had ruled against segregated facilities like bathrooms in public recreational facilities, resistance to integration was rife. Southern states were still not accepting the previous year's decision of *Brown vs. Board of Education* to integrate schools. Anti-miscegenation laws were in effect in these same southern states, what Bradley had called, "today's old Confederacy." In addition to the sixteen southern states, sexual relations or marriage between races was also illegal in eleven states representing the diversity of Americana, from California to Maryland. And, racial violence continued. In Mississippi, in two separate events, two blacks were killed when attempting to enact their voting rights. A fourteen-year-old Chicago boy visiting relatives in that state was killed and the two white men accused of the murder acquitted by an all-white jury. Then, as the year closed, in Montgomery, Alabama, Rosa Parks was arrested for not giving up her seat on a city bus to a white person.

Had Bradley been going over these stories with his dear Isabelle, he would have certainly called to her attention one of life's ironies. Doctors Salk and Francis had announced the discovery of a polio vaccine that year. This vaccine had been developed using cells from a black woman who had died in Baltimore four years earlier and whose unique cell type had been used by medical researchers since her passing. So, white kids in segregated academies in Alabama and Mississippi would be protected by a vaccine built on work using the cells of a black woman. Bradley would have concluded his discussion by saying, "Do ya suppose they'll ever know?".

But there were none of these discussions, none of these articles was even read by Isabelle. She remained introverted, often secluding herself. She rarely went to the Club and when she did, and when she did play cards, she sometimes lost—something that almost never happened. Anne remained fretful but was relegated to the role of spectator as she knew not what to do.

Isabelle conversed, but frequently in monosyllables. There were no more exuberant stories about her travels—no more scathing rants about Democrats or Catholics. She would spend hours reading on the veranda, interspersing this with short walks in the garden as her knee seemed to be bothering her. She and Anne would have their three meals a day at the polished mahogany dinner table, but regardless of how outstandingly Violet had done, Isabelle picked at her food and ate little. From time to time she would call Margaret or Mabel on the phone, having considerably less contact with Helen.

The days swirled around one another and Anne was increasingly concerned. She called Mabel and they agreed Mabel would come to visit to try and pry her dear friend and cousin away from wherever she had gone and bring her back to the here and now.

When Mabel arrived, Isabelle was truly happy to see her. But, contrary to their hopes, she did not open up and immediately regain her old self. She was still closed and withdrawn. Mabel would sit next to her, recalling wonderful things they had done during their journeys, but Isabelle would scarcely acknowledge these events—they definitely did not pick her up. All too often, it was quite the reverse. Mabel would be dramatically remembering one of their adventures, when Isabelle would stand up and say she needed to go to her room. She would mechanically pick up her book, brusquely leave her cousin in the middle of her dialog, go to the veranda outside her room, and begin reading in seclusion.

One day Mabel and Isabelle were slowly walking in the garden, Isabelle's knee noticeably painful, when with clear and piercing eyes, Isabelle turned to face her cousin, saying, "You know, this year I am going to be seventy-seven."

"Of course, dear," Mabel replied. "I've already been there you know."

"Seventy-seven!"

"My dear," Mabel continued, in what she hoped was a soothing voice, "the road we all travel only goes one way."

"George was only sixty-two when he died. Good old Bradley made it to eighty, but he's been gone for almost five years now. I've buried two men, there's only one person left."

"Now dear," Mabel chimed in, being just positive enough, but not too much like Pollyanna, knowing her cousin would detest pseudo optimism, "you have indeed lost loved ones—very dear ones. But you have many loved ones still here who are looking after you, who want you to be happy, who are happy themselves that you are able to do what you do at your age."

"At my age," Isabelle interrupted, "that's it really, isn't it? What can I do at my age?"

"Isabelle, dear," Mabel continued, a bit more softly, "think how lucky you are! It is not only Anne and me who love you and want what's best for you. There's Margaret and her family, Helen and her family, other cousins— why your world is full of people who care."

"Bhaaaaaa," Isabelle almost snorted, "most of those people are happiest to see my backside. I've never warmed up to Helen. Margaret, for her part, has never accepted I married Bradley—and her in-laws—that's almost oil and water for me."

"My dear cousin and dearest friend, let's be honest."

Isabelle nodded her head.

"You are unquestionably no spring chicken, we all agree. You've been more than around the block and you've accumulated some wear and tear through the years. But, at the end of the day, you're in pretty darned good shape."

Isabelle nodded again and did not offer the resistance Mabel was anticipating, so she continued, "I know how much you loved our travels—we were there, side by side, weren't we?"

Isabelle nodded again, still silent.

"They were splendid, the best thing I've done. But, like I told you in Hawaii, as much I'd like to think I could, I know I can't do it anymore. These wondrous journeys are now fabulous memories and, just like they cannot be repeated, they cannot be added-to—my dear, we're just too old."

Isabelle grimaced like she was preparing to intervene, but remained silent, offering only a nearly unintelligible *humpf*.

"However," Mabel continued, "this is not at all to say that we're too old for everything. Why you remember when we were kids and used to go to the pond to go swimming—we're too old for that too—have been for a long time—but that doesn't mean we're too old for living."

Isabelle stared into space.

"You, my dear, are a special and talented person," Mabel tried to wrap things up as she saw she might be losing Isabelle's attention, and certainly her composure, "you have grandchildren to see, you have books to read, you have stories to tell. Get on with it."

Isabelle seemed to hyperventilate. She swallowed hard, then said, "I need a cane, my knee hurts."

"Fine," Mabel added quickly, "so let's go into town and get one now."

From that day, Isabelle walked with a cane.

She walked with a cane into the Club and won all her rubbers. She walked with a cane as she revisited the museums and libraries from which she had been absent for a long period. She walked with a cane to the travel agents, making travel plans to go out west to Margaret's.

It was only after the fact that she called Margaret to tell her she was coming.

Margaret was bewildered. She was not sure how to tell Julian.

Two months after the wedding of Grace Kelly and Rainier III, and even later after the independence of Sudan and Tunisia, Isabelle boarded a train west—reverting to her old standard means of transportation, finding it more comforting and definitely less hectic than the airborne alternative. Reminiscent of days gone by, she was accompanied by Mabel—the two traveling together as far as Des Moines, where Isabelle would celebrate her seventy-seventh birthday with her cousin and a few old acquaintances.

Isabelle spent a fortnight in her old city, most interested how things had changed over the years. Then, by pure serendipity, almost exactly on the two-year anniversary of Percy's death, she took the train to Chicago where she spent a week at the Palmer House, tried desperately to reconnect with Helen and the children, and, as in Des Moines, was astonished at how much had changed in a city she had visited so frequently over the years.

Isabelle had even given thought, during this renaissance rail trip, of going on to Minneapolis to see Bradley's daughter Dorothy but decided this was a bridge too far. She had no desire to open old wounds—be they wounds of the departed or wounds of the bequeathment of the departed.

It was late July when Isabelle disembarked at the train station to be greeted by her daughter.

After a rather limp hug, Margaret took a long stare at her mother, "Welcome, I must say it's a bit of a surprise."

"Well you know," Isabelle almost retorted, "I've been sending stuff here for some time for you to store for me, so I thought I'd follow-up."

"Hmmm," was the best Margaret could offer.

"I figured," her mother went on, "with little Walt starting school in a few weeks, you'd be feeling some sort of emptiness that I could help fill."

Margaret only replied with an even deeper, "Hummmmmmmm."

"So, I hope it's alright?"

"Sure, Mother."

"I mean, if it's a problem, I can get a room at the hotel and then see about getting back to Des Moines or Sarasota?"

"No, Mother."

"Well, OK. Let's get my bags."

"I see you're walking with a cane—everything OK?"

"Fine."

"You sure?"

"You know I'm seventy-seven."

"O.K."

"Let's go."

9

Mother-in-law

MARGARET, WHILE GENERALLY TAKEN aback by her mother's unexpected arrival and apparent plans to stay for a while, had to admit Isabelle had not come totally unannounced—and she was capable of doing so—some might say, even doing so often. The advance warning had given Margaret a chance to try and prepare her family. In spite of their fleeting previous encounters, Margaret realized her children effectively did not know their grandmother. Walt had no real recollection beyond periodic thirty-second exchanges on the phone and a twenty-dollar check that came at Christmas and his birthday. Ann had had more contact with her grandmother, albeit scant. She had a shadowy image of Grandmummie in her mind, knew that many of the dolls in her collection had come from her grandmother's travels, and was also beholden to her for the birthday and Christmas checks. So, from the grandchildren's perspective, relationships with aging kinfolk were pretty much untilled soil.

Julian was a different matter. Julian had initially tried to get close to his mother-in-law—but seemingly failing at all turns to prove that he was worthy of Margaret. Nonetheless, this was almost to be expected. Difficult relationships between a husband and his mother-in-law were legend—considered as the norm and not the exception. Julian was not bothered by not getting along with his mother-in-law—especially if he could keep her at arm's length. He had to admit he felt he had nothing at all in common with the old gal, but his real problem was not his relationship with her, but her relationship with his own parents. He saw her condescending behavior as a way to minimize his parents—particularly his mother. His mother had been a school teacher, raised four children, watched over a sometimes-challenging husband, and, in Julian's eyes, been a saint. He would not tolerate anyone looking down on his mother.

Margaret knew that Julian's health was not what it should be. He was overweight. He took stiff drinks and occasionally smoked a pipe or cigar. Most critically, he was overloaded with stress. He had been sent here to guarantee a constant supply of good quality lumber to the Des Moines plant where it would be cut up to make doors and windows for the still booming housing market. Any delay in arrival in Des Moines or any reduction in quality had a direct impact on the company's bottom line, and thus a direct impact on how the big bosses saw Julian as the mill's boss—the "big boss" no longer Julian's father Robert, who had died after a massive stroke, just a year after Bradley—the company now in the hands of new partners with no family ties.

It was unfortunate Margaret and Julian lived so close to the mill. This made it easy for Julian to be there morning and evening, seven days a week—and he was. He almost appeared to live for that mill—every machine breakdown, every employee dispute, every accident, every little thing bought him to his feet regardless of the time or day. Now, the constant stress was wearing on him. He was tired in the evening. He did not have time for his family. He would come home, eat too much, drink too much, then fall asleep to be up at sunrise, if not before. He was frayed. Margaret feared he would be a lot more frayed now as her own mother added to his load. She was determined to try and minimize Isabelle's bad effects, but she was not sure how effective she could be. It was just hard for Julian to be in the same room with his mother-in-law.

When Margaret had told him of Isabelle's' coming, to his credit, Julian had tried to smile and say, "That's nice."

Margaret, of course, knew it was not. She made her chivalrous husband (as she always saw him—white horse and all) promises she hoped she could keep—promises to do all she could to ensure her mother would not be a millstone around the family's combined neck. In her heart, Margaret knew these were promises she would do everything possible to fulfill. Yet, she knew her mother and knew how hard it would be to minimize—certainly not obviate—her presence.

For the immediate time, she would put her mother in their guest room in the back of the house. This had a separate bathroom and she hoped the long periods Julian spent at work would mean the two would only rarely be in the same place at the same time. They would be together for before-dinner drinks and dinner itself, but she trusted Julian to dose the cocktails so that the two would be a little happier with a cloud of alcohol filming their eyes and ears. But there had to be a better longer-term solution.

For the first few weeks, things ran rather smoothly while Isabelle, with Zelda's help, focused on inventorying her stored possessions. There were varied, and numerous items Isabelle had sent to Margaret for storage over the past several years. There were items sent west when she had moved to and from Tucson. There were items she had sent along the course of her journeys. All these had been carefully wrapped and packed and shipped to herself in care of her daughter.

When these various shipments arrived, most frequently without any forewarning, they had then been painstakingly stacked in what Julian had dubbed (lovingly or not) the Mother-in-law House. Located corral-side, between the tack-room and the stable—these latter structures only used briefly when Ann had had a horse, which she learned quickly was a lot more work than she chose to invest—the Mother-in-law House had no windows, only a heavy, weather-stripped door. But it was electrified with three open bulbs fixed to the rafters. To Margaret, it seemed to be the perfect place to store who knew what for who knew how long.

Now, Margaret knew the day had come. After all the years of collecting "stuff" (as Julian called it), it was time to open the heavy door and see what was really inside.

Isabelle, with Zelda in tow, began meticulously inspecting the contents of the storage facility named in her honor.

Many of Isabelle's items were laboriously wrapped in cotton quilts or packed in cardboard drums with tight covers. Some items, however, were in regular boxes, taped shut—most often with no indications of what was inside. Isabelle decided she needed to categorize all. Margaret was supportive as she felt this would occupy her mother and her mother was at her worst when she was not occupied.

It was August and it was hot. Isabelle thrived in high temperatures—perspiring little (she so hated it when others referred to it as sweating—she always said, "horses sweat, people perspire"). While it was still cool in the morning, Zelda would help Isabelle set aside and open a few containers—the objects of the day's labors. Isabelle would then note on her pad exactly what was in each container, repack and reseal, and write on the outside updated notes with enough information so she would know where to find any specific item on the master packing list. In the evening, Zelda, with a hand from Jimmy, would restock the now inventoried containers. The next day, new items would be set out for Isabelle's undivided attention.

Margaret would check on her mother randomly through the day, warning, "It's hot, don't do too much."

Isabelle would offer a *humpf* or, at most mutter, "Not hot like Tucson or Sarasota—not to mention Bangkok or Columbo."

In what seemed to Margaret as remarkable speed, Isabelle had inventoried her possessions—her daughter unsure of to where her mother would now turn her sights.

Fortunately, soon it was time for Margaret's birthday. The lady of the house decided this would be a good occasion for her to throw a party—more in honor of her mother than of her own birth (self-aggrandizement not among the afflictions that greatly affected Margaret). She would invite Steve and Christine and their children, their Minister, and some of Julian's business colleagues. Then she had an idea. She would also invite card-players from Forest County Club—the one and only establishment of its kind within one hundred miles. She would build bridges for her mother—praying her mother would not burn them down. She would do all she could to get her mother in contact with others she hoped would prove to be equally dedicated to, and adept at, cards so as to attract Isabelle to games on a regular basis.

Unfortunately, she did not know these people. But knowing someone who knew someone was almost as good. Their family doctor, Dr. Brown, who had delivered Walt under such difficult circumstances, had deep roots in the community and his mother, Inez, had grown up here and knew everybody. She could get in touch with Inez through Dr. Brown, and through her she could get a list of targets. She would immediately invite Dr. Brown, his immediate family and his mother to her birthday festivities.

Things went better than she had anticipated. Julian and Isabelle were each so immersed in their immediate duties they seldom saw each other—never without a stout toddy in their hands. Dr. Brown had been his usual helpful self and Margaret took an immediate liking to Inez, if only over the phone—the doctor's mother promising to call back with a list of addicted card players.

With the good services of Zelda, she was able to get a sumptuous menu together, including an ample birthday cake—not homemade, but the excellent local bakery made it taste nearly so. All the invitees showed up, including seven card players who frequented Forest Country Club—five women and two men. Exceptionally, Julian had taken extra time off and had agreed to barbecue hamburgers on his great brick hearth. One of Margaret's friends, who's family ran the local creamery, even came bringing buckets of freshly made ice cream. With blue skies, cool temperatures, it seemed destined to be a success.

There was, nevertheless, one nearly fatal slip. Julian's appreciation, or lack there-of, of his mother-in-law was shared by his younger brother and his family, as with nearly all the Müllers. There seemed to be some inherent animus—some catalytic reaction that, when Isabelle was added to the mix, things could easily boil-over.

It was not a question of beliefs or politics. Julian shared nearly all Isabelle's politics and was a fervent Republican. For reasons into which no one cared to delve, unlike his big brother and sister-in-law, Steve and Christine were equally rabid Democrats. And, both Julian and Steve were devout Christians. There were commonalities and there were differences between brothers, but there seemed to be no lamentable public enmity until Isabelle was added to the equation. Things could then become volatile. This was the close call Margaret experienced.

After her second highball, Isabelle was vociferously and succinctly attacking the Reds. She was now back to her pleasures of digesting all the news she could get. She found the local *Herald* sorely limited, so she had invested in a subscription with the *San Francisco Chronicle*—it came late, but it had a thorough examination of events. She had been reading about the growing problems in the Suez, that dummy Nasser getting chummier and chummier with Khrushchev and America's old Korean War nemesis, Zhou Enlai—Nasser proudly and loudly declaring to the whole world that he was going to buy Soviet arms—everyone thought to attack Israel. Isabelle concluded by advocating an immediate and massive attack on Egypt—even bigger and more devastating than the English and French were considering.

Christine watched Isabelle almost as though she were a one-woman play, shocked at some of the theatrics. Christine was not only very antiwar, having seen the impact WWII had had on Steve, but she was a devout liberal and unwilling to condemn immediately and combatively all socialist ideals. As she too sipped her second drink, she was more than ready, even anxious, to take on her sister-in-law's mother.

Luckily, Margaret saw the pre-attack gleam in Christine's eyes. She quickly pulled Julian aside and he, in turn, got Steve to grab his wife and make momentary excuses that they had to go across the street to urgently check on something at home. They were back in twenty minutes, but the gleam was gone.

Of great importance to Margaret's plans, Isabelle did seem to hit it off with Inez. At more than one moment, Margaret was fearful that her mother's animated antics might be seen as so obnoxious as to eradicate any chance of Isabelle making what she saw as much needed, really essential, relationships if she were to stay in the area. *Maybe*, Margaret thought, *old people are just more tolerant of old people?* She did not know. But for whatever reason, even with Isabelle's outbursts, Inez appeared to nearly instantaneously bond with her co-septuagenarian. So, as she and Zelda were cleaning up the aftermath, Margaret smiled to herself. With a few more smiles from the Roman goddess Fortuna, one of her mother's favorites, things might just work out despite the odds.

And, they did work out pretty well. Isabelle formed strong connections with the players at what was now her new club. She did not go as far to call them friends. She was wont to call nearly any relationship a friendship after feeling deceived by those erstwhile folks she had lived with for so long in Des Moines. But she was making contacts, forming relationships, and finding things to do.

As the holidays neared, it was Isabelle who approached her daughter—to Margaret's great subsequent surprise. Isabelle had decided she should find her own accommodation—an apartment. She had lived under Margaret's roof (she did not mention Julian) for long enough. She now felt she and her grandchildren knew each other. This was important. She also felt she understood better Margaret's life as wife and mother. This too was important. But she was, she admitted, an obstacle—an extra thumb, a fifth wheel, extraneous, or whatever—she was in many ways superfluous. She did not want to be a freeloader. She did not want to hamper the family she now knew so much better and held in such high regard. She needed to find her own way—of course, not straying too far away, she felt she should add.

While this was just the outcome for which Margaret had prayed, she knew it was a difficult decision for her mother and she knew it had to be handled well if it was to last. She had a long talk with Julian and then approached her mother with Julian's counter offer. Isabelle should stay with them until after the new year. They would celebrate together, under one roof, and then they would look for an apartment.

Isabelle greatly appreciated the generosity and accepted without hesitation.

The following February, a week after Valentine's Day, after the inauguration of Dwight Eisenhower for his second term, after the Irish Republican Army launched attacks in Northern Ireland, and after the Alabama Klu Klux Klan forced a black Winn Dixie truck driver to jump off a bridge to his death, Isabelle moved into her apartment. It was spacious, in a quiet part of the town, not far from the city center, but also not more than twenty minutes by car from Margaret's.

Isabelle was once again in her own lodging, surrounded by her own things, setting her own schedule.

Although truly not a materialist, she liked her things and was happy to unpack treasures she had not seen in years. Jimmy had kindly helped greatly by ferrying many things from the Mother-in-law House in his old Chevy pickup. Soon, Isabelle was set up in, even by her standards, fine style.

The one weak link in Margaret's master plan was figuring out how her mother would be able to get about. With her knee, she was not able to walk very far, even with a cane. Furthermore, her knee problem precluded her driving and she had not had a driver's license for nearly five years. Distances between the mill camp, the club, and downtown were considerable. Margaret was troubled as to how her mother could have her own place and not be able to be mobile. But miraculously, this was resolved by Inez. She drove and was more than happy to coordinate activities so she and Isabelle could go out together. It worked wonderfully.

By Easter, when little Walt had completed half of second grade and Ann half her freshman year in high school, their grandmother was embarking on the next phase of her life. Isabelle had a new routine. She and Inez would play cards three days a week. She and Inez were also now members of DAR, Book Club, and PEO—groups Margaret also attended. The two white-haired ladies even joined AAUW. Together they shared a full week.

Every Sunday, after church, Margaret, Julian, and the children would pass by Isabelle's apartment and pick her up for a day at their house. They would have a big afternoon meal, talk, and sometimes play board games. As Margaret's family had a television, a novelty of which Isabelle generally disapproved in principle, but not necessarily in practice, they would wrap up the day watching *The Ed Sullivan Show* together—either Margaret or Julian driving Isabelle home in the early evening. When she left, Margaret sent her mother home with a basket of leftovers which would serve her well, as she knew cooking was not her mother's favorite advocation. In no way seen as repayment, Margaret also sent her mother home with a bag of socks needing darning. Isabelle had proven to be very adept at, and patient with this task that so few did well, and even fewer tolerated. The next Sunday Isabelle would come with a pile of very professionally darned socks, to the consternation of all except Isabelle.

Ann still was not what many might consider as close to her Grandmummie—still, more often than not, referring to her as "grandmother". Ann enjoyed it when they talked about Isabelle's travels or about books. But Ann considered herself a young adult. And, young adults did not need their grandparents. Grandparents were special when you were a child, Walt's age or younger. Grandmummie had not been around then.

Ann was, moreover, particularly disgusted by the darning of socks. She was happy she had brand new socks for dress and for PE. It would be demeaning to go to school, especially in PE class, and be seen wearing socks that had been sewn, repaired, or darned. What an insult. Before she had started high school, she and her mother had bought some bobby socks. She did not wear them too often, but she intended to. She sure hoped Garandmummie would never stick her darning egg in her bobby socks.

10

Visionary

To SAY ANN'S YOUTH was unremarkable would be an understatement. Her concerns over darned socks may actually have been one of the major issues which she considered. She left virtually no bread crumbs along her path to announce her passing. Few would remember she had indeed entered their space.

Her school routine changed little in substance over the years. It became a river that carried her through the grades. There were few changes. In grade school, each school day had started and ended in her mother's car. In high school, each school day started and ended in the school bus. But, when she brought home her report cards, they were also always the same: not good, not bad. She did passably in anything that had to do with reading or writing, faring far less well with anything involving math, science, or PE.

When she entered high school, she was the epitome of the typical student. She was average in all ways—not exceptional nor problematic—just very ordinary. She had no real friends and really cared less if she had any enemies. As was often to be the case with her life, school was an end to a means—a necessary pathway to reach her aim. Each day her intent was to get home and immerse herself in her comfort zone. Each year her intention was to conclude, as painlessly as possible, another step that was inevitably necessary for her to reach her goal of adulthood.

She had no real hobbies or passions. She read. She was still enamored by her books—mostly romantic fiction—nothing heavy or intellectual. She still kept her dolls dusted and polished. But her dolls were now just dolls, just possessions. They were still hers—possessions she jealously protected. But they were no longer an entourage that kept her company. They were now a totem from an earlier phase of life that was to be well kept as if a museum piece.

She neither followed nor played sports. She did fancy herself a horse person and her family had sent her to horse camp where she learned to ride and sleep rough. But when this was over, it too was filed on the shelf, as if part of an archive she was building—never again to ride a horse or camp out.

She was just an average student with a much below average social life.

Over and beyond tolerating school and enjoying the comfort of her home, and even more so, her room, the one thing that became an important part of Ann's life was caring for her little brother.

She had initially hated Walter. She hated sharing. She hated the idea of having to share her parents with another child. She hated the idea that he was a boy. *Were boys better?* She hated the idea that he might actually be better than she—but she did not know how? The family should have stayed a trio and not become a foursome.

However, her feelings changed completely. She saw how worried her parents were for Walter's safety—his survival. He had been premature and come after her mother had lost several babies. Her parents had the fear of God in them—they prayed every day that Walter too would not be taken from them.

This observation prompted an about-face in the young, but already calculating, Ann. If she could be her brother's protector, if she could be the means that assured him the life her parents so wanted, then she would be rewarded. She would receive the praise. She would receive the accolades. She would still be in first place, even if they were now four and not three.

Accordingly, when at home, and when not ensconced in her room, she became her brother's shadow. She would watch him, from near or far, like a barn owl watching a mouse. Whenever he approached any danger, anything that might possibly, in the wildest of dreams, real or imaginary, be danger-ous, she would rush to him, wave her arms, pick him up, and put him down somewhere else—out of harm's way. She would then dash to her parents and tell them, in dramatic detail, how she had just saved Walter from this or that possible disaster.

If Walter were trying to climb a tree, she would pluck him off the trunk and place him safely in a chair on the porch. If he were wandering through the stable, she would drag him, sometimes kicking, to a chair near Zelda in the kitchen. If he were playing with Chip, she would chase the dog away and cajole her brother into the solarium for a cookie. If he were poking about the root house, she would come up behind him, intentionally scare him with a "boo", then wrap him up in her arms and carry him to the dining room. If he were alone by the little fishpond, she would snatch him up and carry him upstairs to sit next to mother in the sewing room. In short, much to Walt's dismay and agitation, his sister became his shepherdess as soon as she got off the bus.

The one snafu in Ann's plan of being her brother's keeper was their difference in age. This had worked fine when she was thirteen and he five. It even worked now when she was fifteen and he was seven. But even now her brother was getting head strong. She could not force or entice him from a pathway she considered, or wished others to consider, as dangerous. She could only start by trying to quietly convince him. This worked increasingly infrequently. She would then yell, warning him as loudly as possible of the terrible things that would befall him if he continued along his present course. Sometimes this worked—mostly when an adult was attracted by her yelling and then ordered Walt to do as he was told. But most often these days, she could not inflict any immediate changes, only make the case to her brother and then run to her parents to complain that her sibling continued to be disobedient and bullheaded. If someone had been keeping score, Ann was uncertain how many points would be chalked up next to her name—she hoped she was winning the match, because this was the most important game of her life.

As Ann moved through high school, she began to develop real affection for her Gandmummie (now, more "grandmummie" than "grandmother") as the two were able to spend more meaningful time together. Isabelle's apartment was only about a ten-minute walk from the school. Ann abhorred the bus with its locker room smell and constant noise from undisciplined students who did not even know who Charlotte Brontë was nor that an *Evzkone* was a Greek soldier, and she had doll to prove it. So, Ann signed up for Latin class. She then convinced her mother she needed tutoring as this was really a most difficult subject. And, who better to tutor than Grandmummie.

It was an easy sale. Two to four times a week, depending on Isabelle's schedule, Ann would come to spend a few hours ostensibly going over Latin—but mostly, if successful, getting her grandmother to talk about her travels and leaving the academic study in the dust. Then, on these special days, Mother would come to pick her up. It was like the old days. She was chauffeured by her mother. She loved it.

Even when she was no longer taking Latin, Ann told her mother she was still taking some advanced classes and had to leave school late—thus, missing the bus. She could, she proposed to Margaret, visit her grandmother, from where her mother could pick her up at her convenience.

Then, in the second half of her junior year, her father found a second-hand in-good-shape 1957 Volkswagen Beetle for his daughter. Ann was thrilled. There were only a handful of kids in her class with cars, and almost no girls—this was excellent. Furthermore, it made it easier for her to visit Isabelle whenever the two chose.

By the time Ann was senior, she felt very close to her Grandmummie. But this was not the love of family closeness one might have for a grandmother who, like Misses Santa, gives her grandchildren all measure of good things. This was almost a teacher-student closeness—a bond of savant and devotee. As much as Ann felt detached from her schooling, including her formal teachers, she saw in her Grandmummie a mentor who would not just open a book and follow a study plan, but who could lead one through learning based on first-hand experiences accentuated with a profound knowledge of ancient civilizations, as well as, present-day humanism.

Isabelle showed Ann how the past guided the future—ancient cultures were not to be forgotten, but to be used as tools to shape our lives. The ancients understood there were true visionaries and there were those representing the wearisome and the workaday—the latter pulling us down, the former pushing us up.

Ann's relationship with Isabelle was one of the cornerstones of her adolescence. School was, of course, another important piece, but one that was endured and definitely not enjoyed. There were two more pieces necessary to frame Ann's youth.

One was her work with her mother. This was housework of all sorts and descriptions. When she had to be, when she wanted to be, Ann was a hard worker. But she had never had a job outside her home. Nevertheless, at home, when there was work to be done, she did it. Nothing was too demanding, too back-breaking, too minacious, or too boring to be unacceptable. Ann knew her path of life was to do as her mother and her Grandmummie had done before her, or as she envisioned, they had done. Her aim was to be an indefatigable housewife who held this title, not as a last resort, but as a first choice. Who held this position with honor and ability. Who knew how to use it for the advancement of herself and her family.

The fourth corner of the frame that Ann built was her inner world. Tangibly, this took place in her room, her inner sanctuary, and the icons were her books and her dolls. Intangibly, this took place in her mind where the milestones were the plans she laid that would keep her and hers on top. She smirked at the girls in her class who wanted to be teachers or nurses. Why, they might as well become nuns. If one wanted to spend one's life working for others, staying on the sidelines, then go ahead and study hard to become a teacher or nurse—or even a nun. But if one wanted to be able to invest in self and in family and the advancement of both, the door for these opportunities lay at the hearth and not the classroom.

She looked at her Grandmummie as the case in point, albeit her mother was in the same arena. Choosing to ignore Isabelle's real abhorrence of domestic chores and duties, Ann painted a very lopsided picture of her grandmother.

Isabelle had a good education. She was truly well educated. But, in Ann's eyes, it was not her education that had got her to where she was today. It was not her education that paid her rent. It was not her education that had carried her around the world. It was not her education that had introduced to her some of the finest spots in the country. It was her wedding vows that had led to where she was. And, she had done it twice.

Ann saw this. She contrasted her grandmother's methods (as she saw them) with her own father's interactions with his family. Perhaps because he was gone at the mill so much, he spent lavishly on gifts for all. He arranged extravagant vacations. He spent a lot of money on his family. In Ann's view, money that was wasted. It was better if a family, if her family, operated like a vacuum, sucking up all that was worthwhile, not dispersing it. The family's wealth should be concentrated, used, as Grandmummie had said, by the visionaries, to generate more wealth for the family—through wealth, power.

Julian was generous. Not only had be bought a VW Beetle for his daughter, he went into town to Derby's Music and bought Isabelle a Magnavox TV. When it was delivered, she nearly had a tantrum, expounding about how communication was all about the written word—this modern technology literally for the birds.

Although her reaction to her son-in-law's gifts was no indication, Isabelle was truly mellowing with age. For one thing, she was changing her so-called intellectual focus. Typically, she had read newspapers, several newspapers with high-quality reporting. She would complement these with some carefully selected magazines. When she was not reading about current events, she would jump way back in time and plunge into her academic area of specialization—the ancient world. However, of late she had set aside both the new and the old in favor of the adventurous and the fictitious. To even her own great surprise, she found herself reading detective novels—what might have been called "dime novels" when she was young. She learned she particularly appreciated the writings of Samuel Dashiell Hammett and Raymond Thornton Chandler.

It was, in a manner of speaking, Hammett and Chandler who converted her to a sporadic TV watcher.

When the damn thing was set up, she had no choice but to see what was on. If Bradley had been there, she might have asked him to help her push it out the front door—that would show Julian. But, she herself could do nothing—so she decided to at least see what all the fuss was about.

By pure luck, when the men from Derby's had gone, leaving the set on, the *Perry Mason* show came on. Isabelle immediately recognized Raymond Burr, having seen him in New York in Patrick Hamilton's *The Duke in Darkness*, a tale she, not surprisingly, enjoyed, recounting a story set in the French civil war in the late sixteenth century. If Raymond Burr was involved, she decided she could change her tone and lower her standards to watch the TV show. She liked it. She really liked it! Soon she never missed Perry Mason.

When Inez learned of her friend's new leisure activity, nearly new passion, she kidded her, saying she was in love with a younger man. She was referring to William Hopper, one of the supporting actors who was rumored to have been a frogman in WWII and who many mature women found very handsome. Sometimes Inez and Isabelle would watch a show together and try to solve the mystery before Perry.

Ann did not like the fact that her Grandmummie now had a TV. She liked even less that her Grandmummie liked *Perry Mason*. She felt the contraption, its shows, and its actors were interlopers. They imposed a more rigid schedule on Grandmummie's time which had heretofore been completely malleable—able to be shaped by Ann's needs or even whims.

Ann also did not like the fact that her Grandmummie had grown attached to Douglas Edward's and *The CBS Evening News*. This meant Isabelle did not rely completely on newspapers for her updates—with newspapers she could pick and choose, avoiding subjects which she found distasteful. Sitting in front of the TV, she was awash with whatever might be the topic of the day. This, too, meant that Ann's ability to interpret current events when discussing with her grandmother was diminished. The more the sources of information inputting into Isabelle's sphere of reference, the more Ann's ability to present the image she wanted was reduced. Ann did not like feeling like she was losing control. She did not like it at all.

Isabelle, for her part, was very happy to join Douglas Edwards for the news. Sometimes she even felt like she was back sharing the day's hottest topics in the garden with Bradley.

Isabelle tended to categorize news into two groupings: there were events, most often gone bad, that were due to incompetent leaders (mostly

Democrats), and there were events with which she might or might not agree, but which were of particular interest because they represented the types of topics she had discussed so wholeheartedly with Bradley as well as with Anne and Mabel—discussions of times gone by that she now missed terribly—sadly Inez (and, certainly not Margaret's family) was no replacement in this domain, in spite of her effective substitution in other key areas like cards.

One piece of news that caught her attention and that fell into the second category was the story of Richard and Mildred Loving—a story, she knew, if she had not seen it, Bradly would surely have pointed it out, priming the pump for an animated discussion. Bradly was always waving flags when the spotlight shone on subjects like racially mixed marriage. Bradly had had such a kind spirit.

Isabelle, from her unwavering stance, fervently knew the Lovings were wrong, having no real patience for their protestations against miscegenation—an act against nature. Yet, she admired what she saw as their spunk. Right or wrong, they were a gutsy couple. But they had been now found legally guilty of interracial marriage and were banished from Virginia, expelled like Hephaestus, the god of the forge, being booted from Olympus. She wondered, were the Lovings and Hephaestus both exiled for events beyond their control? Richard and Mildred found themselves loving someone of a different race. Hephaestus found himself born with a shriveled foot that, perhaps like interracial love, was unacceptable to the gods. This would have been a great exchange with Bradley. She really missed those days. But now she had Ann.

Ann was not so much going through puberty as she was going through a shift. Up to her early teens, she had been able to be daddy's little girl. She could maneuver and arrange things to her advantage and then play innocent: "Ghee daddy, I don't know why Walt broke the vase, he must have been running around the house—I've told him so many times not to run in the house."

She had always been able to directly intervene—to adjust and manipulate situations personally to ensure the desired outcome. Displaying complete guiltlessness for circumstances she orchestrated. She had so often been able to achieve her aims by blaming others while expounding her innocence, and at times her wisdom. Now, unfortunately she found she was too old to simply claim inculpability. Moreover, she was required, by the unavoidable complexities of her daily routine, to be too far away to maintain direct control. She was in less and less frequent contact with Grandmummie. She was equally less the constant companion to her mother, and certainly much less frequently in the same place at the same time as her brother.

Then, in 1960 things became even more complex. Not only did Lucy divorce Desi, France tested their first nuclear bomb in Algeria, the United States sent troops to Vietnam, and Adolf Coors III got kidnapped, but Ann went away to college and her father changed his job.

Everyone hoped this was change for the better.

Julian took a management job at a new mill with a progressive reputation combined with major capital and land resources. Margaret hoped they would all find calmer times by removing her beloved permanently from the excruciating stress of trying to always deliver to Des Moines what was undeliverable. The family moved to a rambling home surrounded by Ponderosa pine trees that Ann hated—her venom for both the house and the trees never concealed.

It was not that she had really liked The Big House—she had not. She really liked the idea of living in The Big House. But, she did not like the house itself nor the neighborhood—too full of family and workers. But this new home was totally unacceptable. It was hidden away in the trees—dark and dreary and overrun with wildlife from the surrounding forest. Even though she had her own room, she was happy she would not be living there.

Nonetheless, this change in venue made things harder to script. There had been so much rote activity in The Big House that, with relative ease, she had been able to anticipate who would do what. This new environment offered no clues.

There were fewer actors. There was no more Zelda and Jimmy—no more Christine and Steve or their kids. When the stage was full, it was an easy feat to play one actor against the other. Now there were but three (not counting her grandmother *cum* mentor) and, for these three, the home was more sleeping quarters than a twenty-four-hour-a-day coliseum. The Big House had always been bustling. The mill was just a few minutes away, people came and went all day, every day. The house, outbuildings, and gardens themselves were big, demanding constant upkeep. Trains went by. Mill whistles and sirens blew. The village was surprisingly vibrant and animated.

The new place was monotonous. There were fewer moving pieces. There were fewer people. It was austere. Father was at work—twenty-five minutes away by car. Mother was generally away doing this or that. Walt was at school. It was only that terrible little Boston Terrier, Francis, who was always at home.

Fortuitously for Ann, her worries about how to pull strings from afar was less of a worry than she had imagined. Her orchestrations were, of course, aimed at always shining a positive light on herself—as she saw it, keeping herself in first position. This was really all about how she was seen by her parents vis-à-vis her little brother. And, here Walt was her greatest ally. He was always doing dumb stuff. He was an excellent student and a serious boy, but he just did dumb things—did dumb things and got caught, more times than not, doing them. The list was endless: throwing erasers in class, roughhousing on the playground, dumping another student in a garbage can, talking in the library, setting off cherry bombs in the boys bathroom, jumping up in the school bus, pulling Samantha's pigtails, hiding one of Jerry's gym shoes, fooling around during dance class, laughing so hard in the cafeteria that milk came out his nose, carving his name in the desk with a pencil sharpener blade—and on and on. Walt seemed endlessly able to do mischief which, in most cases, was reported to his parents.

Moreover, Walt did not, as all had hoped, grow out of it. As he got ready for sixth grade, he was as rambunctious as he had always been. Ann, now at university, regularly heard of her brother's shenanigans during her Sunday phone calls with her mother. They warmed her heart.

By the time Walt finished seventh grade, ready, so he was told, to go to junior high, Ann was finishing her sophomore year. Although Walt's unruly behavior had generated many a sideways glance, and often some stark punishment, his grades were, as always good and he was able to apply for advanced classes in junior high. His sister, however, as was being shown with increasing constancy, was diametrically opposed to her brother. Where he was ornery and puckish, she was controlled and subdued. As well, where he was a good to excellent academic performer, she was average to poor.

Ann's lack of scholastic aptitude had become very apparent as she reached the midpoint of her university education—she had nearly flunked out. It was not that she was not capable of getting at least passing grades, she simply did not care.

A fortnight after she returned home on vacation, her grades arrived by mail. She had foreseen this inevitability but hoped to be able to intercept the offending correspondence, having it disappear forever. Contrary to her plans, her mother got the mail and, as was her habit, opened all the envelopes before taking out the contents one-by-one. Margaret was the billpayer in the family, so this routine helped her in getting all the various settlements carefully organized. But, when she examined the contents of the day's delivery, expecting to see the amount due for electricity or garbage, she found herself looking at her offspring's university grades for her sophomore year—her offspring's failing university grades for her sophomore year.

When Julian got home from work, she corralled her husband and her daughter on the patio while she told Walt to take Francis for a walk in the woods. When all three were seated, she held up the sheet with the university's letterhead, "Well, missy, what do you think I have here?"

With complete *sangfroid*, Ann replied, "Why, my grades of course, glad you got them, thanks."

"And?"

"And what? I guess I didn't do too well. But it was my sophomore year, and everyone knows that the sophomore year is the most difficult—it's the year they try to flunk out a lot of the students because they don't have enough senior level professors if all the students continued for a full four years." All this coming far too fast, clearly rehearsed.

"So," trying to keep her tone flat, Margaret, followed along, "they succeeded, and you've flunked out?"

"Not really."

"Dear." Julian entered the fray for the first time, "surely you know you can do better?"

"Well . . ." Ann started.

"No," a furious Margaret cut in, "it's not about 'could' or 'should'—we all know you're no dummy. You could and should do better. But that doesn't matter. What matters is that you've flunked out. What are you going to do now?"

"Actually, Mother," an indignant Ann replied, with steel in her voice, "I didn't FLUNK OUT. I JUST failed last quarter."

"What?" Margaret and Julian said I'm unison.

"It's true. Look at the card. It gives the grades for the quarter and the accumulative grades. I haven't flunked out."

"So, you're happy with the results?" Margaret almost yelled.

"Now dear," Julian said, addressing more Margaret than Ann.

Not to be hushed, Margaret repeated with added emphasis, "So, my daughter, are you satisfied with what you've done?"

"Well, you know, a lot of others did a whole lot worse. They . . . ."

Again, Margaret cut her daughter short, "You are my daughter. You are the only one I care about. I do not care about others! I care about my daughter and whether or not we are wasting our hard-earned savings putting you through college?"

"You know, Ann," Julian inserted, "in today's world a college degree for a young lady is really quite important."

"But Daddy," she almost sobbed, "Mother and Grandmummie went to college and never did anything with their studies. Why should I go and then do nothing after all the frustration?"

"Ann, dear," Julian continued in a solemn tone, "it's not just about what you do by choice with your degree—it's also what you may be forced to do. Fortunately, your mother and grandmother were not forced—at least so far—to go out and hunt for a job. But, if they had to, the first thing one would ask is, 'where's your degree?' We all expect that you will get married and have your own family. What if you have really bad luck and your husband dies, your parents are dead, and you have children to support? What are you going to do? You need to think about this—and seriously. If you have to get a job to feed your children, by damn you'll get a job, I know it. And if you don't have a college degree, just your high school diploma, you'll be lucky to get a job as a cashier at Safeway—do you want to have to raise your children on the salary of a cashier at Safeway? With a degree you could teach, work in a business, be an accountant, do any number of things. You need—no you must have a degree."

Neither Margaret nor Ann had ever heard Julian speak on such a profound topic for such a long time. They were unsure of what to do next.

"Really, dear," Julian, sensing the silence, felt he should underscore his thoughts—he should really insist, "you need to have a degree, if not for yourself, for your children."

"Daddy, I'm trying."

"Are you sure?" Margaret inserted, feeling she too needed to stress the issue.

"It's hard."

"No one said it would be easy," her mother replied, her pupils now dilating, "this is part of taking responsibility. Is that all you're interested in—that it's easy. Boy, let me tell you, life isn't easy, get used to it. Stand up and do your part!"

Before tempers really flared, Julian made a decision. There needed to be a new option that would reset the dial.

"How about," he enquired, looking at both his wife and his daughter, "we all agree Ann can do better and will do better? How about we wipe the slate clean and start over with her junior year somewhere else where she has a fresh start and can apply herself in a new environment with no ties to past poor performances?"

"Hmmmmmm." This was as nearly the simultaneous reaction for both ladies.

They agreed they would look into another school where Ann could start over. Ann almost curtsied at the end, kissing her father on the forehead, saying with forlorn eyes, "I'm sorry Daddy if I upset you, I would never want to do that."

And, it was over.

11

Meet Howard

LATER THAT FALL, ANN transferred to a small but well-respected college with tuition an order of magnitude higher than the state school where she had passed her first two collegiate years. She managed to pull her grades out of the gutter and kept a solid C+ average. She also met a young man, Howard Newcastle, who was nearly as asocial as she and who was to inherit a small fortune as the only son of a longtime mercantile family that, since statehood, had amassed significant wealth providing the citizenry with everything from plows to notebooks.

In 1964, the first woman was placed in nomination for the United States' presidency, three civil rights workers were murdered in Mississippi, Walt finished his freshman year in high school, and was an usher at his sister's wedding to Howard. Walt was not fazed by the whole marriage ritual that seemed to be so important to everyone else. He continued to follow his interests—as his uncle used to say, "listening to a different drummer." His good grades continued, but he engaged neither in sports nor other extracurricular activities. He spent his free time walking in the woods and otherwise enjoying the great outdoors world that was such a great resource for the West.

Ann had graduated with a degree in teaching and Howard with one in business. Ann's practice teaching during her senior year was so dramatic that she vowed she would never again be seen in front of a class. She told Howard to carry on and find whatever job he wanted, wherever he wanted—her magnanimity purely cosmetic. She knew that whatever Howard would do, it would be unimportant in the big picture—the big picture being inheriting the family fortune.

Howard proved to be even more malleable than any others Ann had sculpted. Howard honestly, in his own words, thought of himself as kind of a doofus. He knew he was not unintelligent, but he just felt he was completely maladroit. He had never had a girlfriend before Ann. He had never thought a girl would look at him, let alone marry him. Then he found Ann. Or, she found him. He was not too sure. She seemed really fond of him. She flattered him. She thought his penchant for photographing old houses was charming. She thought his crewcut was dignified. She did suggest he get out in the sun a bit more to try and darken his pallid complexion.

Margaret and Julian had been less than enthusiastic for their daughter to marry Howard—someone they saw as having low energy and low initiative—characteristics they attributed to coming from an old monied family. They would have been much, much happier if their little girl had agreed to teach for a while and cast a bit wider net to see more clearly with whom she wanted to spend the rest of her life. But Ann was insistent. She was not going to teach. She was going to start HER family—now.

Ann had to muster all her efforts to persuade her folks that it was Howard with whom she would start this family.

Ann feared a frontal assault on her parents would fail, and she did not want to be so severe as to totally erase the pristine image she had spent years building. So, she enlisted the help of her Grandmummie. Ann took great pains to explain to her grandmother that Howard was like Favonius, the Roman god of the West Wind who brought a breeze to cool the land. What others, including her parents, saw as a milquetoast bearing, was actually a timid and humble personality which, if properly encouraged, would rise like a breeze to cool the land.

Isabelle cautioned her granddaughter, suggesting she take a good dose of reality, stressing that power, the end game for all who understood the game (and there were not that many, Isabelle thought, but did not say), could be gained and shifted with stealth and patience. This requires an external calmness and an internal resolve. Masters, like the ancients' gods, were born and not crafted. While all people may be created equal to breathe the air or drink the water, they were not all socially nor intellectually equal—there was great diversity to show different levels like the layers in the bottom of a stream—the mud overlaid by the sand overlaid by the small stones overlaid by the big stones. If you want to be a big stone, you have to be able to sit on top.

While many might tell her it's a man's world, Isabelle alerted Ann, this was pure propaganda. A wise woman could let the man in front think he was leading, when in fact he was being led.

Do not be concerned, she concluded her advice to her granddaughter, that some may look askance at your husband. He is yours, not theirs. If you have picked well, that is all that matters—and the picking is up to you.

Isabelle had been heavily criticized for her choice in men and had considerable personal experience with men who were seen not as a "man's man," but seen as retiring and restrained. Isabelle knew in the case of the men in her family, unobtrusiveness was due to the fact that these men were truly far above their peers in intellectual ability. They preferred to remain silent rather than embarrass others. Isabelle doubted, however, if this analogy applied to Howard, who she also found to be so withdrawn as to be irritating—never feeling at ease because you were always wondering if he were really there. Nevertheless, she also understood the tactics her granddaughter was attempting to apply and the tapestry she was attempting to weave.

It was really not out of love for a grandchild nor a deep conviction that this child was right that made Isabelle support Ann's marriage. It was more applying the pragmatism that had kept Isabel in good stead throughout her life. She really did not see Ann as any great catch. If Howard wanted her, it seemed best for all to acquiesce.

Thus, Isabelle interceded on Ann's behalf. His convictions to the contrary notwithstanding, Julian begrudgingly agreed under great pressure from his wife and mother-in-law. Ann and Howard were married in the Congregational Church with a champagne-filled reception at the Club. Mabel came as did Julian's Aunt Beatrice. Anne sent her regrets that she could not attend, but also sent a lovely antique silver tea service to honor her namesake at her wedding. Helen was not invited.

After the ceremonies, Ann and Howard went on a perfect honeymoon to San Francisco—paid in full by Julian.

Howard's parents attended the wedding events, starting with the dinner for the families on the eve of the church service. Margaret and Julian found them to be just as lack-luster as their son—it was clear to see the origin of his, what Julian had taken to calling "pigeon-hearted" nature. After the reception, they left at the same time as the newlyweds and no one could remember what they looked like.

As Isabelle watched the bride and groom drive off to the airport to get their flight to San Francisco, she silently thought to herself, "I hope her West Wind is strong".

Ann had read in a magazine at the dentist's office that the average family had two children, the first born when the mother was twenty-six years old. If it was good enough for "everyone", it was good enough for her. She put Howard on notice that in four years they needed to be stable for they would start their family.

For his part, the last thing on Howard's mind was starting a family. Prior to graduation, he had gone through several interviews with large national companies. Only one had come through. He received an offer from Sears to enter into their management training program. With no other options, he accepted.

Ann almost hit the ceiling when she heard her husband say he was going to be a Sears salesman. This was completely impossible—unbelievable. But, thinking back to Isabelle's advice, she hid her repugnance at the idea that *her* husband would work for Sears. Making sure her mask was well in place, almost with a smile, she told Howard, who she never thought of calling Howie or any other affectionate pet name (her mother having called her father "Jules honey" for years), this was good news and worth a try.

They were not going out of state, but Howard was starting his training at a store about two hundred miles to the northeast. As this was likely to be the first of several moves, they kept their effects to a minimum and rented a duplex—another young couple occupying the downstairs.

Ann had more free time than that to which she was accustomed. While Howard was at the store, she tried to imagine what to do with her time. She put herself to the task of finding another position for her husband—Sears would NEVER do. If he would not do it, she would. She would go through the want ads, leaving possibilities on the kitchen table next to his breakfast of a soft-boiled egg, toast, and bacon. But Howard never looked at a one. Therefore, Ann started applying under his name, to positions she felt were worthy.

For more than a year, Ann survived miserably in the shadow of the ghost of Richard Warren Sears and his company. Howard seemed neither happy nor sad. He got up, ate breakfast, went to the store, came home, ate dinner, and then watched TV. Ann would try to broach the topic of their future and the need to get somewhere where they had better prospects, but Howard would just mumble something and then get back to his TV show.

Then just a month after the United States began Operation Rolling Thunder, a three-year bombing campaign as part of the Vietnam War, Ann, or more correctly, Ann writing under Howard's name, got an offer for a position with a nationwide insurance company—great benefits, vertically mobile, and choice of offices in which to work.

She made up a story that she had received this news via a colleague she met at the United Way, a charity where she told Howard she volunteered, but where she had actually never set foot. She tried to insist it was really important that he take a quick look, but he left it, as always, untouched.

Ann was unsure what to do. They had to get out of this crazy tailspin.

The solution was amazingly simple. Why had she not thought of it before?

One day, when she and Alex, the husband of the downstairs couple whom they scarcely knew, were entering the duplex at the same time, Ann seemed to slip. She swerved, her hips striking Alex on the thigh. She then appeared to lose her balance, but rebounded cat-like and slapped Alex hard across the jaw, yelling he had tried to grope her.

The poor man became instantly apologetic, trying to calm his neighbor, attesting to his innocence, and apologizing for any completely unintended misinterpretation—after all, it was she who had stumbled into him. But a tearful Ann would have none of it. Through her sobs, she admonished that her husband would deal with this grievous attack.

Howard came home, ready for dinner and TV, to find a blurry-eyed Ann at the kitchen table, through her snivels, telling her husband what had happened, beseeching him to do something.

Howard, knowing his wife better than she realized, felt this was nothing being blown up into something. But he also knew better than to cross his wife. She was decided. Thus, grudgingly he went downstairs to confront Alex—or at least make some sort of show that he was following orders.

Less than five minutes later, he was back at Ann's side, assuring her Alex sincerely sent his excuses for any confusion arising from their totally accidental encounter that afternoon. Their neighbor was so extremely sorry the stumble had led to any distress on Ann's part. Alex and his wife offered to take them both out for drinks to help forget the unfortunate event.

Ann exploded. There was no accident. There was no stumble. There was no confusion. He had groped her. They had to leave. They could not stay here. She could not live in a duplex with a sex offender. If they did not find a way to get out, then she would have no recourse but to go to the police and make a formal complaint against Alex.

Howard had no desire to fan the flames of a fire that was already more than he could handle. He promised his wife he would think of something.

She then almost miraculously came out of her stupor, saying this was an act of providence. There was this other job opportunity. This was a good chance to leave Sears, leave this dead town, leave this dismal duplex, leave the downstairs sexual pervert, and turn a new page.

Howard could only agree.

Ann silently thanked the goddess Antevorte, the goddess of the future, for assuring they take a new path and leave this atrocious place and these atrocious conditions.

Howard did get the insurance job. There was some training and an apprenticeship. But by the end of 1966, shortly after the first black was elected to the United States Senate since Reconstruction, Howard was a full-fledged agent. He then accepted, or he obtained Ann's benediction for an assignment where he would be the Assistant Manager in an office, still in-state and closer to Ann's parents. They bought a three-bedroom ranch-style house and a 1966 tan Ford Galaxie.

The next year, while Ronald Regan governed California, the first North Sea gas reached shore, there were coups in Togo and Sierra Leone, and, in the case of *Loving vs. Virginia*, the Supreme Court overturned laws prohibiting interracial marriage, Ann and Howard put down roots. By Thanksgiving, Ann was pregnant.

In the summer of 1968, three months after the assassination of Martin Luther King Jr, the signing of the Civil Rights Act, and the testing of a major nuclear device in Nevada, approaching her twenty-sixth birthday, Ann delivered a seven-and-a-half-pound baby boy. They named him Robert after his paternal Great Grandfather.

Six weeks after Robert's birth, Walt entered his senior year in high school. He was as equivocal about being an uncle as he had been about his sister's marriage.

Ann, however, was secretly on the verge of collapse. Throughout her married life, she had maintained the habits she had established in college—regularly calling home. In school, she called every Sunday—starting when she had been a freshman calling from the payphone in the closet next to the communal showers in her dormitory. When she became a married woman, with a yellow touch tone Princess phone in the kitchen and a classic black desk rotary in the bedroom, she called every Monday and Friday as well as any other day when there was a crisis—which was nearly every day. So much of housekeeping and married life was fundamentally foreign to her that she needed her mother's nearly constant guidance. Her mother had been her constant chaperone—even if from afar.

Now as a mother herself, she was panicking. Where was her chaperone? She was responsible for a baby—her baby. And, she had no idea what to do. Every move or sound the baby made, she was on the phone to Margaret, often on the verge of becoming hysterical—she was petrified her baby could get sick or die—she was petrified her baby could be anything but exceptional.

Margaret was forthright to a fault. Yet, exceptionally, she did not share with her husband the fact that she was providing nearly continuous instruction and guidance to their daughter. She knew Julian's convictions were that new couples must, as they themselves had done, stand upright on their own feet—build their own lives. She knew he would not like the fact that Margaret was still taking such an active role in their child's adult life. She decided, painfully for her, the least said the better.

She did not want to dampen her husband's exuberance. Julian was delighted to be a grandfather—and a boy! A boy named after his father. It was all wonderful. His misgivings of, and ill feelings for Howard vaporized. Ann and Howard were now the perfect family and they had given him the perfect gift.

The crowning glory of the gift was when Ann informed her parents that she and Howard wanted little Robert christened in their church. They would come home for the baptismal. Everyone would be invited.

But once the shine had worn off the newborn and he was just a baby for whom to care and protect, life changed completely for Ann and Howard. The weeks and months seemed to transpose into unending battles for survival of her child—or for the survival of their mental health. Little Robby would cry at all times of the night, get colicky, vomit, poo, scream, turn red, perspire rivers, and spew voluminous quantities of saliva.

Howard was either at work or asleep—there only being a few hours a day when he could, if he so wished, lend a helping hand. It was all on Ann. And a distraught Ann called her mother again and again:

"He won't eat."

"What?"

"Robby," Ann wailed, "he won't eat!"

"Maybe he's just a little fussy?"

"It's not fussy! He won't eat!"

"Now, Honey." Margaret tried with calm voice, "how is the little fella doing?"

"He won't eat."

"I understand," her mother continued, "but is he alright otherwise? Is he active? Is he crying?"

"He seems OK."

"Well, is he active like on most days?"

"I guess so."

"How's his color?"

"Looks fine."

"Does he have a temperature?"

"Don't know."

"Well, if you really think it could be a problem, maybe you should take his temperature? Do you have a thermometer?"

"Yes."

"So, what's the problem?"

"MOTHER! I said, he won't eat?"

"Calm down dear," Margaret tried to sooth, "he won't eat at all or won't eat something?"

"Carrots!"

"Hmmm, carrots?"

"Uh-huh, carrots. I was feeding him lunch and he refused to swallow the carrots—just kept spitting them out. He ate the peas, sweet potatoes, and the peaches, but not the carrots. What am I to do?"

"Well, Honey, try feeding a little less and don't push the carrots for a while."

And, it was not just child rearing. Ann was befuddled by so much—again seeking the aid of her mother:

"Damn it, Mother," Ann agitatedly complained once again, "Howard comes home with all sorts of stains on his good white shirts and I can't seem to get them out."

"It's OK dear," Margaret, now accustomed to the daily and sometimes hourly dramas, tried to mollify her flustered offspring, "have you tried lemon?"

"Huh?"

"Take a lemon and some salt," Margaret spoke softly, trying to quench her daughter's obviously tight nerves, "squeeze the lemon on the stains, rub some salt over them, let it sit a while before you launder."

"Thanks, you're wonderful."

"Just doin' my job—as you're learning, you're a mother for life."

"Hmmm, Mother, there's one more thing."

"Yes, dear."

"I tried to make spaghetti and meatballs for Howard, it's one of his favorites."

"Yes," Margaret interjected, knowing that Ann really disliked spaghetti with any sauce.

"Well, I put in too much salt. I don't want to throw the sauce away. It took far too long to prepare. But it's too salty. What can I do?"

"It's OK, honey," Margaret said, trying her best to unburden her daughter, "do you know how to make a simple wheat flour dough?"

"I guess so."

"Fine. Make some and roll it into little balls about half the size of ping-pong balls," Margaret was going to say balls about three-quarters of an inch in diameter, but realized before she spoke, that this was not a reference that would be easy for her daughter—visualizing numbers and dimensions had never been easy for her.

"Guess I can do that."

"Put two or three balls in your sauce. Wait ten to fifteen minutes and taste it. If it's still too salty, add two or three new balls of dough."

"And then what?"

"That's it."

"I can serve it to Howard?"

"Well, taste it first."

Margaret was a little concerned. She had certainly had a lot to learn when she and Julian had first been married. But she had not hung on her mother's shirttail to get by—she had just learned to do what she had to do. In fact, even if she had wanted to lean on Isabelle, it would not have carried her very far. No one was less domestic than her own mother. She was really in awe of the fact that her mother had been able to raise two children, because this required skills that were really not readily available in Isabelle's toolbox. Her mother had many positive, and some unique attributes. But, being the quintessential mother, wife, and housewife was not one. Margaret felt, in many ways, the best thing for her daughter would be to have to do what she had done: move far away. Sure, there were telephones, but psychologically Ann knew her mother was close—if Ann called for help, Margaret would come running. However, if they were separated by, say the Mississippi River, this would not be so easy.

Margaret could not share her concerns with anyone. Opening this topic would open a tempest with her mother. This discussion would also force her husband to become defensive and protective of his daughter—still his little girl. Accordingly, as she had had to do more and more often these days, she kept these misgivings to herself and carried on with a smile on her face so that the casual observer thought she had nary a worry in the world.

While all the family hoopla was concentrated on Ann and baby Robby, Walt had graduated from high school and gone on to college. He did not embark on this path to seek greater knowledge nor to obtain qualifications for a great career. He had already spent much of his recent out-of-school time working in the mill—the new mill where his father worked. There seemed to be a tacit assumption on the part of everyone that he had already found his place in life—like his father and grandfather before him, following the family tradition of working with wood. He did not know who made this assumption, nor did he know if he agreed with it. For the moment, he was following the flow of the river—when you graduated from high school, you went to college. The details would work themselves out later.

Walt had been a good, but rather apathetic student in high school. Good grades came easily, yet he was rarely intellectually stimulated by any of the subject matter. Surprisingly, when he got to college, this all changed. After his freshman year, wandering aimlessly through the corridors of the State's largest university, he awoke as from a daze and decided he knew what he wanted to do. He wanted to be a scientist.

Walt realized "scientist" was a catch-all. He did not want just to be any scientist. He wanted to be a biologist who helped the world through difficult times—it sounded naive and grandiose, but he was sincere. He had, for the first time in his life, begun reading. Paul Ehrlich's 1968 bestseller, *The Population Bomb*. This had had a great impact on him. He had also read Rachel Carson's *The Sea Around Us*, as well as her 1962 work, *Silent Spring*; both these latter works reinforced his decision to orient his studies for a career that helped this world house, as well as possible, all the extra bodies that were coming far too soon. He wanted to house them, but moreover, house them in such a way as to ensure Mother Nature would be cared for, to ensure the birds would still sing.

It sounded pompous—nearly flamboyant. But it was true.

Walt had taken a required freshman psychology class where the professor had talked about population studies with rats. If you just kept throwing more and more rats into the cage, they became aggressive, they fought, they competed for food and water—their lives became complete disorder. Walt equated this with President Johnson following General Westmorland's recommendations for expanding the war in Vietnam—throwing in more and more GIs. Walt did not see this through the prism of capitalism vs. communism, world hegemony, or even right vs. wrong. He simply saw it as a clear sign of too many people, and more to come.

That summer, when Walt came home over school holidays to work at the mill, that summer when Judy Garland died and Teddy Kennedy drove off a bridge, Walt announced to his parents that he wanted to transfer out-of-state. He wanted to start his sophomore year at a school where he could study as he now knew he needed to study. He wanted to go to the University of Chicago.

In some ways, Margaret and Julian were pleased to see their son invigorated about his university studies. They even welcomed the chance for him to experience a part of the country where they had grown up. But this effectively put him out of touch. Nonetheless, seeing what they were going through with Ann's continued dependence, they decided to cast no aspersions on his plans.

The same level of support could not be attributed to his sister. She adamantly opposed her little brother going off half way across the country—might as well be across the world. She argued strenuously with her parents that Walt was ill prepared to face living totally alone at this time in his life. She recalled, he had been so premature, he had been so weak, and so behind others. She felt this still influenced his life, right up to the present day. He had, in her view, never really been able to go it alone. Why, she reminded for her parents, she herself had often had to intervene when he was trying to make friendships—delicately (or not) persuading him not to associate with disreputable people—people below his standing, including those who would ultimately drag him down. If he were far, far away, who would help him? Who would guide him? Who would protect him? Who would help him choose his friends, make his decisions, get on with becoming a man? Ann underlined how, as her wonderful parents knew so well, life was tough. Ann herself was struggling. How much more difficult would it be for poor premature Walt?

Ann's enunciations were more about Ann than Walt—albeit, it was unclear if her parents had any notion of this fact. Ann still managed to exert considerable influence over her mother and father by long distance—the distances, after all, not being that great. She still, in her numerous chats with her mother, managed to bring up her brother in a variety of contexts—always disparaging, always highlighting his seeming weaknesses versus her self-proclaimed strengths. This would be almost impossible if he got away to Chicago. There would be no way, if he moved east, she would have an inkling of what or how he was doing—no way she could twist and turn these tales to her advantage. No, this was not a good turn of events—she was solidly against it and she made her feelings known.

Walt was completely unaware of these discussions, ostensibly about his wellbeing. Had he known, he would have been ill-prepared to interpret their rational. He was simply satisfied his parents agreed with his plans—plans he was now setting in motion.

By the summer of 1970, Walt was well settled in Chicago and Ann, having waited the acceptable two years, announced she was again pregnant. Elsewhere in the country—although Ann was totally unaware—a white man killed his pregnant wife and two daughters and a little later a black man was beaten and killed, reportedly by a white man and his son, four students protesting the war in southeast Asia were killed at Kent State in Ohio, fourteen officers were charged with offenses relating to the My Lai massacre, and the first female became a general in the United States military.

Walt's studies progressed normally as did Ann's pregnancy.

By his junior year, Walt had focused his scholastic program on population biology; receiving top marks and finding himself in the upper ten percent in his academic department. He had transformed into a very erudite, some might even say dull, young man from the rather carefree wanderer of his youth.

Walt, unlike his sibling, felt very strong ties to family—not the conjugal family, but the wider extended family which he felt was responsible for so much of the family's character, as he liked to call it. By the time he arrived in Chicago, his Aunt Helen had passed away and his cousins had blown away to the far corners of the earth—one in South Africa and the other in Great Britain. However, there was still a considerable block of his father's family in Des Moines as well as his Great Aunt Mabel. Walt, really the first in his immediate family, made overtures to these relations and then carefully nurtured these links by visiting Iowa at least twice a year.

While Walt was studying how to mitigate the population crisis, and at the same time trying to build bridges to previously overlooked extended family members, Ann was nursing her pregnancy and trying to see how, given her lack of physical proximity, she could remain at the epicenter of her nuclear family. Each was devoting no small part of their energies to the tasks at hand. Each was, in turn, obtaining at least modest positive results.

Among the various tasks in play, the most direct cause and effect was that of giving birth. A week before Palm Sunday, Ann gave birth to an eight-pound baby girl they named Lillian, Lilly for short, in honor of her great great grandmother, Isabelle's grandmother—Ann hoping the honorific name would keep the bonds with her family at home strong and reliable.

Margaret and Julian were, for a second time, ecstatic. A granddaughter and a grandson—what more could one ask for. Ann was making her parents very happy.

The second child, as usual, proved to be much less distressing for the parents than the nerve-racking first. Ann's reliance on her mother's tutelage was greatly reduced, but she still called at least three times a week. She could not bear to think that the "out of sight, out of mind" phenomena could affect her relationship with her parents.

A few months after Lilly's arrival, Howard's father suffered a brief, but very dramatic illness—he passed away hopefully finding death a relief after the tortures he underwent in his last days. Howard's mother was devoured by her husband's illness—almost as though she too suffered from the same ailments. She was no longer able to keep up the old family home and, with the encouragement of her son and daughter-in-law, she decided to move to a retirement community in Arizona where she too succumbed before Lilly's first birthday.

Shortly after his niece's first birthday, Walt graduated with honors, immediately entering a graduate program at Washington University in St. Louis.

While Ann coddled her daughter and Walt dove into his studies, Margaret and Julian breathed deeply, feeling they had done well, things were working out, their children were now on their paths to establishing their own lives and their own dreams.

Margaret had one misgiving still to resolve. Her mother was not good for her husband's increasingly fragile health. Julian had developed a heart problem brought on by years of neglecting his own health in favor of devoting all his strength to his family and his work. True to his Germanic roots, he was willing to give it all for the greater good—even at the cost of his health.

Increasingly, Julian and Isabelle seemed to irritate each other simply by being together. Isabelle was Isabelle and there was little her daughter could do to change her into a kinder and gentler mother-in-law. She expressed her views adamantly—doubling down if confronted. She demanded others conform to her way of thinking and her way of living—claiming it to be the right of old age. She was, Margaret knew, just being herself.

But, whereas Julian had been able to rebuff these irritating tendencies as just mother-in-law foibles a few years ago, they now really got under his skin. He had a hard time keeping silent. The harder he tried, the more he became frustrated. The more he became frustrated, the more his blood pressure rose. Margaret knew it was up to her to seek a remedy.

Julian's health continued to worsen. His doctor prescribed new medication but advised Margaret that the road to health was controlled by more than medications—even more than by diet and exercise combined with medications. Julian needed less stress in his life if he was to regain most of his health.

Margaret felt she had no choice but to act. Yet, she did not know how to act. She started making enquiries, talking to people, seeing what other did when they had aging parents. Ultimately, the sole choice seemed to be to persuade Isabelle to enter what was naively called a retirement center.

Margaret canvased the area within a hundred-mile radius and found a very reputable and apparently comfortable establishment not sixty miles away. It was beautifully situated on a hilltop with a magnificent view of the river valley below. This would be a wonderful place for Isabelle—wonderful, at least, in Margaret's eyes. But she doubted if her mother would share this vision.

There was no real way to address this topic diplomatically. It was just a matter of fact, Isabelle had to move if Julian was to stay alive. When Margaret delivered the news to her mother, she was surprised by the equanimity with which Isabelle took the declaration that would require her to be banished. Unbeknownst to her daughter, upon hearing the pronouncement, Isabelle, with a sad smile, was silently recalling to herself her thoughts about how Hephaestus and the Lovings had been banished—she was now joining their ranks.

Out of guilt, Margaret decided to arrange a party for her mother—she could not call it a send-off nor an *au revoir*—in the smartly printed invitation, she called it a celebration of life. She invited everyone. Mabel was in too poor health to travel but sent a lovely bouquet. Anne also sent her sister her loving regards *in absentia*. Margaret marveled at how these three old gals managed to keep hanging on.

Ann announced she would come home for her Grandmummie's party—bringing Lilly but leaving Robby with Howard. Walt sent regrets, his research requiring his full attention. Inez played a pivotal role, helping Margaret with all the arrangements. They catered the event at the Club to ensure all Isabelle's card players would be in attendance.

The party was well attended and apparently enjoyed by all if the consumption of alcohol was any gauge of success. For most of the time, Isabelle sat in a large chair in one decorated corner of the room, looking like a queen reviewing her subjects. However, for about thirty minutes, Isabelle picked up her cane and walked over to sit next to her granddaughter. She and Ann had a heart-to-heart.

"Ann, dear," Isabelle started, "I so hope you and your family are doing well."

"Yes, we are, Grandmummie."

"I hope you're keeping that husband of your in line."

"Howard's doing well."

"Remember, dear, when we studied the Greek gods and goddesses?"

"Of course, Grandmummie."

"Do you remember the goddess Anake—the Mother of the Fates?"

"Yes."

"Anake was the only one who could control the Fates. You are Anake. You control your fate. Do you understand?"

"Yes."

"Your fate is not to be one of the masses—one of the commoners. You come from a long line of strong women. You are even stronger than your mother. You are part of an elite—one of the chosen. You have right on your side as long as you do what you know is right. You are Anake."

"I do understand, Grandmummie. I now understand much better than I did when we were studying together all those years ago. And, I know what is right. You have my word, I will do what is right."

"You must, and you must help Lilly understand—she is your responsibility as I do not think her grandmother will be able to provide the necessary stewardship."

"Lilly and I will do the right thing."

"You must be unwavering—unbending. Once you sway, you will lose your way."

"I understand."

"There are always those who will want to divert you, to try to convince you to do otherwise, to shame you, or to make you feel guilty. Do not let this happen. You are my legacy."

"I understand."

Then, in a matter of days, Isabelle was residing on her hilltop with her memories. There were card games. There were plenty of people with whom to chat. But everyone was old. Everyone was tired. And, most were not up to her standards. Unfortunately, these were not the elite with whom Isabelle could bond, they were just other orphans like herself with whom she could try and survive.

Over the next few years, a new equilibrium was established. Julian's health stabilized. Margaret drove over the mountain and visited her mother every Friday—exchanging her weekly visit to the hair dresser with a weekly maternal rendezvous. Walt expanded his research and decided to continue in graduate school, pursuing a doctorate. Ann fussed over her children while also fussing over the fact that Howard's upward mobility seemed to be a long time coming.

Just before Lilly turned four, as her brother prepared to enter first grade, their Great Great Aunt Anne, whom they had never met, died. Neither Isabelle nor Mabel was able to go to Sarasota for the funeral. Margaret and Julian went. After the burial, there was a reading of the will. With no foreshadowing, this was when Margaret learned, with the exception of a generous stipend for Violet, she was the sole inheritor of a rather substantive bequest. Anne had invested wisely. She not only had her home, which had skyrocketed in value in recent years; there were orange groves, antiques, and stocks. All told, Margaret had just become a wealthy woman.

It was almost as though the dominos had begun to fall. Within six months of Anne's passing, Mabel was hospitalized in critical condition, passing away herself within two days of entering the hospital. Again, Julian and Margaret attended the funeral. Again, Margaret was the sole inheritor—this time to a considerably more modest estate.

Julian used the rare visit to his hometown to spend some time with his own family. His mother was doing well for her age. While Steve was still out west, his other siblings were close at hand, making sure the matron of their family was well cared for.

However, two years later, shortly after Walt received his PhD, when Jimmy Carter was president and when the Save Our Children crusade pushed the state of Florida to rescind gay rights, within three months of each other, the in-laws, Mrs. Martha Müller and Mrs. Isabelle Hardy Baker, died—closer in death than in life.

Julian, Margaret, Ann, and Walt attended both funerals.

Martha's mourners filled her Lutheran Church in Des Moines. There were accolades and praises for her many kindnesses. There was a well-attended wake where all her favorite German dishes were served. The family cried together, then celebrated Martha's reunion with her beloved Robert.

Isabelle's obsequies were, to say the least, more sedate. There was no one except the immediate family in attendance—Isabelle had outlived all her close friends and family of her generation. There was a brief, almost scripted service in the nondenominational chapel in the center on the hill—the center that Isabelle had called "the home" and that was her home in her final days.

Isabelle's testament, in addition to declaring she should be buried next to Bradly, stipulated that her daughter would be her sole inheritor. While Isabelle's bequeathal added considerably to Margaret's already substantial wealth, her burial requirements were hard for Margaret to accept. Margaret had never accepted Bradley and she was not about to accept him as her mother's partner in the afterlife. Defying her mother's wishes, she accompanied the coffin to Des Moines and had her mother interred next to her father.

As the family adjusted to a new life without grandmothers, Walt accepted a position at the Institute of Applied Population Dynamics in Washington, DC. IAPD was one of the leading groups examining the impact of ballooning population on the globe. It was considered as one of the top think tanks on this subject—a prestigious and meaningful place to work.

Ann was concerned about her brother's growing professional status. Her insecurities bloomed as she saw her little brother move into what might be considered the limelight. She realized his growing recognition as an expert in his field could easily eclipse her family's commonplace existence—even though she adamantly maintained it was anything but commonplace. Nonetheless, she felt the possibility Walt would outshine her in the eyes of her parents was remote. She was satisfied her brother was far enough away and working in a subject totally foreign to her parents that his advancement was scarcely noticed.

Ann decided to fence-off her brother for the moment—a fence she could peek through so as to make sure he was posing no imminent threats. She concentrated on building the image of her family—in her eyes and critically, in the eyes of others.

Lilly was now in first grade and Robby in third. Ann had managed to oversee her children's lives to the point where they had been able to enter primary school as healthy, and she was sure, in all ways, normal kids. Howard had also, at long last, received a promotion. For Ann, things were going smoothly.

Howard, as an only child, had inherited his parent's estate. Now, unexpectedly Ann's mother had so endeared herself to the wider family that she had, fortuitously if unintendedly, consolidated the estates of all those members of Grandmummie's generation—all that remained was for Ann herself to replace her mother as executor of these endowments. Yes, things were moving smoothly.

Then the Greek goddess Tyke, the goddess of province and fortune, smiled on Ann—she was convinced this being arranged by her Grandmummie's spirit. Her destiny got even brighter.

She could always count on her brother to put his foot in his mouth or burn his own bridges. He was just too honest and forthright. He believed too much in people being good. He had listened too closely when their mother had chanted, "Do unto others as you will have others do unto you."

Ann knew things did not work this way. But she also knew her brother, regardless of all, still thought this way. He was naive. He was doomed.

Two years after starting at IAPD, Walt took a real vacation, one of his first. He came home to see his parents. He came home to give his parents the news: he was engaged. He was so proud and happy. He wanted to share with his parents the joy he felt at being so lucky that Emma had accepted his offer of marriage.

As they sat in the living room having one of his father's stout cocktails, Walt cheerfully filled his parents in, "Honestly, I never thought it would happen. With all the work of school, then the new job, it just didn't seem possible."

"Well, tell us all about her, honey," Margaret gushed.

"Yes, son, Tell us. Did you meet her at work?" Julian added.

"No, not at all," Walt started, "I always go to the same café for lunch . . ."

"Don't you make your own? It's better for you, you know," Margaret interrupted.

"Don't interrupt, dear." Julian scowled. "And let the boy alone about food, you have me to control—that's enough."

"OK, OK," Margaret acknowledged, "so honey, you and she eat at the same place?"

"Not really, but maybe, I'm not sure," Walt replied.

The quizzical look on his parents' faces told the story. Walt expanded, "Emma works at the café."

"You're saying she's a waitress?"

"Yes."

"You mean she waits tables while she goes to school?"

"No."

"Well what do you mean?"

"I mean," Walt said succinctly, "she's a waitress—that's what she does—she's a waitress."

"But, like, this is temporary while she looks for something else?"

"I don't know."

"What do you mean you don't know? When a college girl is a waitress, there's some reason. Now you're going to marry her, and you don't know?"

"Well." Walt was unsure the conversation would take this bend. "Actually she's not a college girl. She's never been to college."

"What!"

"No, never been to college."

"But, you're a doctor—got a PhD—and you're dating someone who's never been to college?"

"Yep."

"This doesn't make sense. There's lottsa girls out there."

"Probably, but I love Emma."

"But . . ."

"Wait, there's more. If you've a problem with her education, you may have even more of a problem with her. She's black."

"My God—NO!"

"Well, you raised me. You told me everyone was equal."

"Yes, but . . ."

"She's wonderful. We love each other. What more is necessary?"

"I bet she's after your money. You know how these people are. We'll offer her a settlement."

"Listen, she's not after anything. She was even very hesitant to date me and even more so to marry me. I've been the mover all along."

"But you can't . . ."

"You should meet her."

"You can't . . ."

"Listen, she's great. Give her a chance."

"You can't . . ."

"Please listen to me."

"There's nothing more to say."

"I'm sorry your feel that way."

"I said, there's nothing more to say."

Margaret seemed to shake off the shock of what she had just heard, realizing her husband and son were on the verge of blowing-up. She needed to provide some sort of buffer or reprieve, "Let's just put all this on hold for the moment. We're all tired. We'll take about it tomorrow."

Without further words, Walt went out for a walk and Julian went to his bedroom. Each appeared ready to follow Margaret's advice and at least cool things down for a while.

The next morning over breakfast, the subject was never mentioned. Julian went to work, and Walt went off to visit a childhood friend he had not seen in years. Walt and his friend were going to meet for a cup of coffee, so he did not plan on being gone long. When he returned before lunch, he found his mother sitting at the dining table sobbing terribly. She could not speak.

When, finally, she regained some of her wits and was able to talk, she told her son, "Your father's dead."

Slowly and painfully she managed to tell him enough for him to put the pieces together. His mother had received a call from Julian's office just before Walt had got home. His father had collapsed at work. They had called an ambulance, but Julian was declared dead on the spot.

Walt called Ann and Uncle Steve. Both would be coming as quickly as possible.

It was the next day before they arrived. Walt and his mother had visited his father at the mortuary. Then, when the others arrived, they conferred on Uncle Steve the arrangements for the funeral while Walt, Ann, and Margaret—all in deep shock—sat and stared into space.

Finally, as the reality sunk in, Ann began to ask Walt about his visit home. It came out rather quickly that Walt was engaged—engaged to a black woman.

"I cannot accept that!" Ann almost howled.

"You need to meet her."

"No," Ann continued, "I can never accept that. Not you. Not my brother. Not a BLACK woman. No, no. no."

"You need to give us a chance."

"No."

"Ann."

"No."

"Please."

"No!"

So, it ended. There would be no tolerance. There would be no acceptance. There would be no flexibility. There would only be "no."

Once the trauma of losing her father had become a constant throb and no longer violent, burning pain, Ann realized that, even in these heartbreaking circumstances, she was set to have a double win.

It was impossible, simply impossible, the family could accept Walter marrying a black woman. This would never be tolerated. *Never!* So, if her brother steadfastly (and, if he was anything, he was headstrong) maintained this action, he would, in the best of scenarios, be seen in the worst possible light. If Ann were able to twist things about a bit, she could probably hold

Walter accountable for their father's untimely death—the possibility of having someone black in the family too great an injury for his weakened heart. She would certainly be able to use this blatant example of irresponsible behavior as a fact reconfirming her brother's basic inability to be a rational adult.

It would test her powers of persuasion, but if she were completely successful, she would be able to persuade her mother to come and live with her, thereby ensuring that she would control the family and its wealth—two goals scored.

Her father's death was a catastrophic loss. But her mother was now extremely vulnerable. This vulnerability could be the fulcrum Ann needed to tilt the family fully in her favor—guaranteeing her situation for the rest of her life as well as for Robby and Lilly.

She needed to plan carefully and move with care. She would not bring Howard into the affair at this time. If, however, things were moving in the right direction, she would quickly solicit his help to expedite the processes.

All these thoughts happened even before her father was buried. His death had been so unexpected that it took some time to arrange the funeral. In the end, no one from Des Moines came. But, before all was organized for the burial, Ann had organized her tactics. Before her father went one last time to the Congregational Church, Ann had already prepared the ground. She commiserated with her mother, astounded at her brother's insensitive and carelessly immature behavior, and insisted her mother, now alone in a harsh and sometimes ruthless world, needed to move to be closer to Ann and her family.

It worked. Margaret, totally vulnerable as Ann knew, was susceptible to her daughter's pushes and pulls. Steve tried to advise his sister-in-law to go slowly—not to make any irreversible changes until her heart, her mind, and her soul had adjusted to this terrible loss. But Margaret was decided. She needed Ann. She could not go on without Ann. As soon as she could, she would move to be close to Ann.

The only slight correction Margaret made was to refuse to move into Ann's home. She knew Ann had the space. But Margaret also knew from painful personal experience what can happen with mothers-in-law. She did not want to be to Howard what Isabelle had been to Julian. She would have her own home. Her own home, as close as possible to Ann's.

Accordingly, after the ceremonies were all completed—Walt flew back to DC, Steve and Christine left, Howard and the kids went home, and Ann stayed to help her mother prepare for the move.

Walt had valiantly tried to convince his mother that Uncle Steve was right: she should go slowly, let her emotions heal. Margaret would have none of it. She was going to Ann.

Walt's mother was subdued. She looked beaten, but in true Margaret fashion, kept her head high—never leaving her bedroom without being correctly attired—the tracks of tears on her cheeks carefully covered by a tasteful dusting of makeup. Although she was gentle, almost condescending, to her son, Walt could see his mother was someone transformed by pain. Uncharacteristically, she remained almost mute—sharing little from her heart or soul. He left never really knowing her feelings about his own plans for the future—unsure but fearing for the worst. Approval, or even receptivity, was unlikely.

His mother would listen to no one but Ann. And, Ann had become a skilled puppet master pulling delicately, almost unnoticeably, on the marionette's strings.

Within three months, Margaret had moved into a home a block away from Ann's.

On the other side of the country, Walt gave Emma a quick review of the goings-on when he went home—no gory details, just the synopsis. Ultimately, it all boiled down to his family being less than enthusiastic about their boy entering into a mixed racial marriage.

This was all new ground for his mother and sister. This was, Walt stressed, completely outside their way of thinking. They would have to learn and, when they did, when they knew Emma, they would love her as he did. He knew they would come around.

12

Meet Emma

EMMA HAD NO PRECONCEIVED ideas about what would happen if and when she married a white man. What she knew was that it would not be easy and that a lot of folks would be against it. And, she had not set out to have a white boyfriend. She had dated a lot of black guys. When she had first met Walt, she had never imagined that she might actually fall in love with him. But she knew the strangest things often happened—one such being the fact that she did find herself being in love with Walt and he with her. Thus, family support or no family support, they had a special connection that was too unique, too important to throw away. Despite totally different backgrounds, they found themselves with so much in common—so much pleasure in each other. They needed to take the next step. Emma and Walt agreed they should get married and they did.

They had a civil ceremony. They found a larger apartment. She kept working at the café and he at IAPD. On weekends they enjoyed all the special sights and sounds DC offered; sometimes going north or south along the seaboard to taste new treats and enjoy new panoramas. But much of their time was spent just enjoying each other.

While Walt and Emma got to know each other and the Mid-Atlantic States, Margaret was taking Ann and her family on a variety of luxurious vacations from the Bahamas to Switzerland to Hawaii. She bought Ann a new car. She paid for braces for Robby's teeth and dance lessons for Lilly. She paid country club dues for Howard, so he could play golf. In short, although she had her own home, she was an *ad hoc* member of the Ann and Howard Newcastle family—she had lunch and dinner with them, went shopping with them, went with Ann to pick the kids up at school or after soccer practice. She went to church with them, went to the grocery store with them (where she often paid as a dutiful roommate), even went to the circus with them. As much as she did not want to turn into her mother, for better for worse, she became the omnipresent mother-in-law.

Margaret was always there. She became the intrepid cornerstone of a five-member team. She was definitely not the team captain, but she felt she was a valued member—she contributed. And, by choice, she did all this in total ignorance of what was happening with her son. She did not want to know—so she did not ask.

Margaret would send her son a Christmas card—addressed to him alone. She would call Walt two or three times a year. If he did not answer the phone, she would coldly ask, "May I speak with Walter please?"

Like a throbbing beacon, the name EMMA, EMMA, EMMA flashed in her brain. She tried to turn it off. She tried to jettison it like some unwanted scrap. She tried, but she could not get rid of it—but she could and did ignore it.

Ann, the acknowledged captain, thought it was fantastic that her mother was by her side. She thought it was wonderful that her children would have a chance to get to know their grandmother so well. Howard, somewhat less heartily, echoed his wife's opinion—it was good to have Margaret around. Of course, it was also good to have Margaret around to pick up the tab on so much and to arrange so many special events for the family—events that Howard would never have thought of in a thousand years. For Howard, it was a big outing to go bowling or to a high school football game. He concluded Margaret may well have been a plus for the Newcastle's, even if this meant letting her own life (like his) be domineered by her daughter.

But for Margaret, the hardest part was not the over influence of Ann. Margaret had always seen herself in a supporting role—be it with her own mother or her dearly departed husband. This was just a different script for the same character. The real challenge was not confronting the grip of her daughter in terms of deciding what to do and where to go. The real challenge was dealing with her daughter's uncompromising intolerance that accepted no alternatives.

It was not possible to have a thoughtful discussion with Ann on a topic once Ann had made up her mind. Ultimately, Ann boiled things down to black or white (no pun intended with regard to her new unacknowledged sister-in-law, whom none had yet met). Having done this, she obstinately chose black or white—no further discussion accepted, no other options on the table.

This approach to life was antithetical to the way Margaret had lived. Both Isabelle and Julian, not to mention a score of others with whom she had had friendships and associations, were strong-minded—even narrow-minded. But they at least let others say their piece—even if they insulted them in the process. For Ann, there was no piece nor peace. There was but one way. And, Margaret had to get used to it.

However, it was hard to get used to.

Margaret had been an empathetic person all her life—perhaps too empathetic. Certainly, overly empathetic considering the company she most frequently kept—including family. Margaret liked people. Her own mother had never been able to indoctrinate her into the value of an oligarchy in terms of it being the best way of getting the best out of the best.

In spite of the seeming contradiction, Margaret believed people were genuinely good despite the fact that she could not open her arms nor her heart to a woman she knew was her daughter-in-law. Unlike her own mother, she cherished her ties with old friends and comrades. She wanted to stay in touch. She wanted to do good. She wanted to help.

As her wounds became less acute, she tried to be more introspective. There were so many times now when Margaret realized she and her daughter were simply so different—as though they were chiseled from different stone. Ann would accompany her mother to church on Sunday—sometimes with the rest of the family. While for Margaret it was a spiritual time to try and keep her thoughts and emotions in synchrony with the teachings of Christ, for Ann it was a social event. A time to be seen and, hopefully, appreciated if not envied. Ann had no Christian beliefs. As her grandmother, she could just as easily have been an ancient Egyptian polytheist worshiping Osiris, Anubis, and Horus. Grandmother and granddaughter believed there was a power, probably even a religious power, that promoted and protected the capable, the chosen elite, for the betterment of all—they, of course, being part of the peerage.

Ann was bathing her children in the ether of this plutocratic mind set.

Initially Margaret tried to counterbalance her daughter's asymmetrical view of life.

"Honey," she said one day, "when the children complain the poor grades are because the teacher is unfair, maybe this is just a pretext. Maybe they need to work a little harder."

"They're doing fine. It's the teachers these days. You remember, I was in front of a class. It's a hard job and the pay is nothing. What's it all mean? It means the only people who teach are second class folks who can't get a job elsewhere. They just wait for their paycheck and to hell with the kids."

"Now dear." Margaret tried to keep a level tone. "It really isn't like that. You know. There may be some poor teachers, just like there are poor mechanics and poor politicians. But, look at your father's mother; a terrific teacher. In general, teachers are noble people who do an often-thankless job that is so important to all of us."

"Mother," Ann responded tersely, "that may have been so in your day. Times have changed. School has changed."

"Ann." Margaret tried to bring at least one point home. "Things do change, but principles remain. What was right for my grandmother is still right for my granddaughter. There is a right way."

"Mother," Ann continued, more sternly, "there may have been a right way once. Now it's everyone for himself. Everyone wants to see how much they can get—how much they can get for free—how much they can get off the backs of others. Most of these kids in school with Robby and Lilly are just like their parents—trying to get by, doing the least while gaining the most from the hard work of others like us. They're parasites."

"Ann, dear, I hope you don't really think that."

"Think that? Mother, I know that."

"But honey, look at your father. He worked hard—so hard it killed him. But he totally respected all the men in the mill, from the guy who swept the floor to the one who ran the most complex machinery—he said they all worked hard and earned every dime they made."

"Again, Mother," Ann said acerbically, "that was then, this is now. And let me correct you in this too. Father did not die from mill work. Father died from a broken heart. His son broke his heart when he told him he was whimsically thinking of marrying a Negress."

"Ann, we don't know that."

"I know."

"Ann, you have to be more open."

"Mother." Ann was approaching new heights of being caustic, "just remember your own mother. She was one of the most brilliant and worldly people our family produced in generations. You know as well as I. Grandmummie would never have tolerated a black woman in this family. That's what killed Daddy and that's the mentality that keeps my kids down at school—ignorant, incompetent people who have no place being where they are nor where they want to be."

Margaret stopped, not while she was ahead, but while she still had control of her temper. She knew he daughter was right about her own mother's views. But, in no way did this mean these views were right. Isabelle made many, many mistakes—as did everyone. She just never admitted them.

Margaret remembered the Spanish proverb Aunt Anne used to enjoy reciting: *It is better to manage with a stubborn mule than to carry the wood on one's own back*. She had made her choice. She had rebuffed her brother-in-law and left her home and town quickly, in all likelihood, too quickly. But there was no way back. Ann was helping her carry her load. She had to repay this by suffering Ann's stubbornness. She had to defend this by still believing that, in her heart, Ann was the lady she had been raised to be—a good person.

What was troubling Margaret more and more was this question of goodness. She missed her husband terribly. She knew he had been, and hoped he still was, wherever he was, a good person. But she was less sure about her mother. Had Isabelle really been a good person? She did not know. Isabelle had been smart, very smart. Isabelle had been opinionated, very opinionated. But, had she really been a good person? Probably, like most people, she had been a mix of good and bad—but it sadly seemed that Ann was fixated on the more negative part of Isabelle's character.

Margaret knew her own father had learned to love her mother regardless of her, what some might delicately call, humanistic deficiencies. Isabelle was not always kind. But her father chose the good over the bad—trying to make the good shine through. Truth be known, Margaret suspected the same thing had happened with Bradley. Someone, anyone, could really not be with Isabelle very long if they did not make the clear decision that they were going to let a lot of the unattractive things go by unnoticed—focusing on the positive.

Now, it seemed Ann had reversed things. Possibly because of her really rather limited contact with her grandmother. Possibly because, at least at one time, she viewed her with the awe that any grandchild viewed her grandmother. Possibly because she did not know the context nor the background. For whatever reason, Ann had, Margaret felt, warped Isabelle's views. But Margaret had to admit also, she was not sure if these were warped. It depended upon which lens one used to look at Isabelle. Margaret's lens filtered out the dark side. Ann's lens seemed to magnify it. Margaret no longer knew which lens was right—hers, Ann's, or both.

Margaret decided the only safe thing to do was to carefully put her lens away. She could not stand to be torn between door one and door two—pulled by the forces of yin and yang. She desperately needed to sleep, awaken, and find herself in a new life where the hollow ache in her gut was gone. She needed to find peace—not pandemonium. And, pandemonium would be the result if she tried to analyze her daughter's deeds and motives. There are stones best left unturned. Oh, how she missed Julian.

Margaret felt as though she were at the county fair. She remembered clearly her mother telling her of being at the fair as a little girl, listening to the steam calliope. Isabelle had been mesmerized by the breathtaking contraption. It produced loud, if a bit astringent, music with no one playing the keys. It was like a giant version of Lillian's precious Austrian music box. The marvel was that the music was even played rather than the quality of the melody.

The calliope was a joy to watch—probably more pleasant for the eyes than the ears. Crowds, large crowds, would gather around it's huffing and tooting spot on the fairgrounds, spontaneously applauding at the wonders of modern technology. The group of onlookers was transfixed, almost respectful, as if part of a congregation in church. Then the flow of steam would hiccup, as if the machine had to take a breath and swallow. This prompted a loud squawk that was unpleasant to even the most tolerant of ears.

The yelp from the machine prompted a dissolution of the group, the dry grassy vicinity in front of the contrivance vacated until a new group formed and the process repeated itself.

Margaret felt her recovery, a new life in a new town and a new house, was like her mother's esteemed calliope. Not only did her transfigured circumstances sometimes shriek unpleasant tones, but the cycle of these transfigurations produced recurrent highs and lows, like the fair crowds flowing to and from the mythical, nearly mammoth musical instrument.

Margaret's highs and lows, interspersed with dramatic, at times traumatic, howls, turned like a cyclone around Ann's family—the buffeting winds driven by Ann's control over her loved ones. Ann, the overseer, had uncompromising attitudes as to how all, except she herself, should comport themselves. She, practically unknowingly, seemed to be trying to reenact a version of Isabelle's sardonic view of life without having her grandmother's savvy upon which to base this position. Overall, and surprisingly contrary to the overseer's hoped-for image, Ann's mundane, and when seen by the casual outside observer, completely conventional lifestyle (albeit, Ann would have railed against such a classification) provoked a mental maelstrom for Margaret—she felt like one of her mother's favorite characters, Don Quixote, the Man of La Mancha, jousting at windmills while the calliope screamed in the background. She felt crushed as she tried to placate her daughter while following her better angels.

The ups and downs of Margaret's spirit, intertwined with the random cries of the world around her, led to growing uncertainties. Disquiet seeped into unprotected spaces in her brain. Always trying to do right, had she done right? There was a deep-seated flutter, like an itch you could not reach. She was not calm. Truly, Julian's passing was still an open wound. Yet, it was more. She was not calm. She decided she had but one choice: she put all in God's hands.

Before Julian's death, Margaret had been a believer—but, kind of a hands-off devotee. Alone, without Julian, with little real solace from Ann, Margaret progressively turned more and more to her God. She looked to Him for answers she herself could not find.

Margaret loved her daughter, she adored her grandchildren, and she was even slowly gaining affection for her son-in-law. Margaret was, in most ways, glad she had left the home she had shared with her dearest Julian for so many years—a home with so many memories. Nonetheless, she was troubled.

As long as she concentrated on now, things were all right. The grand-children, like all kids, had nearly daily obstacles with which frequently Margaret was better equipped to assist than their mother—Ann often minimizing these concerns, reacting to them as though they were trivial childhood nuisances that did not warrant any significant level of her time or effort—although, it was hard to see where Ann invested most of her time and effort. The grandchildren were her salvation. And, maybe in some way, she was theirs.

Ann's mothering routinely took big, and now well-know, swings resembling the swings in her mother's emotions. At times Ann was com-pletely overbearing; even panicking about her child's health, happiness, or wellbeing. At other times, Ann was callus and dismissive—virtually ready to tell her troubled offspring, "Pull up your boots, get out there, and get it done." Ann seemed to vacillate between feeling her progeny were well-born, able to handle any and all challenges almost by divine right, and feeling her children were totally susceptible to the perils of daily life, needing a protec-tive bubble to make it through the day.

Margaret could not allow herself to analyze her daughter. If she did, it just dug a deeper and deeper hole in her soul. She forced herself to put this subject in a mental vault and file it away. She forced herself to concentrate on now—helping her grandchildren, keeping up her own home and garden, and taking care of, as an elixir for her angst, a black shepherd mix named Lucy she got, against Ann's wishes, from the pound.

The calliope played on. The highs and lows surged forward. Howard got another promotion. Robby and Lilly moved through the grades, being students much in the mold of their parents. Ann fretted. Ann preened. Ann planned.

Ann used every opportunity to bring up her brother, then immediately tarnish his actions or behavior. If her mother mentioned Walt, Ann was quick with a retort—most often stressing her sibling's less than sterling qualities.

"Honey," Margaret had said to her daughter, as many times before, when getting a letter from her son, she tried to bring Ann into the conversation, "your brother seems to be doing well. He says they're working on some really important research analyzing populations and that sort of thing. He's now head of a new special team that is doing cutting-edge work. And, at long last, Emma has quit her job at the café. Walt says she is now working at some sort of community center helping handicapped kids. Isn't that wonderful?"

"Hmmmm Mother," Ann replied with the coolness of a winter gust, "glad you got news from him. He doesn't write very often, so I'm glad he did at least, for once, do a little to keep his mother informed."

"Dear, you know how busy he is."

"Actually, I don't."

"Come on. Sure, you know. He's always been a hard worker, that brother of yours."

"Well, because he did well sweeping the floor at the mill doesn't mean much."

"Ann, honey," Margaret almost pouted, "don't be so tough on your brother. His life, too, hasn't been easy."

"Mother." Ann took over with a firm voice and a stoic look, "I hadn't really wanted to go into this now, but do you remember Colleen."

"Not really."

"Well, she was my roommate my junior year," Ann prevaricated.

"Well, maybe I do recall you mentioning her name. Go on."

"Well, she's been working in Washington for the World Bank for the last few years," Ann expanded the prevarication.

"Well, that's fine, dear."

"No. You don't see the point. I don't know if it's fine or not that she's working somewhere. But she is living in the same city as Walt. She just sent me a note, worried. She'd seen in the paper where some W. Müller had been arrested for driving drunk—do you think it's Walt. You know how he likes to drink and drink a lot."

"Of course, it's not your brother, Ann," Margaret vigorously replied, "I know, like his father before him, Walt likes a drink—but he has self-control. Don't worry."

"It's our reputation I'm worried about. You know, obviously, that Walt is now undoubtedly mixed up with that whole black community in that city—and there are a lot of them—and, the drugs, the prostitution, the immorality—there's just no imagining it all."

"I know nothing of the kind. He's working as a population biologist and doing a lot of good work. That's what I know."

"Yes. He's that. He's also married to a black. A Negress, so I hear, from the local ghettos. Don't think for a minute his PhD will pull him up. That woman will pull him down!"

"Now, Ann."

"It's true, mother. Just ask Colleen. We all tried to reason with him. He's just too bullheaded."

"But maybe she's a nice girl."

"She's BLACK!"

"Well, Ann, we pray, and we do what we can do."

"But mother, is it enough?"

"What do you mean?"

"Think of Daddy, think of Grandmmmie, think of Grandfather Robert. Think of all those people going back all those years. Every single one worked their fingers to the bone to get ahead—to make a good reputation for the family. You know so well seeing what happened after Daddy died. You can spend your whole life building something that is destroyed in the blink of an eye."

"Honestly Ann, your father's efforts have not been destroyed—the mill is still there and doing better for all the improvements he made."

"I'm not talking about the mill. You spent your adult life there. I grew up there. Daddy died there. But, has anyone from our old hometown even come to see you or call you on the phone. You're as dead to all those you thought of as dear friends as Daddy is."

"It's not that, honey. All those fine people we knew so well and lived with for so long, they all knew us as a couple: as Julian and Margaret. Take away half and you have no whole. I just don't fit in any more, that's all."

"No that isn't it at all. You're put out because your daughter-in-law is BLACK. Name one other person in that whole town, one other white person who is married to a BLACK. They know. They all know. You need to accept this and do something. It's not acceptable to us, and it's not acceptable to them."

"Ann, dear, let's pick this up another day and worry more right now about that Swiss steak you're planning on having for dinner."

Margaret's circumvention was in no way a sign that she did not take this issue very seriously. She did. But she could not argue with her daughter.

They would go round and round, but Ann would never accept to see even the slightest variation from the story she believed to be true. Margaret believed Ann sincerely believed what she said. But her lens, like a telescope, only saw a small part of a faraway image. Margaret was trying to see more, understand more. However, she now had to accept that she too saw little else. Walt had made his choice, but this was not a good choice for the family and Margaret's prime responsibility was for the family and its wellbeing.

She had always believed in treating one's children equally. Margaret had always been disturbed by families where one sibling was the obvious favorite—this just was not right. Nevertheless, now she had to face her own truth. Walt was behaving in a way that was detrimental to himself and to the family. Margaret had to protect the greater good. She had to think of the lives of those darling children, Robby and Lilly.

Margaret contacted her lawyer. She instructed him to recast her will. She could no longer be content with her estate being equally shared by her two children when one was so clearly out of bounds. Following her instructions, her testament now declared that her daughter would be sole inheritor. This was sad. But it needed to be done.

Walt never knew.

Walt had few misgivings. When he and Emma had started getting serious, they realized there were a lot of people out there who thought God had made the races so they could be easily identified and kept apart—feeling it was a sin against Nature for the races to intermingle, even socially, not to mention sexually. The young couple knew, even if they could not fully understand, that there was a lot of racism. They knew their very actions of being together would push them away from many. Nevertheless, Walt had felt, and Emma had chosen to believe, that his family would ultimately see how good the two of them were for each other and accept their union, even if it were multiracial.

Emma had what could perversely be seen as an advantage. Her parents were dead. She did not have a living black father and mother to whom to explain why her boyfriend was white and why she was not going out with one of the guys from the neighborhood. Her parents had died in an automobile accident when she was fifteen and, to a large extent, she had looked after herself thereafter—albeit, an aunt had been legally responsible for her actions until she was no longer a minor.

Emma was a pragmatist. She doubted Walt's family would truly come around. But she loved him. She had seen too many couples where there was not deep, abiding love to blithely close the door on their own loving relationship simply because the two of them happened to have different complexions. Like many marriages, theirs too might fail. But she was going to do all she could to ensure success. If their union was blessed, she would open her arms to those giving the blessing. If their union were damned, she would do her best to graciously ignore the condemner—though she knew this would be hard.

Like a couple putting their head down to walk through a blizzard, Emma and Walt clung to each other and plunged ahead with their lives—learning quickly the imprudence of asking too many questions or peeling off too many scabs. They moved ahead, and they did well.

Walt was well respected in his profession.

Emma was equally well-appreciated when she started work at the community center.

Walt wrote or called his mother once a week. He tried to find the right balance of boring her with tales of their life in DC, while making sure she knew enough to know that she could be proud of him.

For more than a decade Walt and Emma focused on their lives, their activities, at the Nation's Capital. They bought a house. They planted a garden. Walt wrote three books. Emma received a special service award. Although they had no children, they had many friends, and were intrenched in a very active and diverse social life.

Then, in 1990, out of the blue, Margaret wrote to Walt and Emma, asking if she could come and visit and celebrate with them Walt's fortieth birthday. They agreed immediately.

It was, at the very least, a strange visit. Margaret was now seventy-four years old—in surprisingly good health, but inevitably showing signs of age—signs that were more noticeable for Walt who had not seen his mother for years.

Margaret greeted Emma at the airport with a dispassionate embrace—the first time the two ladies have ever met face-to-face. On the drive from Dulles to their home in Silver Spring, Margaret solemnly announced that she had not really come because she wanted to—they both knew, or should have known, that there was a lot of friction, to put it mildly, about a mixed marriage in the family. This was real and hard to rectify. This was a predicament, according to Margaret, that never should have happened. But it had happened. Now, putting this aside, forty was a landmark in someone's life. Margaret felt, regardless of the unpleasant impasse that seemed to plague the family, it was her maternal responsibility to assist her son meet this important life threshold. She was, thus, doing her duty regardless of her personal feelings.

Neither Walt nor Emma were prepared for such a blunt and candid preface to a much belated family visit. They really had no comeback.

Walt just said, "OK, Mother."

Emma, trying to be a bit more diplomatic and welcoming, took a positive tack as was generally her custom. "Well, Mother, I hope you don't mind me calling you 'Mother', we are so glad you have finally come to see us and hope you will have a good time while you're here in Washington—we surely enjoy living here and hope we can share a bit of this joy with you."

Emma's overture seemed to have put a small crack in the wall of stoicism and Margaret permitted herself to say, with a slight smile, "I'm not really, of course, your mother. But I called Julian's mother 'Mother', so I guess you've the same possibility if you want."

After that, the subject of any family problems or complexities was not mentioned—the three of them spending the next week visiting all the well-known tourist sites of the Capital as well as a number of special places that Emma and Walt had discovered in their peregrinations through the city and its environs over the years.

The days went by, each evening the simple meals shared at the Müller home being a little more cordial, a little more warmhearted than the day before. By the time Emma and Walt dropped Margaret back at Dulles, Margaret realized that she was leaving with a very different impression than that with which she had arrived.

Her son and daughter-in-law were, obviously, a mixed-race couple. But they were not derelicts, deviates, druggies, nor drunks. They had a charming and well-kept home. They had friends and neighbors who spoke well of them. She had even visited Walt's office and met his team—they all seemed honestly impressed and satisfied with Walt's skills and leadership. Emma and Walt were different: one black, one white. But they were not ogres nor misfits. They were hardworking intelligent people who wanted to make a difference.

Before she hugged them goodbye, much more affectionately this time, she asked if she could come again next year to celebrate Emma's fortieth birthday. Emma and Walt were delighted, and the date set on the spot.

When Margaret got home, her daughter came by to welcome her and see if she had had a good trip.

"Mother," Ann said, cheerfully, "welcome back, I hope it wasn't too terrible."

"Oh, honey," Margaret immediately responded, "it was really very pleasant—nothing at all terrible about it. Your brother and sister-in-law are really special people. Washington is a lovely city. We saw so much, did so much. I am really glad I went."

Ann was shocked. She had counted on her brother's well-honed habits of doing the wrong thing at the wrong time to reinforce the image she had carefully been crafting. She had counted on Walt to be vindictive and incriminating—these reactions surely shining an ill light on her brother. But he had let her down. Apparently, he had been controlled and engaging, his Negress wife apparently also able to behave in an acceptable way. Things had not gone as planned.

"Mother," Ann attempted to calmly interject, "it's good you had this trip and saw first-hand Walt, his wife, and home. I'm so happy they are OK. They deserve to be OK, as living a life in a mixed marriage—a condition that was illegal up to a short time ago—cannot be easy. It cannot be easy to have friends, to be respected at work, to have any kind of normal social life—thank God they don't have any children who have to suffer through these unpleasant conditions."

Margaret was tired. It had been a long flight. She saw her daughter's conversation begin to focus on her main theme—the despicableness of interracial marriage. She was now uncertain of her own views. But she was certain she was tired.

"Ann, honey," Margaret said, putting on her most tired face, which was not difficult at all, "I'm very tired. We'll talk more tomorrow, but I have three hours of jet lag to get over and I need to do that in my bed."

Ann left, worried. She was distressed. Had she built from her family relations a bastion that would support her as clearly the one sibling who merited the succor of the all-important family, or had she built a house of cards?

Margaret's life, by her own admission, became discombobulated. Since Julian's death, her daughter had been her safeguard. Ann had been the crutch that kept her from crumbling into the dust and trying to crawl into Julian's coffin with him. The great and piercing hole in her heart and soul was even now not healed—just scabbed. Ann was the person who had given her the courage to move ahead one day at a time. Ann's children—their wellbeing and their future—had been the motivation for her to keep herself healthy and active. Ann's protection against the unpleasant, often hurtful, realities had allowed her to get up and greet each new day. She relied completely on her daughter.

Now she was plagued by doubt. She had seen with her own eyes the lives led by her son and his wife. She had spoken, eaten, laughed, and even cried with them. She felt, for the first time, she knew them—including for the first time really knowing her son. She felt like a queen whose standard had been rolled and hidden in a dark corner—this standard only now unfurling on a fresh breeze—only now seeing the light of day.

Her emblem, her colors were the colors of her family—the family she had created with Julian. It was a family with two children—not one. The family flag should embrace and protect all the family—not just some of the family.

She needed to do the right thing.

But how could she balance what she had just seen and experienced with what her daughter had been saying for years? She had been raised to be an honest person. She and Julian had raised their children to be honest people. She could not accept that her daughter, that Julian's daughter, was inherently dishonest—a fabricator, by even some measure, a liar. This was too much. Ann might embellish, yes. But she would not lie.

Still, Margaret could not reconcile the facts. She turned to higher powers. She turned more and more to prayer. She redoubled her efforts—trying to understand and absorb rather than rotely react. She began reading the Bible. She spent several hours a day in her room, reading scripture. She wanted a solution, but she was scared. She did not want to hurt anyone. She began saying to herself, "It's God's Will. It's God's Will." She prayed for wisdom. She prayed for guidance. She prayed for serenity. Then she went to Ann's for dinner.

As always with age, time seemed to run on fast forward, and it was soon summer again and time for her to go east for Emma's birthday. Ann tried various tactics to dissuade her mother, including proposing a vacation that was a must do at the same time Margaret was scheduled to travel to Washington.

Margaret was unwavering. She took little heed of her daughter's denunciations and theatrics. These fell on blind eyes and deaf ears as Margaret was totally focused on trying to find answers of how to heal and reunite her entire family.

When she was in the car, going from Dulles to Silver Spring for the second time, she again had a short speech for her son and daughter-in-law. She wanted to get it out right now at the beginning of her visit. She knew all was not well and that there were still ill feelings in the family. She hoped with all her heart these would heal and she wanted them to know she had put this morass, as she saw it, in God's Hands.

Emma was almost overjoyed with her mother-in-law's declaration, she felt she had been accepted and that things, finally, were moving as she and Walt had hoped they would. After all, her mother-in-law would not consider their racial imbroglio as an issue that needed God's help if she were truly opposed. She had slowly but surely come to see both sides of the story.

Walt, for his part, was glad to see this change in his mother's outlook but was unsure what role God's Hands would play. He had lived under his sister's penetrating glare, single-minded dogmas, and toxic control for his whole life. He knew the topography. He knew the actors. He crossed his fingers (literally) and hoped his mother would be able to take on Goliath.

With Margaret's strategic declaration at the very beginning of her visit, the subject was never broached again—except once. Walt had taken a day off while Emma was at the Center and was shopping with his mother, looking for presents for Ann and her family. Margaret was looking at a Georgetown hooded sweatshirt for Robby. She suddenly hugged it to her breast, looked Walt straight in the eye with her own moist eyes, and said, "I hope God and I can do something—we must try harder."

Walt had no comeback.

Margaret was not expecting one.

With this poignant exception, their time was spent sightseeing, visiting nice restaurants, and celebrating Emma's birthday with great fanfare. When they were *en route* to take Margaret back to Dulles, she thanked her children, as she called them now, for a lovely time and once again asked if she could come back next year—making this into an annual adventure. Emma and Walt were once again delighted.

The next visit came surprisingly quickly. This time, there were no declarations upon arrival, no pregnant pauses, no awkward moments. The trio just had a genuinely good time; concentrating totally on today, with no mention of yesterday or tomorrow. To all, those days took on a special glow, seeming to play in slow motion, with a velvety radiance as if seen through gossamer curtains. For them, the days seemed bathed in a new-found peace of mind. When Margaret left for the third time, it was less the painful cramps of separation, and more the profound thankfulness for having shared special experiences.

When Margaret got home, she called Annabelle. Over the years, Annabelle had become more than a distant sister-in-law—she had become a sounding board, a confidante. This was a discussion she could not have with her daughter, and, one that could not wait.

"Sweetie," Margaret started, knowing her sister-in-law enjoyed the intimacy of a sobriquet, "I need your advice."

"Of course, dear."

"I'm just back from a trip to Washington to see Walt and Emma."

"Wonderful."

"Yes, it was. I had a truly wonderful time with our son and his wife (she often used plural pronouns as though her husband were still alive). You know, this is the third visit and I feel, for the first time, I really know them well."

"And, are they worth knowing?"

"Oh yes! They really are very good people—honest, sincere, serious. I know I'm sounding like a proud mother, and maybe that's what I am. But it's been a long time since I let myself be proud of my son."

"Margaret, dear," Annabelle consoled, "you're living in difficult circumstances, still mourning my brother, your husband, and trying so hard not to be a thorn in the side of your daughter and her family, who have become your buttress."

"That's just it," Margaret almost sobbed, "I still miss Julian so, oh so, so much. Ann was there when I needed someone—maybe anyone. But, you know, she is not the easiest person. Looking back, even if I moved here, I probably should have ensured a little more distance between Ann and myself—but I can't undo anything."

"Ann has many of our family's attributes." Annabelle tried to mollify her sister-in-law. "You know, our family is German through and through. We have that German stubbornness. We can really be unbending. I think Ann may have inherited an overly strong dose of our Germanic genes. She's always been unwavering, even when she was a little girl here in Des Moines."

"Ahh, that she has. And, it's only gotten more so with age."

"Uh-huh, so you see, it's rather like walking a tight rope isn't it?"

"Boy is it."

"But you have to be careful. You have to take care of yourself. You have to watch where you walk, so you don't fall off the rope."

"Well, that's just it. It was so easy before I got to know Walt and Emma. Ann pretty much kept me apprised of things and I just knew she had my interests at heart, so I followed her lead."

"Understandable."

"Then, when Walt and Emma went ahead and actually got married and Ann was so completely against it, making what seemed like very valid arguments, I just didn't see how I could go along with our son marrying a black woman—knowing that the shock of even this possibility may have pushed my Julian over the edge. Ann understood. She saw the egregiousness of it all—it was, as we all thought, just plain wrong."

"We live in changing times—sometimes it's difficult to know what is right and what is wrong."

"I didn't understand then. I relied on Ann. I thought she understood. It all seemed wrong. I felt it was so very wrong. So, you know what I did, I disinherited him."

"Margaret, honey, that's pretty severe. Does he know?"

"No, I never told him."

"Does Ann know?"

"Of course, she supported the idea."

"Well, to me it seems pretty harsh—he is your son, regardless of who he marries, where he lives, or what he does."

"I know."

"So?"

"Well, I think I made a mistake."

"It's not really for me to say, dear, but I have a feeling you are right— you made a mistake."

"I think I'd best undo it?"

"It's up to you, but you need to do the right thing."

"I know. But I don't know what's right. I was so sure he was wrong."

"And now you are proud of your son?"

"Yes."

"Well, do the right thing."

"I will. I'll call my lawyer tomorrow and undo what I've done. I've been so wrong."

"Now, dear, just think of what you've been going through. It has been terrible—in many ways still is. It's understandable you would be unsure of what to do, react strongly to your son's choices—even seek to punish some-one who had done ill to you and our dear Julian. But, to me, it doesn't seem as though Walt has really done ill. He has followed his heart as we all have. He has turned out to be a pretty good guy, despite the skin color of his wife or his political affiliations. If you're proud of him—and you should be—then accept him fully as your son."

"I will."

As promised, the next day Margaret called her lawyer, instructing him to redraft her will, dividing all assets equally among her two children.

Four days later, the day the new will arrived in her mailbox, Margaret was found dead in her kitchen by a neighbor.

13

Adieu Margaret

ANN CALLED HER BROTHER, the first time the two had spoken in a long time, telling him their mother had passed away—apparently from choking on a slice of ham she had been eating.

Walt was in shock and soon so was Emma. They howled and cursed the gods. Burning tears washed their faces. They were angry, they were sad, they were shattered.

Ann too was grieved by the loss of Margaret, whom she saw as *her* mother. Margaret had looked surprisingly young for her years, while Ann had exactly the opposite appearance. The result was that sometimes the two were confused as sisters. In many ways, Ann thought of Margaret as her sister—a younger sister who had to be steered and protected from the hidden pitfalls of a dangerous life. Margaret had become a fixture in Ann's life. She was now gone.

Regardless of the grief, which was nearly biological, Ann had a sense of satisfaction. Her family was going to do well. She had to show an adequate level of bereavement for her children, as they were shattered with the passing of their dearly loved grandmother. But Ann was well aware that she had now succeeded in consolidating the endowments of Howard's and her parents in one plump account in her name.

Margaret's lawyer had innocently called her when redrawing the will to confirm Ann's address as one of the co-inheritors. Ann, of course, had been well aware that she had been heretofore the sole beneficiary. With her mother's death, she had appropriated the unopened letter from the lawyer that had still been in the mailbox. No one ever saw the redraft.

Ann had told her brother, and all interested family and friends, that Margaret's funeral had to be postponed a few weeks due to a particularly busy calendar at the church. She had then used this period to make all necessary arrangements so that the estate would be expeditiously settled in her name alone. She had also used this time to have Margaret cremated. She appreciated the risk. Anyone who had known her mother well, would have known that she was strenuously opposed to cremation. But, under the circumstances, it seemed a risk worth taking.

She knew her mother wanted to be buried next to her father, so she went back to her hometown and made all the arrangements as quietly as possible. She then announced to everyone that the funeral date would have to be changed, again blaming the church's busy schedule—brought forward by five days. This meant that no one had more than three days' notice—those needing to travel any distance, including Annabelle, finding it very difficult to change their plans at the last minute to attend the funeral.

Although Walt and Emma were coming the furthest distance, they were accustomed to dealing with critical issues in short order and managed to get on a flight west in time to make the funeral.

It was only after the internment that Walt and Emma had a calm moment to try and sit down with Ann and Howard—upon their arrival, they had only really had time to exchange brief at-arm's-length, light embraces with their in-laws during the hectic hours leading up to the ceremonies. When the needful for Margaret had been done, the siblings and their spouses arranged to have a drink in the bar of the motel where Walt and Emma were staying. When they were all four seated in the corner booth, silence reigned—whether due to sorrow or discomfort, it was unclear.

Walt decided he needed to open the conversation, "I guess there's no need for formal introductions at this time, although it is the first time you've seen Emma, but we are glad that we've had this chance to be together—of course, wishing it would have been under happier conditions."

Howard stared at a place halfway between the tip of his nose and the corner of the booth.

Ann, feeling compelled to do something, managed to say, "Well, there's so much to do. You know, of course, this is such a terrible shock and surprise and all the things that have to be done, have to be done by me."

"I'd be happy to help," Walt inserted.

"Really not necessary. I'm sure you've got so much awaiting your attention back east," Ann rebuffed, "And, Walt, I am not sure when the right time is, nor who is the right person, but since we're all sitting here, I guess it, as usual, is up to me. You do understand, don't you, that Mother left everything to me."

"Gosh, I'd never even thought about it."

"Well, think about it. Mother had become a real part of Howard's and my family and I guess she wanted to thank us for shoring her up all these years after Daddy's death—after Daddy died when he heard about your plans—but I'll say no more."

"Like I said, I never really thought about it."

"Well, it's what she wanted."

"Emma and I have never even discussed it."

"Well, Mother did discuss it with her lawyer and it's all done now."

"We've understood. That's not, of course, why we came. We really reconnected with Mother over these last few years—and we never ever talked about her estate."

"It's what she wanted."

"Fine. There's nothing anyone can do now, is there? If we could do something, and we can't, we'd want to bring her back, wouldn't we?"

"Uh-huh."

"We didn't really want to talk about this, just to make sure we all knew each other."

"Well, we all know each other."

"Yes."

"You know, Walt," Ann changed tack, thinking some sort of appeasement might be in order, "I know many of your things going back to high school were at Mother's. I have to deal with everything, like I said. But, if you send me a list of things that you specially might like to have, I'll see what I can do."

"We're not really interested . . ."

"No, really, do this."

"There's really nothing . . ."

"Really, just do this."

"Well, I guess . . ."

"Fine. We're all decided. Well, Howard and I have to go and see the minister to make sure there's no loose ends after the services. Have a safe trip back."

No hugs. No handshakes. It was over.

Walt and Emma did go home. They continued to cry on each other's shoulders and feel a great void that couldn't be filled—all the more bittersweet because, it was only over the past few years, their relationship with Margaret had become one that could leave a void. To them, this was still a young liaison that needed to be nourished to become what, under normal settings, would have been a parental relationship that had been built over a lifetime and not three years.

As the grief subsided, Walt did devote some time to thinking back to all those things that had been stored in his mother's attic. His guns when he had been a teenager and avid hunter. His cross-country skis, his scuba gear, his high school and college text books, his butterfly collection, his electric train, his rock collection, his fishing rods and reels—there was a lot of stuff. Stuff upon which he had not laid eyes in almost two decades. Stuff that was certainly superfluous to the lifestyle he and Emma were now leading. But his stuff, nonetheless.

He, also, mentally floated around his mother's home—like a spirit entering a haunted house. He visited each room and looked at everything; the carpets on the floor, the pictures on the wall, the furniture, the curios—everything that had made his mother's home her home. Many of these things were things that had been in his family's home when he had been born—old, comfortable things that somehow reflected his life.

He then sat down and put pen to paper, listing those special old and comfortable things as well as those things he considered his stuff—things, following his sister's suggestion, that he would like to have sent to them.

He mailed his list to Ann. Two weeks later, he called to see if she had received it. She confirmed she had. She informed him she would take care of it—in no way reacting to the items he had highlighted.

Walt, in fact, heard nothing more from his sister or her family. He and Emma fell back in their old routine—in all practicality, a relatively young married couple with no family, making a go of it in the Nation's capital.

Almost a year after his mother had died, a moving van pulled up in front of their home in Silver Spring. By pure chance, this happened to be a day when both Emma and he had taken the day off to take care of some home repairs that were badly needing attention. So, when the van pulled up, Walt was on the ladder cleaning a gutter, Emma holding the base.

The van driver came over to the couple, introducing himself. He had a shipment for Mr. Walter Müller that had come all the way from the West Coast—a COD shipment. He informed Emma and Walt that he needed full payment before he could unload—the payment including nine months of storage fees.

Astonished, but finding no alternative, Walt and Emma gave the driver a check—his crew then offloading the cargo into their garage. Walt reviewed the packing list, seeing items cited similar to those he had requested. However, when he began checking the contents, it was clear that the packing list was overly optimistic—the boxes mostly contained things that otherwise would have been donated to a rummage sale.

Thinking, but doubting, there could be a mistake, he called his sister.

"Ann, the truck just dropped off the stuff you sent."

"OK."

"Well, it would have been nice to have some advance warning—it was only by dumb luck that Emma and I were home."

"OK."

"But say, it doesn't seem like this is what we were expecting."

Silence.

"You know, there were a lot of my personal things there at Mother's, and I'd indicated a few keepsakes from when we were kids that would be nice to have as souvenirs—but most of this seems to be absent."

"I did the best I could."

"But you know, there was the oriental rug from my room, the dresser from there too, my stereo . . ."

"I said, I did the best I could."

"But . . ."

"Everything else is gone. Nothing can be done. I did my best."

"But . . ."

"It's finished."

She hung up.

There was obviously nothing more to be said or done.

Walt and Emma decided to go through one carton, box, or wrapped item a day—they were in no hurry to uncover what was mostly junk. After closer examination, it was clear that Ann was using this as just another way to take a jab at them. What was marked on the packing list as a patio table turned out to be a two-by-three-foot rickety aluminum table. The refrigerator was an old piece of thirty-year-old scarp—who knew where Ann had found it—definitely not at Margaret's house. What was labeled simply as "collections" turned out to be stones—just plain old every-day stones. Hats were sent without hatbands, watches without watch fobs. In short, it was none of what they had expected.

One evening they were unwrapping what turned out to be a bedside table—incongruously, to Walt's surprise, he recognized this as one of a pair of tables that had been in his parent's bedroom. He now knew his sister would not intentionally send an item of value—especially an item that had been one of their mother's personal possessions. The movers must have made a mistake and picked up something they were not supposed to. But, regardless, it was now here. And, even though a very nice piece of furniture, they had no use for it now. It would accompany the other less prized items in their attic.

Walt was wiping off the marble-topped table before re-wrapping, when he opened its small drawer. To his great amazement, inside he found a letter addressed in his mother's hand to "My Dear Emma and Walt."

He and Emma sat on a box in the garage and read the letter out loud, together.

My Dearest Children,

I am writing this, not really sure if I will ever mail it. I have just returned home from the wonderful visit I just had with you both. I believe, through these visits over recent years, I have finally understood each of you and understood how little I had indeed really understood myself. I guess what I am trying to say is that, if I am honest, I was not willing to open my eyes and really see my own son and his wife. I have now done this, and you have opened my eyes. You are fine young people and I apologize for not giving you the benefit of the doubt, for not loving you as a mother should love her son and her daughter-in-law. I am sorry, very sorry.

I thought about this all the way home on the plane. I have decided it is necessary that I be as honest with you as you have always been with me. I did blame you for my darling Julian's death. I did blame you for being so thoughtless as to even consider entering into a mixed marriage. I guess, I did blame you for, in spite of everything, being true to yourself—for following the Golden Rule as we had tried to teach you. I was angry. I was heartbroken. I was lost.

I leaned on your sister. I relied on her words. I felt I could not go on without her hand on my shoulder.

Your sister, too, blamed you for all these things—and probably for being what she never could be.

At the end of the day, my pain was so great, my need to do something so pressing, that, after consultation with your sister, I decided to disown you. Yes, I disowned you. I am horribly ashamed. I deeply regret this act of vengeance—attacking the wrong person for the wrong reasons. I am so sorry. I was so wrong.

I know this is a shock. I know you may hate me for doing what I should not have done. I know I probably no longer deserve your love. But, please do accept the fact that I am so sorry and that I have tried to rectify things.

When I got home, having been working on this problem for hours, I called your Aunt Annabelle. She chastised me for my actions. She tried her best to explain how my overreaction may have been normal but was not right. She asked me to undo what I had done, and I agreed.

I immediately contacted our lawyer and gave him instructions. You and your sister are to, as always should have been the case, share equally in all things. I know this decision will make your sister very angry. I fear she will likely explode—but I believe she will ultimately accept my decision. Really, short of killing me, what choice does she have? She knows that I, like she, have two children, and I should not be asked by anyone to choose between my children.

If you ask me why I am writing this letter, I can only say that I honestly don't know. With your father's untimely death, I have learned not to count on tomorrow. I feel pushed and pulled by my family responsibilities, loyalties, and love. And, since I do not know what might happen in the next hour, let alone the next day, I wanted to tell you both in my own words what I have done, how sorry I am, and how I have tried to make amends.

I am proud of you both and hope you will find it in your hearts to pardon me for my terrible actions, knowing that you are loved by me as my only son and daughter-in-law.

The letter was unsigned. They wondered if it were unfinished. Walt could not imagine how it had found its way into the drawer. He really had no idea if it were even really from his mother. However, Emma encouraged him to accept it as the real thing, and he knew her judgement in such matters was far keener than his.

The question was what to do.

He consulted with their lawyer. They decided to contact Margaret's estate and ask for a formal copy of her Last Will and Testament. When this arrived, it was dated 1980 and clearly designated Ann as the sole beneficiary—equally clearly disowning Walt for the shame he had brought on the family. It was all duly signed and notarized.

Emma and Walt asked their lawyer if there were any options. The lawyer's reply was encapsulated in his conclusion, "Life ain't fair." There were ample reasons to believe this was an injustice. There were possible legal grounds in regard to undue influence and perhaps even human rights violations based on race. But the honest truth was that any legal course of action would be expensive and have very little chance of success. Like the old adage, "possession is nine-tenths of the law," Ann held all the cards—she possessed all, physically and seemingly legally.

Emma and Walt decided to cut their losses. They remembered the proverb, "broad experiences lead to great tolerance." Ann's myopic views were surely not based on broad experience, but on fables and lies. There was no way they could set things right—no way to convince others of the outrageous offenses Ann had committed—covering them all with a smile and nod. Before all this unfortunate business, they had had their lives and their jobs. They still had their lives and their jobs. It was best to move ahead.

They simply cut the slender threads that remained connecting them to Ann, never speaking to her again.

Nine years later, Walt was startled to receive a call from Howard. Ann was dead. During a severe storm, she had apparently got out of bed in the middle of the night and fell over dead. Walt asked if he could attend the funeral. Howard, obviously uncertain of what to say, agreed. He said they had moved—giving the new address on Bainbridge Island, west of Seattle—a very swanky neighborhood indeed. The church service would be held at the Eagle Harbor Congregational Church with a reception at their home following the religious ceremonies. However, Ann's wishes were to be buried next to her mother, so the actual internment would take place in their old hometown.

Emma and Walt decided for their own self-respect, they should be represented at the funeral. But it was not necessary to subject Emma to any unnecessary stress. Therefore, Walt would fly out to Seattle by himself, attend the church service and reception, then fly back the next day—one final sacrifice for the woman who had already so disrupted their lives.

Walt rented a car upon arrival at Seattle-Tacoma Airport, taking the ferry to Bainbridge. Onboard, he looked over the tourist brochures on display for those traveling for happier reasons. He noted that Bainbridge Island was cited as being the second-best place to live in the United States. Just like his sister to aim for the top—he wondered where the best place was and why she had not gone there.

Following the GPS in this car, he found himself at a relatively modest and somewhat rustic church where he met Howard, Robby, and Lilly. There was also Ann's hairdresser and a few neighbors, but it was a small turnout to celebrate the death of a relative newcomer. It was clear Ann had never been to the church in life, the minister having a difficult time talking in any personal way about someone who had only been a parishioner in death.

Walt then followed the others for about five miles, where they entered a large gated residence sitting on, what Walt estimated to be, about ten acres of mixed pasture and forest. The fenced-in areas seemed to be home to a mishmash of animals; a potbellied pig, a pony, a llama, and even some peacocks. His sister, never an animal nor nature lover, must have felt these critters somehow added to the status of the manner.

The house itself was of a certain age and immense; three floors, six bedrooms, ten baths, green house, and stable. It put The Big House of their childhood to shame. There was a large circular drive with a shining late model Range Rover parked at the apex, adorned with a black ribbon—certainly Ann's personal means of conveyance—subdued as always.

Inside the house, Walt declined a tour, knowing he would surely recognize so much that he felt rightly belonged to him.

The weather was pleasant and the invitees, though they were few in number, sat on a large patio while caterers served drinks and ornate light snacks. Walt chose a bourbon on the rocks and sat quietly in a shady corner. This was truly an *acte de présence* for him—he had no desire to socialize, chat, or know any more about anything.

He was enjoying the burn of the whisky as it trickled down his throat, deep in thought about the pointlessness of so much in life, when he was bewildered to find Lilly at his shoulder. He really did not know his niece and had never spent any time with her. In fact, he did not think he had ever spoken to her.

Lilly smiled, "Uncle Walt, do you want to know something?"

"Oh, hi Lilly, you surprised me. My mind was far away. Sure. What do you have to tell me?"

"I am a dreamer."

"That's great. We all need to have dreams—then see how we can achieve these dreams."

"No, not those kinds of dreams. Sleeping type of dreams."

"OK, that's great, too."

"Somehow, I dream of things that have happened."

"That's special."

"Honestly. My dreams are real—real, true things."

"That's unusual—but some people are special."

"The things I dream are things that have really happened, but no one knows they've happened."

"Well, I guess, that's even more special."

"Do you believe me?"

"Of course."

"Uncle Walt, I dreamed my mother killed my grandmother."

Walt had no comeback.

Postscript

ANN WAS INTERRED WITH her parents, on the hill that, at the time of her father's death, overlooked the sawmill where he had died. However, the lumber industry had passed through a big slump, the mill had closed years ago, the site had been razed, a new investor sought, but soil pollution levels were too high for reuse approval. Therefore, the view from the hill was now desolate—one of acres of crumbling asphalt and naked, red soil. There was little to see except small dirt devils filled with aged sawdust rising from the tundra-like land when the afternoon breeze strengthened over the lake.

Walt returned to Washington and gave Emma a great hug. He continued his work, the next year authoring a tome, *Influence of Tolerance on Population Impacts*.

Emma continued at the Community Center, receiving more awards for meritorious service.

Howard married a young woman twenty years his junior, sold the estate, and moved to Las Vegas.

Robby contracted a little-known illness, dying a year after his mother—fulfilling her worst worries about the precariousness of his life.

Lilly continued to dream—too often discovering the truth in her visions—her prognostications frequently weighing heavily on her—wishing she could free people from the inevitable. After getting a degree in psychology at Saint Martin's University, she became a counselor at the Washington Corrections Center for Women in Gig Harbor.

Lucy, Margaret's shepherd mix, who, for a brief period was part of the menagerie at Howard's villa, found herself an orphan when Howard moved to Nevada. Emma and Walt adopted her. Lucy thoroughly enjoyed her new home in Silver Spring—Emma and Walt thoroughly enjoyed having her.